NURSE KITTY: AFTER THE WAR

NURSE KITTY: AFTER THE WAR

Maggie Campbell

First published in Great Britain in 2024 by Orion Fiction,
an imprint of The Orion Publishing Group Ltd.
Carmelite House, 50 Victoria Embankment
London EC4Y 0DZ

An Hachette UK Company

1 3 5 7 9 10 8 6 4 2

A CIP catalogue record for this book is available from the British Library.

ISBN (Mass Market Paperback) 978 1 4091 9183 4
ISBN (eBook) 978 1 4091 9184 1

Typeset by Born Group
Printed and bound in Great Britain by Clays Ltd, Elcograf S.p.A.

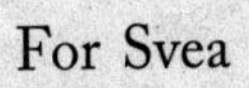

For Svea

1950

Chapter 1

'Come on, get a move on!' Kitty said beneath her breath. Frowning, she looked down the aisle of the bus, wishing she could get a glimpse of the driver in his cab to see what on earth was keeping him from pulling away from the stop. Kitty checked the wristwatch James had given her as a birthday present and balked. 'Quarter of an hour, I've been sat here like Piffy on a rock bun,' she said to the woman on the opposite side of the aisle. 'I'm going to be late for work.'

'It's not on, is it, love?' the woman said, clutching her shopping bag on her knee. 'My bacon's going to go off if I don't get it in the larder soon.'

Outside, Manchester had been enshrouded not just in the early evening gloom, but also in thick fog – the pea-soup kind that reduced the city to nothing more than fuzzy shapes and the suggestion of life.

Kitty turned around to see if other passengers shared her irritation and spotted the bus conductor, standing on the edge of the rear platform, where the lower deck was open to the elements. He clung to the pole, hanging at an awkward angle off the back of the bus, clearly trying to get a good look at what was going on, further down the street.

'Lovey,' she called out. 'Are you there?'

The conductor righted himself, but he was still craning his neck, his attention clearly on the street and not her. He put his index finger to his lips, signalling the need for hush.

Kitty frowned at the conductor's perplexing behaviour. 'What's going on? Can you tell us why we're stuck here? Only I'm a nursing sister at Park Hospital, and my shift started three minutes ago.' She tapped the face of her watch insistently. Having finally been promoted to Sister, the last thing she wanted was for Matron to think her a poor time-keeper.

The conductor opened his mouth to answer, but his response was drowned out by a din of raised voices, disturbing the foggy stillness. Suddenly, the front half of the bus was surrounded by men, who hammered on the windows with their fists – two rival groups, jeering at each other from opposite sides, with Kitty and the other passengers as terrified go-betweens.

When Kitty noticed that several of the men on one side were wielding the red standard of the fascist Union Movement, featuring the unmistakeable white lightning bolt in a blue circle, her heart beat a frenzied tattoo inside her chest. 'Missus! Get into the aisle!' Kitty shouted at an elderly woman who had been snoozing against a window.

The old lady shuffled across her seat just as two brawling men hurtled into the side of the bus. All Kitty could make out was a jumble of flailing fists. Then a crow bar came into view, there was a loud bang, and the window where the lady had been sitting only moments before cracked.

'Flipping Nora! It's a full-on riot!' Kitty yelled. She got to her feet, ran to the front of the bus and thumped on the partition that separated the passengers from the cab. 'Driver! Get going!'

But the engine was still merely idling.

Glancing back at the bewildered-looking conductor, Kitty balked as a young man leaped onto the platform, barrelling into the conductor. The dark-haired man looked a little like

Kitty's fiancé, James, though this was no doctor. Dressed in shabby grey slacks and a red boiled-wool jumper, he looked more like a student from the university. His face was a picture of terror.

'Steady on, lad! What do you think you're doing?' the conductor said, adjusting his hat.

The conductor reached out to take a fistful of the man's red jumper just as a fascist leaped aboard the bus. The fascist shouted a shocking slur at the man, wrapped a meaty arm around his waist and dragged him back into the street.

Gripping the handrail of the seat in front, Kitty couldn't believe the melee that they were caught up in. Mercifully though, the fog seemed to claim the fracas back and the bus thrummed properly into life. The conductor rang the bell, and they pulled away at some speed.

Safe in her makeshift office on the ward, with trembling fingers Kitty tried to fasten a fresh apron around her waist but found she couldn't tie the knot.

Grace put down the file she had been leafing through. 'You're shaking like jelly,' she said. She enveloped Kitty in a warm hug. 'There, there. Tell me what's the matter.'

Kitty exhaled long and hard, drinking in the comforting smell of the coconut oil that her soon-to-be sister-in-law used to smooth the tight curls of her hair into a neat bun. 'Oh, you're a good'un, our Grace.' She broke free of the embrace, patted Grace on the arm and wiped away a tear that had taken her by surprise. 'Thanks. I needed that.' She sat behind her desk, which, even in this brave new decade, was still just a table-top that had been put over a freestanding bath in her 'office' – an office that doubled as the ward's bathroom. 'Where do I start?'

'At the beginning?' Grace leaned against shelving that held stacks of snowy white, clean towels. She folded her arms and smiled encouragingly.

Kitty shook her head. 'Well, I was coming back from Mam's. One minute, I'm on the bus, wondering why we haven't left the stop in ages. Next, there's this . . . riot comes out of the fog, and we're caught right in the middle of it.'

'A riot?'

Nodding ruefully, Kitty exhaled hard. 'Blackshirts. Well, I say Blackshirts, but actually it's not the ones that were marching on the streets when I was a little girl, wearing black uniforms like military men. Oswald Mosley's still behind their antics, but these are new'uns, waving flags with a lightning bolt on them. Conductor said they'd been blocking the road, holding some sort of protest.'

'Over people like me? Immigrants. That's what fascists normally get riled up about.'

Kitty bit the inside of her cheek. She fingered the nurse's watch on the crisp starched bib of her uniform. 'I'm really embarrassed this is the welcome you've been given, after leaving behind everything and everyone you love in beautiful Barbados.'

A wistful look passed over Grace's face, but she waved her hand dismissively. 'It's not so bad. Manchester weather's growing on me.'

'Ha. Fungus would grow on you before the weather did.' Kitty grinned. 'Heaven knows, it's damp and drizzly enough! It might be 1950, but I don't think better weather in the north-west comes as standard with a new atomic age.'

'Well, at least I'm managing to send a little bit of money home,' Grace said, tidying some towels that had been left on a trolley by a junior nurse. 'I'm making a name for myself in the new National Health Service and I've got the man I love right here.' She looked down at her modest engagement ring.

'Our Ned!' Kitty said quietly, thinking about her wayward brother who would soon be tying the knot with Grace. She rolled her eyes. 'By heck, he's no Montgomery Clift, that's for sure. You've got your work cut out for you there, Grace, or my name's not Kitty Longthorne.'

'You'll be Mrs James Williams soon.' Grace winked and retrieved the file she'd been leafing through. 'A doctor's wife, no less.' She curtseyed dramatically. 'Will you still speak to me and Ned, when you swap a single bed in the nurses' home for a fancy house in Cheshire, living it up with Manchester's finest plastic surgeon?'

Kitty laughed. 'Give over, you daft beggar.' She got to her feet and now deftly knotted her apron. 'Listen, I understand we've got a new arrival in from Casualty. Let's see what they've sent us.'

The mixed ward was full and thrummed with the chatter of the new nursing recruits, Lakshmi and Tasmia, from India and Malay, handing out dinner to the patients.

'Here you go, Mrs Baxter,' Lakshmi said. 'Tripe and onions today.'

'You what? Say that again,' one of the elderly patients shouted, holding her cupped hand to her ear and eyeing the Indian nurse with undisguised disdain.

'Tripe and onions, Mrs Baxter. Here, let me get you some fresh water.' Lakshmi kept smiling, despite the old lady's unfriendly behaviour. She set the steaming plate onto the patient's wheeled table and picked up her empty jug.

Mrs Baxter turned to the woman in the next bed. 'Can you understand what she's saying, Fanny? Because I haven't got a clue.'

Fanny shook her head. 'No, I can't understand any of them.'

Watching the scene unfold, Kitty marched up to the bed. 'Everything all right here, Nurse Argawal?'

'Yes, Sister.' Lakshmi smiled and nodded, though the tightness around her eyes made it clear she was feeling uncomfortable.

Kitty took the jug from Lakshmi's hands and poured Mrs Baxter a glass of water. She held the glass to her lips.

'Ta, love,' the old lady said, sipping gratefully. She nodded her head towards Lakshmi. 'Can't you get an English nurse to look after me? Only when this one talks, all I can hear is gobbledegook.'

Setting the jug down, Kitty leaned in and spoke softly to the patient. 'I think your ears must be blocked with wax, Mrs Baxter, because I can understand Nurse Argawal perfectly.' She patted the old woman's hand. 'Shall we get your ears syringed? Or can this lovely nurse do her job and look after you?'

Mrs Baxter glared at Kitty, but Kitty smiled and held her gaze long enough for the anger to leach from the old woman's wizened features.

'I suppose I could eat some tripe and onions,' she said, turning her attention to the plate of grey food. Then, she tap-tap-tapped the table with her index finger. 'But what I want to know is when are we going to get something decent to eat? A lovely lamb chop. Real eggs.'

Fanny, the woman in the next bed, started to nod enthusiastically. 'Aye. She's right, Sister. We're sick and tired of all this rationing nonsense, aren't we, Mabel? The war ended five years ago, and we're *still* eating sweepings-up and sawdust.'

'I voted Labour in the last general election, but maybe I'll think twice in the next,' Mrs. Baxter said.

Fanny folded her arms tightly, her mouth downturned at the corners. 'The communists can whistle for my vote if all we've got to look forward to is rusk sausage and—'

'You don't know what you're talking about, you silly old bat!' A man's raised voice sliced through the hubbub on the ward.

Kitty got to her feet and turned to find the voice's owner was her latest admission. She strode to the other side of the ward and picked up the notes, hanging from the end of the man's iron bed frame. 'Mr Tom Stockwell?' She eyed his arm, encased in plaster, and his right leg, similarly in a solid cast, raised by a winch above the bed. His face was battered and bruised, his lip split and swollen to double its normal size, and his torso was encased in wrappings. 'Seems you've had quite a time,' she said. 'Broken arm, broken leg, two cracked ribs, not to mention the state of your face. Have you been ten rounds with Bruce Woodcock? Or did you call a lady from the Barbary Coast a silly old bat too?'

The cackle of laughter could be heard from the patients in the surrounding beds.

'The likes of him has probably never set foot in Salford docks,' one of the other male patients said. 'Flipping commie.'

Kitty briefly wondered at how her mother had lived in Salford's notorious 'Barbary Coast' for a couple of years, quite happily. Only Kitty's father's recent death had motivated her dear old mam to up sticks and move to the lovely council housing estate in the recently created area of Wythenshawe. At least this time, James had borrowed a van to move her few belongings. Her mam's days of moving house on a handcart were over, mercifully.

'Can we all just pipe down about politics?' she said, looking round at her patients. 'What is it with you lot today?' She turned back to her new arrival, and it struck her then that he was familiar somehow. It was his hair. It was the same shade as James's, in exactly the same Brylcreemed short-back-and-sides style. She caught sight of a red boiled wool jumper, folded on the man's nightstand. 'I know you!' she said. 'You were the lad who tried to get on my bus, on my way to the hospital. You were one of the rioters that kept me from starting my shift on time. Some Union Movement thug dragged you back onto the street.'

Even though his skin was cut and bruised, it was clear that Tom Stockwell was blushing. 'That was me, all right. I gave him as good as I got.'

'Is that right, Mr Fisticuffs? Maybe that fascist was taken to the Infirmary, then, eh, because I can't see him in here. But I can hear you're well spoken. Are you a student at the university?'

'Guilty as charged,' Tom said.

'Well, if you're so clever, why on earth did you get involved in that nonsense?' Kitty asked. 'Haven't you heard there's war brewing in Korea? A war to *stop* the communists! Mark my words, British lads will get pulled into fighting by the end of the year, if the commies won't back down. That's what I've heard.'

'How else are we going to stop Moseley and his new lot of fascists?' Tom said. 'You saw all those hoodlums – Blackshirts in everything but name. They take it upon themselves to march in our streets, spouting vile things about anyone who isn't true blue British. Waving flags like they're going to war. We may not have the brave 43 Group in Manchester, but there's still a good number of us willing to take a stand against an army of ignorant thugs!'

The middle-aged man in the adjacent bed caught Kitty's eye as he swung his legs out of bed, got to his feet and staggered over to Tom. 'Ignorant thugs, are we? I'll give you thug, you commie toerag.'

Before Kitty could react, the patient yanked at the winch that held Tom's plastered leg aloft and sent it crashing down onto the mattress.

Tom yelped in agony.

'That's quite enough of that!' Kitty bellowed, using the tone that she'd heard Matron use so many times with wayward patients. 'Get back to your bed, sir! I will not have patients assaulting each other on my ward. Get in bed, *now*, or I'll telephone the police myself.'

She called for Grace, who left the bedside of the patient she was tending to.

'Yes, Sister Longthorne?'

'Can you tend to this poor chap's broken leg, please, Nurse? Our appendectomy patient in the neighbouring bed seems to think the mixed ward of Park Hospital is an appropriate place to start a brawl.'

Kitty strode to the fascist's bed and checked his notes. 'You're due for discharge tomorrow, Mr Collins. Good job, I'd say. You mind you keep a civil tongue in your head until then, please.'

Mr Collins, however, was not listening. He began hurling insults at Grace, so biting, that Kitty watched in dismay as her sister-in-law righted Tom's leg and then fled the ward in tears.

When her shift ended and the morning staff began to arrive, Kitty made her way over to her fiancé's clinic, where she knew he'd be reading notes, ahead of his consultations.

'James!' she said.

He greeted her with a dazzling smile. 'Kitty, my darling. Good morning. How was your—?'

Kitty was in no mood for chit-chat, however. 'James, we've got to talk.'

Chapter 2

'I need you to speak to the board about the way patients – and some of the staff – talk to the new recruits from the colonies,' Kitty said, marching up to his desk and placing her hands territorially on the polished oak desktop. 'It's gone beyond a joke. I've just had to referee a ding-dong between a communist and a Union Movement fascist. Some of the language coming out of the Mosleyite . . . ! It could have stripped paint. Poor Grace ran off in floods.' She looked into James' warm brown eyes. 'It's happening too often, and it's got to stop.'

James got to his feet and walked around to meet her. This early in the morning, he looked pristine and smelled of the TCP he gargled with as well as Brylcreem. He put his arms around her. 'I love it when you're all hot under the collar. Sister Kitty, my warrior queen. You're quite formidable when you want to be. Do you know that?'

Irritated that he didn't seem to be taking her seriously, Kitty pushed him away. 'Aren't you listening to me? I've got old ladies making fun of the new nurses' accents. It's beyond the pale.'

Sighing, James perched on the edge of his desk and glanced at the clock on the wall that showed it was approaching half past seven in the morning. He locked eyes with Kitty. 'Darling, we're dealing with a polio epidemic. Have you seen the numbers of children being admitted? It's dizzying – three times the number of children with polio we saw in 1948.' He ran a hand through his dark hair and thumbed his freshly shaven chin. 'We barely have enough iron lungs to accommodate them all.' He held his hands up as if in surrender. '*That's* the main worry for the board at the moment.'

'Oh, come off it, James! Matron's told me what goes on in those board meetings. You have agendas and that. There's no way you only discuss one topic.' She grabbed his forearm, savouring the feel of his starched shirtsleeves when she felt so unkempt after a full shift on a busy ward. 'You can be the champion of Park Hospital's new nurses from the colonies. They've come to help build our National Health Service, but what are we giving them? Lower wages than advertised, longer hours. Most of them are the equivalent of State Registered Nurses, but we've relegated them to washing out bedpans and changing sheets. The least we owe them is the right to be treated as equals on the wards.'

James took Kitty's face in his warm hands and planted a gentle kiss on her forehead. 'You're right, my love. No patient or staff member should be making someone like Grace flee the ward in tears, just because of where she's from.' He looked up to a corner of the high ceiling, his eyebrows bunching together. 'I tell you what, I'll ask Professor Baird-Murray if you can sit in on the board meeting so you can give a first-hand account of what you've seen. How does that sound?'

Nodding, Kitty tried to visualise sitting in on the meeting at that huge table, surrounded by all the senior medical men in the hospital. 'I'd better let Matron know. She won't want me treading on her toes.'

'She's retiring in a couple of weeks – I doubt she'll give a fig. Just you make sure you turn up in time for the meeting at five.'

As Kitty made her way over to the nurses' home, her feet stinging and her back aching from having another full shift under her belt, she wondered if, now that she was a Sister, the likes of Professor Baird-Murray would deign to listen to what she had to say about how Park Hospital was being run. Somehow, she doubted it.

When the alarm went off on her clock, Kitty rose and dressed quickly. Her head was still heavy with fatigue since she'd cut her sleep somewhat short. No matter though. The anticipation of sitting in on a board meeting was enough to get her going.

Downstairs, she found Matron sitting in her office – not at her desk, though, where she would normally be, if she wasn't walking the floors of the hospital, inspecting the nurses' work and keeping the doctors in check. That afternoon, Matron was sitting in her armchair with her feet up, reading a book.

'Knock, knock,' Kitty said, standing hesitantly in the doorway. She stifled a yawn.

Matron turned to face her and smiled. 'Kitty, my dear. Do come in.'

'I'm surprised to find you here, actually. I thought you'd be on the wards.'

Putting a bookmark between the pages of her book and setting it down on the side table by her armchair, Matron motioned Kitty to sit in the visitor's chair. 'I'm gathering my strength – the calm before the storm.' She chuckled to herself. 'A new matron means the outgoing matron has an awful lot of affairs to set in order in a very short space of time.'

'When does the new matron start?' Kitty asked, realising that her beloved mentor suddenly looked old. It was as if the stresses of overseeing Park Hospital's evolution from a brand-new hospital that served the people of Davyhulme to a military hospital, during the war years, and then to the first NHS hospital in the country, had finally permeated her tough exterior.

'In three days, would you believe it? And there's a hand-over period that's going to be rather frenetic, I think.'

'If you need any assistance, you can count on me, Matron.'

Matron leaned forwards and patted Kitty's hand. 'I know that, *Sister* Longthorne. You are one of my biggest successes.' She winked. 'Not bad for a girl from Hulme, eh?'

Kitty blushed. 'Actually, I'm glad I found you. I needed to get your permission to speak to the board about the shoddy treatment of the new nurses from the colonies by some of the other staff and the patients. I didn't want to tread on your toes, seeing it's normally you—'

'You brought the new nurses here, Kitty.'

'Not all of them, I didn't. I only brought one!'

'Well, you were our recruiting champion in the West Indies, travelling the high seas to bring foreign talent to Davyhulme. You got the ball rolling. It makes sense you should fight their corner at today's meeting, if that's what you're minded to do.' Matron grunted as she got to her feet. 'Tea?'

Kitty looked at her watch. She had only five minutes before the meeting began. 'No thanks, Matron. I'd best get going.'

Taking her leave from Matron and crossing the grounds of the hospital, Kitty was struck by a pang of sorrow. So much of her own story had come to pass in these hospital grounds, and so much of it had involved Matron.

Walking beneath the sturdy Art-Deco clock tower, she remembered how her estranged father had shown up at the nurses' home in the middle of the night on VE Day, drunk and demanding to see Kitty . . . until Matron had locked him in a cupboard. Bert Longthorne, the errant father who had always taken, rarely giving anything more than sleepless nights and a bad reputation to the entire family, had been tamed only by Matron. And then there was James . . . Kitty remembered her fiancé sneaking around the nurses' home in a bid to look after her when she'd been ill; always on the lookout for Matron, who patrolled the floors to check no nurse had a gentleman caller in her room.

As she entered the hospital and passed the casualty department, making for the stairs, she mused that the infamous, inimitable Bert Longthorne was dead, and Matron was leaving. Matron, who had supported her when her devious pal, Violet, had betrayed and belittled her; Matron, who had taught her how to be the best nurse she could be and rise above her poverty-stricken Hulme roots; Matron, who had turned Kitty the girl, into Kitty the woman.

'By heck,' Kitty muttered, wiping a tear from her eye. 'Pull yourself together, Kitty Longthorne. There's work to do.'

The board room was already full and almost foggy with the smoke from cigars, pipes and cigarettes when Kitty arrived. She looked for James among the consultants and spotted him sitting by the open window, with Mr Galbraith, the heart and lung surgeon, to his left, and an empty seat to his right.

James patted the place next to him, and Kitty filed past the board members, who continued to chat animatedly, barely batting an eye that a woman was in their midst.

One turned to Kitty, just as she was about to take her seat. 'I say, Nurse. Fetch us some tea, there's a good girl,' he said.

Kitty recognised him as a general surgeon, who had removed many a gangrenous limb from wounded servicemen. She'd assisted him in theatre several times. Yet this surgeon obviously had no idea who she was. 'Oh, I'm not here to serve the tea, Mr Latimer,' Kitty said. 'I'm here to talk to you all in my capacity as Ward Sister.' She felt her cheeks burn but steeled herself to adopt the non-nonsense manner that she'd seen Matron so successfully deploy whenever the consultants tried to take liberties.

Taking her seat by James, Kitty sensed that Mr Latimer was staring at her, aghast, but she turned her focus to what she might say in front of these powerful men, who weren't used to listening to women.

Professor Baird-Murray tapped his signet ring on his tumbler of whisky and the room fell silent. He put his burning cigar into a large cut-glass ashtray, positioned by his notes.

'Gentlemen. Let us commence our meeting.' He glanced back at his bespectacled secretary, who was sitting primly at a separate side table, taking shorthand notes in a pad. He gave her the nod.

At her side, James cleared his throat. 'Er, Professor, before we begin . . .'

'What is it, Williams?'

Beneath the table, James squeezed Kitty's knee. 'I'd like to remind you that you agreed that Sister Longthorne, here, could address the board about behaviour in the hospital.

There's a problem with the new nursing and auxiliary staff from overseas.'

'Acting up, are they?' the professor said, sucking on his cigar. 'What more can you expect from their kind? Small wonder we've seen the fall of the Raj in our lifetime, eh?' He wheezed with mirth, looking around, perhaps to check that his best chum and senior consultant radiologist, Sir Basil Ryder-Smith, was chuckling along with him.

On her uncomfortable seat, Kitty wriggled, itching to take Baird-Murray and Ryder-Smith down a peg or two. She knew it wasn't her place to criticise the hospital's senior management, however, especially not a professor and a Knight of the Realm.

Baird-Murray waved his cigar towards her. 'Cathy, my dear—'

'It's Kitty, Professor,' Kitty said, clamping her molars tightly together until they squeaked with tension.

'Actually, it's *Sister Longthorne,*' James said, placing his hand on hers.

Kitty withdrew her hand and silently cursed the blush that spread across her cheeks and up from the base of her neck.

'Yes, yes. Of course,' Baird-Murray said. 'What I was about to say was, that if the Sister wishes to address the board, she'll have to wait until the end, assuming we've got time.' He turned to a quiet, tweed-clad consultant immunologist – Dr Bourke – who oversaw treatment for polio. 'Dr Bourke, I believe item one on the agenda pertains to your field of expertise. Do apprise us of the latest on the polio calamity.'

Dr Bourke straightened his bow tie and sat up straight in his seat. 'Professor . . . gentlemen, I do hope you're ready for this, because I have momentous news.'

Chapter 3

'The results are in from Hilary Koprowski's orally administered polio vaccine trial in America,' Dr Bourke said, steepling his fingers and looking around the table.

'Well?' Baird-Murray said. 'Don't keep us on tenterhooks, man. We're drowning in polio cases.'

Dr Bourke nodded and a smile lit up his wan face. 'Well, he only tested it on twenty children from a disabled home in New York state . . .'

The board members looked positively underwhelmed.

'Twenty?' Ryder-Smith said. 'That's hardly a trial worth talking about.'

'On the contrary, Sir Basil,' Dr Bourke said. He punched the air, awkwardly. 'All pulled through with *no* complications. It's positive news. The vaccine works.'

Kitty watched as the board members broke into rapturous applause.

'Jolly good show,' James said, nodding at Dr Bourke. 'What's the word on how quickly a mass-produced vaccine might follow?'

In answer, Dr Bourke merely shrugged. 'Can't be long, can it? There are the efforts of Albert Sabin to consider too, who's apparently sharing the attenuated virus that Koprowski's used. And that fellow, Salk – he's trialling injections. One of them is sure to have a breakthrough, and we'll get a mass-produced vaccine sooner rather than later. Lord knows, I'll be following the progress with bated breath. It grieves me to see so many children being admitted with the disease. Half of Manchester's youth will be limping around in leg callipers and braces . . . assuming they survive.' He looked sideways to a board member sitting on his left, whom Kitty recognised as Dr Benny Silver, the paediatrician.

Dr Silver nodded. 'Bourke's right. We're in a state of near emergency. An entire section of the children's ward has had to be dedicated to polio patients.'

Professor Baird-Murray glanced down at his notes. 'And where are we with iron lungs?'

'Ah, that's another bit of good news,' Dr Silver said. 'We've got four new iron lungs coming in later this week. They might be cumbersome, but at least the little blighters will be able to breathe and have more of a fighting chance of recovery.'

'Bally good news,' the professor said. 'Perhaps when the iron lungs arrive, we should name them after the last four horses to win at Ascot on Ladies' Day. Give them a soupcon of glamour. Ha!'

Kitty wondered if she would get her chance to speak next, but the professor turned to Mr Galbraith.

'Now, Galbraith. You're the next item on the agenda. What do you have to share with us about this new atomic medicine?'

Mr Galbraith, always a serious sort, nodded curtly at the professor, but Kitty could see that his eyes shone almost as brightly as his bald pate, gleaming beneath the board room lights.

He stroked his pencil moustache with a perfectly manicured index finger and looked around the table at the other board members. 'Many of you already know I'm waiting for news on the Canadian trial of the Cobalt 60 Isotope to treat cancer. Well, results haven't been published yet, but the rumours on the grapevine are that it's looking promising.' He nodded and finished with a fleeting smile. 'I'm not a superstitious man, but I'll be keeping my fingers crossed.'

There was a chummer of enthusiasm around the table.

'It's a brave new world,' Sir Basil said.

Would Kitty get her chance to speak now? Alas, it was James who spoke next.

'Gentlemen, I'd like to draw your attention to the next agenda item. Road accidents.' James folded his arms and waited for his announcement to register among his colleagues.

'What of them?' the professor asked.

Unfolding his arms, James read out a set of statistics that caused a few raised eyebrows among the consultants. 'As you can see, that sort of a percentage increase of road accident victims, turning up in my clinic needing facial reconstructive surgery, is just unprecedented. We have a new modern-day problem, gentlemen.'

One of the consultant surgeons, Mr Thistlethwaite, whom Kitty knew specialised in leg, arm and back injuries and who often worked in casualty, nodded. 'James is right. We're inundated with major trauma from road accidents. One can only think it's down to there being so many more motor-cycles and cars on the roads since the end of the war. We get them in quickly enough, but I'm losing patients left, right and centre. If I'm honest, we're not entirely certain why.'

Just as the room buzzed anew with concerned chatter, James cleared his throat. 'Then I propose that those coming into contact with trauma patients keep their eyes peeled for reasons why these patients might be dying.'

'Perhaps more are dying because more are being admitted with major trauma,' Sir Basil said. He turned to Professor Baird-Murray, chuckled and winked. 'Simple mathematics, what?! And this chap is supposed to be one of our brightest and best, eh? Could have fooled me.'

Watching Professor Baird-Murray guffaw through his cigar smoke, Kitty balled her fists beneath the table. She was desperate to speak out in support of her fiancé.

James, however, needed no assistance in that regard. 'Laugh all you like, Basil, but with new medication and treatments being discovered every day,' he said, 'it's very clear to me that what we call "modern medicine" is still tottering around in its infancy. We have no idea of the extent of our own ignorance, and it may yet be that we simply haven't looked at our care of trauma patients *in the right way* to find a means of lowering mortality rates. There could be something obvious, right under our very noses, and it's our duty to look for it in a systematic manner.'

Before James had even finished speaking, Professor Baird-Murray had become engaged in a private tête à tête with Sir Basil. Kitty leaned forwards, listening hard to what the two men were saying, and she was sure they were talking about single malt whisky.

She turned to James. 'Is it always like this?' she asked.

James shrugged. 'The end always descends into organised chaos. I don't let it bother me anymore.'

'Well, I'm not here for the good of my health,' Kitty said. She got to her feet and spoke as loudly as she could without shouting. 'Professor, might I now address the board about my concerns?'

The board members around the table fell silent, at last.

Baird-Murray took his fob watch out of his pocket and looked at the time. 'Yes, I suppose so. But do keep it brief, Sister. We are all very busy men.'

Ignoring the burning sensation in her cheeks, Kitty swallowed hard and began to speak. 'It's about the treatment of our new nurses from the colonies by the English staff and patients. I've witnessed some shocking racialist behaviour on the part of the English folk – name calling and such like – and I've had new nurses fleeing the ward in tears. I just don't think it's on, and we need to bring in some sort of formal code—'

Holding his hand up, Mr Latimer spoke over her. 'Why are you addressing the board, Sister Longthorne? Is this not the job of Matron?' He looked around. 'In fact, where is Matron?'

'Matron's . . .' Kitty tried to find a suitable answer, but in truth, she could only assume Matron had not attended because her heart was no longer in it.

'I really think we ought to hear of complaints of this nature from Matron,' Baird-Murray said. 'That's the normal etiquette for these sorts of thing. And if Matron didn't see fit to bring it to our attention, well then . . .' He started to shuffle his papers and pulled his large briefcase onto the table, as if the meeting was already over.

Kitty stared at him, open-mouthed in disbelief. Was that it? Had she been dismissed without even having the opportunity to explain the situation?

James squeezed her hand. 'We are *very* busy, darling. I'm sorry. I did try.'

When the board meeting ended, leaving James behind to talk to Galbraith about the promise of atomic medicine,

Kitty made her way out of the hospital building and into the freezing February early-evening. In the eerie yellow of the external lighting, she could see that the forlorn-looking rose gardens were sodden and stripped of all foliage. Above her, there was no moon. The overcast night sky had a strange pink hue, as if snow threatened.

Clutching her cloak around her, Kitty hurried towards the nurses' home, trying to beat the sleet or snow that she could almost smell on the air. She was just about break into a run when she spotted a couple sitting on one of the benches that were dotted along the pathway. Narrowing her eyes in the gloom, she was certain she recognised them.

'Ned? Grace?'

Her brother's disfigured face was unmistakeable, even in the poor light. 'Just the woman we've been waiting for.'

At his side, Grace blew her nose loudly on a giant man's handkerchief. 'Kitty. How did it go?'

The two got to their feet.

Kitty kissed her brother on his freezing cold cheek and then put her arm around Grace. 'There, there, Grace. You're shivering like jelly. You shouldn't be out here, dressed so flimsily.' She turned to Ned and tugged at the coat he was wearing – the same expensive overcoat he'd stolen from Kitty's former squeeze, the anaesthetist, Richard Collins. 'Blimey, our Ned. The age of chivalry's certainly dead where you're concerned. Dead and flaming buried. Give her your coat, for heaven's sake! Why didn't you take Grace to a pub to keep warm?' She immediately regretted asking him the question.

'Well, if you could lend us a couple of bob . . .' Ned removed his coat, chuckling all the while.

'Ooh, you're such a cheapskate, Ned Longthorne,' Kitty said. 'By heck, Dad might be dead but his apple didn't fall far from the tree.'

'Speak for yourself,' Ned said, putting his coat around Grace and kissing his fiancée's cheek.

Grace pushed him away. 'Kitty's right. Think on, Ned. I expect you to behave like a gentleman if we're going to tie the knot. It shouldn't take your sister to point out your thoughtless ways.'

'Hey! I'm being defamed here.'

'Who de cap fit, let he draw de string,' Grace said. 'You're acting like a guilty man.'

Ned put his arms around Grace and held her close. 'Ooh, I love it when you come over all Barbados. Give us a kiss.'

Kitty could no longer feel her toes in the biting cold. 'Right. That's enough of your mucking around, Ned Longthorne. You came a long way for a canoodle, but canoodling time's over. Grace needs to come inside with me before she gets frozen to the marrow.'

Grace's teeth chattered. 'Actually, Kitty, Ned didn't just come for a canoodle. We *both* want to hear what was said in the board meeting. It's not just me that it affects, is it? We're an interracial couple. Any children we have will be affected too.' She wiped a fresh tear from her cheek. 'We know people don't approve of us.'

'Don't be daft,' Kitty said. 'Nobody's ever—'

'Dishonesty doesn't suit you,' Ned said. 'Are you telling me, not a one of James's posh pals haven't commented that his betrothed has got a brother who's marrying a lass from the West Indies? Come on, Kitty! Pull the other one. It's got bells on!'

Grace grabbed her by the forearm. 'It's our responsibility – me and Ned – to make sure our babies and your future nieces or nephews don't get treated like second-class citizens.'

Kitty nodded. Then, she shook her head. She spoke in a quiet voice. 'Well, I'm sorry to say I didn't have much luck getting the board to listen to me. But I'm going to keep trying. I swear.'

Chapter 4

'Ladies, pay attention!' Matron said, clapping her hands. 'I have an important announcement.'

At the end of a busy week, when Kitty's overnight stint had finally come to an end and she had embarked on a new day shift on the children's polio ward, she'd headed to the nurses' dining room – not just in the hope of snatching a hasty bite to eat, but at the insistence of Matron. Now, the place was filled to bursting point with every nurse in Park Hospital. Even those yawning and exhausted-looking women who were due to work the night shift had abandoned their daytime sleep to join the throng. Matron could barely be heard over the excited chatter.

'Silence!' Matron shouted.

A deathly hush finally descended. The nurses faced forwards to give Matron their full attention. The only sound was the odd clank or tinkle of a cup being placed on a saucer or a piece of cutlery being laid on a plate.

Kitty stood in a row along with the other ward sisters, to the left of Matron. She laid a hand over her growling stomach and leaned forwards, catching a glimpse of the reason for the momentous meeting – the new matron. Kitty's hunger was immediately vanquished by curiosity and excitement. Who was this new, grim-looking, grey-faced woman who would control their day-to-day lives and the fortunes of Park Hospital's nursing family?

'Right, gals,' Matron said. 'As you know, I retire in just a few weeks.'

There was the sound of genuine sorrow rippling around the room. Nurses called out, 'We're going to miss you, Matron!' and 'Don't leave us!'

Matron smiled sadly. 'Thank you for your kind words, gals.' She looked down at hands that looked like they'd seen their fair share of hot soapy water and scrubbing brushes. 'But all good things must come to an end, and my knees aren't what they used to be.' Her smile turned into a frown, but it had no real bite to it. 'Anyway, I haven't gone yet, you cheeky young whippersnappers. So, how about we save the farewells for another day? Right now, I am delighted to introduce you to my replacement. Please put your hands together for the new matron.' Matron beamed at the newcomer and beckoned her forwards.

Kitty watched as the new woman strode forwards with obvious confidence and shook Matron's hand like a man.

'Thank you, Matron.' She turned to the nursing staff. 'Good afternoon, ladies. My name is Dorothy Pratt, and I'm delighted to start what I hope will be a long and happy stint at Manchester's famous and much-loved Park Hospital.' Her accent was genteel, but there was an obvious north-western lilt to it, audible in those flat vowels.

Kitty was so used to hearing senior staff who spoke like landed gentry that she was taken aback by the new matron's regional accent. *She sounds a little bit like me*, she thought, inadvertently raising an eyebrow. *Well, I never!*

As she applauded, Kitty noticed the younger nurses turning to one another, all mouthing the incoming matron's second name – Pratt. She was certain she could hear snorts of laughter above the clapping. Glowing with embarrassment at the thought of the disrespectful reception the new woman was encountering, Kitty glared at the junior nurses until they stopped.

The new matron either hid her hurt well or else had not noticed the young nurses ridiculing her. Wearing a serious expression, she held up her hand until the clapping subsided. 'Now, I'm sure quite a few of you are wondering what sort of a matron I'll be. Well, let me tell you ladies straight, I've come from Manchester Royal Infirmary and I expect things done properly. I'm an ordinary local woman, originally from the market town of Bury, to the north. But I've got where I've got from diligence and discipline. I believe that nurses are more than just glorified teasmades and bed-makers. We're an essential part of the medical staff, and what I'm personally interested in is how nurses on the other side of the Atlantic are starting to study for diplomas in their field. They're commanding respect and they're getting better paid.' Dorothy Pratt looked around the room, apparently studying each and every woman's face for a reaction.

Kitty felt a frisson of excitement at the thought of nurses in America, forging ahead with study and professional qualifications. She pictured herself standing on the steps of Manchester University, wearing a cap and gown and clutching some rolled-up certificate. Was it even possible?

One of the senior nurses put her hand up to ask a question.

'I'll take questions at the end,' Dorothy Pratt said. The authority in her voice was undeniable. 'For now, I need you ladies to listen. Over the next few weeks, your existing matron will be handing over the reins to me. To avoid confusion, you will call me Matron Pratt.'

A couple of sniggers could be heard. Kitty looked around and saw that quite a few of the younger nurses had their hands over their mouths and their shoulders were shaking as they stifled laughter.

The new matron stood in silence, eyeing the wayward nurses with obvious disapproval.

Kitty felt duty-bound to do something to salvage the reputation of Park Hospital's junior nursing staff. After all, these giggling girls reflected badly on the outgoing matron as well as on her and the other sisters. Digging her nails in the palms of her hands, she pondered which was the lesser of two evils – allowing the insubordination to continue or stepping out of line to take charge of the situation? *Come on, Kitty. You're a Sister now. Show this new matron what sort of stuff you're made of.*

Taking a deep breath, Kitty broke ranks and approached the group of giggling nurses. She grabbed one of them, Sally Townley, whom she knew to be a ringleader of sorts, but whispered sharply to them all. 'You stop this nonsense right now or you leave the room.'

'Sorry, Sister,' a couple of the nurses said.

Sally Townley, however, shook her arm loose. 'You're not my Sister. What are you going to do? Tell on us to the new prat?'

'Out! Now!' Kitty laid her hands on the girl's shoulders, turned her to face the door and pushed her forwards. 'I'll deal with you later, Nurse Townley. Come to see me in my office before the end of your shift.' She turned to the rest of the sniggering girls. 'And you lot can pipe down, or I'll pass your names on to the new matron, and you'll soon find out exactly how hilarious she is.'

The girls' faces fell. They all muttered apologies and stood straight, facing front.

Kitty made her way back to the line of Sisters at the front of the room. As she did so, she glanced over to Matron

Pratt. She was looking directly at Kitty. Kitty's heart quailed. Was the new matron cross with her for causing a to-do?

Kitty turned to face the room and prayed nobody could see her chest rise and fall with the thunderous beating of her heart.

Matron Pratt finally started to address the nurses once more. 'This hospital was the first National Health Service hospital, and as such, it's a jewel in the city's crown.'

There was a sea of nodding heads.

'I expect all of you to prove yourselves to me,' Matron Pratt said, casting her eyes over each and every girl. 'You need to demonstrate that you're worthy of that nurse's uniform. It doesn't matter a jot to me if you have a good reputation with the outgoing matron. I'm not the outgoing matron. So, as far as I'm concerned, you *all* have a blank sheet . . .' She paused, her expression positively dour. 'And I will not tolerate any blots on your copybooks. In return for your excellent service and loyalty, I will lobby the hospital's management for better pay and regular training.' Finally, her near-grimace softened into an almost-smile. 'Any questions?'

The senior nurse, who had raised her hand earlier, thrust her hand into the air again.

Matron Pratt pointed to her. 'You. Yes, you.'

In a faltering voice, the senior nurse spoke. 'Do you think us lot will start getting qualifications like the Yanks? And if we do, will we get respect, more like the doctors?'

'What you need to understand right now, nurses, is that this is 1950,' Matron Pratt said. 'Things are changing all the time. We've got new treatments and heaps of medical research going on. We're finding cures all the time, and having a centralised body that governs and funds all hospitals makes it easier for innovation to ripple out from the labs and onto the wards fast. America seems to be leading the way, so improvements for nurses are definitely on the horizon.' She held her finger up. '*But*, and I say *but*, the National Health Service is already running out of money. In fact, we might even see people having to pay for spectacles, dentures and prescriptions again.'

The was a murmur of disgruntled agreement in the dining room. Kitty thought about how Mam had been complaining about the very same prospect only the other day. 'If they make us pay for specs and the dentist,' Mam had said, 'I'm back to stumbling around and getting my teeth yanked the minute I get a bit of toothache. Imagine that, our Kitty! Your Mam will be blind as a bat and all gums. Good job my Bert isn't around to see *that*!'

As the meeting came to an end, Kitty wondered what the future would have in store for her.

Following the other sisters and the two matrons out of the dining room, she observed the ramrod-straight back and surefooted stride of Matron Pratt, next to the small, round figure of the outgoing matron, recognisable as ready for retirement with her swollen ankles and stiff gait. Could the new matron sanction Kitty staying on as a Sister after she and James had married? How much sway did this new dour woman have over the rules that governed the nursing body?

Kitty was jolted out of her reverie by her long-standing colleague and friend, Lily Schwartz, touching her elbow.

'Hey! What do you think of this new woman?' Lily asked. 'Do you think she'll clamp down on some of the prejudice of the English nurses and patients?'

'Who knows?' Kitty said, still visualising herself standing on those university steps, clutching her diploma whilst also wearing a shining wedding band on her left hand, James with his arm around her, beaming proudly at the camera. 'She certainly sounds like she's all in favour of progress, doesn't she?'

Lily shook her head and frowned. 'Well, I've been putting up with it for years, but I'm just one five-foot-nothing German Jew in a modest nursing post. I've never been able to shout loud enough on my own. But it's got even worse since the new nurses arrived. It's brazen, and I'm sick to the back teeth of it.'

Kitty rubbed Lily's upper arm, sorry to see her friend so agitated. 'I did tell you I approached the board about this, didn't I?'

'Yes. You're a good'un.' Lily patted her hand. 'But you told me they wouldn't let you get a word in edgeways.'

'Are you surprised? You know what they're like – a bunch of overgrown spoiled public schoolboys. It doesn't affect them, so they don't give a stuff. But maybe the new matron will listen. I'm a Sister now, so I can have a word. But really, Lil, you ladies also need to speak up for yourselves. There's strength in numbers. Maybe you and Grace could get organised, get the new girls involved and approach the new matron together. See if she'll take it to the board a second time.'

Lily looked ruefully at Matron Pratt and started to nod slowly. 'Let's hope she's not Pratt by name and prat by nature. She can't be any more deaf to the problem than old matron.'

Kitty raised an eyebrow and patted Lily on the back. 'The old guard is retiring. Who knows what the future will bring?'

The two friends parted company to return to their respective wards. Noting with regret that lunch had all been packed away, Kitty then remembered she had sent one of the junior nurses out for behaving disrespectfully during Matron Pratt's introduction. Heading for the dining room's exit to find the girl and chastise her properly, Kitty was surprised to feel a hand on her shoulder.

'Sister? Have you got a minute?'

Kitty turned around to find Matron Pratt standing behind her. 'Oh, er, hello.' Her pulse sped up to a gallop as she wondered why on earth the new matron would single her out before the woman had even started her first Park Hospital shift. *Be confident*, she thought. *You're a Sister now. Act like one.* Kitty stuck out her hand. 'Pleased to meet you, Matron Pratt.'

Matron Pratt stood in silence, clearly waiting for the nurses and the other sisters to file out quickly. Presently, Kitty was standing alone with the new matron. The old matron approached and took her place at Matron Pratt's side.

'This is Sister Kitty Longthorne,' the old matron said. 'I told you about her. She's one of my greatest success stories. A very dedicated and skilled nurse.'

Kitty felt her cheeks glowing red hot. 'Oh, Matron. You flatter me.'

'Nonsense,' the old matron said. She turned to Matron Pratt. 'Kitty was also responsible for Park Hospital's recruitment drive in the West Indies. She's our intrepid adventurer.'

The only sign that Dorothy Pratt had taken the old matron's high praise to heart was that she nodded and her eyebrows shot towards her hairline. Did she doubt Kitty's achievements? 'Interesting,' she said.

She fixed Kitty with a gaze so direct and penetrating that Kitty had to steel herself not to look away. Yet Matron Pratt fell silent again and started to look pointedly at the old matron. Was she waiting for the old matron to leave?

'Right. Well, ladies. I suppose I have handover notes to continue writing. I'll leave you both to it.' Sure enough, the old matron gave Matron Pratt a weak smile and left the dining room looking somewhat bewildered.

Kitty couldn't believe how much authority this new woman wielded with so few words. She dug her index finger behind her stiff collar and swallowed hard. Was she about to be given a dressing down?

Chapter 5

Finally, Matron Pratt spoke. 'I saw how you dealt with those giggling junior nurses, Sister.'

'Oh, I, er . . . Well, they know better than to behave like little children when a senior member of staff is addressing them. I thought I just couldn't—'

'You did the right thing. You showed strength of character and upheld the order of things. That's absolutely essential in a place where we deal with matters of life and death, round the clock.' Dorothy Pratt stood even taller than before, towering over Kitty like a forbidding but impressive statue. 'The staff of the National Health Service is an army. I am the commander of the nursing battalion. Every single one of us must know our place and fulfil our duty.'

'I completely agree, Matron Pratt. Duty first.'

The new matron nodded thoughtfully, as if passing judgement on Kitty. 'I may have a surname that marks me out as a figure to be poked fun at, but I am a serious woman, Sister Longthorne. I have serious ambition for the nursing profession and the standard of nursing in this hospital.'

'Smashing. I'm all for progress. Us younger nurses – we all are. We want to make a difference to the health of the nation.'

'You strike me as a leader.'

Kitty opened her mouth to respond, but her words were whipped clean off the tip of her tongue by self-doubt. Would she come across as boastful if she agreed? If she took this as an opportunity to mention the plight of the nurses from overseas or mentioned nurses' right to marry and remain in the profession, would Matron Pratt see her as a complainer and a troublemaker, running with tales and making demands? No. It could keep. 'Thank you.'

'The outgoing matron seems to think very highly of you, and her reputation for good judgement and high standards precedes her. I shall be keeping my eye on you, Sister Longthorne.'

The new matron strode out of the dining room, leaving Kitty feeling like she had been put through the proverbial wringer. Whatever did Matron Pratt mean by 'keeping an eye' on her?

Back on the ward, Kitty wended her way through the rows of iron lungs to continue to get to know her young patients and to see how they were faring. The hiss and sigh of the giant machines made it seem like the entire room was one giant breathing organism.

'Afternoon, love,' she said to a little boy with a shock of white-blond hair and a ghostly pale complexion to match. 'Now, I don't believe we've met. Who have we got here?'

She checked the boy's notes and saw that he was six years old, admitted a week ago, and had only just pulled round from the peak of his polio infection. 'Archibald Davies. Hello, Master Davies. Can I call you Archie? I'm Sister Longthorne, but you can call me Sister Kitty.'

Little Archie could only blink in response.

She turned back to his notes and could see that he'd undergone a tracheotomy to drain the mucus from his paralysed lungs. At least the cumbersome iron lung that encased him up to the neck was forcing him to breathe again.

Kitty turned to Rijuta Ghosh, one of the new nurses from India, who was gently wiping the boy's face with a flannel. 'How is Archie's tracheotomy wound healing, Nurse Ghosh?'

The nurse nodded and smiled. 'Very well, Sister. Very well. Dr Bourke is hoping Archie will be able to tell us himself how he's feeling, very soon.' She stroked the boy's hair. 'Brave boy.'

'Let's hope so. Carry on the good work, Nurse.'

Moving down the ward, Kitty greeted the children and observed the tender care that the nurses were giving to each one. Some were reading to the young patients. Others were helping them to drink from a straw. All that was visible of these gravely ill children was their small heads, propped on a single cushion. Their faces were only visible through the angled mirrors that were mounted above them.

Despite years of experience as a nurse, Kitty had never known anything like the polio epidemic of the last two years, and she would never get used to seeing children trussed up inside these giant whooshing machines.

At the far end of the ward were the children who were out of the iron lungs and on the road to recovery. Yet their story was still one of pain and inconvenience, as they were encased from head to toe in plaster.

'How are you this afternoon, Gordon?' Kitty asked a little boy whose casts were about to come off.

'A bit fed up, if I'm honest, Sister Kitty.' Gordon bit the inside of his cheek. His mouth was downturned. He screwed up his blue, blue eyes and spoke as if he were sharing some great secret with Kitty. 'My leg's itching like mad, and I can't scratch it. And my big brother said I look like an Egyptian mummy.'

Kitty ruffled his bright red hair. 'Ooh, your brother sounds a meanie. And you look nothing like a mummy. Mummies don't have hair that glows like a Belisha Beacon, for a start. You're brightening up this dull old ward with that lovely ginger mop of yours.'

Gordon smiled.

'And doesn't your brother realise these casts are there to make your bones grow nice and straight?'

The boy shrugged. 'They still itch like mad, Sister.'

'I'll get Nurse Ghosh to take a look. See if there's something she can do for the itching. Anyway, Dr Bourke has written in your notes that you'll be free of this lot in another couple of days. And a little birdie tells me your birthday's coming up. Is that right?'

Gordon smiled. 'Next Monday. I'm going to be nine. My mam said she'd bring me in a book about cowboys and Indians.'

'Cracking,' Kitty said. 'I'll come and read it to you myself, if you like.' Kitty checked the notes on the end of his bed. 'And your casts will definitely be off in time for your birthday.'

The lad punched the air. 'Yesssss.'

'You'll begin some special exercises. It's called physiotherapy.'

'Phys-what?'

'Physiotherapy. It's like magic. You do exercises and it strengthens all the muscles in your arms and legs. We're going to get you walking again, Gordon.'

'Will I be able to play football, Sister Kitty?'

Kitty nodded, picturing the boy wearing a leg iron and callipers like the other sufferers of polio – the children who had been lucky enough to escape with their lives, though not their full range of mobility. 'I'd put a shilling on it, Gordon. You'll be kicking a ball around in no time.'

She turned to the little boy next to him, who was almost as new to the ward as she was. His head peeped out from the top of his iron lung, which hissed and whooshed as the concealed bellows within sucked his lungs in and out in the vacuum they created.

Smiling at the boy's reflection in his overhead mirror, Kitty noted the boy's dark curls, big brown eyes and olive skin. 'And who do we have here?' she asked, wondering what his story would be. Might he be Italian or even Romany?

The boy's expression was utterly hangdog. 'Sammy. Sammy Levine.'

'Pleased to meet you, Sammy. I'm Sister Kitty.' Kitty glanced at his notes and saw he'd contracted polio in all likelihood at the municipal baths. His given religion was Jewish. He was down to receive Kosher meals. She made a mental note to check the kitchens knew of his dietary requirements. 'I understand you've just arrived at Park Hospital, and you're in one of our fancy, brand-new iron lungs.' She appraised the new piece of equipment. This iron lung had holes in the sides, like the portholes on a ship, to allow the nurses to tend to the patients without having to remove them entirely from the machine. 'Is it comfy in there?'

Sammy looked at her through the mirror. Tears stood in his eyes. 'Not really. I want to get out. I want my mam and dad. Do they know I've been moved to a new hospital? They never came to visit last night.'

Kitty turned to one of the senior nurses, Faye McNamara, who was taking the temperature of a child in the adjacent iron lung. 'Nurse McNamara! Does this patient's parents know he's been transferred from the infirmary?'

Nurse McNamara glanced at Sammy and smiled. 'Oh yes, Sister. Dr Bourke said they were sent a telegram. I've no doubt they'll be in to visit this evening. I believe they only live in Wythenshawe. It's not too far for them to travel.'

Turning back to the boy, Kitty stroked his cheek. 'There you go, Sammy. Your parents are sure to turn up this evening. In the meantime, you've got us to look after you.'

Sammy managed an unconvincing smile. 'Am I going to get better, Sister Kitty? Am I ever going to get out of this machine?'

Kitty searched for an answer that would offer some hope. 'Well, the good news is that you're not contagious anymore. All you children on this ward are over the worst of it.' The reality was, however, that the boy was currently paralysed and couldn't breathe for himself. What else could she say to cheer him that wouldn't be a lie? She remembered the discussion that had taken place at the board meeting. 'And the clever scientists are working on a vaccine as we speak. Polio will soon be a thing of the past.' Would this satisfy this inquisitive boy? She was sure he was studying her with the sort of sharp-eyed cynicism she was used to seeing only in intelligent adults. He seemed much older than his tender ten years.

'But a vaccine won't work on me because I've already got polio,' he said. 'I need medicine to fix me. Have they found a cure?'

'Blimey, Sammy. There's no flies on you!' Kitty chuckled awkwardly, wondering how much more of the difficult truth she dare share with Sammy, given he had already hit the nail on the head. 'I tell you what, I'll ask Dr Bourke to tell you all about it on his rounds.'

Casting her mind back to but a few nightmarish years earlier, when tuberculosis had had the deadliest grip of all on Manchester, Kitty paced along the central aisle of the polio ward with a surprisingly heavy heart. Medicine was advancing, new antibiotics were being discovered with each passing year, but it felt like they were constantly merely swapping one killer disease for another.

She observed the scores of children in their iron lungs, gasping for breath mechanically on their behalf. The Royal Infirmary was bearing the brunt of the outbreak; its polio wards were filled with still-contagious children, many of whom wouldn't make it. At least these children at Park Hospital stood a chance of recovery and were being treated for free. But what would happen if the National Health Service failed? What would happen if there were cutbacks because the government coffers had already run dry?

Kitty blinked the thought away and turned her attention to preparing notes for Dr Bourke's evening rounds.

Visiting time arrived, and Kitty was still writing at her desk when there was a knock on her open door.

She looked up to find a man standing in her doorway. Dressed in trousers and an overcoat that looked too big for him, he had the same dark curls as Sammy Levine. Behind him stood a woman who was standing on her tiptoes, eyeing the small patients in their iron lungs. 'Can I help you?' Kitty asked.

'We've come to visit Samuel Levine,' the man said. 'We're his parents. I'm Dovid Levine.' He turned and inclined his head towards the woman. 'This is my wife, Esther.'

Kitty got to her feet. 'I'm Sister Longthorne. Come with me. I met Sammy earlier. He's a very bright boy.'

Esther Levine nodded. 'Oh, yes. He's always been sharp as a tack has our Sammy.' Her friendly expression faltered. She looked suddenly afraid. 'Tell us, Sister. How's he getting on? We were beside ourselves when we got news that he'd been moved. We thought it was bad news.'

'Not at all,' Kitty said, beckoning them to follow her. 'He's been moved here to recover.' They made their way past the other children, some of whom had parents visiting, and others, who were alone and left to stare at their bedfellows through their own mirrors. 'We've just taken delivery of some lovely new iron lungs, and your Sammy is tucked up inside one.'

'Thank you so much, Sister. We feel so lucky to be in a country where our boy's getting the best that modern medicine can offer,' Dovid said. 'And for free, thanks to the National Health Service. Imagine! It could have been a lot worse if Sammy had got ill when he was younger.'

'That's true,' Kitty said. 'I know only too well the heartbreak of having a sick loved one and not being able to pay for their treatment. We're living in an age of miracles.'

As Kitty led Sammy's parents to his machine, she noticed that young Gordon's parents were also visiting. Gordon's flame-haired father had positioned his chair so that it blocked the way to Sammy's head.

'Oh, you must be Mr Spencer, Gordon's daddy,' Kitty said. 'I'm Sister Longthorne, in charge of the ward.'

Gordon's father barely glanced her way. He was too busy scrutinising the Levines through narrowed eyes. 'Oh, aye?'

'Would you mind moving your chair to the other side of your son's bed so that Mr and Mrs Levine here can see their son? Please.'

At her side, Esther was waving to Sammy through his mirror. She spoke in a language that Kitty didn't understand but which she recognised as Yiddish.

Gordon's father shot Esther a venomous look. Reluctantly, he scraped the legs of his chair along the polished wooden floor. 'Don't be making friends with that one,' he told Gordon, jerking his thumb towards Sammy. 'I'll speak to the doctor and get you moved, son. You don't want to be mixing with four-by-twos.'

Kitty felt certain the Levines had not heard the uncharitable remarks. She was relieved to see that they were busy chatting to their son. She knew, however, that the issue of bad behaviour on the ward still needed addressing, and urgently at that.

Later that evening, when the visitors had left, and the ward was silent but for the whoosh and wheeze of the iron lungs, Kitty made her way back down to where Sammy and Gordon both lay; one encased in his breathing machine, and the other, prone on the bed, with limbs encased in thick plaster. The little boys were whispering excitedly to one another about *The Beano* comic books.

'Now, now, gentlemen,' Kitty said softly. 'Time for you two to get some sleep.'

'Sorry, Sister,' Sammy said.

'Will the nurses read to us tomorrow, Sister?' Gordon asked.

Kitty ruffled his hair. 'You bet your bottom dollar they will.' She was privately pleased to see that the tension between both sets of parents wasn't affecting the camaraderie between the boys. 'Night-night, sleep tight, don't let the bed bugs bite.'

She padded quietly back down the ward, but stopped short when she reached Archie's iron lung. In the dim light that shone from the Sister's office, she could see his cheeks were wet.

'Are you crying, lovey?' she asked, crouching until her face was level with the boy's. She looked up into his mirror and they locked eyes with one another in the almost-dark. 'There, there,' she said, stroking the flaxen locks on his head. She took a clean handkerchief from the pocket of her apron and patted his eyes and cheeks gently dry. 'Try not to get upset, son. If you're missing your mam and dad and maybe your sisters and brothers too, that's only natural. Don't worry, flower. You'll be back home in no time.' Clearly, forgetful sleep was failing to find this new arrival on the ward. Kitty racked her brains for a way in which she could soothe the boy. 'Hey, I know. Would you like me to read to you? I usually leave it to my nurses to do the reading, but seeing as it's you, Archie, I'll read to you myself. How about that? A bedtime story from the Sister.'

Kitty turned to Archie and angled her head so that they could look at each other properly. When she saw Archie blink, she smiled. 'Back in a jiffy.'

She retrieved a dog-eared book from the bookshelf on the other side of the ward, fetched a small torch from her office that she kept for power cuts, and returned to Archie. 'Will *Noddy Goes to Toyland* do you? It's quite new, this. I love a bit of Enid Blyton, me. Do you like Noddy?'

Archie blinked twice.

Kitty pulled up a chair and positioned herself right by the head of his iron lung so that the boy would hear her above the noisy contraption that was helping him to breathe. She kept her voice low enough to avoid waking the others, and for the next ten minutes, she read the children's book by the light of her small torch.

After a while, she glanced over to her young patient. She realised that he was finally sleeping. Kitty closed the book and stroked Archie's hair, wondering if there would be any end to the polio epidemic that had begun waging its war on British families as the Nazis had surrendered.

Chapter 6

'Where on earth do we begin?' James said, laying the ingredients for Sunday lunch out onto his Formica kitchen worktop. He yawned and scratched his stubbled chin. 'I've been working such long hours for so long, eating so much canteen food, that I can barely remember how to cook a roast.'

'You see to the chicken and I'll peel the potatoes,' Kitty said, wrapping her arms around her fiancé from behind and resting her cheek on his broad back. 'Many hands make light work.'

James turned around and stroked her brow tenderly. 'We're a winning team, you and I. And I can't wait to introduce the woman I'm going to marry to one of my oldest and best friends. George is going to love you.' He planted a kiss on her lips.

Kitty pushed him away as her lips burned. 'Ooh, get a shave! It's like kissing sandpaper.' She giggled as he tried to smother her in prickly kisses. 'But seriously, I don't know what one of your fancy Cambridge pals is going to make of me – Kitty Longthorne of Hulme.' She announced her name and family's origin, as though she were announcing the arrival of a duchess at a society ball.

'He'll love you. I guarantee it. The question is, what will you make of him?'

*

They prepared the meal together, chatting about their working week. James bemoaned the spike in numbers of patients coming in with terrible facial injuries from road accidents; Kitty told him all about Dorothy Pratt and the reception she'd been given by the nurses.

Just as Kitty was basting the roasting tin full of almost-golden potatoes with the melted lard, the doorbell rang loudly throughout James's bachelor flat.

Almost jumping out of her skin, she glanced at the clock. She could feel panic rolling in like bad weather. 'Heavens to Betsy! He's here early. I haven't even put any tutty on.'

James untied the knot of his apron and hung it on the back of the galley kitchen door. 'You don't need make-up, my darling. You're naturally beautiful.'

As James let his friend in, Kitty hastily turned down the gas beneath the pan of swedes and turnips that was bubbling away on the stove. Desperate to know if she passed muster as a charming hostess, she tried to check her reflection in a polished spoon.

'I'll have to do,' she muttered, trying to shape her eyebrows with her finger. 'It's not like we're entertaining the King.'

Worrying that she smelled of lard and cabbage, Kitty made her way through to the living room, wearing a rictus grin. She could hear James and his guest chatting on the staircase, and the painful memory of the wedding-that-never-was, where James had almost married Kitty's fellow nurse Violet, came flooding back. She could still conjure the sneering tones of James's best man, Timothy. Tim, the upper-class twit who had warned her not to get in the way of James's planned marriage to a rich girl who was a better match. Would this George be any better? He sounded no different.

Kitty took a step backwards as George appeared in the doorway to the flat, unwinding a college scarf from around his neck. She forced herself to walk forwards to meet him and stuck out her hand. 'Hello, George. You must be George. I mean, you are George. I'm Kitty. Kitty Longthorne. Oh, flipping heck. Will you listen to me? I'm making a right hash of saying a simple hello!' She tittered nervously, cringing inwardly that she was still so bad at this sort of thing.

George chuckled and seized her hand between his, giving it a hearty shake. 'Jolly pleased to meet you, Kitty. I've heard so much about you from Jimmy-boy here. All good things! All good things, what?!' He cocked his head to the side, frowned and then shouted 'Ah!' as though he'd forgotten himself. 'And I'm George Hardy, of course.' This time, it was he who stuck out his hand, and they shook again.

He's as bad at this as I am, Kitty thought, immediately feeling a little more relaxed. 'Can I take your coat?'

Shrugging off his overcoat, George handed her his things. 'You're so kind.' He turned to James, 'Good Lord! You are a lucky, lucky man, James Williams. What have you done to deserve such a charming fiancée?'

'I often ask myself the same thing, George. I am indeed the luckiest man alive.' He waved at the leather and chrome Bauhaus settees that Kitty thought so uncomfortable. 'Now, make yourself at home, old chap. Let me fix you a stiff gin and tonic.'

As Kitty hung George's coat up, she rubbed the thick camel fabric between her fingers. The coat was a little thread-bare and shiny around the elbows but she could see it was of the finest quality and cut. The scarf's label said it was from Ede & Ravenscroft, by appointment to His Majesty the King. The garments were from a different world. How could she, from a terraced street in Hulme, fit in with the likes of George Hardy and whatever rich girl he would eventually marry?

'That's defeatist talk, Kitty,' she whispered to herself. 'And don't be so quick to mark him out as a snob, just because he's a toff. That's too much of Bert Longthorne talking, and he's pushing up daisies.'

Returning to the living room, Kitty perched on the edge of one of the settees, trying to arrange her legs in a way she thought a girl who had been to finishing school in Switzerland would. When James handed a gin and tonic to her, she took a large gulp, hoping it would give her a little Dutch courage.

'So, tell us how you two met,' she said.

'Ah well, Cambridge, of course,' George said. 'Jimmy-boy, a chap called Timothy – have you met him? – and yours truly were at Trinity College. We all went up in the same year. James and Timothy were these two terribly, terribly serious medical students . . .' He pulled what was clearly his 'terribly serious' frowning face for Kitty and said the words in a deep, almost slurring voice that sounded just like Professor Baird-Murray. Then he winked. 'And I was—'

'You graduated in rowing, drinking the college cellars dry and gadding about, I seem to recall,' James said, chuckling.

George ran a hand through his dishevelled hair, which needed a good cut, Kitty decided privately. 'That sounds about right,' he said. He turned to Kitty. 'I read Physical Natural Sciences, if you must know. Ohm's law and the theory of relativity and all that. I think Sir Isaac Newton must have been spinning in his grave, though, ha ha. I don't recall turning up to a single supervision. But I *did* get a Cambridge blue in rowing and captained the men's eight beautifully.' He kissed the tips of his fingers dramatically, as though he were a chef pronouncing over delicious food. He laced his fingers over his chest and rolled his eyes to the ceiling. '*Ab abusu ad usum non valet consequentia.* And I certainly did misuse my time there . . . to staggeringly good effect.'

'You seem very different from Timothy, I must say,' Kitty said, warming to this positively eccentric and clearly fun-loving man.

Waving dismissively, George sipped his gin. 'Jimmy-Boy and I had more in common, I'd say. Timothy was the spare wheel, still clinging onto James's coat tails after Eton.' He turned to James. 'I know we were the "Notorious New Court Three", but he always did hang around like a bad smell.' When he maligned their mutual friend to Kitty, he did so with a conspiratorial air and winked again.

James breathed in sharply through his teeth. 'Oh, that's brutal! Poor Tim. I always thought he smelled rather nice.'

The two men burst into laughter.

Kitty took her leave to tend to the Sunday roast. She was happy to see that everything was cooked to perfection. As she dished up the steaming food, she eavesdropped on James and George's conversation.

'So what brings you to the rainy north and back into my orbit, old chap?' James asked.

'Well, it's rather fortuitous, actually. I was offered a job at the new Windscale plutonium plant as one of their emeritus physicists in residence, as it were.'

'Emeritus? *You*?' James asked, clearly expressing surprise. 'At the vanguard of nuclear science? Good God, man. Do they have any idea what you're really like?'

George wheezed with laughter. 'I'll have you know I'm one of the finest science minds in all of the north-west.'

James guffawed. 'Haven't you heard that self-praise is no recommendation?'

Straining the gravy through a sieve into the gravy boat, Kitty decided it was time for the men to shelve their conversation. 'James, can you give me a lift taking the food through to the dining table, please?'

'Coming, my love!'

Together, they laid the table and carried the dishes full of vegetables, stuffing, roast potatoes and the all-important chicken through to where George was waiting, rubbing his hands in glee.

'I say, you wouldn't think there was rationing still on in Manchester,' he said.

'Don't kid yourself,' Kitty said, setting out the plates which had been warming in the oven. 'James made good use of his patient network to make sure you wouldn't be sitting down to a bowl of corned-beef hash.'

'I'm honoured,' George said. 'I haven't had a decent roast since Christmas, and that was only because my old man had been on a pheasant shoot and bunged the gamekeeper a few shillings for a nice fat turkey.'

James sharpened the carving knife at the table with some flourish and dug the two-pronged fork deeply into the chicken breast. 'I'm very lucky. I did a farmer a favour and now we never go short of an egg or two or a chicken on special occasions, do we, Kitty?'

'The pleasure shall be all mine,' George said.

Kitty watched James carving the bird, fleetingly imagining how it would be to watch him doing that with two or three of their children sitting at the table in a lovely suburban dining room, looking adoringly up at their capable father with big brown eyes, just like his. Knowing that such a domestic idyll couldn't currently be hers without her abandoning her professional dreams, she sighed wistfully and pushed the fantasy aside. She turned to George. 'Did I overhear you've taken at job at Windscale? Isn't that just up from Blackpool?'

George held his plate out for slices of chicken and helped himself to potatoes. 'Not far. It's just to the west of the Lakes. On the coast.'

'We go up there for breaks when we can, don't we, James?'

'I never say no to a weekend in Windermere,' James said, handing Kitty her plate back.

'Then you shall both have to visit,' George said. 'I've just rented a little cottage with marvellous views. They're still building the Windscale site at the moment, and I'm helping to oversee all that. But I shall be quite lonely when the working week is over.' He smiled sadly at Kitty. 'Ah, a travelling physicist's life is not easy.'

'Maybe you'll meet a lovely local girl,' Kitty said. 'Or maybe there will be female scientists at Windscale.'

Both George and James looked at each other and laughed. Kitty couldn't help but feel niggled that the notion of a woman being a scientist in 1950 was still something to be joked about. Again, she visualised herself on the steps of Manchester University, clutching a diploma.

'Oh, dear Kitty, no need to look so crestfallen. We were only joking,' George said.

'Yes. Sorry, darling,' James said. 'It was a cheap shot.'

'Aye, at the expense of women like me,' Kitty said. The resentful words tumbled from her tongue as if they'd just been waiting for their moment to be spoken aloud. 'Don't think I've forgotten the way my concerns were dismissed in that hospital board meeting, James Williams. A bit more moral support would be nice.'

The smile fell from James's face. He ran a finger around the collar of his shirt. 'Er . . . perhaps we can save that discussion for another time, darling. Let's not bore our guest with work matters.' He looked to George, clearly hoping his university pal might fish him out of an awkward spot.

As if some telepathic communication had taken place between the men, George raised an eyebrow. 'It's not that there are no women scientists, Kitty. There's actually a theoretical physicist called Maria Goeppert Meyer who's working on something called a nuclear shell model.' He looked at her sheepishly. 'I think she might even win a Nobel Prize. But women like her are still few and far between.' The sheepish look turned into a positively wolfish one, then. 'My secretary *is* rather pretty, though . . .' He took a large bite out of a potato, skewered on the end of his fork. He spoke with his mouth full. 'So, it's not all bad news.'

Bite your tongue, Kitty counselled herself. *He's not the first man to treat his secretary like a bauble instead of a colleague . . . and don't pass comment on his terrible table manners. These public schoolboys never had a mother around to teach them how to behave.* 'What were you doing before?' Kitty asked.

'Well, most recently, I've been working in Oxford on some research into various applications of plutonium,' he said.

James booed as he tugged and tugged the cork out of a bottle of wine with a wayward corkscrew. 'Do you mean to tell me you defected to the *other place*?'

''Fraid so,' George said. 'During the war, I'd been working on a jolly interesting spot of research in the Manhattan Project.'

'I say!' James said, pouring George a glass of wine. 'The Manhattan Project? Wasn't that the name for the group of chaps who developed the atomic bomb?'

'The very same. I was lucky enough to be on James Chadwick's team.' George turned to Kitty. 'Chadwick discovered the neutron, back in '32. He's a very bright fellow.'

Kitty nodded, pretending to know what a neutron was. Whatever it was, it was clear that George, despite his protestations that he'd done little but row at university, was quite the scholar. She shuddered at the thought of the atomic bomb, though, remembering reports on *Pathé News* at the local picture house of how the war in the Far East had been stopped only by the Americans dropping atomic bombs on Hiroshima and Nagasaki. The images of giant clouds, mushrooming in the sky made a cold sweat break out on her top lip. She hastily wiped her upper lip with her napkin and kept her distaste to herself.

George continued, clearly enjoying himself. 'Anyway, when I heard there was a professor at Oxford, doing some very interesting research into atomic power, and I felt the lure of a research grant and an easy spot of teaching undergraduates, I thought I'd decamp there for a year or two. Since then, China's fallen into the hands of the communists and here we are in a new atomic era, my friends, with the Yanks racing the Reds to build as many bombs as possible.'

'I do think it's rather disagreeable that the focus is always on weaponry,' James said. He turned to Kitty. 'Don't you, darling?'

Kitty nodded, chewing thoughtfully on a carrot. 'Oh, aye. You can say that again. You try spending the war years patching up wounded airmen and seeing too many of them end up in the cemetery, and you soon start getting pacifist sympathies.'

'Quite,' George said. 'Personally, I'm much more interested in other applications of atomic power.'

James regaled his friend with news of the cardiothoracic surgeon Mr Galbraith's hope that the Cobalt 60 Isotope trial would yield a new treatment for cancer. 'Seems to me that there's no limit to what a spot of radioactivity can do,' he said. 'I'm all for using science to improve man's lot.'

'Indeed.' George shovelled a fork stacked with a little of everything into his mouth and groaned with pleasure. He cleared his palate with some wine. 'Anyhow, when the Windscale offer came along and I was wooed up north by a rather comfortable salary and the prospect of working with plutonium in a civilian capacity, I jumped. I still have my fingers in a few Ministry of Defence pies, obviously, but lighting up the great British nation with atomic power is one hell of a lure for a scientist like me . . .' He leaned in towards Kitty and adopted that tone of confiding in her again. 'Even if it does rain all the time.' He held his hand up with fingers outstretched. 'Webbing's coming along nicely.' Then he winked. 'I think I qualify for *local* status when I become entirely amphibian.'

James shoved his fork into his pile of mashed swedes and turnips, pointing at George with the laden fork. 'What do you think are the odds of the Reds taking over all of Asia?'

George shrugged. 'We're about to find out, but I'm fairly certain our government and the Yanks will be doing their darndest to stop the commies marching over the face of the earth. They're already sowing the seeds of discontent in a post-war Britain.'

Kitty thought about the clash between the modern-day Blackshirts and the anti-fascists. 'I've seen fighting in the streets between Oswald Moseley's new lot and the communists. I have to say, our sister-in-law-to-be is coloured, and I'm from a working-class family, so I'm inclined to side with the communists.'

James looked at her askance. 'Oh, darling. You don't mean that, do you?'

'Well, I'm no fan of the commies, but they do seem to be the lesser of two evils, don't they?' Kitty said, pushing a piece of roast potato around her plate, visualising Grace and Lily Schwartz and Sammy Levine on the polio ward. She considered Mam, struggling to make ends meet now that Bert had gone and she was getting too old to work the hours as a machinist that she'd been used to working. 'How many men lost their lives fighting the Nazis? If Britain votes in a load of fascists, what was all that death and destruction for? And where would that leave all the poor?'

George pointed at her with a roast parsnip hanging from his fork. 'An excellent point. At least communists purport to champion *the people*. All men are equal, and all that malarkey. Fascism is entirely divisive.'

'We're not a nation that votes for extremist politicians, though,' James said. 'The communists are as unpalatable as the fascists. Look at Stalin and the Bolsheviks. They wouldn't know democracy if it battered them over the head with . . .' He looked at George's fork. 'A roast parsnip.'

Silence had fallen on the three for a minute or so, when James broke through their reverie.

'All this working with atomic power and sympathising with the commies, George. You'll have to make sure the Reds don't try to recruit you as a spy.' He chuckled at the notion.

'I don't *really* have commie sympathies,' George said. 'I'm playing devil's advocate, of course.' With his plate now empty, he set hit cutlery down. 'I say, have you seen the scandal in the papers recently?'

'I take it you're talking about the Cambridge men who've been caught spying for the Soviets,' James said.

'The very same.'

'Wasn't Douglas Philips a Trinity man from the year above?' James's brow furrowed. 'He always was a quiet sort, if memory serves.'

George nodded vehemently. 'Yes, yes. Dreary Doug . . . lived on the most boring staircase in Great Court. Read Mathematics, as I recall, and smelled of musty old cupboard.' He snorted with derision. 'Went into the civil service, didn't he? Imagine *him* being fingered for spying?' He chuckled.

'Double agent to boot, I read,' James said. 'He's had to defect to avoid being tried for treason. Bet it's cold in Moscow at this time of year.' He pulled a face and shivered visibly.

George locked eyes with Kitty and patted her hand. 'Kitty, my dear. You must think us terrible bores, with all this reminiscing and gossiping like old washerwomen.'

'Not at all,' Kitty said. 'I'm glad to be marrying a man of the world. Until I travelled to the West Indies for work, I'd never known anything at all beyond Trafford. Now, here I am, listening to talk at my fiancé's dinner table about atomic power and spies. It adds a little spice to Sunday lunch, all right.' Again, she pictured their future children seated at the table. 'I want our family to be men and women of the world.'

She turned to James for a reaction, but he was still clearly preoccupied by the strange fate of his college mates.

He helped himself to another slice of chicken and started to nod with narrowed eyes, as if he were solving a conundrum. 'I'd heard rumours that one of the Trinity Fellows was a Soviet recruiter. Turns out the rumours were true.' He raised his glass to his lips and paused, now wearing a look of disbelief on his handsome face. 'How funny! I wouldn't have thought that Dreary Doug had subterfuge in him. Not so dreary, after all.'

As she cleared away the plates after dinner and left James to enjoy a glass of brandy with his old university friend, Kitty thought about the communists and Union Movement fascists who had been fighting on the streets of Trafford. She wondered about the threat of war in Korea and shuddered at the possibility that she and James might once more be patching up wounded soldiers.

Chapter 7

'How was your weekend, Kitty?' Grace asked as they stood next to one another at the sinks in the bathroom of the nurses' home.

Kitty scrubbed at her neck with a scrubbing brush, recoiling at the feel of the boiling hot soapy water that dripped down her freezing cold back. 'Not much better than getting a strip wash at half five on a Monday morning in February.' She soaped her armpits and splashed herself with water from the large ceramic basin. 'James had this friend for Sunday lunch. He was very interesting and all that, but I found it hard to keep up with the conversation, if I'm honest. It was all Cambridge this, and atomic science that. I felt a bit daft.'

Grace took her towel from the burning hot towel rail and started to rub herself dry. 'You're the last person who should be feeling like that. Just because you weren't born with a silver spoon in your mouth doesn't make you stupid.'

'He was very nice, if I'm honest. I'm being unfair. Anyway, James has asked him to be an usher at our wedding. I wish he was the best man, actually, because I prefer him a darn sight more to that pompous prig, Timothy – James's so-called best friend. He doesn't make any secret of the fact that he thinks James is marrying beneath himself.'

Taking her toothbrush out of her washbag, Grace tutted. 'And there was me, thinking Barbados was bad for snobbery with all them plantation owners and hoity-toity coloureds working in the best jobs and lording it over the rest of us! England . . . I've never seen anything like it.' Her eyes widened. 'Imagine what this Timothy would say if you were Black, as well as being poor.'

'Oh, he's nothing but an upper-class twit. You're lucky that when you and Ned get wed, you don't have to think about family politics – which obnoxious berk has to get an invite, just because his parents are college chums with your parents, and your parents are giving you money towards a house. And by that, I mean *James's* parents, because my mam hasn't got two ha-pennies to rub together.'

'Why we putting ourselves through this again?' Grace asked, giggling. 'But I tell you what, you think James's lot aren't cock-a-hoop about you, but you should see what my mumma's been writing to me.'

Kitty looked at Grace askance. 'She doesn't approve of Ned?'

Grace shook her head. 'You surprised? You heard what Ned was living like in Barbados, running whores, lying, gambling . . . *I* know Ned's got a big heart and a good soul, but your brother's name is mud back in Bridgetown. He's the no-good white man with the face like a hog been in a fire. And my mumma's no fool. She heard the rumours about Ned and she knew I was sweet on him before I even got on the boat. She said, "Gracie, if black bird fly wid pigeon, he will get shoot."' She mimicked her mother's strong Bajan accent and castigating tone. Though she chuckled, there was regret in her voice. 'She's got a point. I'll not be able to hold my head up high when I go home. Rich white people don't have exclusive license on snobbery.'

'Love finds a way,' Kitty said, though she could empathise with Grace, given how she was looked down upon by some of James's upper-class friends and family. 'Things'll get easier. It's just that people are taking a while to adjust to change.'

With the change of matron on her mind, Kitty returned to her room and put on her pristine Sister's uniform. Standing before her mirror, she tried to imagine herself wearing pearls in her ears, a fully fashioned twinset and a mink coat over a tailored skirt – the sort of uniform every doctor's wife seemed to wear. She shook her head, uncomfortable at the sight of Mrs James Williams in her mind's eye. Nursing had been in her heart for so long that Kitty wondered if there would be space for the inevitable charity work and coffee mornings that would be expected of her, once married.

'Pack it in, Kitty,' she told her reflection. 'Concentrate on planning a good send-off for Matron.'

Making her way over to the hospital building in the freezing, early morning dark and entering the brightly lit reception with unaccustomed eyes, Kitty made a mental note to speak to the other nurses at lunchtime about a whip-round. Perhaps James could speak to the board about—

Kitty's thoughts were interrupted by the strange sight of two men standing in the corridor up ahead, talking in low, secretive voices. Both sported black eyes, cut lips and arms in slings, as if they were mirror images of one another. Yet both were familiar. One with black curls and the other with terrible scarring on most of his face. Trying to blink away the heavy veil of fatigue that only a strong cup of tea could lift, she realised who the disfigured face of one of the men belonged to.

'Ned? Is that you, our kid?' Quickening her pace, she approached the men.

Ned spotted her, turned on his heel and started to walk swiftly in the opposite direction.

'Hey! Ned Longthorne!' she shouted after him. 'Don't you be throwing me a deaf'un. I can see it's you!'

Stopping in his tracks, Ned turned around and held his free hand in the air as if in surrender. He started to walk back towards her and his wounded compatriot. As Kitty walked forwards, she realised why she'd recognised the other man, too.

'*Mr Levine*?' she said, realising that his black curls were almost identical to those of his son and her new polio patient, Sammy.

'Morning, Sister Longthorne,' Dovid Levine said, his words muffled as he spoke with a fat lip. 'Fancy meeting you here. Ha ha.'

Kitty glared at him. 'I work here. What's your excuse? And why are you standing in the corridor at quarter to six in the morning, looking like you've been knocked down by a truck and whispering sweet nothings to my brother?' As Ned came within reach, she grabbed him by the sleeve and pulled him close.

'Ow!' Ned tried to shake her loose. 'Get off, will you? I'm not a kid, our Kitty.'

'Well, how about you stop acting like one, then? What are you doing, sneaking around with a fat lip, your arm in a sling and the biggest shiner I've seen in a long while? How do you know Dovid, here?'

'I, er, well . . .'

'It's not what you think, Nurse Longthorne.'

'*Sister* Longthorne, not Nurse.' She looked from Dovid to her brother and back again, then glanced down at the knuckles of both men – they were freshly bandaged, but some blood seeped through the dressings. 'You've been fighting. Right, I wasn't born yesterday. Out with it.'

Dovid was the first to talk. 'We've been in a bit of a scuffle with some fascists, if you must know.'

'*We?*' Kitty glanced at her brother and could see a florid rash inching its way up his scarred neck. 'Who's we?'

'No one. Nothing for nosies.' Ned tapped the nose that James had re-formed for him, years earlier, using the latest plastic surgery techniques.

'Why don't you tell her?' Dovid said to Ned. 'There's no need to be ashamed. You're fighting on the right side.'

Kitty may have been dogged by a fatigue that never really left her, but now she was alert enough to work out exactly what sort of men clashed regularly with Mosleyites. She yanked Ned closer still. 'Wait, you're a commie?'

Ned shook his head and shrugged. 'Anti-fascist, not really a commie.'

'I come from a family of proud Bolsheviks,' Dovid said. 'We believe that all men should be treated equally and that all wealth should be shared.'

Feeling red mist descend, Kitty tried to bite her tongue but failed. 'Oh, I know full well what a Bolshevik is, Mr Levine. And what you do is *your* business and for *your* wife and mother to worry about. But my brother, here . . .' She locked eyes with Ned. 'You're addicted to getting into bother, aren't you? Now Dad's dead and you've got Grace, you might have stopped fencing bent gear and running a counterfeiting fiddle, but you had to go looking for some new way of getting your kicks, didn't you?'

'This is about fighting for Grace,' Ned said. He laid his good hand on Dovid's shoulder. 'And all the other good folk who get treated like dirt because they're not true blue.'

'Fighting's not the answer, you daft ha'peth. When was anything solved by brawling in the streets? If the Blackshirts start, call the police!'

Dovid sighed. 'It's not that simple, I'm afraid. The police . . . most of them mean well and take their duties seriously, but as a rule, they don't see defending people like my family and Ned's fiancée as a priority.'

'But siding with the Reds! You're going to get into trouble with the government if you're not careful. Communism's not the answer.' She turned to Ned. 'Honestly, Mam's going to have a heart attack if she thinks you're getting into bed with the commies. Of all the ropey things you've done, Ned Longthorne . . .'

'Look around you, Kitty,' Ned said. 'People are fed up. The rich are getting richer, and the poor are getting poorer.'

'Don't kid yourself. It's always been like that,' Kitty said, eyeing a dark patch of dried blood on Ned's head with concern.

'The country's changing, Kitty, and it's a tinderbox, waiting to go up in flames.' He finally pulled himself free of Kitty's grip. 'The fight's already come to the city. All I had do was to choose which side I was on. And I'm marrying a Black girl, aren't I? So my choice was already made.'

'Jesus,' Kitty said, shaking her head and looking down at the highly polished floor. 'You're both playing with fire.' She looked up and met Dovid Levine's bloodshot gaze.

'I fought in the war against the Nazis,' he said. 'Tanks in Africa. I took a bullet to the shoulder. Made it home by the skin of my teeth. And your brother, here, fought in the Far East and ended up losing his face. That can't all have been for nothing. We didn't put our lives on the line to let the likes of Mosley turn Britain into Nazi Germany.'

Kitty was suddenly beset by light-headedness that threatened to knock her off her feet. She waved at both of them dismissively. 'I can't be doing with this bunkum right now. I've got a ward full of seriously poorly kids, including your son, Dovid. I need a strong brew and then I need to do my job. I'll see you at visiting time.' She turned from Dovid to her brother. 'And . . . well, I don't know when I'll next see you, Ned, but it seems you keep turning up like a bad penny while I'm trying to work. I just hope the next time I see you won't be in the mortuary or a prison cell.'

'Stop being melodramatic!' Ned said, adjusting his arm in its sling. 'I'll see you at Mam's on Tuesday night for tea.'

He blew her a kiss, but Kitty could only roll her eyes and turn away, poised to resume her journey to the polio ward. As she did so, she spotted two police constables heading right for them, and they only had eyes for Ned and Dovid.

Chapter 8

'Take deep breaths, Sister,' Nurse Ghosh said, holding Kitty's hands. She crouched in front of Kitty, wearing a concerned look.

In the relative privacy of her Sister's office, Kitty was sitting on her desk chair, inhaling slowly through her nose and breathing out through her mouth. She nodded, grateful for the Indian woman's kindness and the calming effect of her touch. 'Thanks, Rijuta,' she said. 'I can feel my heartbeat slowing down now. It's just I got such a shock when I saw those coppers. I honestly thought they'd come to arrest my brother and Mr Levine. Turns out they were headed elsewhere.'

'All's well that ends well,' Rijuta said, getting to her feet. 'Do you want me to tell Dr Williams about your funny turn?'

Kitty shook her head vehemently. 'Not on your Nelly. He's got enough on his plate without me panicking him over nothing. I just got a little het up. Do me a favour, though, please don't tell anyone what I told you about Mr Levine being a Bolshevik. It's none of our business, and I don't want any tensions on the ward during visiting time with the other parents.'

'I won't breathe a word,' Rijuta said.

'Not to Grace either, about my brother's involvement. It's his place to tell her. He has to take responsibility for his own actions.'

Rijuta nodded. 'Promise.' She picked up a stack of kidney dishes that she'd been sluicing out and then paused, halfway to the door. She turned back to Kitty. 'Your brother's got a point though. The fascists are making people's lives a misery, especially newcomers like me. I'm lucky enough to live in the nurses' accommodation, where I know I'm safe, apart from the odd sneer from one of the English nurses. They think I don't hear it when they say I smell of curry. But sticks and stones may hurt my bones . . . I know a family that came here in the thirties from the Punjab, though. They run a lovely little café near the university. They are having a hard time of it too. Somebody's got to stand up to the bullies.'

The lights on the ward were still low at the start of the day shift. As she read through the notes left by the Sister who had been in charge overnight, Kitty's thoughts wandered to what Rijuta had said about needing to stand up to bullies. Yet the thought of Ned getting involved with political extremists didn't sit at all well with her. She was reminded of the conversation that had taken place at the weekend between George and James, about their college mate who'd had to defect to the USSR to avoid being hung for treason, after he'd been caught spying for the other side of the Iron Curtain. She shuddered at the prospect of Ned getting in too deep and getting into hot water with the secret service. *Focus on these notes, Kitty!* she told herself. *Ned isn't one of your patients. He's big enough and daft enough to look after himself.*

Heading out onto the ward to check on the children before the day began in earnest and breakfast was served, Kitty was sure she could hear a strange noise, above the hiss and sigh of the iron lungs. She stood still a moment and cocked her head to the side, trying to place the sound. It was an ominous gurgle. She realised then that one of the children was choking.

Walking swiftly down the rows of iron lungs, she inspected each child as she went. When she got to the little boy who'd been admitted a week earlier – Archibald Davies – she knew there was a serious problem.

She looked up to where Rijuta was talking softly to a child who had woken early. She clicked her fingers to get her attention without waking the entire ward. 'Nurse Ghosh,' she whispered loudly.

Rijuta looked up. Kitty beckoned her over. She must have looked quite stricken with fear because Rijuta all but ran to her side.

Kitty spoke as quietly and as calmly as she could. 'Get Dr Bourke immediately. Ask Galbraith to come too, if you can find him. There's something wrong with this child. I think his tracheotomy wound has bled internally, or else the iron lung's not working.'

Rijuta sprinted out of the ward to find the necessary specialists, leaving Kitty to deal with Archie.

'Archie! Archie, can you hear me?' she asked.

The child's eyes opened suddenly, wild and full of terror, but he could not speak. His body started to convulse. He was turning blue rapidly. Kitty could see he was drowning. Using her initiative, she started to slide Archie out of the iron lung, realising her best hope was to turn him on his side to drain whatever was blocking his airways.

By the time she had freed the boy from his iron lung, Dr Bourke was running towards her, with Galbraith close behind.

Bourke and Galbraith examined the boy together, seeming to communicate by nodding to one another.

Galbraith broke the ominous silence. 'This child needs immediate emergency surgery. Do we have a free side room, Nurse?'

'Yes, I'll lead the way.'

Kitty went on ahead as the men wheeled Archie the short distance to the room.

'Close the door, Sister,' Dr Bourke said. 'Let's scrub up.'

Preparing for surgery, Kitty said a silent prayer that Archie would survive. She was to assist the doctors, but the least she could do was keep the boy's spirits up. 'Don't worry, Archie, love,' she said to him. 'You're in good hands. These two kind doctors are going to sort you out, cocker. Just try to think of your favourite football team or your favourite game.'

When she'd lined up the various surgical instruments, Richard Collins, the anaesthetist, entered. He'd brought with him a syringe, which he filled with anaesthetic. 'What's the patient's name?' he asked Kitty.

'Archie.'

He nodded and turned to the boy, who was losing consciousness. 'Hello, Archie. I'm just going to give you something to make sure you float off into a nice sleep full of lovely dreams. You might feel a scratch.'

Together, they worked quickly as a team, trying to save the boy. Almost half an hour had passed in near silence, as the thoracic surgeon, Galbraith, beavered away, trying to drain the mucus and blood that was stopping the boy from breathing.

Kitty's heart started to sink as she saw that the doctors were fighting a losing battle. Today, at least, it seemed as though her prayers wouldn't be answered.

'We're losing him,' Galbraith said.

'Yes, I'm afraid he's beyond our reach,' Dr Bourke said. 'To be honest, I'm surprised that the child made it this far, given the condition he was in when he was first admitted.'

Taking a sharp breath and holding it, Kitty watched as her small patient slipped away. Exhaling hard, she blinked away a tear and said a silent word of apology that she'd not been able to do more for him.

'If only I'd got to the ward early and had realised straight away that he'd got into difficulty,' she said, privately cursing Ned for the drama that had waylaid her for vital minutes. 'It's all my fault.'

Galbraith stood straight with a grunt and held his bloodied hands aloft. He looked drained of all colour, as though Archie had taken something of Galbraith's life force with him to the hereafter. He fixed Kitty with a resigned expression. 'Don't trouble yourself with feelings of guilt, Sister Longthorne. You, of all people, have seen enough patients die on the operating table to know that nothing is straightforward with the human body.'

'Especially not where polio is concerned,' Bourke added. 'We lost five children last week and seven the week before. Poliomyelitis is a killer. That's the sad truth of it. Until we get a vaccine that can be administered en masse, all we can do is our best. And I believe that is exactly what you did.' He looked at the clock and made a note of the time of death.

Richard gathered up his equipment and took his leave. 'Sorry it wasn't a better outcome. See you later, chaps. Kitty.'

Dr Bourke smiled sadly at Kitty. 'There, there, Sister. The young ones are always the hardest to lose. But you'd better send a telegram to his parents, post haste, and make arrangements for the boy to be taken down to the mortuary.'

Left alone with the boy, Kitty allowed herself a few moments to shed a tear and say a prayer for the little boy's soul. She wasn't a particularly practising Catholic, but still hoped that there would be something better awaiting this innocent young soul, if there was such a thing as the other side. She covered his body with a clean sheet, scrubbed her hands and arms and put on a fresh uniform that she had hanging in her office.

On the ward, she whispered to Nurse Ghosh all that had come to pass. 'Can you oversee the start of breakfast for a few minutes, please, Nurse? I have something urgent to attend to.'

Having dealt with the terrible task of sending a telegram containing the worst kind of news to the Davies family, Kitty made her way to the mortuary to inform the porters that Archibald Davies' body needed collecting from the children's polio ward.

The mortuary was a cold and foreboding place that Kitty didn't like at all. She shivered as she walked into the freshly distempered, austere place, feeling that the temperature had dropped by at least a few degrees. Three trolleys were lined up, each holding a body covered by a sheet.

'Hello?' she called out. 'Is anybody there?' Kitty wrapped her arms around herself, sensing the hairs on the back of her neck rising at the eerie silence of the place. The industrial lights that shone overhead flickered on and off. She could hear the buzz of electricity through their circuit. 'Come on, Kitty. Pull yourself together. You're supposed to be a professional woman. The dead can't hurt you.' She pushed herself past the dead bodies and was presently able to hear voices in the examination room beyond.

The voices belonged to two men. One was the mortician, the other . . .

When she caught sight of James, examining a cadaver on the mortician's slab, Kitty had to stifle a yelp of surprise. 'Dr Williams? Whatever are you doing down here?'

Kitty had walked in to find James bending over the body of a man. The man looked to be in his thirties with a badly lacerated face. He had also sustained injuries to his legs, given that they bent in the wrong places and looked to have sustained several nasty breaks.

'I say! Sister Longthorne!' James said, looking up at her. 'Come and look at this and tell me what you think.' He beckoned her close.

'Haven't you got a clinic this morning?' Kitty asked, nodding at the mortician, a bespectacled and odd-looking man in a soiled white coat, the sight of whom always caused a shiver to run down her spine. 'Morning, Derek.' She turned from the mortician back to James. 'Shouldn't you be reading through case notes right now?'

'Oh, yes, I suppose so. But I had a free moment and a blinding flash of inspiration.' When he grinned at her, his face lit up the drab, cold place. 'You know I've been inundated with patients who've been in road accidents, don't you?'

'Yes.'

'And at the board meeting, old Thistlethwaite, our casualty man, backed me up over the surge in deaths, thanks to car and motorcycle accidents and what have you.'

'Yes.'

'Well, it's all very well asking my colleagues to look out for reasons as to why these poor souls are shuffling off their mortal coils in seemingly untrammelled numbers. But when I found myself reading an article in a medical journal about that very phenomenon, I thought I'd come down here and have a look for myself.' He glanced at the mortician. 'Sure enough, Derek here had a fresh one that came in overnight.' James stood tall and pointed to the dead man's leg. 'Now tell me, what can you see there?'

Kitty steeled herself to look at the distended and crooked leg. 'Well, you can see it's been broken in several places, and it looks swollen.'

James clapped his hands together. 'Exactly. Now, what's the nursing procedure when patients come in from a road accident?'

Casting her mind back to her many and various stints in casualty, Kitty remembered the admission of a retired bank manager called Fred, who had been cut out of his car by the fire brigade after a truck had ploughed into the driver's side of his Ford, rendering the Ford a mangled wreck. 'We check for immediately life-threatening injury, and if it's not an obvious matter of life or death, we give them a nice cup of tea with a big dollop of jam. Maybe a biscuit too. The sugar helps with shock.' She smiled with pride. 'Us nurses know to make the patients as comfortable as possible until, say, the orthopaedic surgeon on shift can come and sort whatever's broken.'

Nodding thoughtfully, James seemed to be visualising the nursing procedure and then contemplating the dead man's leg. He poked at the leg with his fountain pen. 'The trouble is, this swelling tells me that blood has been pooling around the various breaks for several hours.' He pointed to a bad burn on the man's arm. 'The arm's swollen too. Massively so. And, all that's happened is that he's been given a nice cup of tea and been told to wait for the doctor. In the meantime, he's died.'

Kitty sighed. 'Look, Dr Williams, I've just lost a young polio patient, and I only came down here to ask if Derek's porters could come and collect the boy's body. I'm busy, James. What are you trying to say?'

'Don't you get it?' James said. 'These patients who've been in car and motorcycle accidents have suffered blood loss internally, at the sites of breakages and burns. Volume blood loss.' He clicked his fingers excitedly and pointed at her with the same pen he'd used to poke at the dead man's leg. 'I'll bet that's why they're dying on us.' He raised a thick black eyebrow. 'These people need blood transfusions and immediate surgery, not a cup of tea.' He put his pen in his breast pocket and punched the air. 'Ha! I'd better tell Baird-Murray straight away. We need to change the protocol in casualty to give my theory a whirl.'

Kitty saw an opportunity to remind James to talk to Baird-Murray about some of the bad behaviour in the hospital. She opened her mouth to speak. 'While you're at it, Dr. Williams—'

'Sorry, Sister Longthorne.' James kissed her on the cheek. 'Got to dash. See you this evening.'

James marched out of the mortuary, leaving Kitty alone with creepy Derek and the dead body.

Chapter 9

'Is that you, Kitty love?'

The door to Mam's new place had been on the latch. Kitty had pushed it open to be greeted by the delicious smell of the chip pan, bubbling away with deep-frying chips. She stepped into the narrow hallway, took off her scarf and hung it on a peg, forcing herself to leave her grief for little Archibald Davies at the door. Her heart had been heavy all day, imagining his parents' gut-wrenching anguish as they'd opened the telegram she'd sent.

Don't bring death in with you, Kitty counselled herself. *You're experienced enough to shove that in a box, for now, and Mam's got enough on her plate as it is.* She took a deep breath, and when she'd finished exhaling, she'd pushed the tragic loss to the back of her mind.

'Hiya, Mam! Smells good.' Kitty's stomach growled. 'I've brought some sponge cake for afters. It's got real eggs in it.' Carrying her parcel of cake in one hand, she slid out of her coat and hung it up with the other, noticing that Richard Collin's stolen overcoat was already there. That could mean only one thing:

'Ned!' Kitty opened the door to the parlour to find Ned sitting on the settee, listening to some horse-racing commentary on the wireless. 'By heck, our Ned. It's like Dad never died, seeing you on that smelly old settee, listening to that boring claptrap. Switch it off, will you?'

She studied her tutting brother. His black eye had started to turn all shades of vivid purple and green overnight. He was still wearing his sling, which already looked grubby. Thankfully, his swollen lip had gone down, leaving more bad bruising in its place.

'What have you told her?' Kitty said, nodding towards the kitchen.

Ned grinned. 'Said I got done over for my wallet by some young lads.'

Kitty shook her head. 'She's not daft, you know.' She kept her voice to a whisper. 'If she gets wind that you're involved with the commies—'

'Anti-fascists.'

'Yes, whatever you want to call them. Mam'll have your guts for garters. She's had a lifetime of police knocking her door down because Dad was into all sorts. Don't put her through that again.'

'Where's my Gracie?' Ned asked.

'Wait your hurry. She had a new admission right before her shift ended. She'll be on her way when she's finished,' Kitty said, stooping to kiss her wayward brother on his head. She cuffed him gently on the ear. 'Idiot.'

'Ow!'

'Did you vote?' The results of the general election were soon to be announced, and Kitty was nervous that Labour would lose power, sending the new National Health Service into chaos. She'd dutifully cast her vote.

Ned shrugged. 'Doesn't make a difference if I voted or not, does it? Nowt much changes for the likes of us Longthornes.'

Kitty frowned. 'Blimey, you really are an idiot, aren't you? If you don't vote, you don't get a say, Ned. You should always get off your backside and put your mark on a ballot paper. For heaven's sake.'

Waving her away, Ned turned toward the wireless once more, as though Kitty had already left the room.

'Oh, that's right. I forgot you're a communist this week. I don't think they stood in the general election.' She didn't bother to keep the sarcasm out of her voice.

Making her way into the kitchen, Kitty found her mother clad in a food-splattered apron, pulling a frying basket full of golden chips out of her blackened, greasy chip pan. She poured the chips onto a plate covered with several layers of the *Manchester Evening News*, which immediately turned transparent on contact with the hot lard. In a giant steel tureen, something foamed and steamed as if the devil himself was taking a bath in the water.

Kitty sniffed the air. 'Bacon ribs?'

'And mushy peas,' her mother said, taking the lid off another bubbling pan and stirring it vigorously. Her words were muffled; her mouth had collapsed, making it clear she wasn't wearing any dentures. 'General election celebration tea! I'm hoping Labour get in because I need a new pair of Newtons.' She pointed to her mouth. 'My other set smashed when I was taking them out of the jam jar I keep them in.'

Wrapping her arms around her mother, Kitty planted an enthusiastic kiss on the old lady's sunken cheek. 'Keep your fingers crossed that Clement Attlee has wiped the floor with Churchill and Davies, eh? Churchill got us through the war, but he's not right for rebuilding the country.' Kitty looked around the little kitchen, with its clean cupboards and its back door out onto the garden. It felt good to see her mother in a house that had the luxury of being detached on one side. 'Ooh, I love Tuesday nights, now you've moved here, Mam. It's so much nicer than the old flat. So spacious and green round here.'

'I know. I've even planted some spuds in the back garden. What about that, eh?' Her mother peered through the kitchen window into the wintry evening darkness. 'I haven't got a clue what I'm doing, and the ground's all but frozen solid, but her next door offered me some spouting King Edward tubers, so I thought I'd have a go at digging for Britain.'

Kitty chuckled. 'I'd say Dad would have been proud, but Dad wouldn't have given a stuff. He didn't know one end of a carrot from another. But *I'm* proud of you. Will that do?'

'I'll say!' Her mother pulled a bottle of malt vinegar out of the cupboard, walked into the tiny dining room and set it on the table. 'What do you think of this for fancy?' she shouted back through to the kitchen. 'A proper dining room!'

'You say that every week,' Kitty said, meeting her on the threshold. 'It's smashing, Mam. Us Longthornes are coming up in the world.'

Her mother looked wistfully at a framed photo of her dead husband – the infamous jailbird Bert Longthorne – that enjoyed pride of place on the mantel of the tiled hearth. The photo had been taken just before his spell in Strangeways Prison, when he'd been in the pub – either gate-crashing some wedding or else somebody's wake in the pub's upstairs reception room. In the photo, Bert had been clutching a pint of stout, with a cigarette wedged between his fingers. He'd been dressed in his Sunday best.

'I wish your dad had lived to see us moved into a house with a dining room and an inside toilet,' Mam said. 'I wonder what he would have made of all this high-living. A front *and* back garden, and fields nearby.' She shook her head and grabbed at the handles of the tureen full of boiling ribs. She poured the water into the stainless steel sink. 'All mod cons, eh?' The steam mushroomed towards the ceiling and fogged up the window. 'I must thank James again for putting in a good word with his contact at the council.'

'You've already done that, Mam. He knows. Just leave it now and enjoy your new house.'

Her mother had dished up the ribs, mushy peas and chips just as Grace came through the door.

'Hello there, Mrs L!' Grace shouted from the hallway. Her voice was bright and full of hopeful anticipation for the family dinner. But when she came into the parlour and caught sight of Ned's face, that all changed. 'Good Lord, what in sweet Jesus's name has happened to you? You look like you've been in a fight with a steam train, and the train won.'

Kitty watched her brother through narrowed eyes, wondering if he would tell his betrothed the truth.

'I got jumped down an alley by some kids,' Ned said, getting to his feet and trying to kiss her.

Grace pushed him away and folded her arms. She looked him up and down. 'You don't fool me so easily, Ned Longthorne.' She grabbed at his hand and pushed the bandage aside, revealing split skin over his knuckles. 'You been fighting, I see.'

Ned looked over his shoulder at the kitchen, where his mother was picking up two full plates. 'Keep it down, will you? I don't want to give the old lady a heart attack. It was fascists, all right? I did it for us.'

Kitty could see that Grace was biting her tongue. Like the happy family her mam so dearly wanted them to be, they sat apparently companionably around the sturdy old oak dining table and smiled as the steaming plates were set in front of them.

'I'll put James's in the oven to keep warm, if he's going to be late?' Mam said.

'Perfect.' Kitty smiled at her mother, but glowered at Ned, wishing she and Grace were able to give him the dressing down he deserved.

They were just about to tuck in when the front door slammed against the wall.

Kitty got to her feet, her heart racing. Was it Mosleyites, bursting their way in to find Ned?

'Only me!' James shouted. He sounded pained.

Rushing out to the hallway, Kitty was bemused to find him carrying a large wooden cabinet. 'What on earth are you . . . ?' It was then that she realised what he was struggling under the weight of. 'Oh, my giddy aunt. Mam! Mam! You're not going to believe this!' She took the bottom of the cabinet, grinning like a fiend at her fiancé. 'Where the heck did you . . . ?'

James shushed her and winked. 'Keep it a surprise.' He kicked the front door shut behind him and turned to open the parlour door with his hip. 'Close your eyes, Elsie,' he said.

Kitty could barely stifle her delighted, excited laughter.

'Aye, aye,' her mam said. 'What's all this to-do? Are you coming in for your tea or what? Your ribs are getting congealed.'

James kept his voice to a whisper. 'On the count of three?'

Kitty nodded.

'One, two, three.' He nudged the parlour door open. 'Surprise!'

Watching Mam's reaction, it was all Kitty could do to stop herself from jumping up and down with jubilation when the old lady realised what James had brought her.

'A television? A television! Jesus, Mary and Joseph. I don't believe it!' Mam was on her feet, clapping her hands excitedly. Tears started to stream down her face.

James beamed as though he'd won a Nobel Prize. 'I believe these are fairly straight-forward to set up. I thought we could watch the general election result on the news. Richard Dimbleby is supposed to be presenting it.'

Mam's face fell slightly. 'Oh, are you taking it back tonight?'

Chuckling, James shook his head as he manoeuvred the set into the corner of the parlour, close to the window. 'Absolutely not. This is for you, Elsie.' He stood up and rolled his shoulders. Then he slapped his hand onto the top of the polished mahogany cabinet that housed the small set. 'There's not an especially great deal to watch at this point, but I'm told there's going to be regular broadcasts, very soon. Dramas, sport, light entertainment.' He grinned at Ned. 'Imagine being able to watch the cricket at Lords from the comfort of your own home.'

'Sounds good to me,' Ned said, carrying his plate over to the settee, sitting down and resolutely putting his legs up on the pouffe.

James plugged the set in and switched it on. Amid much crackling and hissing, he started to tune the set in and looked over his shoulder at Kitty's mother. 'I thought it might keep you company, now Bert's gone. And, of course, if you'll allow Kitty and me to come and watch it on the odd occasion until we buy our own set, that would be just dandy.'

Kitty put her arm around her blushing mother and kissed her on the cheek. 'How about that, Mam?'

'He's a bobby-dazzler, that feller of yours,' Mam said. 'Solid gold.'

Kitty chuckled. 'No, I meant the television.'

'Ooh, cracking. We must be the first people on the estate to get one. I can't wait to tell her next door.'

James finally shed his coat and took it out to the hall. 'I should think you're one of the first people in the whole of Manchester to get one, Elsie.' He returned and put his arm around Kitty, pulling her close. 'But I reasoned that you needed a pick-me-up, since Bert passed away. Anyway, consider it a housewarming gift.' As he appeared to scan the sparsely furnished room, his gaze rested on Ned's injuries. He raised an eyebrow. Then his attention moved back to Kitty's mam. 'Watch out for eye strain, though! I think the recommendation is that you limit your viewing to an hour a day or something.'

Mam touched the corner of her heavy National Health spectacles, where the arm had broken off and she'd affixed it back onto the frame using a sticking plaster. 'Hey, I blooming well hope Labour gets back in because I need new specs as well as dentures, and I've no money to pay.'

'Let's watch the television once we've eaten,' Kitty said. 'And we'll soon find out.'

The meal, albeit stone cold now, tasted heavenly. As they sat around the table, Kitty couldn't help but imagine the whole family around her dining table – one day – tucking into a Christmas dinner that she and James had prepared in their own kitchen, a spacious affair with all mod cons. She made a mental note to speak to the new matron about the possibility of marriage and a nursing career becoming happy bedfellows.

The chat remained cordial and light, mainly revolving around the change of matron at Park Hospital and Ned's hunt for work and a packing job at the biscuit factory he'd heard tell of. Soon it was time to sit in front of the new television, with a mug of strong tea in one hand and a piece of the cake Kitty had brought in the other.

'It's a good picture, James,' Ned said. 'I'll give you that.'

'Everyone's so tiny on that small screen,' Grace said. 'But it's amazing to see moving pictures in your own parlour.'

Kitty watched the presenter, Richard Dimbleby, sitting behind his news desk, looking terribly serious. Several other presenters flanked him, offering commentary on the unfolding results. Behind them was a large map of the country, on which a man wearing a white coat was painting squares either in black, white or half-and-half to show which boroughs had voted for which parties.

'I say,' James said. 'This is worth the licence fee alone! It's terribly exciting.'

Ned tutted and sighed. 'Are you telling me we've got to watch that berk painting in squares until one in the morning before we know who's won?'

Nudging her brother, Kitty scoffed. 'Stop being so cynical, Ned Longthorne.' The picture switched suddenly to a broadcast of people in Trafalgar Square in London. They'd gathered in a large crowd to watch the results being announced on one of the largest screens Kitty had ever seen. 'Blimey! Look at that! It's London. All those people are actually standing around in Trafalgar Square while we're sitting here, supping tea. It's not even a recording. It's actually happening.'

'Give over, Kitty,' Ned said. 'Anyone would think you've never seen the news before. Anyway, you two have got to be back at the nurses' home by curfew. You won't even find out the result until tomorrow.'

'Misery guts,' Kitty said.

'Which way do you think it's going to go, though?' Grace asked. 'It doesn't look like a guaranteed landslide to me.'

Could it be that Grace was right? If she was, and the Conservatives got in, what would that mean for everyone who worked at Park Hospital and for the patients like Sammy Levine, whose life depended on free treatment?

Chapter 10

'How do you like?' Molly Bickerstaff said the following morning, marching by Kitty's side down the freezing corridors of the hospital as they both made their way to their respective wards for the start of the day shift. 'Labour got back in.'

'Really?' Exhausted as she was after a night of fitful sleep, where she'd dreamt about Archibald Davies gasping his last in a side room of the polio ward, Kitty's heart leapt at the news. The new National Health Service was safe – for now, at least.

'Heard it on the wireless in Matron Pratt's office first thing.'

Ignoring Molly's obvious boast that she'd been shooting the breeze with the new matron before the day had even dawned, Kitty nodded to some of the junior nurses, heading towards the exit as they came off the night shift. 'Smashing. At least my mam will be able to get herself rigged up with a new set of gnashers and specs.'

'I bet Dr Williams is disappointed that Churchill lost out again.' There was a gleeful look on Molly's face.

Kitty stopped in her tracks. 'Why do you assume he votes Conservative?'

Molly, however, kept going. 'He's a doctor, isn't he? A public schoolboy, I heard.' The disdain in her voice was clear. She looked over her shoulder back at Kitty.

'They're all the same. You'll be living the high life too, once you're married. So don't pretend you're some working-class heroine, Longthorne.'

Balling her fists, Kitty wanted to shout after Molly that she was rude and presumptuous. Shouting down the corridor, however, was not exactly making a good example for the younger nurses. 'Mind your own business, you judgemental heifer,' she said beneath her breath. Many things had changed for the better over the years at Park Hospital, but Molly Bickerstaff wasn't one of them.

Pushing aside her irritation, Kitty entered the children's polio ward. As she passed the side room where Archibald Davies's emergency surgery had failed so miserably, Kitty prayed that there wouldn't be more deaths. She knew her prayers were futile, however. Until they could vaccinate against a disease like polio, wards like this would always offer a mixture of triumph and despair for the medical staff.

'Right,' she said to the nurses beneath her who had gathered in her office. 'Let's get breakfast served and get some of these recovering children out of their iron lungs and into their day chairs.' Glancing at her diary, she felt her pulse start to race. 'We've got old Matron doing the rounds with Matron Pratt this morning. So I want to see this ward shipshape and Bristol fashion.'

The nurses all nodded. 'Yes, Sister Longthorne,' they said in unison.

'Better not make a prat of yourself,' one of the junior nurses said, giggling as the group of women turned to make their way back onto the ward.

Kitty clapped her hands. 'Er, not so fast, ladies.' She pointed to the young nurse who had made the joke. 'Gladys Ernshaw, what did I just hear you say?'

Gladys looked down at her short fingernails. 'Nowt.'

'I beg your pardon?' Kitty emerged from behind her desk and stood toe to toe with the gangling girl. '*Nowt?* What kind of an answer is "*nowt*"?'

The girl shrugged. 'I mean, "nothing", Sister.'

'Well it's funny, that, because I distinctly heard you coming out with a pun on the new matron's name.' Kitty looked around at the other nurses, many of whom sported florid cheeks and barely concealed grins on their youthful faces. She pointed to them, one by one. 'Let me put this plainly. Anyone caught making fun of the new matron's name will get their wages docked. I'll see to it personally.' She made sure to look directly into the eyes of each girl as she cast her gaze critically around the office. She'd seen old Matron do this time and again to ensure she had the attention of her charges.

'Sorry, Sister,' Gladys muttered.

Some of the other nurses who had been giggling followed suit, uttering quiet apologies.

'This profession . . . these patients and their families rely on us being professional and showing respect to our superiors.' Kitty folded her arms. 'We're an army – the Park Hospital army – and we obey orders. Matron Pratt is our commander, and if this hospital is to run like a well-oiled machine, you will give her the respect she's due. Do I make myself absolutely clear?'

'Yes, Sister.'

'Yes.'

'Sorry, Sister.'

The smiles were gone now. Kitty could see the nurses steeling themselves to look her in the eye, straightening up, as though they were indeed soldiers on parade.

Satisfied that they had taken her words to heart, Kitty turned to the doorway and balked at an unexpected sight. Matron Pratt was standing there, stock-still as if she was a waxwork figure from Madame Tussauds.

'Matron Pratt,' Kitty said, flummoxed by the sight of her new superior. Had she seen all that had just come to pass? 'Morning. I, er . . . The girls were just, erm. Breakfast time for the patients, so I was, er . . .' She turned to her charges. 'Nurses, get to work!'

The nurses filed out in absolute silence, exchanging nervous glances as they passed the new matron.

Once Kitty was alone, Matron Pratt entered the makeshift office, flanked by the old matron – as short and round as Matron Pratt was tall and thin.

'Good morning, Sister Longthorne,' the old matron said. 'I'm taking Matron Pratt on a guided tour of all the wards, and where better than to start with you, my dear?' She smiled. There was a relaxed warmth to her expression that Kitty had not often glimpsed over the years.

Kitty realised that Matron had the relieved yet determined look of a runner nearing the finish line. She felt a pang of tenderness towards her mentor. Could she ever enjoy such a connection with this austere replacement?

Matron Pratt looked at the eccentric rig-up of the desktop perched on the bath and frowned. 'I think it's time we got you a proper office, Sister.'

'Lovely idea. But where would you put it?' Kitty asked. 'We're short on space as it is. We looked at putting a desk at the top of the ward, but that would mean fewer beds.'

The new matron pursed her lips. 'Leave that to me. Now, how often do the patients bathe?'

Suddenly, Kitty's mouth was dry. She reached for the words

but they seemed to have vanished. *Come on, Kitty. Don't be intimidated by her, just because she's new*, Kitty thought. You're no wet-behind-the-ears trainee. 'Once a week, normally. Obviously on this ward, the children are mainly in iron lungs. Some of them are able to come out during the day, so they can be bathed carefully, if they're fit to get in the bath. But the ones who have to be in the machines around the clock . . . well, we've got new iron lungs with portholes in the side that let us reach in and tend to their hygiene needs.'

Matron took up the file that contained the notes from overnight – observations about the patients that would be conveyed to Dr Bourke when he did his rounds. 'May I?'

Kitty nodded. 'By all means. I haven't had chance to finish going over the night shift notes yet, but my counterpart, Sister Shaw, always does a verbal handover before she leaves.'

Matron Pratt's eyes moved from side to side as she read what had been written in the file. 'I understand you lost a patient yesterday.'

'Archibald Davies. Yes. It was tragic. Dr Bourke and Mr Galbraith tried to save him, but . . . it's the nature of the disease. We did do everything we could, though.'

The new matron nodded. 'Keep your fingers and toes crossed for that vaccine.' She continued to read. 'Lots of young patients making progress. Good.'

'My nurses do more than meet these children's complex medical needs. They're excellent at reading and talking to them. Some of these poor little blighters are on the ward for months and months, even after they're fit to be out of the iron lungs. They don't all see their families on a regular basis, for a variety of reasons. They get terribly homesick too. I believe rehabilitation is hard on their minds as well as their muscles, so . . .'

Matron Pratt locked eyes with her. 'Don't you maintain clinical detachment? What if nurses get too involved?'

Was she being tested? 'They're children. Matron has always insisted we do our caring duties to the highest level, and in my book, caring includes offering words of comfort and listening to patients. They recover more quickly when they're being treated with kindness and dignity.'

'I see.' Matron Pratt continued to read the notes in silence until her slender eyebrows shot up towards her brow. 'Hang on. It says here there was a scuffle between two sets of parents at visiting time.'

Kitty balked at the news. 'Sister Shaw made no mention of that.' She held her hand out to see what had been written in the notes. When she saw Sandra Shaw's neat handwriting, she immediately honed in on the names Spencer and Levine. 'Ah. Gordon and Sammy's fathers.' She nodded and exhaled heavily. 'The Levines are Jewish, and Bolsheviks, at that. Mr Spencer seemed to be looking for an argument the other night, during visiting time. So, my guess is he either has a thing about Jews or else he's not a fan of Bolshevism.'

'Or both,' Matron Pratt said.

Shrugging, Kitty looked to the old matron for comment, hoping she'd make mention of some of the tensions between English-born patients and staff and those who were of immigrant stock.

'I do hope Sister Shaw called for assistance,' the old matron said, clearly having other ideas. 'We can't have unrest spilling from the streets into the wards.'

Kitty wondered if she should take matters into her own hands. Perhaps now was the time to mention to Matron Pratt her attempts to bring the problem of racial prejudice in the hospital to the attention of the board. She opened her mouth to speak.

'Take me to meet your patients and the nurses under your jurisdiction, Sister,' Matron Pratt said, marching out of the office before Kitty could say a word.

Introducing the nurses one by one, Kitty felt proud of her little team, however new she was to the shift. The ward gleamed from top to bottom. Every child was being attended to by nursing staff who were courteous, friendly and immaculately clad in their pristine uniform.

'I run a tight ship,' Kitty said. 'I don't suffer insubordination from the girls, and in return, I support them properly.'

Matron moved among the iron lungs, greeting each child individually, though she was anything but warm and motherly.

'Your name?' she asked a little girl through her angled mirror.

'Veronica Gamble,' the little girl said. Her cheeks were pale and her voice was meek.

'How long have you been here?'

'Since before last Christmas. Which wasn't bad at first, because Santa brought us all books to read.'

'What's the best thing about this hospital?'

The little girl smiled and some colour blossomed in her cheeks. 'Oh, I *love* breakfast. I'm always starving when I wake up, and we usually get nowt at home because Mam's skint and has to go out to work cleaning at the crack of dawn. Nurse Ghosh said she's bringing me porridge in a bit, made with gold-top milk with sugar sprinkled on top. And she spoon-feeds it to me because I'm poorly and can't sit up. We've got nice stripey straws to drink. And I like being read to.'

'And the worst thing?' The new matron's expression never softened.

'I'm itchy but I can't reach my leg. And I miss home.' Tears welled in her big hazel eyes. 'I miss Mam and Dad and our Kevin and our Patrick and baby Maureen and my nana.'

'I see. Well, let's make sure Nurse Ghosh gives your leg a good old scratch this morning and . . .' She turned around to see one of the junior nurses, pushing a cart from the kitchens that contained the children's breakfasts. 'I believe some lovely creamy porridge is on its way.' She smiled quickly, and it was like the brightest light flashing on and off, putting Kitty in mind of a lighthouse's beacon, strobing through inky storm clouds.

Matron Pratt seemed to have eyes for everything, from the standard of the bed-making to the sluicing of the bedpans for those children who were out of their iron lungs but encased in plaster. She observed how medicine was administered and how well ventilated the ward was. She ran her finger over nightstands and the wooden floors beneath the iron lungs, checking for dust.

'I told you, didn't I?' old Matron said. 'The girls' standards are as high as any in the land. Sister Longthorne is one of my biggest successes. A very bright young woman. Very hard-working, and even the colonials on her team seem to be pulling their weight admirably.'

Matron Pratt came to a halt, and turned to look at the old matron. She raised an eyebrow. 'Am I not seeing that the Indian and Malay nurses are working harder than their local counterparts, despite their being paid less for their professional attainments?'

The old matron walked on ahead, clearly ignoring Matron Pratt's pointed comment. Kitty's cheeks burned as though she'd eaten a bowl of hot porridge herself. She bit her tongue, not wanting to get embroiled in a battle over authority between the old and the new matrons.

Finally, Matron Pratt reached Gordon and Sammy, side-by-side at the end of the ward.

'Hello, boys,' she said. 'Spencer and Levine, am I right? I'm Matron Pratt, and before you ask, I'm not a prat.'

The boys giggled so hard and for so long that Sammy started to cough.

'That's quite enough of that, boys.' She put her face close to one boy after the other. 'Are you two arguing?'

'No, miss,' Gordon said. 'Sammy's my pal.'

Sammy shook his head and met her gaze through the mirror. 'Gordon's fun.' He looked sheepish. 'But our dads have been arguing. They said we shouldn't talk to each other.'

'Would you like me to tell them to stop and mind their own business?' she asked. 'So that you two boys can get on with being friends in peace?'

The boys both nodded in earnest.

The new matron folded her arms tightly. 'Very well. You be good for Sister Longthorne, here, won't you?'

Together the three marched back through the ward to Kitty's office.

'Can I have a word with Sister Longthorne, please, Matron?' Matron Pratt asked.

Clearly crestfallen, the old matron took her leave, casting one last rueful glance back at Matron Pratt.

'Sister Longthorne,' Matron Pratt said. 'I saw how you dealt with the silliness of the junior nurses earlier.'

Kitty took a deep breath and held it. She nodded silently.

'I thought you did well. You do run a tight ship. So tight, that I may have a proposition for you. Come to see me in my office when your shift has ended.'

Chapter 11

'What do you think she wants to talk to me about?' Kitty asked Lily as she held her plate out for some shepherd's pie that looked distinctly light on the meat.

'Search me,' Lily said. 'Taking on more responsibility? Training courses, maybe.' She looked at Kitty and nodded. 'I bet that's it. I bet she wants you to do some formal teaching thing for junior nurses. Maybe the new ones from abroad.'

As Lily went in search for a free table, the dinner lady slapped a large spoonful of grey slop onto Kitty's plate. She wore an utterly blank expression.

'Thank you, Nelly,' Kitty said, trying to make eye contact with her. She waved her hand in front of the dinner lady's face.

Nelly shook her head. 'Sorry, love. I were miles away. I went to see *The Blue Lamp* at the flicks last night, and I can't stop thinking about it.'

'Oh, was it good?' asked Kitty, thinking that it had been a long while since she and James had been to the cinema.

'Not bad. That handsome young actor Dirk Bogarde were in it. Jack Warner was playing this copper, and there was this dog that kept nicking food. He called the dog Strachey – like the Minister for Food, John Strachey.' She frowned and cocked her head to the side. 'Do you think they were trying to say something about rationing?' She then looked pointedly at the large tray of grey shepherd's pie, which was clearly full of rusk, minced offal and gristle.

Kitty's stomach growled. 'I'll bet. Don't know about you, Nel, but I could murder a proper meal with proper ingredients. My mam's sick of trying to cook with powdered this and substitute that.' She rolled her eyes. 'Anyone would think we're still at war, eh?'

Nelly curled her lip and raised her pencilled in eyebrows. 'Welcome to 1950. Enjoy your pie, love.'

Taking her place next to Lily at an empty table, Kitty checked her fob watch. 'I've not got long to shovel this down.'

Lily looked disparagingly at her pile of boiled vegetables. 'At least you can eat the pie. Look at what I'm left with! And I bet the new Indian and Malay nurses aren't doing much better.'

'How come?' Kitty asked.

'The Hindus can't eat beef, Rijuta told me, and the Muslims can't eat any of the meat because it's not . . . what's it called again? Hillel? Hull— Halla . . .? Halal. That's it, Halal. That's what I've heard, anyway. I think Halal's the same thing as me not being able to eat meat that isn't Kosher. Those girls must reckon the British have got the worst diet in the world.' She poked her fork at a pile of over-boiled spouts.

Ordinarily, Kitty might have joined in with some comment about the food she'd eaten in Barbados, but her mind was on Matron Pratt's cryptic proposition. 'I hope I'm not in trouble.'

Grace joined them, carrying a tray that contained only a Spam sandwich, a glass of water and an apple. 'Hello, girls. What's the gossip? Talking about the election?'

'No. The new matron,' Kitty said. 'I don't know what to make of her.' She spooned her tasteless shepherd's pie into her mouth, thankful, at least, for the heat of the meal that sent the February chill packing. 'She seems a right miserable so-and-so, but if she's going to fight our corner for change, so that we're properly valued as medical staff, as well as emptiers of bedpans and general wiper-uppers, I'm on her side.' She placed her cutlery across her plate. 'Who knows? Maybe she'll let us both keep our jobs, even after we're married.'

Biting into her sandwich, Grace chewed in silence as Lily started to talk about old Matron's leaving-party plans.

'One of the girls has made a card, and we're having a whip-round. What do you think we should get her as a leaving present?' she asked.

Kitty glanced at her fob watch yet again, realising she ought to get back to the ward. 'The board will get her a gold wristwatch or a carriage clock, obviously.' She thought about the few personal effects that Matron kept in her office. Framed photos and the odd book that wasn't a medical or nursing publication. 'She's given her entire life to nursing, hasn't she? I've been here since I left school, and I still couldn't tell you if she had a hobby in her spare time.' She drank from her glass of water. 'In fact, I don't think she has spare time. I'm not even sure where she'll live when she leaves. Park Hospital's her world.'

'How about a framed photograph of all the nurses then?' Grace asked. 'You know? Professionally taken and properly framed with all our names written underneath. I've seen them do that sort of thing for the West Indian cricket team.'

Kitty thought about the large framed photograph she'd seen in James's flat. It had been taken of his entire year, as they'd graduated from Trinity College – row upon row of serious-looking young men, wearing scholars' gowns and posed in front of some ancient-looking pale-stone building. James held that photo dear, and it took pride of place in his lounge. She was sure Matron wouldn't appreciate something quite so formal and posed, but a group portrait of all of the nurses she'd taught over the years, standing in front of Park Hospital's imposing clock tower, would make quite a memento.

'Cracking idea, our Grace,' she said. 'If you look into a photographer, I can get in touch with the nurses that have left over the years to get married. We can get them all back one Saturday lunchtime, maybe, and throw a party with cake and that.' She cast her mind back to the excruciating afternoon tea she and James had once shared with her mam, dad and James's parents at the Midland Hotel in Manchester. Her dad had made fun of the dainty sandwiches that had had the crusts removed. Kitty had thought them elegant. 'Nice Victoria sponges and little afternoon tea-type butties,' she said. 'Cucumber sandwiches. They're cheap and everybody likes those, don't they?'

Lily got to her feet and picked up her tray. 'You'll have to be quick tracking down all those ex-nurses, then. The old matron retires soon.'

'What do you think then, Dr Bourke?' Kitty said later that afternoon. 'Can little Gordon here come out of his casts and start physiotherapy to get moving again?'

Dr Bourke stood at the foot of Gordon's bed and examined the notes that had been written about the child. 'Yes. I think he's ready for rehabilitation. Speak to the therapy girls when they come round later. Let's get this brave little soldier walking, eh?' He gave Gordon a curt smile before moving onto Sammy Levine.

'And how is young Master Levine doing on this cold and frosty morning?' Dr Bourke asked, staring solemnly into the angled mirror that reflected Sammy's face.

Unexpectedly, a tear rolled from Sammy's eye, tracking its way into his ear. Kitty took a clean handkerchief out of her pocket and wiped his face.

'There there, sweetie. Why the tears?' she asked.

The boy's bottom lip wobbled. 'I'm fed up. I'm *so* fed up. I've got an itchy arm and an itchy foot, everything aches, I keep choking when I try to eat or drink because I can't get the hang of when to swallow. And it's boring. I want to get out of here. And I'm worried my dad won't be able to visit me anymore because . . .' His eyes flicked over to Gordon. 'Can me and you still be friends, even though our dads were rowing yesterday?'

Gordon rubbed his lips together and cocked his head to the side. 'Not sure. Dad said I'll be for the high jump if I get pally with the likes of you. He said if I lie with dogs, I'll get fleas.'

Sammy sniffed. 'My dad said the same thing to me.' He looked at Kitty through the mirror, his face a picture of misery. 'Sister, can't me and Gordon be friends?'

Kitty stroked his brow. 'There's no good reason why you two boys can't chat to each other all day long. I'm going to have a word with both of your parents tonight. We must have good behaviour on this ward – from mams and dads, as well as you children. Leave it to me.'

Dr Bourke was reading Sammy's notes in silence, peering over the top of his heavy round spectacles, which had slid almost to the end of his nose. After a while, he looked up and turned to Kitty, pushing the spectacles up. 'I think we might take Samuel out of the iron lung for an hour and see how he fares. Ideally, we want to get him to the point where he can be out of the machine during the day, and just be returned to it to sleep. Beyond that, well, we'll just have to see . . .'

Sammy managed a hopeful smile. 'Ooh, yes please. I'm getting better every day, Doctor. Honest.'

'I'll be the judge of that, young man.' Dr Bourke winked at the boy. 'But I certainly hope you are.'

Together, Kitty and Dr Bourke continued the rounds until the progress of all of the children had been checked.

Dr Bourke turned to Kitty just by the door to the ward, out of earshot of the patients. 'Er, if you're having issues with the fathers of those two boys, then you might do well to separate the children. Move Samuel Levine closer to your office, perhaps. We can't have brawling on the wards, no matter the excuses and apologies given. These children are invalids. They need tranquillity if they're to recover.'

'If you don't mind,' Kitty said, 'I'm going to play it by ear until I've had words with both men. The boys have been getting along lovely. It's a shame to separate them just because of their fathers' misdemeanours.'

Dr Bourke nodded, departing just as the two women who conducted physiotherapy – Daisy and Alice – arrived.

'Ah, perfect timing,' Kitty said. 'We've got a new recruit for you today. Gordon Spencer. Follow me.'

Kitty led Daisy and Alice to the end of the ward to where Gordon was laughing at something Sammy had said. 'Did you hear what Dr Bourke said, Gordon? We're going to get those casts off for an hour and see how you get on with Daisy and Alice, here. They're going to get you on your feet.'

Kitty summoned Rijuta to assist, and together they freed Gordon's limbs.

The little lad tried to shake himself loose of Rijuta's supportive grip, and almost fell to the floor.

'Oh, Gordon,' Rijuta said. 'Are you hurt, love?'

'Steady on, Gordon,' Kitty said. 'Let Nurse Ghosh help you into a wheelchair before you try to run off.'

Rijuta leaned over to pull the boy up, but Gordon reached out and grabbed Kitty.

'You can help me. Not her,' he said.

Exhaling heavily, Kitty gestured that Rijuta should take him under one arm, while she took the other. 'That's quite enough of that, young man. I don't know what your father's been telling you, but all of the nurses on my ward are the best in the National Health Service. So, let's get you into your wheelchair, and you can go and have some fun with Daisy and Alice. Right?' She kept her tone firm but friendly.

Alice took the handles of the wheelchair and Daisy knelt to greet Gordon.

'Take no notice,' Kitty whispered to Rijuta, rubbing her arm affectionately.

Rijuta took a step back, out of Gordon's earshot. 'It's very hard to do a heavy and difficult job when you feel nobody really wants your help. I could have stayed in Delhi.'

'He's only a little boy and he seems a nice one, at that. They learn stuff like that at the knee. Don't worry. I'm having a word with his dad tonight.' Kitty raised an eyebrow. 'Now, get a junior nurse to help you get Sammy Levine out of his iron lung and onto a day chair. See how he goes, eh?'

Kitty turned and made her way back to her office and almost jumped with fright at the sight of Matron Pratt. The new matron was sitting behind Kitty's desk, her back ramrod-straight as usual and her fingers steepled together.

'About that proposition,' she said.

Swallowing hard, Kitty took a seat in the visitor's chair. 'Yes, Matron Pratt?'

'I've heard you're an intrepid traveller. Matron told me all about your voyage to the West Indies to recruit new nurses.'

Kitty smiled nervously. 'It was the most exciting thing I've ever done. I'm honoured to have represented our hospital and the National Health Service.'

'Would you do it again?' Matron Pratt asked, leaning forwards and narrowing her eyes.

'How do you mean?' Kitty asked, at once feeling the thrill at the prospect of travel and the dread of leaving James and her family behind.

'I'm talking about a nurses' convention in New York. How would you like to go to America, Sister Longthorne?'

Chapter 12

'I do love the Lake District in the spring,' James said, steering his Ford Anglia along the winding road that was leading them up into the hills. 'Don't you?'

'I'll say. It's balm for the soul, this place.' Kitty peered out of the passenger window at the hawthorn hedgerows to their left, bursting into fresh, pale green leaf. Up the steep slopes beyond the drystone walls, the bracken was finally coming back to life after a harsh winter, replacing all that was brown and shrivelled with green and springy growth. 'I can't wait to see the lovely little churches we've shortlisted for the wedding.'

A light rain was falling on the fells, but the inclement weather didn't dim the beauty of the pastures she saw through the windscreen and driver's side window. They were full of nodding daffodils and baby lambs, frolicking by their mothers' sides.

Kitty saw how the road ahead started to climb even steeper. 'Slow down!' she said. 'There's a big fat sheep has got out of its paddock. Look!'

James dropped his speed to a crawl, as they navigated past the rogue sheep. 'You have to have your wits about you, driving round here,' he said. 'Are you sure having the wedding in the Lake District is a good idea?'

'I am,' Kitty said, giggling. 'Better than boring old flat-as-a-pancake Cheshire or, even worse, Davyhulme. We're waiting a long time to get wed. When we do eventually tie the knot, I want it to be special. I want it to feel like a real day out for everyone. Mam's never *ever* been to the Lakes. Did you know that?'

James patted her thigh. 'She'll love it. I only hope Ned doesn't scare the sheep.'

Kitty nudged him. 'Cheeky!'

Watching the bucolic splendour as it unfolded, she thought about the proposition Matron Pratt had put to her a week earlier. Deliberately peering out of the passenger window, lest James notice she was blushing, she thought about how every time she'd tried to mention the proposed trip to America, words had failed her. On her return from her trip to Barbados, she'd promised that her wanderlust had been satisfied; that focusing on their relationship and planning for their marriage – however far in the future it may be – would be her priority. Yet now that New York was on the table . . .

'You're very quiet all of a sudden,' James said, glancing at her. 'Are you feeling queasy with all the sharp bends?'

Flustered, Kitty took a deep breath and flapped her hand in front of her face. 'Yes. 'Fraid so.' She rolled down the window by a couple of inches. 'A bit of fresh air's all I need.' Blinking hard, she realised she did feel quite sick. It wasn't the bends that were at fault, however. It was the problem of being torn both by the pull of adventure and her commitment to the man she loved. Kitty stared straight ahead at the road as it rose to meet a low-lying cloud. 'How much longer to George's place?'

James glanced down at his wristwatch. 'I'd say we'll be there by lunchtime, but first I thought we could swing by one of the churches on our list.'

The road twisted this way and that, climbing ever steeper. They were in thick fog as they passed a pub on the summit of a steep fell on one side and a tiny road called The Struggle on the other. Kitty saw from the sign that it led all the way back down to Ambleside.

'Are we going to Glenridding?' she asked. 'The little village by Ullswater?'

'The very same,' James said, grinning. 'I don't think we've got time for a trip on the paddle-steamer today, though. Maybe next time. I think now that George is living in the West Lakes we may find ourselves up here even more. Maybe we could put a deposit down on a holiday cottage.'

Kitty scoffed. 'We've got to get married and buy a family home first. Let's not jump the gun.'

They drove through the quiet, desolate, rocky hamlet of Patterdale, passing The White Lion pub to their right and a number of walkers, clutching their walking sticks and clad in trousers that had been tucked into lumpy woollen socks. A little further along, as the ground flattened out, Glenridding Church came into view. It was a small stone and flint church, set in grassland as green as anything Kitty had seen, with an old cemetery out front.

James parked the car and they got out. 'Well, darling?' he said, offering her his arm. 'First impression?'

Kitty was glad to be out of the car with its hot engine smell and its uncomfortable, vinyl seats. She inhaled the crystal-clear air of the Lakeland setting, so high in altitude, it was almost above the treeline. The bleating of the spring lambs and their mothers was the only thing that competed with the birdsong. 'It's dreamy. Come on, let's go inside.'

On a Saturday morning, the church was unlocked but empty. Kitty walked in and immediately felt the temperature drop. She pulled her coat closed and fastened the buttons. The heels of her shoes made a click-clack noise on the stone flags that echoed around the vaulted ceiling. 'It's pretty gloomy.' She looked up and around at the ancient supporting beams and looked down at the pews, trying to imagine their wedding guests, sitting in rows.

'The windows are lovely, though.' James came to a standstill in the aisle and reached out for her hand. 'I get the impression you're not keen. Are you quite all right? Is there something the matter?'

'No, I'm fine.'

'Jolly good. Let's get going, then. It's still quite a drive to the West Lakes.' James started to walk away from her.

Was now the time to come clean with James about Matron's proposition? Kitty privately chastised herself for being so secretive. *Just tell him,* her inner voice said. *How can you have a good marriage to this man if you have to keep secrets?*

James was already standing by the open door, the cold light of a cloudy, wet day casting him in near-silhouette.

'Hang on, love,' she said. She walked back up the aisle towards him. 'There's something I need to tell you.'

'Oh? That doesn't sound good.' James's smile faltered. 'Are you pregnant?'

'No, don't be daft. We learned our lesson, last time.'

His thick eyebrows bunched together and his brow furrowed. 'You aren't breaking our engagement off, are you?'

''Course not!' Kitty passed by him and walked out into the churchyard, glad to be in the open and to hear the sounds of nature again.

James followed and took a hold of her elbow. 'Out with it.'

Kitty sighed and rolled her eyes. 'If you must know, the new matron has offered me the opportunity to go to a nursing conference in New York. On behalf of the hospital, like.'

'New York? Why can't she go? She's the matron.' Was he annoyed or supportive of the idea? James's expression was inscrutable.

'She's got to settle in, I suppose, and a week away is more than she can afford if she's trying to get her feet under the table. But she's all in favour of the American style of nursing, so . . .'

'When is it?'

'The summer.'

Now, his face fell. 'But I thought we might get married in the summer.'

Kitty's innards tightened. 'It's a week! A measly week!'

'But the planning . . .'

'What do you mean, the planning? I can plan a wedding with about fifty guests, James. Why shouldn't I go? It's New York! Maybe you can arrange to attend one of those plastic surgery conferences you're always on about, at the same time.'

James looked at the battleship grey heavens as he opened the car door for her. 'If you're representing Matron at a big nursing conference, Kitty, it means you're still totally committed to being a nurse. And we both know you have to leave the profession when we get married.'

Feeling frustration building within her, Kitty sank heavily onto the passenger seat and stared straight ahead, clutching her handbag on her knee. 'We're not married *yet*. And I haven't left the profession *yet*.' She turned to him, blinking back tears. 'Nobody's asking *you* to give up anything. How many times do we have to have this conversation?'

Slamming her door shut, James walked around to the driver's side and got into the car. Momentarily, he clutched the steering wheel and gazed dolefully through the windscreen. 'I'm just desperate to start our family life together, Kitty.' He turned to her and wiped her angry tears away. 'You're right. It's only a week. Go. New York's incredible. And I'll see if there's a plastic surgery conference or training thing on at the same time.' He chuckled. 'Actually, that's an incredible idea. Who knows? Maybe we can convince the board that you should keep your job, and a jaunt over the pond can be our honeymoon. We can fly down to Florida while we're at it.'

'Fly? Ooh, I've never been on an aeroplane.'

'You'll love it. It feels dreadfully Hollywood. And I hear a trip to the Helena Rubenstein salon in uptown New York is a must for stylish doctors' wives, too.'

Finally, the angry ball of fire in Kitty's stomach was extinguished by the thought of another trip of a lifetime, and they were able to continue their journey in good spirits.

'I really do think change for the better is just round the corner, James,' she said, as they skirted around Derwentwater. 'And I'm talking about nurses' working rights as well as our marriage. I have a feeling they're going to lift the ban on getting married sooner than we thought.'

'I don't think either of us should hold our breath, but one can only hope, darling.' James reached across and stroked her hair.

'But hoping's not enough, is it?' Kitty felt a mixture of exasperation and desperate longing churn in her empty stomach. 'Hope's not going to get us to the church on time *and* keep my hospital nursing career going. How about we make change happen? You and me.'

'Whatever do you mean, darling?' The furrows in James' brow deepened.

'I mean, I want to have my cake and eat it . . . same as you fellers. Will you show your support if I push the new matron on it?' Kitty studied her handsome fiancé's features for signs of his commitment. Was it uncertainty she could see in his warm brown eyes? 'Would you approach the board with me and state the case for me staying on after we're married?' She wrapped her chilly fingers around his hand.

James brought her hand to his lips and kissed her gently. 'I'd move mountains for you, Kitty Longthorne. Let's hatch a plan when we get back to Manchester. Right now, we've got a George to find.'

Chapter 13

'Is this it?' Kitty asked, when they drove up a rutted, muddy track, and an old stone cottage came into view.

'I believe so,' James said, pushing the engine hard to traverse a particularly claggy patch. 'My word, this really is splendid isolation.'

Just as the car jolted suddenly forwards and then stalled, George opened the front door of the cottage and greeted them with a merry wave. Wearing wellington boots, he came out to meet them.

'Greetings! Greetings!'

James spoke through the half-open driver's side window. 'Hello, Professor Particles. I thought you said you'd moved to the Lake District, not the edge of the earth.'

'Just leave her there, old chap. She'll be fine.' George patted the car's bonnet.

Clearly flustered, James grimaced through the windows at the rugged terrain and complete absence of a parking space. He turned back to his friend. 'But I don't want to be stuck in the mud in the dark when we're trying to leave. Honestly, George, whatever possessed you to live in the middle of nowhere?' He looked up at George's car, which had been fitted with tyres which were deeply ridged, like the tractors Kitty had seen chugging along the country lanes.

'Oh, don't worry about that. I'll help you push her out when it's time to leave.' George turned to Kitty. 'Kitty, my dear, are you coming in? I've made lamb. I need you to tell me if I've seasoned it enough.'

Kitty swung her legs out of the car but caught sight of the deep crests of earth that the car had dredged up. She looked at her inadequate shoes and then at the mud. 'Er . . .'

George laughed. 'You city folk! I thought you said you went walking in the Lakes regularly, James. Neither of you are dressed for the countryside, are you?'

James emerged from the car, stepping gingerly around the bonnet. 'I'll help you, darling.'

'No need!' George said. He trudged forwards in his rubber boots and stretched his arms out to lift Kitty from the car.

Kitty yelped. 'By heck, George. Go easy!'

'You're as light as a feather,' he said, plucking her from the car with apparent ease. 'And we don't want those dainty shoes covered in mud like James's brogues.'

He carried her to the path and set her down. Kitty didn't know whether to whack her saviour with her handbag or thank him profusely.

'Steady on, old chap,' James said. 'That's my fiancée you're manhandling, there.'

George clapped James on the back. 'Next time, bring wellingtons, eh?'

Inside, the cottage's cosy kitchen was heated by a big old cast-iron range. George opened the door and, wearing the thickest oven gloves Kitty had ever seen, he removed a roasting tin that contained a delicious-smelling shoulder of lamb.

Kitty's mouth watered. 'I feel like I've gone to heaven. Look at that! I haven't had proper lamb in years.' Her stomach growled loud enough to set James and George off laughing.

'The joys of living in Cumbria,' George said. He nodded to the small kitchen window. 'A few miles that way, and

I'm in the future, processing plutonium at Windscale.' He nodded towards the back door. 'Half a mile that way, and you're into some of the best farmland in the country. The rules are different here. It's a lonely life at the weekend, but I love it. No cinema for miles, though. Good job I've got a decent library.'

They ate around a chunky pine table and drank honey-flavoured ale that George had apparently brewed with Lakeland water.

'I do declare you're a changed man, old chap,' James said, raising his glass to his friend. 'Gormless George, who couldn't boil an egg as an undergraduate, is now a culinary genius. Praise be!'

They discussed churches in the vicinity that might be ideal spots for Kitty and James's wedding, and talk turned to village life.

'So, how do the sick get taken care of in such a remote place?' Kitty asked. 'Do you have district nurses and health visitors and that?'

George dug his tongue into a molar thoughtfully and frowned. 'Why, yes. I've seen the district nurse on her pushbike, visiting the old girl next door. And there's a health visitor attached to the local doctor's surgery. All the nursing types round here are married with children of their own, as far as I know. I've been to church once or twice and I've seen them with their families.'

Kitty nodded, trying to imagine the change, from tending patients in a hospital setting – a privilege only unmarried women were currently allowed to enjoy – to visiting the sick at home, the sort of professional backstop she knew was foisted on nurses who left hospital jobs to marry. Would it be as fulfilling?

'I tell you what,' George said, setting his knife and fork on his empty plate and wiping his mouth with a napkin. 'What do you say we go for a nice long ramble? Walk off the lunch, eh? I can take you down to the boundary of Windscale and you can see for yourselves quite what an impressive endeavour it is.'

'Sounds like an excellent plan,' James said. He turned to Kitty. 'Will you be quite all right in your shoes, darling?'

Glancing over to James's mud-encrusted brogues, which had been left by the door, she got to her feet. 'I think I should be asking you that.' She turned to George. 'Can I use your loo, please? Is it outdoors?'

'Ah, that's one luxury I have insisted on,' he said. 'No outdoor facilities for me.' He pointed to a door that led to the far end of the long house. 'Through the living room and past the study. It was the only place to put the smallest room.'

Trying to orient herself in a strange house with uneven levels between the rooms, Kitty found herself in a cosy living room lined with bookshelves. She lingered there a while, reading the spines of the books, amazed that a physicist should have such a keen interest in literature, art and poetry. She pictured James's sole bookcase in his flat, which contained only medical journals and textbooks. It was a world away from this library, stacked with tomes by Shakespeare, James Joyce, Bertolt Brecht, Franz Kafka, Karl Marx and Dostoyevsky.

'Flipping heck,' Kitty said to herself. 'What doesn't George know?'

There were texts in foreign languages she recognised as French, Latin, maybe Spanish or was it Italian. German, certainly, and perhaps Russian – or was it Modern Greek? The two always looked the same to Kitty. There was art on the wall that appeared to be the real thing. The sort of angular, abstract stuff that she knew intellectuals liked. There was the odd thing that looked Chinese, too – a beautiful silk embroidery of some Far Eastern calligraphy. The furniture, though, was battered and old and looked as though it was Victorian hand-me-downs. On the stone flagged floor was a threadbare Persian rug. Everything reeked of old money. She imagined it was not dissimilar to the rooms in Cambridge, where James and his pals had lived and been taught.

'It's a different world,' she muttered, wondering what Mam and Ned would make of such a place.

A small hallway led from the lounge to two identical-looking doors. She tried the handle on one, but it was locked. *It must be his study*, she thought. She tried the next and found a perfect little indoor toilet. The stone cottage was cold, but Kitty still didn't take for granted the joys of an indoor toilet. One day, she thought, she'd have a house with an indoor toilet and a library full of books, which she'd encourage her children to read. Kitty felt a sudden pang of grief at all she'd never learned and would never learn because of the type of family she'd been born into.

'Crikey, feel that wind coming off the sea!' Kitty yelled, trying to make herself heard as they stood on a fell, looking out at Windscale. It stretched before them, all the way down to the coast.

'It's quite a place to work,' George shouted.

Gulls squawked overhead, and the long grass was flattened. Suddenly, this corner of Cumbria didn't feel quite so springlike at all. Kitty gazed down at what was half built and what was still under construction.

'It's massive,' she said. 'Where do you work?'

George pointed at an ugly concrete tower that seemed to sprout from the ground like a strange plant. 'Windscale Pile Number 1,' he said. 'I've been helping to oversee the final stages of construction. They started it three years ago, but it's going to be finished, hopefully by October.' He pointed to another tower, starting to emerge from the concrete sprawl of the site. 'See that? That's Pile Number 2. That's going to be operational by next year.'

Kitty covered her ears with the palms of her hands, hoping to stave off earache from the freezing wind. How she wished she'd worn more layers. 'What exactly are you doing with the towers, then?'

Shoving his hands into his trouser pockets, looking every bit the country squire and not the physicist, George smiled and raised an eyebrow. 'We're making weapons-grade plutonium.'

James turned away from the site and started to walk back up the hill.

'You feeling well, old bean? Too much walking?' George shouted after him.

Had James heard his friend? Kitty trotted after him and linked his arm. 'Whatever's the matter?' she asked.

George caught them up in a couple of strides and slapped a hand on James's shoulder. 'I think your fiancé here is a pacifist, Kitty.'

James glowered at him – it was a look that seemed to be loaded with meaning. Kitty tried to guess what was going in his thoughts. When they got over the summit and back into a lane where the wind had eased, he finally spoke.

'I'm sorry, George. I didn't mean to walk away like that, it's just . . . I'm in the business of saving lives, not ending them. I didn't feel comfortable looking down at all that . . . those government-sanctioned plans for destruction.'

'What do you think physicists do for a living nowadays, Jimmy-boy? Do you think I can choose my job?'

Nodding, James came to a standstill and peered off at the distant, glittering Irish Sea. 'Nothing against you, old boy, but you could . . . I don't know . . . use your knowledge for good.'

'You can't unsplit the atom, James.'

James shrugged. 'If I were a physicist, I'd much, much rather be developing nuclear science that could be used in medicine, like the chaps using nuclear isotopes for experimental cancer treatments. I'd sleep much better at night than I would if I were working on new bombs for the military.'

Kitty was starting to feel not only cold but uncomfortable with the direction the conversation was taking. 'Lads, can we get back, please? We need to pull the Ford out of that mud before it gets dark. It's a long way back to Manchester.'

The men weren't listening, however. James stalked off again.

George walked after him. 'What would you rather the government do? Stop military research and development in Blighty, when the Ruskies have already engaged the West in an arms race? Supposing they won . . . What happens to our hard fought-for freedoms, then? Are you happy to become a communist?'

'Of course not,' James said. 'Don't be so facile.'

'And what about the side-product of this research? We're going to be able to light up the National Grid with nuclear power soon. Think of the good it will do to get rid of all those foul power station towers and chimneys on every house in every street in the country, pumping out thick black smoke and choking the nation. Imagine! Clean fuel at a low cost, all thanks to physicists like me, James. It's not all bad.' He turned to Kitty. 'Tell him, Kitty. There's a good girl. I find women are so more pragmatic in these situations.'

Kitty chuckled. 'Oh, don't get me involved in talk like this. I didn't go to Cambridge. I don't have opinions on things I don't understand, though I do hate the fog we get in winter because of all those coke fires. And it was flipping cold during the war, when we couldn't get fuel. I know my mam would lap up clean, cheap heating.'

Making their way back to George's cottage and James's car was an uncomfortable undertaking. Kitty could feel the tension in the air between the two men, yet because she wasn't a scientist, she felt there was nothing she could say to alleviate that tension. She knew the old friends had to work out their differences by themselves.

'Come in for a quick cup of tea to thaw out?' George asked, putting his hand on the roof of the Ford.

James looked around at the setting sun, which had finally emerged from the thick cloud. 'I don't think so, old chap. It's a long drive back.'

George and James stood awkwardly facing one another in the twilight.

'Are we still friends, Jimmy-boy?' George asked, smiling uncertainly.

James looked down at his mud-encrusted shoes. When he lifted his head, he wore a wry smile. 'Of course. We'll agree to differ like the gentlemen we are.' He stuck out his hand and George shook it.

'Marvellous. Marvellous. So, I haven't been sacked as your usher?'

'Absolutely not,' said Kitty. 'Not when you roast a potato like that. Your spuds are the best I've ever eaten.'

James chuckled. 'I don't suppose you can help being an idiot physicist, either. I can hardly blame you for scientific progress.'

George clapped his hand onto James's shoulder. 'You wait until doctors are using radioactive material to diagnose and treat this, that and the other. You'll be thanking physicists then.'

The drive home took them back through Ambleside and Windermere, where Kitty drank in the sight of the giant lake through the bare trees – a silver disc in the moonlight. The day out had been meant to bring them closer to their wedding plans, but talk of progress had only served to sow seeds of doubt about setting a date for that summer. Kitty wondered if James would actually deliver on his promise to approach the board about her staying on after marriage. Was it even conceivable that they could change the course of nursing history?

Chapter 14

'Are you going to keep your political beliefs to yourself on my ward?' Kitty asked Dovid Levine. 'I'm not going to have to separate those boys, am I? Because they've made friends, and I think that's healthy.'

The working week had swung around yet again, and Kitty was already exhausted, coming to the end of a long shift. Visiting hours were upon them, and Gordon Spencer's parents were already sitting by their son's bed.

Sammy's father pointedly lifted his arm, which was still in a sling. 'We already had this discussion, and I apologised and gave you my word. My word is good, Sister.' He nodded in the direction of Gordon's father. 'I hope you've asked the same of that Blackshirt.'

'Of course I have. I don't take sides when it comes to politics,' Kitty said. 'Most of all, I also don't take kindly to men pushing each other around on a children's ward.'

Esther Levine laid her hand on Kitty's arm. 'But this isn't politics, Sister. Spencer attacked my husband because we're Jews. If I told you the slur he used against us, it would make your toes curl.'

As if the care of scores of sick children wasn't responsibility enough, Kitty felt almost overwhelmed by the cultural turmoil that was raging inside the hospital and in Manchester, her beloved city.

She patted Esther's hand and sighed heavily. 'Go and comfort your son.'

Visiting time passed without event, and her shift came to an end. Kitty made her way back to the nurses' home and collected her personal post. In her sparsely furnished room, she sat on her hard bed and opened the scores of letters with a knife.

Dear Sister Longthorne,

I'm so sorry to hear that Matron's retiring. Of course I'd love to be in a commemorative photo. I look forward to meeting you on the day!

Yours sincerely
Marjorie Balfour

Dearest Kitty,

How lovely to hear from you after all this time! Yes, Scott and I are well and now have our own little family. Mable is three and Toby is eighteen months old. I'm working as a health visitor in Liverpool, but I would love to come back for the photo and the party, if you'll have me.

Kind regards
Florrie Finney

Dear Kitty,

I hadn't expected to ever hear from you again. I'm sorry to hear that Matron's retiring, but all good things must come to an end. I'm afraid I won't be able to take part in the photograph because I've recently moved to London with my husband, Dr Charles Moorhouse, the consultant paediatrician. Charles has just been transferred from Manchester Royal Infirmary to Guy's Hospital, where he heads up all of paediatric medicine. We're expecting our first child in August. Sorry to hear

through the grapevine that you are still not the doctor's wife you'd hoped to be. Do remember me to James.
Sincerely
Violet

Kitty stopped reading momentarily to digest the missive from her one-time friend, Violet. After all of the trouble that Violet had caused, coming between her and James at the very start of their romance, Violet had still never apologised. Now, not only was she unwilling to say goodbye to Matron, but she had taken the opportunity to boast unashamedly about her marital achievements.

'You always were nothing but a vain and insincere berk, Violet. I hope your child turns out better than you,' Kitty said, filing the letter along with the other handful of regretful respondents.

Picking up the sheaf of correspondence from those who were coming, Kitty felt a thrill of anticipation. The photograph was going to be a roaring success, she was sure. The only conundrum was how to get the old matron out of the way for an hour or two, while all of the nurses from Matron's Park Hospital career crowded into the rose garden in front of the clock tower.

'Matron Pratt,' Kitty said, picturing the new incumbent. Would this austere woman play along with such a light-hearted ruse?

Having put her uniform back on, Kitty found Matron Pratt in casualty, observing the work of the junior nurses at the start of their night shift, who in a flurry of brisk efficiency, were bringing bedpans to the immobile patients, taking temperatures and measuring blood pressures.

'So you see, Matron Pratt,' old Matron said, 'the nursing body is the very engine room of the good ship Park Hospital. What we're still short of, however, is more skilled pairs of hands on deck.'

How on earth could Kitty get Matron Pratt on her own? Kitty had passed a pair of squabbling nurses in the corridor, both of whom she knew were fighting over Richard Collins, the eligible but tedious anaesthetist. Might that be a suitable distraction? It was worth a try.

She approached the old matron and whispered in her ear. 'Matron, I noticed Nurse Callaghan and Nurse Ancaster having a set-to in the corridor by orthopaedic outpatients. I tried to intervene, but . . . I wondered if you might go and have a word. I didn't want Matron Pratt to get the impression that the younger girls are anything but—'

'Leave it to me, Sister Longthorne,' she said, patting Kitty's hand and winking.

It was only a half-lie and in a good cause, wasn't it?

The old matron turned to Matron Pratt. 'I have something to attend to. Longthorne, here, will take my place. She knows all the gals on shift.'

As soon as Matron was out of earshot, Kitty faced Matron Pratt with a heart beating so wildly, it felt as though it might punch its way out of her chest and through her starched apron at any moment.

The new matron looked at her with a bemused expression. 'Are you quite all right, Sister? You look as though you're about to pass out.'

Kitty looked over her shoulder to check the old matron had left. She turned to Matron Pratt. 'Forgive me for wasting your time with a bit of a frippery, but it's about the old matron's leaving present. I need your help.'

She told Matron Pratt about the photograph and the role the new matron would need to play to keep the old matron away from the grounds of the hospital during the gathering of the nurses and the taking of the photograph. 'I'd say with that number of women, we'd need about half an hour in the middle of the day.'

'When is it?' It was hard to tell if Matron Pratt's flinty face was a picture of annoyance or intrigue. Was she going to play along or reprimand Kitty for being frivolous?

Kitty told her. 'I've told the photographer he's got to be quick so the girls are away from their duties for as short a period as possible. We'll do it at lunch, and the night staff have said they'll set their alarms so they don't miss it.'

Matron Pratt's lips thinned to a mean line and her face seemed sterner than ever. 'Tell me you'll go to New York on that conference, and I'll make sure I take the old matron for afternoon tea.' She winked.

Feeling her cheeks glow, Kitty grinned. 'It's a deal.' Feeling utterly daring, she winked back. Her plan was coming together.

Caught up in a whirl of long shifts and some overtime she barely had the energy for, the day of the photograph came around faster than Kitty could believe. It was a freezing cold, sunny morning. As she fulfilled her duties on the children's polio ward and the hands of the clock edged towards midday, through the windows she could see women who had previously worked at the hospital arriving and bumping into each other. They squealed with delight at the reunion, embracing each other.

'I really hope the old matron doesn't notice them,' Kitty told Rijuta. 'Else all my sneaking around will be for nothing.'

As the clock on the clock tower struck twelve, Kitty stood by a window and saw Matron Pratt and the old matron heading out of the main entrance, clutching their capes close against the cold. She gave the nod to Rijuta, who had volunteered to stay behind and keep an eye on the children, given she'd only been at the hospital for a matter of months.

'You're in charge for half an hour. Shout if you need anything. I'm only outside.'

'Best of luck,' Rijuta said, giving Kitty the thumbs-up.

Buoyed by adrenalin, Kitty hastened outside to find the photographer waiting with his equipment behind a bush.

'Ready?' she asked.

'Just as soon as you pay me, love.' He held his hand out.

Kitty took out the money taken from the whip-round fund and dropped it into his hand. 'I'll get everyone together. You make it snappy and make it a good'un.'

Looking around at the women – some in nursing uniform and others wearing their civvies – who were crowding the rose garden, Kitty stood on a bench and clapped her hands together. The crowd fell silent.

'Good to see so many of you girls.' Could they hear the nervous waver in her voice? Kitty hoped not. 'Thank you especially to our old nurses for answering my invitation and for coming back. I think you all know how important it is to show the outgoing matron our appreciation. She's a credit to nursing, and she's been our stand-in mother since this hospital opened for business in 1929.'

She looked out at a sea of expectant faces. They were all applauding her words. Her nervousness had gone now, and she allowed herself a satisfied smile as she studied the gathering to see who had turned up. Her eyes came to rest on a familiar redhead whom she hadn't expected to be there at all. Violet, dressed in a mink coat and wearing satin gloves that gleamed in the winter sun.

The two adversaries locked eyes, but Kitty surreptitiously touched her engagement ring with the tip of her thumb and moved her focus onto the others. If Violet had hoped to be the centre of attention, she had another thing coming. Kitty did, however, glance over to the window behind which James's clinic waiting room was situated. Had he seen his ex-squeeze? Perhaps not. Nobody was standing at the window.

Kitty turned back to the gathering of current and past nursing staff. 'Now, do as the photographer says, please,' Kitty shouted. 'We've got hardly any time at all before Matron's back from lunch.' She climbed down from the bench and gave the photographer the nod.

The photographer emerged from the bushes swiftly, carrying his cumbersome equipment. 'Get together, girls. Tallest ones at the back, please, and those in the front, make sure you show us a nice bit of shapely leg.'

Kitty tapped him on the shoulder. 'Hey, we're nurses, not beauty queens. Try to show some decorum when you're speaking to these ladies. They've saved many a serviceman from a painful and early death and they've seen more blood in a week than you'll see in a lifetime, pal.'

The photographer's Adam's apple rose and fell in his skinny neck. He nodded and got on with the task of herding the women into the right formation without further ado.

Feeling proud of the gathering she was responsible for, Kitty took her place at the end of the front row.

'Remember to say cheese, girls, even if it's on ration,' Kitty said.

A ripple of laughter seemed to vibrate on the cold spring air, warming it just enough to stop the women's eyes from watering and their noses from turning red in the wind.

'Cheese!' they all shouted.

Several flashbulbs popped and the photo was done. The crowd started to disperse rapidly as nurses returned to their wards or their beds or their families and new jobs, leaving Kitty standing face-to-face with Violet for the first time in years.

'Kitty,' Violet said. A smile spread across her perfectly made-up face, though it didn't reach her eyes.

'I thought you were living in London,' Kitty said. 'I thought you weren't coming.'

Violet was wearing expensive-looking shoes that showed off her dainty ankles, and beneath the mink coat, it was clear she was wearing some designer gown or other in the New Look style that Christian Dior favoured – the same style Violet had once selected for her planned marriage to James.

'I had a change of heart,' Violet said, taking off her satin gloves with some ceremony to reveal an engagement and wedding ring combination that Kitty felt sure could take out a man's eye. 'I realised I wouldn't miss it for the world. So, my husband – Charles – booked me onto the Pullman. First class makes travelling that sort of distance a little easier, I find.'

Kitty looked at her one-time friend, wondering what to say. Was Violet expecting some kind of confrontation over how her planned wedding had ended? Well, Kitty decided that she wasn't going to give her the satisfaction. Violet had always been the sort of spoiled girl from a wealthy family who was used to getting her way. Kitty wasn't about to indulge her further.

'If you need to call a taxi back to Piccadilly, I'm sure they'll call you one from reception,' Kitty said. She turned to leave.

'You're a Sister now?' Violet shouted after her.

Kitty turned around and touched her starched cap. 'Yes. I was promoted in the new year.'

'And James?' Violet's eyes brightened.

'He's very well. I'll tell him you asked after him.' Again, Kitty shot a glance towards James's clinic, but the window was empty but for a bedraggled spider plant on the window sill. 'I'll tell him when I see him for dinner this evening.'

'Oh.' Violet touched her rings and then her belly, beneath the lustrous fur coat. 'So you got back together?'

Should she just leave Violet standing there, Kitty wondered? Did she owe her answers, when Violet had been the one to first obstruct true love's path? Or should she tell her their wedding plans and revel in the satisfaction that Violet's efforts to drive a wedge between her and James had been futile, after all?

'We've been engaged for a good while,' Kitty said, fingering her engagement ring, which she'd slid back on for the photo. 'We should have married last year, but I went to Barbados on a nursing recruitment drive, and got promoted soon after I got back.'

Violet smiled. 'Still a spinster really then?'

'We're getting married this summer instead. But I'm surprised you're showing such an interest, Violet, given how you're happily married yourself and have a baby on the way.' She narrowed her eyes and tried to put her finger on why Violet had embarked on a four hundred-mile round trip for a half hour's visit to the rose garden of Park Hospital. 'All that travelling for a matron who you hated and who never liked you? Anyone would say you'd come hoping for a glimpse of James.' She smiled at her sympathetically. 'It's a long way to come to lay eyes on somebody else's fiancé. Must be hard, knowing that you've got it all, but it still isn't what you actually wanted.'

Kitty walked back towards the nurses' home, feeling sullied by her own vengeful words but glad that she had finally laid the ghost of Violet and James's ill-fated romance to rest.

'Be careful what you wish for, Kitty Longthorne,' Violet shouted after her. 'If he could break my heart, he could break yours.'

With Violet's sour words ringing in her ears for the rest of the week, Kitty was left wondering if her ex-friend would prove to be right.

Chapter 15

'You wouldn't recognise Manchester if you'd come here before the war,' Kitty said, as she and Grace made their way up Princess Street, heading for Albert Square and the city centre shops beyond. 'See this bombed out shell?' She pointed to a glorious 1850s façade that was miraculously still standing – the only remnant after the Blitz of what had been the Free Trade Hall. 'Imagine all the bomb sites around the city, filled with smart old buildings like this, and you can imagine what it was like.'

'I bet it was impressive,' Grace said. 'All that Victorian money pouring in from the textile industry.'

Kitty linked arms with her future sister-in-law, marching her past what was about to become an enormous building site. 'Now look at it.' She shook her head. 'Still, apparently Princess Margaret is coming to Manchester in a couple of weeks to lay the foundation stone for the new Free Trade Hall. They're rebuilding the innards.'

Grace sighed heavily. 'Ned said he could have got a job working as a labourer in there,' she said. 'They're recruiting for the building trade all over the city, especially to put up these new prefabricated houses. But only my Ned could get work at the biscuit factory instead.'

'What's wrong with that?' Kitty said, relieved to hear her brother had actually found paid work.

'Haven't you heard?' Grace looked at her askance as they crossed the road, narrowly dodging a Rolls Royce that glided by, presumably ferrying its owners to the Midland Hotel. 'He's got involved in the trade union. He's been there five minutes, and he's already spouting this, that and the other about workers' rights and strike action.'

'That's good, isn't it? A fair day's work, a fair day's pay? One of the things I like about Matron Pratt is that she's keen to improve nurses' lot – pay, training, our standing. Hey, maybe we'll even get some of those lovely modern uniforms that they wear in America. They're a darn sight more stylish than ours.'

'Ned isn't Matron Pratt,' Grace said. 'If there's trouble, Ned will find it. He came to the Band on the Wall to see me sing the other week and got into an almighty ruckus with some lads from out of town.'

'Not again!' Kitty said. 'He's only just been patched up after his run-in with the fascists.'

Grace shook her head. 'It's politics, isn't it? Ned's suddenly got a bee in his bonnet about the Bolsheviks. He thinks communism is the only way to make Britain a fair place for all.'

Kitty thought about how the returning Labour government had just announced that prescriptions would be charged for, despite the initial promise that everything would be free for everyone. 'Well, there's definitely a problem with there being a few "haves" that have got a lot more money than the "have-nots". Mam can't afford to get new dentures and get her specs fixed, yet there's rich folk swanning round in Rolls Royces, going for afternoon tea at the Midland Hotel. But communism's dangerous. It's not the answer. Ned's going to get himself into hot water with the police – not for the first time. Except if they decide you're a traitor – they don't just chuck you into Strangeways for a spell. They hang you.'

In contemplative silence, they crossed Albert Square, passing beneath the Victorian gothic splendour of the Town Hall. Kitty tried to think of a way she could pull Ned aside to give him a good talking to – sister to brother, and out of Grace's earshot.

'What time are we meeting the boys again?' she asked.

'After the match. It'll take them a while to get back into town, though. Especially after an FA Cup semi-final.'

Kitty nodded, catching their reflection in the shop window of a gentleman's outfitter. Behind them, she could see two elderly women pointing at the spectacle of a white woman and a Black woman linking arms. *Idiots*, she thought, hoping Grace hadn't caught sight of their disapproving looks. 'I wish they weren't going, if I'm honest. James doesn't even like football. He's a cricket man. And Ned . . . Well, let's hope they keep out of mischief. Maine Road's going to be crammed with Liverpool and Everton supporters, all gunning for a fight the minute the opposite side scores.'

'On my birthday outing, too!' Grace said, tutting. 'Boys are so selfish.'

Pulling Grace closer to her, Kitty winked. 'Come on, Gracie. I'll make it up to you. Let's nip the Kardomah and get a nice coffee and a piece of cake. It's not often us nurses get time to ourselves. And then we can look in the shops at the new fashions.'

Grace laughed. 'I can't afford anything but the clothes I'm stood in on my wages.'

'It doesn't cost to look, our Grace.'

The afternoon passed in a whirlwind of peering in shop windows at dresses they couldn't possibly afford.

'I love the new full skirts and nipped in waists,' Kitty said, standing in front of a shop front where the mannequin wore a brightly coloured floral-print dress. The short-sleeved bodice was tightly fitting over the mannequin's perky bosom. Kitty undid her coat and squeezed her handknitted jumper in at the middle. 'What do you think? Could I carry one of those off?'

Grace chuckled. 'There's so many underskirts beneath that dress, a tiny gust of wind could carry you off in one of them.' She unbuttoned her coat and looked down at her own chest. 'Maybe Ned could do with buying me one of those new conical bras for my birthday. I'm sick of this grey old utility thing.'

'You think that's ropey,' Kitty said. 'Mam got my corselette from a jumble.'

They started to giggle, striking poses like magazine fashion models in the gleaming shop windows. Though with her heavy woollen coat on and her scarf tied beneath her chin, Kitty felt like an old washerwoman.

'No Christian Dior for us when we walk down the aisle,' she said. 'Good job Mam's a seamstress. We'd better pray she gets new specs before she makes our dresses or we'll end up looking like dented lampshades.'

Kitty dragged Grace to C&A, Lewis's and even Kendal Milne, where they tittered at the rich women in their furs and pearls, who spoke to the shop assistants as though they were lowly servants.

'I like to stroke their furs as I walk past,' Kitty said. 'They feel amazing. I bet you can't stroke that posh old bag's mink without her noticing.'

Grace sidled up to a wealthy-looking woman who was wearing a full-length Persian lamb coat, trimmed with silver mink collar and cuffs. The woman was leaning over the make-up counter, examining an Elizabeth Arden powder compact. Glancing back at Kitty, Grace reached out and stroked the woman's fur cuffs. She wrinkled her nose. 'Gold teet don't suit hog mout.'

The woman turned to look at Grace, balked and moved a couple of feet to her left, as though Grace was emitting a bad smell.

Walking away briskly, Grace snorted and burst into laughter.

'My turn next,' Kitty said. She looked around the shop-floor and spied an assistant giving away samples of L'Air du Temps perfume, which was all the rage since it had been launched a couple of years earlier. A beautiful young woman, who looked like an actress and who was dressed in much the same way as Violet had been, in a rich brown mink coat with pearls in her ears and around her neck, stopped to engage the assistant in conversation about the perfume. Kitty watched as the assistant sprayed the woman's wrist from the bottle. 'Watch this.'

Feeling like her giggles might burst out and give the game away, Kitty hurried over to the perfume assistant and the fur-clad young woman. She glanced back at Grace and gave her the nod. Then, she ran her hand gently down the back of the mink coat, stuck out her free hand, snatched a sample and scarpered, barely able to contain her laughter.

'And there's me thinking you're all sensible now you're a Sister,' Grace said.

Kitty produced a tiny glass vial of the expensive perfume. 'I read that Ingrid Bergman wears this. Here you go.' She gave the perfume to Grace.

'Ooh, lovely. I'll smell like a West Indian plantation owner!'

Grace pocketed the perfume, but not before a security guard started walking across the shopfloor towards them, wearing a stern look.

'Hey up. Look lively.' Kitty dragged Grace out of Kendal Milne and onto Deansgate, where the two of them fell about in fits of laughter.

'I haven't had so much fun in a long time,' Kitty said.

Before the shops closed for business, Kitty and Grace made their way to the back street framing company, where the commemorative portrait of all the Park Hospital nursing staff had been framed. The shopkeeper brought out the finished article.

'Are you happy with that, love?' he said, holding it up for her to see.

The large photograph had been mounted on white card, on which all the nurses' names had been written in tiny copperplate script. Kitty ran her hand over the traditional gold-coloured wooden frame and looked at Park Hospital's imposing clock tower in the background with a pang of such strong affection in her heart that she felt a lump in her throat. Would she feel like this when she left to marry?

'It's marvellous,' she said. She turned to Grace. 'What do you think?'

Grace nodded. 'Smashing. I think it's going to take two of us to carry this thing to James's car, though. It's enormous.'

Together, they carried the giant portrait to Moseley Street, where they had arranged to rendezvous with James and Ned. Kitty was relieved to see the Ford Anglia parked outside the new Ping Hong Chinese restaurant that had not long been open.

James got out of the car. 'Ah, there you are, girls. We've been waiting for you.' He opened the boot of the car and took the portrait from them, carefully laying it down and covering it with a woollen blanket. He looked up at Grace. 'Many happy returns, Gracie. How does twenty-five feel?'

'Much like twenty-four.' Grace smiled as James handed her a birthday card.

'Dinner's on me,' he said.

'That's very kind. Now, where's that man of mine?'

Kitty didn't need James to tell them where Ned had got to. She could see he was asleep, his head resting against the passenger side window. Knocking on the glass, when Ned woke with a start, even in the twilight, even though his face was badly disfigured, she could see he'd had one ale too many.

'Out of the car, Ned Longthorne,' she said, hands on her hips. Kitty turned to James. 'How can you let him get like this? You know it's Grace's special day.'

James shrugged. 'Ned's a grown man. What can I tell you? He'd been in the pub before we even met.'

Grace gently moved Kitty out of the way and opened the door of the Ford Anglia with such force that Ned almost fell out onto the street. 'Ned Longthorne, you're drunk as a lord. How could you show me up? On my birthday too!'

Ned held his hands up and tried to embrace Grace. 'I only had a couple. I'm not drunk, I promise.'

'You're lying!' Grace took a swipe at Ned, who lolled against the car, smiling.

'Don't worry, Grace,' James said. 'We'll get some tea and food in him. He'll be fine.'

They bundled Ned into the Chinese restaurant with a warning that he had to behave. Kitty brought up the rear, drinking in the delicious smell of food she'd never before eaten in her life. They were shown to a table by a Chinese waitress wearing what appeared to be jewel-coloured silk pyjamas. The waitress offered them menus and bowed low.

'Is this like what you had to eat in the Japanese prisoner-of-war camp, Ned?' she asked.

Ned, however, was trying to read the menu upside down.

Kitty snatched the menu from him and shoved it back into his hands, the right way up. 'Idiot.'

'Go easy on him,' James said. 'He has had rather a day of it.'

'How do you mean?' Grace asked.

James looked furtively around at the other guests in the restaurant, as though he were checking that nobody was eavesdropping. 'Ned got drunk at the pub for Dutch courage. He thought he was being followed.'

Ned nodded and squinted at the menu. 'I didn't think it. I was followed.'

Kitty felt her lips prickle cold with unease. 'What did he look like, this feller?' She turned to James. 'Did you see him, or is Ned just stringing us a line to get away with turning up to Grace's birthday meal three sheets to the wind?'

The waitress returned to take their order, and they fell silent.

James ordered fried rice and spring rolls for them all. When the waitress went away, he turned to Kitty and spoke softly with an eyebrow raised. 'I'm afraid I did see this chap at the football ground. He looked pretty ordinary – hat pulled low, coat collar up. Unsurprising in this weather. But he was standing a few rows behind and he was definitely watching us. Every time I turned around, he had eyes for Ned and then looked away quickly when he noticed I was watching. He moved closer in the middle of the match to within earshot, and when we scarpered to a different part of the stadium at half-time, he moved too.'

Kitty gasped and looked at Grace, who clasped her hands to her mouth, wide-eyed. 'Who do you think he was?'

James shrugged. 'What sort of chap follows someone like Ned, who's been rubbing shoulders with communists? A fascist? The police? A spy? It's beyond me.'

Kitty turned to Ned.

'Ned Longthorne, if you've got men following you at football matches, you're in trouble. What the hell have you been up to now?'

Chapter 16

'Make sure she doesn't know what we're up to,' Kitty whispered to Molly Bickerstaff in the corridor outside her ward, on the morning of Matron's big retirement send-off.

'Mum's the word,' Molly said, nodding. 'I'll bring her down at half past eleven, and tell her there's a problem with the kitchens; that Cook's asked specifically for her. Hopefully she won't suspect a thing.'

Kitty patted Molly's arm. 'Good work. Lily's going to make sure the cake's in place, and I've hidden the framed portrait in Cook's office. It's all wrapped up in nice paper, and I've stuck the card to it.'

'What time are the other girls getting there?' Molly asked.

'Everyone knows to be there ten minutes early, just to be on the safe side, and everyone knows to be absolutely silent until the light goes on.'

Kitty returned to her ward.

Attending to her duties on Matron's last morning wasn't proving easy. She'd been taken aback by how much she was dreading the change. Though Matron Pratt was proving to be positively inspirational, with her modern views and her firm but fair ways, losing the old matron felt rather like losing a parent. Kitty realised that the early years of her own career were well and truly over. The old guard slowly retiring, one by one, meant that that likes of her and James were now rising to be the senior medical staff members that people looked up to.

'Ah, Sister Longthorne,' Dr Bourke said as he entered the ward. 'Good morning. How are my patients doing today?' He adjusted his bow tie and looked along the rows of iron lungs that hissed and wheezed in unison.

Kitty fetched her notebook from her office, where she'd written any developments of note that the night shift Sister had informed her of. 'There are a few real triumphs, actually. Several children have just started going all day outside of their iron lungs. A few are starting to walk with assistance.'

She looked down the ward and her gaze came to rest on Sammy Levine at the far end, who was sitting in a visitor's chair next to his iron lung, reading a book. His colour had improved, and though his limbs were still too weak to allow him to walk, he could at least breathe for himself during the day.

'Sammy Levine and his neighbour, Gordon, have both come on in leaps and bounds.'

'Didn't you have trouble with the fathers?'

'Yes. But I think the boys' unlikely friendship suits them both very well. Gordon's walking well with leg callipers and braces now. Sammy's at least able to get out of his iron lung for a bit. They keep each other company and encourage each other. It's nice to see.'

Dr Bourke grunted his approval. 'Any deteriorations?'

'Thankfully not. We've not lost a child since Archibald Davies sadly passed away. Some of the rehabilitated children have been discharged home to their families and GP care. There's constant replacements, obviously, but . . .'

'Excellent. Excellent. Let's keep our fingers crossed for a vaccine, and one day, this ward can be given over to other childhood afflictions – hopefully less ruinous ones.'

*

Dr Bourke's rounds went smoothly and soon it was time for Kitty to make her way to the dining room, where she found most of the nurses in the hospital chatting loudly.

Kitty stood on a chair and clapped her hands. 'Now, ladies. Pipe down! Matron's going to be here in just a few minutes and we want to keep it a surprise.'

The senior nurses were the first to fall silent, clearly keen to lead by example. The ebullient junior nurses were the last to stop chattering. A few continued, oblivious to Kitty's disapproving glare.

Kitty clapped her hands again. 'Enough!'

The startled juniors fell silent then, and looked up at Kitty, wearing deferential expressions on their youthful faces.

'Sorry, Sister,' they said.

Kitty climbed down off the chair, pressing her index finger to her lips. She retrieved the portrait from Cook's office in silence. Lily Schwartz wheeled in a two-tiered sponge cake, beautifully piped in pink with fresh grape hyacinths and a daffodil, arranged in a posy on the top.

'Blimey. Where did you get that?' Kitty whispered. 'Cook didn't make it, did she?' She had visions of cutting into a dry sponge full of hard, floury lumps.

Lily shook her head. 'You're joking, aren't you?' she said. 'We're trying to show gratitude to Matron, not poison her.'

Kitty started to laugh, but then, one of the senior nurses burst into the dining room.

'She's coming!' she said. 'About a minute away.'

Excited chatter struck up anew among the girls.

'Quick! Draw the curtains! Switch off the lights,' Kitty said. 'Everybody, hold your tongues and keep absolutely still as statues until she's turned on the lights.'

Watching the handle on the door turn in the dim light that came through cracks above and at the sides of the curtains, Kitty felt the blood rushing in her ears. She couldn't help but grin excitedly.

Matron walked in and switched on the lights.

'Surprise!' Every single nurse in the dining room yelled in unison.

At first, Matron looked as though she'd seen a ghost, but quickly, her shocked expression turned into a look of wonder and then, a broad smile. She laid her hand on her chest. 'My word. Look at this! Look at you all. Aren't you wonderful. My girls!'

Kitty approached Matron and brought her up to the front of the dining room. She banged a spoon on a glass until the room fell silent again. She turned to Matron and though she'd written her speech days earlier and had rehearsed it a couple of times, the words failed her at first. Kitty could only think of the lump in her throat and the tears pricking the backs of her eyes.

Come on, Kitty, she told herself. *Take a deep breath and get on with it. All these nurses are watching you, relying on you to speak for them. Find some courage, and don't cry like a twit.*

Taking a deep breath, she finally spoke – jittery at first, and then with more confidence. 'Now, all of these women have gathered here today, not just to give you the send-off you deserve, Matron, but to say thanks. Thank you for everything that you've done for Park Hospital, generally. Thank you most of all for everything you've done for all of us nurses.'

There was a rapturous round of applause, and then the nurses all fell silent once more.

'You've been there for us from the minute we started as trainee nurses. You've taught us to care for patients, to assist the doctors, to act like professionals. You've taught us self-discipline and self-respect.' She turned to the onlookers. 'Hasn't she, girls?'

There were whistles and cat-calls of agreement.

Matron was blushing now and looking down at the polished floor. 'Oh, well, I . . . er . . .'

Kitty took Matron's hands into hers. 'You've made Park Hospital an institution *so* admired nationally, that Aneurin Bevan picked this place to be the first-ever National Health Service hospital. You're our heroine, Matron. You championed nurses and the domestic staff when the doctors were taking liberties.'

Her comment was greeted by whoops and cheers until Kitty looked pointedly at her rowdy compatriots, and they fell silent again.

'You championed the comfort, safety and dignity of the patients. You championed professional pride in this nursing body, dragging the daftest and laziest trainees up to your standards, leading by example with decades of solid graft.'

As she contemplated her next words, Kitty felt emotion start to overwhelm her. 'And I have to say personally, Matron, that under your stewardship, nursing in Park Hospital has lost a lot of its snobbery. When I started training just before the war, most of the nurses were well-to-do girls who were just doing a suitable job to fill the years before they left to get married. But now? Now I'm so glad to see so many working-class girls wearing their aprons, caps and capes with pride. Nursing is about bright, dedicated young women, whether they're from good families or families like mine.' She chuckled. 'And believe me, there's not much good about *my* family. But Matron, you've always seen the potential in young nursing recruits, regardless of how much money their mams or dads have got in the bank. You've worked your socks off to raise us all as your nursing daughters to become amazing medical women in our own right. And for this, we want to thank you, Matron. Thank you for dedicating your working life to making us nurses as good as we can be.'

The applause from the room was rapturous. Kitty scanned her colleagues' delighted faces and felt the love and gratitude pouring out of everyone, from the trainees to the Sisters who had held senior posts for decades. She turned to Matron and saw that this formidable woman was crying, despite the smile.

Kitty turned to Molly Bickerstaff and mouthed, 'Flowers.' Molly marched out from the shadows with a giant bouquet of iris, tulips and early season roses. She handed them to Kitty, who presented the heavenly smelling bouquet to Matron.

'Oh, thank you, my dear. Thank you, Molly.' Matron turned to the rest of the room. 'Thank you all.'

'We've got you another gift that I hope will serve as a lasting reminder of us all,' Kitty said. She tipped the wink to Lily and Molly, who carried the large, wrapped photograph in from Cook's office. Kitty helped them carry it to the table.

'What on earth is this?' Matron asked.

'Open it and see.'

Matron removed the paper carefully and gasped when she saw the beautifully framed portrait. She read the names listed on the bottom of the mount in silence, wiping a tear from her eyes. Then, she looked at Kitty and nodded. 'It's wonderful. You're so thoughtful.'

'It's from us all,' Kitty said. 'With heartfelt thanks. There's a card as well.' She handed over a large retirement card.

Clutching the card, Matron pressed her lips together in a doleful smile and turned to the nurses who had gathered together to say goodbye.

Kitty banged on the glass with the spoon once more, and the clapping abated.

'For once, I'm speechless,' Matron said. 'Almost.'

The nurses burst into laughter.

Matron cleared her throat. 'Girls, girls, my girls. Thank you *so* much for this heart-warming gesture. But really, it is I who should thank you. Nursing was always my dream job when I was a little girl. I used to dress up as a nurse, pilfering my mother's apron and wearing my father's handkerchief on my head. Caring for the sick is one of the noblest and most Christian things any of us can do. We work long, tiring hours for little pay or prestige, but we are the ones who are there, by patients' bedsides throughout the night, tending to their needs in the operating theatre and on the wards, at the end, when the doctors have lost their good fight. Nurses are the most selfless people I have ever met, and I am honoured to have spent my working life surrounded by you all. Training and working with the nurses of Park Hospital has been the privilege and the highlight of my career. It has made me a better person, and together we have saved thousands of lives. Thank you from the bottom of my heart. I shall treasure this photo. I only hope those less-than-divine creatures, the doctors, haven't had the same idea, because if they presented me with a portrait of their ugly faces, I think I should have to hang it in the privy.'

Kitty burst into hearty laughter at the unexpectedly daring and funny comment. She put her arm around the old matron and whispered, 'We'll never forget you.'

'Nor I you, Kitty Longthorne.' Matron smiled back, leaned over and kissed her on the cheek. 'Nor I you.'

It was the end of an era, and Kitty had never felt so equally cursed and blessed.

Chapter 17

'Where shall we go first?' Kitty asked James, looking up at a signpost that showed in which direction the many and varied attractions of Belle Vue lay. 'The zoo, or a walk round the gardens, or the funfair?'

'Well, I've never been to Belle Vue before, darling. It's entirely your choice. You're the one who needs cheering up.'

Two months had passed since Matron had left Park Hospital, and Kitty had been feeling surprisingly low with her old mentor gone. Matron Pratt always bristled with brisk efficiency and seemed more than a worthy replacement, but Kitty privately acknowledged that a malaise had set in – in her, if not noticeably in the other nursing staff. Whether it was pure fatigue or grief at losing another important person in her life so soon after her father's death, she couldn't rightfully say. But she'd definitely needed a pick-me-up, and Mam had suggested James take her to Belle Vue.

'Well, it's not long since breakfast, so maybe leave the fair until our grub has gone down. How about we start with the zoo? I love the giraffes.'

'Giraffes it is then,' James said, taking her hand and kissing her fingers.

Kitty turned into the May sunshine with her eyes closed, relishing the warmth on her face. 'The Murray Theatre Girls are on in the fairground later. It's going to be a smashing day out. I can feel it in my bones.'

Hand in hand, she and James strolled through the gardens to the zoo and visited the animal enclosures. Kitty laughed with delight at the sight of the hippos begging to be fed. She watched with some distaste as the big cats dined on what appeared to be horse meat, judging by the size of the leg they were tearing the flesh from. When she went looking for the penguins with the sort of childish delight she hadn't felt since she was a child, however, she couldn't find them.

Kitty approached one of the zookeepers and tapped him on the shoulder. 'Excuse me, but how come there's so few animals, compared to before the war? Where's the sea lions and penguins and that?'

The zookeeper looked at her sympathetically. 'Sorry, love, it's rationing. A lot of the animals . . . we just can't be feeding them things like bananas and fish. They're either too pricey or we just can't get hold of 'em. The sea lions . . . we tried to give them beef, covered in cod liver oil, but they got ulcers and died. Same with the penguins. You can't feed a penguin potatoes, can you?' He shrugged. 'We lost a lioness and her cubs, and all because we couldn't put the heating on. What can you do? At least the place didn't get badly bombed.'

Kitty looked at James in dismay. 'I never thought of that. What a shame.'

'We see a lot worse in the hospital, my dear. And that's human beings.' He squeezed her hand and then put his arm around her. He turned to the zookeeper. 'Please tell us the giraffes are still alive and well.'

The zookeeper smiled and pointed to the giraffe enclosure. 'See for yourselves.'

Feeling her mood soar when she spotted the long-necked, long-lashed beauties, Kitty ran to the railing that separated the public from her childhood favourite animal. She turned to tell James about how she'd fed them the last time she'd visited Belle Vue, as a child, but he was standing several feet away, staring into the distance with a puzzled look on his face.

'What's got into you?' she asked.

James frowned. 'I could have sworn I caught sight of a chap watching us while we were talking to the zookeeper. He looked devilishly like the man who seemed to be following Ned and me at Maine Road on the day of the FA Cup semi-final.'

Kitty immediately felt a shiver run down her spine. She pulled her cardigan closed and looked in the same direction as James. 'No sign of him now.'

'No.'

'Are you sure someone was there?'

'Yes. Quite sure.' After a few moments, James's frown dissipated, and he sighed. 'Perhaps I'm just overwrought. Same as you. We work too darn hard, you and I.' He kissed her head and they turned their attention back to the giraffes.

After the tour of the zoo, Kitty opted to tackle the funfair. 'I want to go on the rollercoaster,' she said.

James looked up at the giant wooden structure that snaked its way through and around the sprawling Belle Vue site in an undulating string of peaks and troughs. 'Really? Must we? I mean, it looks rather daunting, and I'm satisfied my job is thrilling enough.'

As if to prove his point, a string of carriages hurtled towards the peak closest to them at top speed, rattling as it scudded down, down, down the previous peak. The passengers screamed with terrified delight, their hands in the air and grimaces on their wind-flattened faces as the carriages almost crashed to the bottom, only to be fired back up, up, up to the summit. Again, they hurtled down, doing a good sixty miles per hour, Kitty reckoned.

'Oh, come on, you big spoilsport. All the mad things you do in the operating theatre, and you can't face a thrill ride?' She nudged him playfully. 'It'll be just like your driving in the Lakes.'

Finding the start of the queue, they were chatting enthusiastically about the prospect of toffee apples after the ride and their impending trip to New York, when four men, dressed in black suits, surrounded them.

'Dr James Williams? Catherine Longthorne? Come with us, please,' one of the men said. He didn't sound like a local man at all.

'You!' James said, pointing to one of the men, who wore a trilby low on his head. 'You're the fellow who was watching me at the football. What on earth—?'

'Put your hands behind your backs,' the man said. He too spoke with a London accent, and took out a set of handcuffs, as did the man who'd spoken first.

'Are we under arrest?' Kitty asked, feeling so lightheaded with panic, she wondered if she might faint at any moment.

The first man grabbed her hands roughly and snapped the cuffs onto her. The cold metal bit into her skin.

When the second man cuffed James, James wriggled, trying to turn and face his captor. 'Who the hell are you people?' he asked. He looked around at the other funfair revellers, who had backed away but were still watching, clearly agog. 'Do you see this?' James shouted at them. 'We're being arrested and we don't even know who by or what for. Call the *Evening News* and tell the news desk. This is an infringement of our civil liberties as British citizens. I am a doctor and this is my fiancée, a nursing Sister. We both work at the Park Hospital in Davyhulme. We're pillars of the community, I tell you.'

'We're just having a day out,' Kitty said, unsure whether she was about to burst into tears or bite her own captor in a fit of pique. 'What on earth do you want with us?'

Finally, the man who'd spoken first took out what looked like a black leather wallet. He opened it and showed her some form of identification, but he closed it again so quickly, she didn't have time to register what it had said. She had, however, seen the Royal Coat of Arms on the card.

'You're government,' she said. She turned to James. 'They're secret service.' Her legs went weak.

'Come with us,' one of the other men said. 'Don't make a fuss or it will be worse for you.'

'Steady on,' James said, pulling away from his captor's grip. 'We're not in George Orwell's *1984*. You can't just snatch us in a public place, clap us in handcuffs and not even tell us *why* we're under arrest and under whose authority we're being arrested. I demand to speak to a solicitor.'

'Get moving.' The man who held him kicked James's ankles and started to push him in the direction of the exit.

Kitty followed, though she tried to wrench her elbow out of the pincer-like grip of the secret service agent who held her. Walking through Belle Vue, she could see that people had noticed she and James were being frog-marched out by officials. She was at once cringing with embarrassment and at the same time livid that this was happening to two innocent people.

They passed beneath the sign for Belle Vue, through the gates and into the street. Kitty caught sight of a Black Maria van, which she was being marched towards.

'No! No! This can't be happening. I've done nothing wrong.' The heel on her shoe broke off as she was dragged along.

'Get in the van,' the fourth man said, pulling the door open.

'You shall hear about this when I've spoken to my solicitor,' James said. 'This is an outrage.'

His words sounded brave enough, but Kitty could see from his ashen face and the waxy sheen to his skin that he was just as frightened as she was. Shivering with shock, she clambered into the van and sat on the hard wooden bench. Two of the men got in with them.

'Now, look here!' James began.

'Shut it,' the agent said. 'You two have got some explaining to do, but you're going to have plenty of time to do it at His Majesty's leisure.'

They arrived outside an anonymous-looking building. Looking around at the street, trying to spot a familiar landmark, Kitty realised that she had no idea where they were.

'Just stay calm, darling,' James said. 'This will all be over in a jiffy. We've nothing to hide. We just need to stick together. I'll protect you.'

Kitty nodded. She was still quaking with cold and adrenalin. Her teeth chattered.

'You're not protecting anyone, lover boy. You're coming with me,' James's captor said.

James was marched inside the building.

'James! James!' Kitty shouted after him, but the heavy iron door slammed shut and her fiancé was out of sight.

'Where are you taking me?' Kitty asked, craning her neck to get a better look at the agent who held her. 'Don't hurt me!'

'Walk,' he simply said.

One of the other men held open the heavy iron door and she was taken down a dank-smelling flight of stone steps to a basement.

'James! James!' she shouted. 'Can you hear me?'

A door was opened and Kitty was pushed inside a room that was set up for an interrogation, complete with a table, three chairs and a bright light, mounted on a tripod. Her heart beat so wildly that she swayed back and forth with the force of it.

'Sit,' the man said.

He and one of his colleagues pulled out their chairs on the opposite side of the table, scraping the legs against the concrete floor, and they sat down. One had his arms folded. The other took out a file and put it on the table. They both leaned forwards in a menacing manner.

'I don't know what all this is about, but I can assure you—'

'I'm Agent Riley,' her captor said.

'And I'm Agent Townsend,' the other said, opening the file and taking a pen from his breast pocket.

Agent Riley looked at his watch and announced the time. Agent Townsend wrote it in on a clean sheet of paper in what was otherwise a surprisingly thick file.

'Now, Miss Longthorne. We've been keeping an eye on you and your family and associates, and it's come to our attention that there's a potential risk to national security.'

Suddenly, Kitty felt infused with a little Bert Longthorne belligerence, as though her father was in the room, encouraging her to stick up for herself. 'How? I don't get any time to do much apart from tend sick and dying children in iron lungs. How on earth can *I* pose a national threat? And my fiancé, Dr Williams . . . he spends his day trying to put the faces of war veterans back together. Does that sound like the actions of anything but a patriot?'

'Tell us about your brother Edward's involvement with the Communist Party.'

Kitty felt the blood drain from her face. *Bloody Ned!* She opened her mouth to answer, but no words would come.

Chapter 18

'I honestly don't know what my brother gets up to in his spare time,' Kitty said, her mind racing with thoughts of how Ned had admitted fighting in the streets alongside the local chapter of the Communist Party against Oswald Mosley's new band of fascists. 'He's always been a law unto himself, and I'm not his keeper.'

'Yet you see each other at least once a week,' Agent Riley said.

Kitty's eyes widened. 'You've been following me? Hey! How long have you been tracking my movements? That's an infringement of my privacy, that is.' She poked herself in the chest emphatically. 'It's a free country, and *I've* done nothing wrong.'

Agent Riley pressed his lips together until they became a thin white line. 'Yet here you are. Consorting with not just one known communist but two.'

'Two?' Kitty sifted through her memories, trying to recall one of a Red in her social circle. She shook her head, baffled. 'Who do you mean?'

'I'll get onto that in a moment. Now tell me about your brother.'

'Well, our Ned's got a good heart, but he's easily led.'

Agent Riley narrowed his eyes at her. 'Tell us about the injuries he was admitted to Park Hospital with.'

'He wasn't admitted,' Kitty said. 'He went to casualty and was patched up as an outpatient.'

'Don't try to be clever, Miss Longthorne,' Riley said. 'That kind of attitude will get you into trouble. And this is a very serious matter of national security. Do you know what the penalty is for treason?'

Kitty swallowed hard, imagining her entire family swinging from the gallows while onlookers jeered. 'There's no way my brother's a national threat. He's not a threat to anyone but himself and our mother's sanity.'

'Let's try again,' Agent Townsend, who presided over the note-taking, said. 'Now, tell us the extent of your brother's involvement with the Communist Party.' He looked up from his file and fixed her with a penetrating stare.

Feeling as though the very flesh had been blasted from her bones by his intense scrutiny, Kitty realised she had to tell them as much as she knew. 'Our Ned's marrying a lovely girl called Grace – my colleague at the hospital. She happens to be Black and from Barbados. Right? That's it, as far as I know. Ned's worried. He's upset by the Union Movement yobs that are marching on a regular basis. Oswald Mosley and his latest cronies are anti-anything that isn't true blue, and our Ned's taken it upon himself to defend his fiancée's honour.' She shrugged. 'It just so happens that the ones fighting the fascists on the streets are the communists. My guess is he's joined them so he can do his bit for anti-fascism. If it had been clowns getting into fisticuffs with the Mosleyites, he'd be walking around wearing big shoes and a red nose by now. Honestly, I think that's as far as it goes for him.'

Agent Townsend nodded. Did that mean he was satisfied with her response?

'Can I go now?' she asked. 'I've told you all I know.'

Agent Riley held his hand up. 'No. Because I think you're not giving us the whole picture.'

'Good lord, what more do you want me to say? Just because we meet up at my mam's for dinner once a week, and Ned and Grace sometimes come for Sunday lunch to my fiancé's place, doesn't mean anyone is running with secrets behind the Iron Curtain.'

'But is it a family get-together?' he asked. 'Or are you all involved in some strategic plan to spread communist thought among Manchester's working class and weaken the British way of life?'

Kitty inhaled sharply. She studied the thin-lipped, dead-eyed agent, searching for some sign that this was all a misunderstanding or even some big joke. 'Wait! You think my mam's sausage, mash and gravy is some kind of ruse for a secret political gathering? Are you crackers?'

'I'd watch your tone, if I were you, miss,' Townsend said.

'Or what?' Kitty could feel her temper igniting as if these two agents were flints knocking together and she were the tinder, trapped beneath them. She leaned towards them. Her voice was hoarse from dehydration. 'Are you going to sling me into prison for telling you how preposterous this arrest is? Listen, if you want to know what I voted in the general election, it was Labour. Like most of the population. I work for the National Health Service and I happen to think it's the best thing since sliced bread because poor people get treated and it costs them nowt. A Labour government is not going to get rid of its own creation, now, is it? If you ask me what I think James voted, I reckon it was Liberal. But he didn't say because he believes secret voting ballots are . . . what does he always say?' She tried to remember James's turn of phrase, whenever one of the other doctors tried to quiz him on his political allegiance. 'Oh yes, that's it. *A cornerstone of a functioning democracy* – those are his words. A man's vote is between him and the ballot box. Hell, maybe he even voted Conservative, but I doubt it. I can tell you straight, though, my intended is no communist sympathiser, and neither am I.'

'Do you know your brother is heavily involved in trade unionism?'

Kitty slapped the sides of her head and screwed her face up in frustration. 'I'm not his keeper, for heaven's sake.' She took a deep breath and faced her accusers. 'Anyway, how can he be heavily involved in a union? He's only just got off his backside and got himself a new job in the biscuit works. I think he's taking broken biscuits out of the perfect stock to be sold as "Misshapes". Some revolutionary!'

'All right. Let's go about this another way,' Agent Townsend said. 'Tell us about your involvement with Professor George Hardy.'

'George?' Now, Kitty's brain knew something that the rest of her had been slow to cotton onto. Her fingers went icy cold and she felt lightheaded. She chuckled nervously. 'He's James's pal from Cambridge. He's going to be usher at our wedding.'

Kitty saw the Windscale complex in her mind's eye and she realised the enormity of what George had said he was doing for a living – producing plutonium. What had his precise words been? 'We're making weapons-grade plutonium.' She felt the ground shift beneath her and the air grow thick. She could barely hear the agent talking to her as she remembered the books on his bookshelves – Russian authors. Books written in Russian. Books with Bolshevik themes. Could it be?

'Are you listening, Miss Longthorne?' Agent Townsend was clicking his fingers in front of her face. 'I asked you what you knew about George Hardy's work at Windscale. We know that you've been to Cumbria. We know he took you to the site.'

'He didn't,' Kitty said. 'We went for a ramble and he showed us the building site from the vantage point of a hill, a good mile away. That was it. And, to be honest, I don't know George as well as you think. I've only met him twice. And before he came to lunch at James's flat, I don't think James had seen him since university. He's mentioned George, but only in passing.'

'Yet he's going to be usher at your wedding.'

Kitty shrugged. 'I think James just thought it would be a nice gesture. I know he misses his old college chums. The male camaraderie and that. He works such long hours at the hospital – we both do – and he's so far away from his family, down south . . . Thinking about it, James doesn't really have any friends in Manchester. That's why he'll go to the odd footy match with Ned, and when my father was still alive, they'd go to the cricket.'

'So there's very little you actually know about your fiancé, isn't there, Miss Longthorne?'

'Wait. *What?*' Kitty looked at him, incredulous. 'Now just hold your horses one minute, mister.'

'Do you know Douglas Philips?'

'No.'

'But clearly, you know of him. Has James ever mentioned or fraternised with Douglas Philips?'

Casting her mind back, Kitty did remember James and George mentioning the old college chum, who had defected to the USSR after he'd been found spying. Hadn't Douglas been a double agent? She couldn't remember. How much should she tell the agent? She didn't like the way the conversation had switched from an interrogation about Ned to naked suspicion of James. Was it possible that James was, in fact, involved in some sinister communist subterfuge? *Don't be a berk, Kitty*, she told herself. *They're trying to make out up is down, and down is up. Be strong.*

'I have no memory of that name,' she lied, suddenly wondering if her room in the nurses' home and James's flat had been bugged, as if they were caught up in some spy film. Was being bugged even possible? Were these men capable of inflicting such strange and intrusive things on normal folk? 'The only people James has ever mentioned to me from his Cambridge days are his best buddy, Timothy, and more recently, George Hardy.'

Steeling herself to be as brave as possible, she got to her feet. 'Now, have you finished asking me these daft questions, because I'd like to go now? Or are you going to make me sit here for the rest of the weekend, asking the same thing and getting the same answers? Maybe you'd like to shine that light into my face, for good measure?'

The agents looked at one another.

Then, Agent Townsend put the cap on his fountain pen and slid his pen back into his breast pocket. He smoothed his thin moustache with a manicured finger. 'I think we've got what we need for now, but don't leave the country. We may need to speak to you again.'

Kitty thought of her trip to New York. 'I was supposed to go to America for work in June.'

'We prefer that you don't. We are on His Majesty's business, here. I'd advise you to take this very seriously indeed.' Agent Riley handed her a business card that contained a London telephone number and business address. 'Call me if you get any information that you think we might be interested in. Remember, Miss Longthorne, the security of these great British Isles and our colonies depends on our keeping extremist political affinities at bay, while communism is on the march all over the globe. Your brother is playing with fire. He needs to leave Bolshevism for the Ruskies and the Chinese.'

'What about George?' she asked.

Agent Townsend touched his perfectly styled hair. 'Professor Hardy is of great interest to us. If you spot anything untoward, do your duty as a British subject. Call that number.'

When she emerged from the interrogation room, blinking in the bright sunlight and desperate for a drink and to freshen up after spending time in that dank place, Kitty was escorted back into the van. She was forced to wait in the windowless space for what seemed like an age before the door was flung open and James was bundled onto the bench at her side. Her heart quailed when she saw grazing on his cheekbone.

'James! They hit you!'

He touched the wound and winced. 'We'll talk about this when we get back to the car,' he said, eyeing Agent Riley, who had sat in the back with them.

The journey passed in uncomfortable silence, where Kitty's emotional state swung between anger at feeling as if she'd been falsely accused of treachery, and terror at the thought of her words being misconstrued by the secret service, finding herself condemned to imprisonment or worse. Was it possible that this man who sat beside her – the serious-minded, moral and well-respected doctor whom she adored with every fibre of her being – was leading some terrible secret double life?

Eventually, the van's brakes squealed, she felt the vehicle lurch to the left, and they came to a halt.

'Out,' Agent Riley said. 'And don't forget what you were told.'

Wordlessly, stumbling on legs that felt like jelly after her ordeal, Kitty followed James back to his Ford Anglia. He unlocked the doors and they climbed in.

Kitty turned to her fiancé. 'What in God's name just happened?'

James shook his head. 'I don't know, I don't know,' he said softly.

She could see his hands were shaking. Kitty put her face close to his until he looked her in the eye. 'We need to get back to yours and have a stiff brandy,' she said. 'And then, we need to talk, James Williams.'

Chapter 19

'What do you mean, *what have I been up to*?' James said, handing her a drink. His voice had a hard, bitter edge to it. 'I haven't been *up to* anything, unless you count spending every waking moment working for the betterment of my patients or else with you.'

'I didn't mean it like that, James,' Kitty said, exhausted, confused, worried that her world was about to fall apart. 'It's just . . .'

'Those agents were out to sow discord between us,' James said, flinging himself onto his settee and exhaling hard. He took a hefty gulp of the brandy and gasped. 'Don't let them. All that's happened here is that Ned's been up to his usual tricks. He's been mixing with the wrong kind. It's not as if he hasn't done it a thousand times before.'

'I'm not disputing that,' Kitty said, sipping the brandy and feeling it burn her throat but warm her. 'Trouble has always found Ned. He's no different from my dad. But this . . .? This is a bit different from fencing stolen goods and counterfeiting or even running a brothel. This is . . . By crikey, when you have the secret service dragging you off the street and interrogating you in some grimy, damp basement in the middle of nowhere . . .' She looked at the graze on James's cheekbone. 'I've never been so terrified in all my life, and that's saying something, considering I nearly drowned in the Bermuda Triangle!'

James set his brandy down and shuffled in his seat so that he was directly facing her. He took her glass and put it on the glass table next to his. Then, he took her hands into his and looked into her eyes. 'Right. Before you say another word, you need to know that I have nothing to do with this. Absolutely nothing.'

'Promise me.' Kitty searched the warm brown of his irises for sincerity and was sure she saw it there. 'It's just, all these spies you read about . . . they've all been to Cambridge.'

James nodded. 'Not just Cambridge. Oxford too. They recruit spies from among the students, and even when I was there, the students gobbled up every word of Karl Marx's manifesto. The Communist Party meetings were hopping. I kept my distance, of course – I swear on my life.'

'But what about George?' Kitty said. 'He had Karl Marx books and books in Russian in his lounge. He's doing stuff with plutonium, for heaven's sake, and he worked on the atomic bomb or something, didn't he?'

'I was grilled solidly about George, mainly, and a bit about Douglas Philips, whom I haven't seen since God was a boy. I told them I hadn't seen him. They must know I wasn't lying if they'd been watching Douglas!'

'Couldn't have been watching him that carefully, else he wouldn't have been able to defect.' Kitty pulled her hands from his grasp and stroked the skin around his graze. 'Can you believe how ludicrous it is that we're even having this conversation?'

James nodded. 'We're living in strange times, my darling. Anyway, I think they believed me when I said I had no idea what George was up to, beyond what he'd told us. And I swear that's true, Kitty. He's a physicist, after all. Why wouldn't I believe that he's legitimately working in the field of atomic research?'

He got to his feet and crossed his living room to the framed photograph on the wall of his Trinity College fellow students. For a few moments, he studied the portrait. Sighing, he turned back to Kitty. 'First things first. We're going to have to confront Ned because that's the most pressing issue here. We see Ned on a weekly basis, and if he's plotting the downfall of Westminster or something potty like that, it puts us, your mother and Grace at risk.'

'You leave Ned to me,' Kitty said.

'No. We face him together, as a couple. And you ought to tell Grace separately. She deserves to know what she's letting herself in for. A rehabilitated petty criminal is one thing, but an enemy of the realm is quite another.'

With the day out to Belle Vue nothing but a peculiar and unpleasant memory, Kitty walked over to James and embraced him in the calming golden light of the standard lamp. She could smell that dank basement on him, but the warmth of his body through the fabric of his shirt felt reassuring and real. *Do I believe him?* she asked herself. *Yes. I do. He's honest as the day is long, and I mustn't tar him with the same brush as Ned. But George . . .?*

'I think we should distance ourselves from George,' she said.

James held her face and pressed his nose to hers. He stood awhile in silence and then broke away, shaking his head. 'I don't know what to make of it all. They might be wrongly maligning him. The George I knew at Cambridge wasn't political in the slightest. The secret service can't know everything.'

'Oh, come on! Pull the other one. It's got bells on. You saw those fellers. They're not your average wet-behind-the-ears bobby on the beat. They're intelligence agents.'

James walked away from her and retrieved his drink. 'I just have a feeling that they might be scrutinising all physicists working with plutonium, what with the unrest in Korea, and Moscow racing the West to acquire atomic capability. How do we know they haven't interrogated the friends and family of *all* the scientists working in Windscale and projects like it?'

'There's no smoke without fire, James,' Kitty said.

'Let me speak to him. I'll try to get to the truth of the matter. It's only fair. Innocent until proven guilty, Kitty.'

'No! Keep your distance, for God's sake. Let sleeping dogs lie.'

Kitty walked into the kitchen to put the kettle on, irritated by James's even-handed approach to his old friend. With stakes this high, could they afford to give George Hardy the benefit of the doubt? He wasn't family, so she felt strongly their friendship with him ought to be put on the back burner.

Ned, however, was her flesh and blood. If Ned thought he could drag her family to hell without a thought for any of them, he could think again.

Chapter 20

'You! Come here!' Kitty said, marching up to her brother as he emerged from the biscuit factory gates. 'I want a word with you.'

'Hey up, Kitty. What's eating you?'

'*You*, Ned Longthorne. You're what's eating me.' She dragged Ned down the street by his collar, just as she had done when they'd been small and Ned had done something dangerous, silly or both.

He shook himself loose, pulling Richard Collins's stolen overcoat back on straight. 'How do you mean? What am I supposed to have done?'

Kitty looked up and down the busy road and spotted a side street that looked altogether quieter. 'Walk. What I need to say to you doesn't need an audience.'

In silence, they walked away from the biscuit factory, from which workers were still streaming at the end of their weekend shift. Kitty held her tongue until the side street opened out into a large park. Only once they were in the open, with nobody within earshot, did Kitty come to a standstill and turn to her brother.

She punched him in the arm. 'You're in bed with the communists in a big way, aren't you?' She studied her brother's heavily scarred face, trying to gauge his reaction. It was no mean feat, given the extent of his disfigurement and the corrective surgery he'd undertaken.

'Ow!' Ned clutched at his arm. He took two steps backwards. 'I don't know what you mean.'

'Rubbish.' Kitty drew close to him and grabbed his collar again. She locked eyes with him, hoping he could see the ferocity behind hers. 'Me and James got pulled off the street by four secret service agents. At Belle Vue, for God's sake.'

'Get away!' The colour in Ned's face drained, leaving his skin ashen and covered with a visible film of sweat.

'We were queuing for the rollercoaster. They came out of nowhere, cuffed us and slung us in the back of a Black Maria. In broad daylight. Four of them, Ned. Four, built like brick outhouses. We got taken to some damp, dark basement – no idea where. They grilled the both of us separately for hours. Know who they were asking questions about?' She poked him in the stomach. 'You! You, you bloody mischievous, lying idiot. So, don't tell me, "I don't know what you mean".'

Ned opened and closed his mouth. He exhaled heavily through his reconstructed nose and his shoulders sank. 'I'm just doing what's right for me and Gracie and the kids we'll have. Mosley and his fascists . . . they're turning Manchester into a place I don't recognise, Kitty.'

'Give over. There's always been people from all walks of life in Manchester, and there's always been racialism. I agree, the Mosleyites do need to crawl back under their rock, but it doesn't mean you personally have to get tangled up with the Communist Party, does it?'

'The communists are the only ones fighting them.'

Kitty shook her head and looked at the freshly green cherry trees in the park. All around, birds were in song in the flowering horse chestnut trees, and emerging daisies and buttercups made the grass seem to glow with sunshine.

Spring had sprung, but Kitty felt trapped in an eternal winter of worry.

'You're so naïve, Ned,' she said. 'I got stuck on the bus in the middle of a Mosleyite scuffle, and I'll bet most of the lads giving them what-for weren't Bolsheviks or communists or whatever the heck you want to call the Reds. We just won a war against fascism. Most Brits will be against it. You don't have to get involved in dangerous politics to do the right thing by Grace. Or is it that you're covering up something even more stupid?'

'How do you mean?'

'Come on, Ned, I wasn't born yesterday.' She checked over their shoulder to make sure they were still alone. There was no sign of anyone following them. 'Secret agents don't take an interest in ugly sods that fight in the street with bully boys. They take an interest in people who threaten the stability of the country. What the hell have you got involved in, outside of the brawling? Is it to do with this trade union business?'

Ned glared at her and dug his hands deep in the pockets of his coat. 'How should I know? This is supposed to be a free country, but here I am, having to explain myself to you.' He started to march off back towards the bus stop. 'Nobody made you my boss.'

She ran after him, grabbing him by his elbow, pleased to see that he didn't try to shake her off. 'No, but the *King* is your boss, and the secret service works for the crown. And me and James are being dragged out of Belle Vue on our day off and forced to answer questions with handcuffs on – like common criminals – because of your actions. We could lose our jobs! What you do affects us all, Ned.'

'Does it heckers like.'

Kitty had to stifle the urge to shake her obstinate brother. 'Do you want to swing from the gallows for treason?' She was shouting now.

A woman walking by, pushing a pram, shot her a startled look and hurried on her way.

Kitty turned back to Ned, who was looking blankly back at her. 'Well? Do you? Do you want to see us hang too, because those agents decide me and Mam and James and Grace are all in cahoots with you?'

Ned turned again and trudged away. 'I'm not a kid, Kitty,' he said over his shoulder. 'You can't blackmail me like that.'

'Oh, my giddy aunt. You've been brainwashed, haven't you?' she said. 'Right, that's it, Ned Longthorne, Kitty was shouting anew, balling her fists. It was all she could do to stop herself from running after her errant brother. 'Me and you are *finished* unless you drop this nonsense. You keep away from me and James, and don't you *dare* go near our mam.'

Ned stopped in his tracks and turned back to her. 'I live with Mam, unless you'd forgotten.'

'Well, you've got a new job, so you can afford digs. And I thought commies shared everything, anyway, so how about you ask one of your trade union cronies to put you up on their communal settee?'

He waved her away dismissively, and continued on his way.

Kitty was aware of local residents in the houses that edged the park coming out of their front doors and walking to their gates. Women, wearing their washday aprons, with scarves on their heads like turbans, stood and watched the family drama unfold, their meaty arms crossed and eyebrows raised.

Kitty didn't care that she was making a spectacle of herself. She was too incensed. 'But if I catch you so much as standing by Mam's garden gate, *looking* at the house,' she yelled, 'I'll give you the hiding of your life. Do you hear me?' Ned was getting further and further away from her now. 'You'll need a new bloody plastic surgeon, Ned Longthorne. I mean it.'

'Where is it?' Kitty asked, lifting her mattress to see if she could find a bug. She had no idea what a bug might look like, but she was sure she'd know one if she spotted it. 'Come on, you eavesdroppers. I know you're listening in. You don't fool me.'

She got onto her knees and checked beneath the bedstead. Might something have been affixed to the slats that held the lumpy, thin mattress? No. She checked her bedside cabinet next, even taking out the little drawer, emptying it of its contents and turning it upside down, as she'd seen actors do in the movies. Was there anything stuck to the underside? No.

Kitty looked around her small room in the nurses' home – a room she'd slept in for all of her adult life, so far – and realised that suddenly the place didn't feel like home. She could sense strangers having rifled through her meagre possessions, dissecting her life in a bid to find evidence of civic misdeeds.

'Fireplace,' she said. She marched over to the small, tiled fireplace and felt beneath the lip of the mantel. Nothing. She even dirtied her hands, trying to feel inside the grate. It was clear. She was about to pick apart her chest of drawers when there was a knock on her door.

'Come in,' she said. Getting to her feet, she ran the back of her forearm over her clammy brow.

'Kitty, what on earth are you doing? You're covered in muck.' Grace stood on the threshold, staring at her with undisguised bemusement.

Kitty pressed her index finger to her mouth and pulled Grace out of her room and into the shared bathroom.

'What's with all the hush-hush, and why are we in the bathroom?' Grace asked. She pressed her hand to Kitty's forehead. 'Are you well?'

Taking a deep breath and momentarily closing her eyes while she found the words, Kitty held both of Grace's hands. She kept her voice low. 'Now, I'm going to tell you something that sounds mad. But you've got to listen, and I'm being deadly serious. None of it is a joke.'

'I don't like the sound of this. Go on.' Grace's brow furrowed. She looked over her shoulder and onto the landing.

'Look at me, Grace.' Kitty waited until her friend's attention was fully on her. 'I think, in fact, I *know* I'm under government surveillance. We all are. Me, you, Ned, James, maybe even Mam.'

'*What?* What do you—?'

'You need to listen to what I'm about to say. Just let me speak.' Kitty took a deep breath, and then, in the relative privacy of the otherwise empty bathroom, she told Grace about the arrest. She took Agent Riley's business card out of her pocket. 'See?'

Grace took the card from her and ran her finger over the embossed Royal coat of arms. She made a sucking noise with her teeth. 'Sweet Jesus. What has my Ned got into? He told me he was just defending my honour. Trying to make the city right for a couple like us.'

Kitty squeezed Grace's hands. 'How much does any of us really know about Ned and the shenanigans he gets up to?'

'I do know him!' Grace's bottom lip started to wobble. Her chin dimpled and her eyes filled with tears. 'Well, I thought I did.'

'Look, he's my brother,' Kitty said, wondering if she was doing more harm than good by making Grace face the truth. She could see her friend's heart start to break. Yet wasn't it better to tell her the truth than let her get deeper into a relationship that could see her swinging from the gallows? 'I've known Ned for the whole of his life, and I'm telling you straight, Grace – you can never truly know Ned. He's always been a magnet for trouble. Always. And his heart is good.' She released Grace's hands and thumped herself in her chest. 'He's full of love, and he means so well. He really does. But, it's like he can't help himself. He falls in with the wrong sorts and he lies, thinking he's protecting us.'

Grace shook her head. A tear fell from her eye and tracked down her face. 'My Ned's good. He loves me.'

Kitty nodded vehemently. 'Yes, he does love you. He really does. But that doesn't mean he isn't constantly lured down the unrighteous path by bad people and temptation. Ever since we were kids, he's done the wrong things for the right reasons – stealing to keep money in Mam's pocket; getting involved in criminal dealings to help my dad out; getting into fights to defend something he believes in. He's addicted to it. But this . . .?'

Grace raised her fists to her temples. Her face was a picture of anguish and irritation 'We don't even know what "this" is.'

'Exactly. We both work such long hours. How can we know what he's up to when he's not under our noses? I just don't think government agents would make it up. Ned's into something big. I don't want to know what it is but I've told him it's got to stop. And if you know what's good for you, Grace, you should think twice about tying the knot in a hurry.'

Touching her wedding ring finger, Grace sobbed and turned away. 'How can you say this to me, Kitty? How can you bring all my dreams crashing down?'

'I'm doing you a favour.' Kitty tried to put her arm around Grace, but Grace shrank away. 'I'm his sister. I love the bones of my brother. But he's wilful and naïve and stupid and he thinks the rules don't apply to him. And that's selfish, because it affects the rest of us. Don't let him drag you down, Grace. Don't sacrifice everything you've worked for for Ned. He's my flesh and blood, but I won't swing from the gallows because of his bad decisions. I've put up with an awful lot from our Ned over the years, but I draw the line at this commie shenanigans. And so should you.'

Kitty took some Izal toilet paper from a toilet cubicle and held it out. 'Here. Dry your eyes.'

Grace turned and looked at the hard, unabsorbent paper. 'If I want to injure myself, I'll get my emery board and rub it on my eyelids.' She tittered.

Kitty started to laugh, feeling like there was a way forward for the friendship she had forged with Grace, despite her having been the bearer of the worst kind of news about the love of Grace's life.

'What will you do?' she asked.

Grace shrugged. 'What will *you* do?'

Chapter 21

'I can't go to New York,' Kitty told Matron Pratt. 'I'm so sorry.' She studied her superior's face for signs of a reaction.

The new matron looked up from her desk and merely closed her eyes and exhaled heavily through her nose. Her eyes snapped open again and Kitty felt as though she were being X-rayed.

'Why?' Matron said. 'The ticket and hotel have already been bought and paid for.'

'I'm so, so sorry to mess you about.' Kitty felt like the contents of her stomach had turned to lead. Would she be in trouble? This new matron was so different from her old mentor that even the office in the nurses' home was unrecognisable. Gone was the clutter and memorabilia from a long career and a life spent nurturing women. Gone was the flowery winged armchair by the fire and the mismatched, saggy-cushioned chair for the many nurses and guests who had gone to her for advice, consolation or merely a glass of the sweet sherry that the old matron had so enjoyed. Matron Pratt had turned the office into a businesslike, aseptic-feeling place, with the bookshelves filled only with medical tomes. No photographs on the shelves, no paintings on the wall, no trinkets given as gifts by others, no ornaments whatsoever. Even the desk was neat as a pin, with the paperwork in two orderly stacks. Yet, Kitty had to learn to confide in this seemingly unknowable woman. 'It's a long story.'

Matron looked down at her nurses' watch and pressed her lips together. 'I've got time. This paperwork can wait. Sit.' She pointed to the visitor's chair, which was now nothing more than an old wooden straight-backed dining chair. 'Tell me why one of my best Sisters can't go on an all-expenses-paid trip to the Big Apple?'

Kitty took her seat, almost swaying from exhaustion given she'd just finished a long and difficult shift. In truth, she was still reeling from the abortive trip to Belle Vue and the ensuing sleepless nights. 'My brother's in trouble.'

'Go on.'

Kitty mulled over how much to tell the matron. Would she jeopardise her and James's jobs and professional reputations if she told the truth? 'He's got himself tangled up in some goings-on and is in a spot of bother with the authorities. I can't leave the country. I'm sorry.'

'Can't, or won't?' Matron Pratt raised an eyebrow, but her mouth remained a straight line.

'Can't. Definitely. I would have loved to go, but . . .'

The new matron breathed in sharply. 'You would have loved to go, *but*? All that National Health Service expenditure on your travel, and you can't give me a reason why your brother's misdemeanours should affect your ability to get on a boat and leave the country for a fortnight?' She turned to face Kitty directly and folded her slender arms over her flat bosom. 'Out with it. Has Dr Williams put the kibosh on it?' She unfolded her arms and leaned forwards, giving their conversation an air of secrecy. 'Anything you say to me in here will be confidential.'

'It's nothing like that,' Kitty said. 'Dr Williams is in favour of me going. He's been waiting to marry me for years, because he understands that my job means too much to me to just walk away from it.' Kitty saw an opportunity to sidestep Matron Pratt's question about Ned. 'Actually, that reminds me. There is something I've been wanting to ask you.' She reached out to run her fingers over the smooth, highly polished edge of the desk. 'I read in the newspaper about this male nurse in Derbyshire who tied the knot with a female nurse.' She looked hopefully at Matron Pratt.

The matron sat back in her uncomfortable-looking chair. 'Are you asking me if I think the rules are going to change about nurses having to leave their jobs when they marry?'

Kitty nodded. 'I'd quite like to have my cake and eat it, same as the doctors.'

Looking through her window to the hospital gardens that were bursting with spring life and colour, the matron shrugged. 'I don't know about Derbyshire and I don't know about that news story. Maybe the female nurse had already stopped work and had got a job as a health visitor or such like. Perhaps the reporter just reported it incorrectly. As far as I'm aware, our health authority still insists nurses leave when they marry.'

'Do you think it will change soon?'

'Who can say?' She picked up her fountain pen and put the lid on. Then, she pointed it at Kitty. 'Why don't you just become a health visitor or a district nurse? I'm sure that will give you the same sense of fulfilment. In Salford, they're needing more and more health visitors to look after the elderly . . . helping with bathing and laundry and such like. The powers that be want to keep them out of hospital and keep them up on their feet and fit and healthy.'

Kitty tried her best not to roll her eyes. 'I'm a Sister. I've worked in theatre. I've saved countless lives. I train junior nurses and run a busy ward. Why would I want to swap all that to wash old folk's laundry?'

'Well, I hear Sir Henry Cohen is chairing a committee to look into general practitioner care. Everybody knows it's appalling. I mean, where my family lives they don't even have an examination couch in the surgery, let alone a proper waiting room with chairs. But I've heard through the grapevine that this committee is going to focus on general practitioners. And Dr Joseph Collings has written a damning report on the subject in *The Lancet*.'

She rose to her feet and thumbed through some of the medical journals and periodicals on her bookshelf. 'Here we go.' Taking out a copy of *The Lancet*, which was dated 25 March 1950, she leafed through to an article, simply entitled 'The Collings Report' and showed it to Kitty. 'He recommends group practices in new premises, where doctors, nurses, social workers and other support staff all work together. If the National Health Service implements his recommendations, the nurses and health visitors working there will be at the vanguard of progress.'

'I don't want to work in a group practice for a general practitioner,' Kitty said. 'I want to stay here.'

The matron pressed the journal into Kitty's hands. 'Here. Borrow it and read the report. Bring it back when you've finished.'

Not wanting to insult Matron, Kitty took the journal and got to her feet. 'I've wasted enough of your time. I'm sorry.'

'Er, not so fast, Sister Longthorne,' Matron said. She drummed her fingers on the desktop. 'You still haven't given me a good enough reason for cancelling New York at such short notice.'

Kitty sighed. 'I've been told to stay in the country by the authorities. My brother has got himself in deep with the Communist Party, and I'm afraid they're keeping an eye on his movements and family. That includes Grace, too.'

The matron looked taken aback. 'Eh? Grace? How . . .?'

'You didn't know Grace was engaged to my brother?'

'Why would I?'

'Look, please don't let my idiot brother's poor judgement reflect badly on me or Grace. We're both utterly dedicated to our jobs, and I've tried to talk Grace out of spending time with my brother for a while.'

Matron Pratt nodded. 'You can't choose your family.'

'Precisely.'

The rest of the working day was mercifully busy enough to distract Kitty from her terrifying brush with the authorities and from the conundrum of what to do about Ned.

'Now, gather round, ladies,' she said to the nurses who had just begun their shift on the children's polio ward, which had come to feel a little like home to Kitty. 'We've got five new admissions, two of which are complicated by lung infections.'

Rijuta raised her hand.

'Yes, Nurse Ghosh,' Kitty said.

'I'm finding that the sulphonamides we're using in some of the children coming in with chest infections aren't working the way they used to. Some seem resistant to penicillin, too,' she said.

Kitty nodded. 'Yes, I've heard from some of the doctors that overuse of these medications might be behind them not working as efficiently as they did. There's not much we can do about that until new treatments come along.'

'What about this new cortisone stuff?' a senior nurse who was new to the ward asked. 'Professor Baird-Murray was banging on about that on the orthopaedic ward. He said it can take down inflammation, like rheumatoid arthritis and that. Is it worth mentioning to Dr Bourke when he does his rounds this evening? Only, some of these children have got inflammation of all sorts from lying in those iron lungs. Maybe it would help with their chests, too.'

Casting her mind back to a report on cortisone that she'd read in one of James's medical journals, Kitty realised why the suggestion could never become a practical solution. 'I like your thinking, Nurse Holliday, but I understand that cortisone has to be extracted from ox bile, and it takes forty heads of cattle to make just one day's treatment. So, I wouldn't hold your breath. And it's worth remembering that we're nurses, not doctors or pharmacologists. How about we just do our jobs, and let the scientists and doctors do theirs?'

She looked down at her list. 'Right, so let's get our new admissions settled in. And then I believe three of the children are well enough to start physiotherapy today.' She saw Sammy Levine's name listed and smiled. 'I'm looking forward to seeing their progress, so make sure you liaise with the physiotherapy ladies.'

With the nurses given their orders, Kitty made her way along the central aisle of the ward, saying good morning to the children and checking their needs were being met. It still broke her heart to see these tiny patients imprisoned in their cumbersome iron lungs and lying stoically all day and all night long, observing their limited world through an angled mirror.

'Good morning, Albert,' she said to the first child, at the head of the ward. 'How are you today?'

'Morning, Sister Kitty,' Albert said. 'I'm fine, thanks, except my foot's hurting. Like cramp.'

'Well, it's encouraging that you can feel your foot,' Kitty said, scanning the notes that had been written by the night staff on the clipboard, hooked onto his iron lung. 'I'll ask one of the nurses to give you a good foot massage when she cleans you up.' She gave Albert a warm smile, trying to push away the encroaching mental image of agents Townsend and Riley.

'Thanks, Sister.'

She moved on to the next child. 'Good morning, Winifred. How are you today?'

Winifred had only been on the ward for three days. Slight for her age, thanks to malnourishment that Kitty knew was common in the poorest children, she was only six. Winifred's chest rattled – audible even above the noise of the iron lung. Her little face crumpled into a look of pure despair. 'I want to go home,' she cried. 'I want my mam and dad.'

'We're going to work really hard to get you better, Winifred,' Kitty said. She knew she couldn't promise that they would get the girl better. Too many children had already been lost to polio the world over to make that anything but a lie. 'All these lovely nurses are here to do as much as they can to keep you comfortable in the meantime. And I'm sure your mam and dad will come and visit you very soon.'

'They've not been at all,' the girl sobbed.

Kitty crouched so that she was at the girl's eye level. 'How many brothers and sisters have you got, Winifred?'

'Four big brothers, one big sister, two little sisters and baby Tommy.'

'Eight brothers and sisters? My word. Well, it's no wonder you've not seen your mam and dad yet. They're busy looking after everyone. And until they come, you've got the nurses and the other children to chat to. How about that?' What could she say to put a smile on this little girl's face. 'Do you like jelly?'

'Yes.' Immediately, Winifred's face brightened up.

Kitty winked. 'How about I sneak you some jelly from the nurses' canteen, and you can have it after your lunch? Our secret.'

Winifred finally gave her a weak smile. 'Thanks, Sister Kitty.'

Making her way slowly down the ward, Kitty wondered how she could possibly leave the hospital environment to work in a general practitioner's surgery or one of the proposed health centres. She took a moment to look around at the high-ceilinged ward, with its polished floors and welcoming fireplace. She observed the children, so vulnerable yet so brave, being lovingly and selflessly tended by her often-exhausted nurses – nurses whom she trained and managed. She peered through the windows at the grounds, where the rose bushes were coming into bloom, and beyond, to the further reaches of the hospital. She knew exactly what was going on behind each window: wounds being cleaned, infections being tackled, lives being saved. Park Hospital had become her world. Could she really turn her back on it?

'Morning, Sister Kitty!' Sammy said, as she returned her focus to the task in hand. 'Is it true I'm going to start walking again today?'

Kitty nodded. 'It certainly is, young man.' She moved over to where he was sitting in a day chair, clutching a coloured pencil and a Roy Rogers colouring book. She complimented his work. 'You're managing to colour inside the lines, I see. That's a good sign that you're getting better.'

Sammy looked up at her with rather more sparkle to his eyes than he'd had when she'd first encountered him back in March. 'I know. I do feel lots better. But I'm worried I won't be able to walk again. Me and Gordon want to have a game of football when we get out of here, don't we, Gordon?'

'You bet!' Gordon got up from his chair and grabbed his crutches.

Kitty watched as the ginger-haired lad supported his weight on his left leg whilst pretending to kick a ball with his right. Both legs were encased in callipers and braces, but on the end of his right foot, he wore a much larger boot, where the sole had been built up to accommodate one leg being shorter in length than the other, thanks to a curvature of his spine. Kitty winced inwardly at the lifelong disabilities that these children would be left with because of the disease.

'But I'm worried the exercises won't work, and I'll be stuck in a wheelchair.'

'Do you know what, Sammy?' she asked the little boy. 'I'm going to come and watch you take your first steps.'

When Sammy had been wheeled off for his treatment, Kitty left Nurse Holliday in charge so she could check on the boy's progress. She found Sammy in the physiotherapy room, which looked rather like a gymnasium. He was on his feet, with his legs strapped into brand-new callipers and braces.

'Come on, Sammy!' Diana, the therapist, said. 'You're doing smashing. Now, hold onto the rails and try to put one foot in front of the other.'

Sammy looked to be gripping the parallel bars with all his might as he tried to keep himself upright. He was red in the face already, even though Kitty could see he was right at the beginning of the bars.

'Sister Kitty!' Sammy looked up at her, beaming. 'Look at me! I'm walking.' He promptly lost his grip and collapsed in a heap on the floor.

'Ooh, what a to-do,' Diana said. 'Did they put brandy in your porridge this morning, Samuel?' She laughed kindly. 'Not to worry. Let's get you back on your feet. If at first you don't succeed, try, try again, eh?' She grabbed Sammy beneath his arms and hefted him to standing position. 'Try not to let Sister Longthorne distract you, now.'

Kitty took a seat off to the side. Sammy wasn't the only young patient in the room. There was another girl, learning to walk with a prosthetic limb, and there was a teenaged lad being taught by one of the other therapists how to use his new wheelchair. As she watched them all make painful progress, Kitty marvelled at the many areas of modern medicine that were developing now that the war was behind them.

'I'm going to do it this time, Sister Kitty,' Sammy said. 'You watch me.' The little boy stuck his tongue out thoughtfully as he grabbed at the rails and started to pull himself forwards.

'Don't just drag yourself along, Samuel,' Diana said. 'Try to put the weight on your legs, lovey, else your arms are going to get mighty tired, very quickly. Tighten your tummy muscles to support your upper body.'

Kitty checked her fob watch. She had ten minutes to spare before she had to return to the ward. It wasn't long enough to see Sammy learn to walk perfectly, but she did at least witness the boy standing confidently and moving a couple of steps.

Just as she was about to leave, he collapsed again, this time bursting into frustrated tears.

'It's no good. I'm never going to walk again.' He sat on the floor with his callipered legs outstretched, his doleful face a picture of defeat.

Kitty strode over to him and sat cross-legged by his side. She put her arm around him. 'Do you know what, Sammy Levine?'

Sammy looked up at her with tears in his eyes and wet tracks down his cheeks. 'What?'

She offered him a handkerchief. 'I think that was one of the best first attempts at walking after polio I've ever seen.' She looked at the therapist and winked. 'Isn't that right, Di?'

Diana nodded. 'She's not wrong, chuck. You'll be whizzing around here in no time. You'll see.'

Satisfied that her words had placated the boy, Kitty got to her feet. 'I'll see you back on the ward, Sammy. Keep up the good work.'

Sammy looked so cheered by her encouraging words that he reached out to Diana. 'Let me try one more time?'

Kitty walked away, feeling glad that she made such a difference to her patients. That knowledge made the prospect of leaving her hospital career to marry so incredibly hard.

On the way back to the ward, she bumped into Grace, who was carrying a pile of freshly laundered sheets.

'Kitty! I was just thinking about you,' Grace said.

'Oh, aye? All good, I hope.' Kitty smiled uncertainly at her future sister-in-law. Were they still to be friends?

Grace looked absently at a hospital noticeboard, covered in leaflets. 'Well, I was thinking about my future with Ned, really, and what you said.'

'And? Are you really ready to give up the job you travelled thousands of miles to do for a man who can't stay on the right side of the law?' Kitty asked.

Grace's chest rose and fell. She met Kitty's gaze and then looked away again. The sadness was clear to see in the furrows of her brow, her downturned mouth and the uncharacteristic dullness of her eyes. 'No.'

'Oh, Gracie. I'm so sorry.'

'I feel so alone and so far from home.'

Grace's shoulders started to heave with wracking sobs. Kitty put her arms around her and tried to offer what comfort she could to her homesick, broken-hearted friend. She couldn't help but wonder if her own relationship would survive the strain of the secret service investigation, not to mention the personal demands of a career that wasn't moving fast enough to keep pace with modern women's aspirations.

1951

Chapter 22

'Is the theatre prepped and ready to go?' James asked Kitty as they stood together by the exit of the hospital, looking up at the grey skies.

'All ready. All hands on deck. Are you sure you want me to assist you in theatre?' Kitty asked. 'You could have had any of the other nurses.'

James looked at her, his brown eyes smiling, and placed his hand on the small of her back. 'It will be just like old days.' He faced the sky again. 'Actually, I wish that weren't so.'

The whacka-whacka sound of blades rotating in the air was suddenly audible, though still a way off.

Kitty felt butterflies in her stomach take flight. 'I have to say, I'm very excited about this. A helicopter ambulance! Who'd have thought it? Worth working on my day off just to see one close up.'

James started to walk out to where it had been arranged that the helicopter would land, in Park Hospital's extensive grounds. He beckoned her to follow him. 'If the Korean War has done anything positive for medical science, it's the increased use of air ambulances. I hear they're saving thousands of servicemen this way.'

Kitty gathered her cape around her against the chill wind. She held her cap on, running to catch up with James. The army helicopter had come into view – a black blob in the overcast sky, growing larger by the second as it approached the hospital, until it became clearer and transformed into what appeared to be a mechanised flying insect. 'So, who are these two men?' she asked, shuddering at the sight of the helicopter.

Raising his voice to be heard above the sound of the helicopter, James looked up. 'Two RAF servicemen fresh in from Korea. I've been reading about it in *The Times*. Their Meteor F8s were apparently outmanoeuvred by the Koreans' MiGs, and they were shot down. These chaps are being transferred from a military airbase in Kent. That's all I know. Apparently they've both sustained terrible facial injuries and need immediate surgery.'

The giant military helicopter was hovering overhead now, creating a hefty down-draught that almost blew Kitty off her feet. It started to descend. The noise of the engine and the whirr of the blades was so deafening that Kitty put her hands over her ears.

'This gives me a terrible sense of déjà vu,' she shouted, casting her mind back to the countless British and American servicemen who had come though Park Hospital's doors. Many had sadly never made it out alive, so severe had been their injuries and so scant had been the effective remedies available to them. 'I thought I'd left my wartime duties behind when the war ended. Now here we are again. Only our lads are fighting on the other side of the world.'

'The legacy of 1945,' James shouted. 'Who could have known that, when the Japanese surrendered and the Soviets and Yanks moved into the Korean Peninsula, the place would be split apart? With Pyongyang turning Red!'

An RAF serviceman hung out of the open window of the helicopter and shouted, 'Stand back and keep your heads low 'til the blades stop rotating.' He pointed to James. 'You Dr Williams?'

'Yes. We're ready for your boys.' James squinted up into the gusting wind that the blades whipped up. 'Just follow me and Sister Longthorne here. We'll take them straight to surgery.'

The huge bulk of the helicopter settled on the rain-sodden Mancunian ground like an enormous metal hornet. Kitty was rendered speechless by the sight of it. She had only ever seen such aircraft on *Pathé News* or in films.

'Crikey. If my dad were still alive to see this . . .' she said beneath her breath.

Standing awkwardly by, she watched the airmen on board the helicopter stretcher out their wounded compatriots. The patients were whimpering in pain and wrapped in bloody bandages.

'I hope you can fix up these fine pilots,' the first airman said, marching past James as he carried his end of one of the stretchers towards the hospital entrance.

Kitty and James walked briskly to keep up as the airman briefed them.

'They're in a bad way, I'm afraid. Their planes went down and burst into flames, so there's burns and blast injuries to contend with. It's a miracle they survived. Squadron Leader John Bristow's jaw has detached entirely. Flight Lieutenant Matthew Hanrahan has lost one side of his face.'

'I won't know their prospects until I've seen the injuries for myself,' James said. He looked down at both men, who were clearly awake and suffering mightily beneath their bandaging. 'Don't worry, chaps. We'll do our very best to restore your matinee-idol looks for the girls.'

'You're in safe hands,' Kitty said. 'Our Dr Williams is the cream of the crop. And me and my nurses will take the finest care of you. You wouldn't get better care if you were King George himself.'

*

In the operating theatre, once they had scrubbed their arms and hands and donned their protective garb, Richard Collins was already waiting with his equipment at the ready to put the airmen to sleep.

'Dr Williams, Sister Longthorne,' he said, nodding by way of a greeting.

He narrowed his eyes at James. Kitty was sure she could see the sneer hidden beneath his surgical mask.

James didn't even look Richard in the eye when he nodded back. 'Dr Collins. Right. Let's see what we're dealing with here. I think we can start by giving these fine gentlemen some morphine. Then we can get their bandages off.'

Richard administered morphine to both men with a syringe. He asked the airmen if they could feel anything, and it was clear the strong drug had rendered them pain-free.

'Once I know what I'm up against, I'll decide who's going first and we can pack them off for a lovely long nap.' He looked up at the clock that showed ten past eleven on the morning of Wednesday, 4 April 1951. 'I suspect we'll be here for some hours.'

As she unwrapped the bandages on the squadron leader, whose jaw had apparently detached, Kitty was certain that there was still tension in the air between the anaesthetist and James. Yet, years had passed since she'd rebuffed Richard's advances, before reuniting with her fiancé. Now was not the time for Richard to be harbouring grudges or regret, however. She ignored the hurt looks that Richard kept shooting her and tended to the task in hand.

Squadron Leader Bristow's face was barely recognisable as such. Kitty had seen horrific injuries like it when servicemen had been brought to Park Hospital from the front, only six years earlier. Over the years, she had trained herself not to show any kind of a reaction. The old matron had drilled into her nurses the need to be calm at all times, so that the patient wouldn't panic. She merely smiled at the patient beneath her surgical mask, knowing he'd see the friendliness in her eyes and perhaps be comforted.

'Try not to worry, love. Dr William's knows what he's doing,' Kitty said, patting his hand. 'My brother came back looking like a bag of potato peelings after he'd been in a Japanese prisoner-of-war camp, and Dr Williams here fixed him right up. Gave him a new nose and everything.'

James leaned over the squadron leader, studying the extent of the damage.

The glare of the overhead operating theatre lights beat down on the scene, reflecting off the shining white tiles on the walls and the floor and the gleaming instruments laid out on a polished steel table at James's side. The brightness rendered the patient's fresh blood so florid a red that Kitty almost couldn't bear to look at it without shielding her eyes.

She observed James as he scrutinised the injuries, frowning and saying the odd, 'Hmm' while he contemplated how to proceed. She was almost overcome with pride and gratitude that she was marrying this brilliant surgeon.

James straightened up and changed his surgical gloves. 'All right. Now let's take a look at Flight Lieutenant Hanrahan.

He began to examine the second patient's injuries, which were even more devastating than the squadron leader's.

'We're going to need a lot of reconstructive surgery here. A prosthetic eye. Skin grafts. A new nose.' James frowned. 'I foresee many surgeries over several years for both, but I think this chap's needs are really very complex.'

Kitty marvelled that human beings could be so torn apart by injury and devastated by fire and yet still survive. She knew, however, that even James's careful ministrations would never give these men back the faces they had previously taken for granted. Ned had certainly never been the same since the torpedo that blew up his boat home from the Far East had robbed him of his looks.

Not for the first time did Kitty privately bemoan the fighting that always seemed inevitable when one group of men wanted to assert their authority over another. If women were in charge, would Nagasaki and Hiroshima have been the logical endpoint of splitting the atom? More to the point, since she was sure the secret service was still watching them as suspected communists, almost a year after their arrest, would Britain and its allies be racing the Soviets to manufacture nuclear weapons?

'Let's begin on our flight lieutenant,' James said, interrupting her reverie.

The squadron leader was wheeled to a side room, where Kitty's nursing assistants made him comfortable. Only then did the long haul of trying to reconstruct the pilot's face begin.

With the patient asleep, the hours came and went as Kitty passed scalpels and swabs to James. Her back ached and her feet throbbed, but still, she threaded needles and passed him the equipment for cauterising blood vessels and reconnecting sinew, rerouting veins and reinvigorating nerve tissue.

The dense darkness of the early hours of the morning had enveloped Park Hospital by the time James had finished operating on both men and they'd been installed in rooms close to James's clinic.

'Blimey, I could sleep for a year,' Kitty said, stretching, feeling the sting of tension in her shoulders and a dull but insistent ache in her lower back. The balls of her feet felt as though they'd been burned with a cauterising iron. She removed her blood-spattered apron and was thankful for the junior nurses and auxiliaries who were already busy cleaning up the theatre.

'Luckily, we've got all of Thursday to recuperate.' James was scrubbing himself clean at the large sink. In that unforgiving light, his olive skin had paled to make him look positively sickly, with dark shadows beneath his eyes. He shook his head. 'I haven't seen anything like those injuries in six years. I've had a marvellous time, fixing hair lips, pinning back wayward ears and bobbing noses. The most taxing operations I've had have been repairing the damage that facial tumours have done to patients and trying to undo some of the havoc wrought by car crashes. But I've got a nasty feeling this war will drag on, and I'll be getting more war-wounded back through my door.'

'Budge up.' Kitty stood next to him at the sink and took a scrubbing brush. She yawned. 'Let's get clean and go back to yours. There's no way I'm going back to the nurses' home right now. The day shift will be clattering around, getting washed and dressed in an hour. I want some peace and quiet. I doubt Matron Pratt will even notice. She knows we put the wedding on hold for yet another year. I think she's happy to cut us some slack.'

James let the water run on his forearms and studied Kitty's face. He moved aside and started to dry them, never taking his eyes off her. 'Matron hasn't found out *why* we postponed, has she?' he whispered.

Kitty shook her head. 'I said we just wanted to save up a bit more.'

All this while, Kitty hadn't told James that Matron Pratt knew all about Ned's involvement with the Communist Party. She knew Matron was worldly wise enough to realise the postponement of their wedding had been down to the cloud of a secret service investigation hanging over them. Matron seemed discreet and trustworthy, however, and Kitty hadn't wanted to worry James needlessly. 'Ned's behaving himself, from what I can tell. Grace is just getting on with her work since their break-up. What with that Julius and Ethel Rosenberg being convicted of espionage in New York last week, none of us wants to give the government any excuse to interrogate us again, never mind arrest us and falsely charge us with treason.'

'But the Rosenbergs aren't just idiots like Ned, getting involved in local Communist Party scuffles with Union Movement thugs. They were found guilty of passing atom bomb blueprints to the Russians,' James whispered, glancing over his shoulder. 'They're being sentenced later today, I believe.'

'Well, we're all keeping our heads below the parapet. None of us fancies being accused of being a Soviet spy.'

Later that Thursday, the bell of the local church struck midday. Kitty was the first to wake. Not wanting to disturb James, she put on her clothes and made her way down to the communal lobby, where she found *The Times* newspaper in James's pigeon hole.

Unfurling the paper, she read the headline about the Rosenbergs' sentencing, and it sent a shiver down her spine.

Chapter 23

'How's the picture now?' James said, adjusting the aerial.

The screen was still hissing with static. 'Try turning it to the left,' Kitty said. She sat on the uncomfortable leather settee, folding James's spare woollen dressing gown beneath her legs. On the screen, a picture was suddenly visible and crystal-clear in black and white. 'That's right. Leave it right there. I can see the news. Bingo.'

Just over a week had passed since James had operated on the airmen who had been shot down in Korea. On the same day, the infamous Rosenbergs had been convicted of sharing atom bomb plans with the Soviets. Now, James and Kitty sat together after long shifts at work, ready to watch *Pathé News* on James's brand-new television set.

James sat beside Kitty and put his arm around her. She noticed that he was looking drawn, of late. Concerned that he was working too hard and worrying too much, Kitty nestled her head against his chest and listened to the slow beat of his heart.

'Here we go.' They broke apart and he sat forwards. 'It's the Rosenbergs.'

The presenter spoke over footage of Julius Rosenberg being led from the New York courtroom in handcuffs, and his wife, Ethel, looking into the cameras with a look of resignation . . . or was it bewilderment, Kitty wondered? The presenter was telling viewers that, 'For the first time,

American citizens would pay the extreme price for espionage on behalf of a foreign power.'

'Sentenced to death? Ooh, I don't like it one bit,' Kitty said. 'I know they've done terrible things, and the judge accused them of being responsible for over fifty thousand deaths in the Korean War and altering the course of history and all that, but . . .'

James ran his hand through his hair and shook his head. He looked back at Kitty. 'The electric chair. Imagine! It's so ghastly and final. What if they were wrongly convicted? What if it was Ned, or us, and the government agencies just . . .' He bit his lip. 'I feel terribly conflicted over this, as a doctor. First, do no harm. Yet what they did was undoubtedly treachery.'

Kitty held her arm out and James relaxed back into her embrace. She savoured the smell of his hair and his warm skin beneath the cotton of his pyjamas. It was rare for them to have this time together away from the hospital, especially since more wounded British airmen were being sent to James from Korea for reconstructive surgery.

'Ooh, hang on. There's something about the war,' Kitty said.

Together, they watched the report of how the Americans were flying on air missions over the hills of Korea, accompanied by a Chinese interpreter.

'They're flying within rifle range,' James said. 'That must take some courage. Can you imagine?'

A loudspeaker hung from the US military aircraft, and through it, the Chinese interpreter was addressing the Reds below, urging them to surrender.

'Look at that!' Kitty said. 'The speaker's absolutely peppered with bullet holes.' She wrinkled her nose and tightened her embrace. 'I'm so relieved and thankful that you're a doctor, safe and well in rainy old Manchester. I don't know what I'd have done if you'd been called up during the Second World War.'

'We were just friends, during *that* war,' James said, chuckling and reaching back to stroke her hair.

'Didn't mean I hadn't already fallen head over heels for you, James Williams.'

He smiled, and some of the colour returned to his cheeks. 'And I you, darling.'

Kitty's thoughts turned to their marriage. 'We've still not set another date for the wedding, and we're already in April.' She grabbed her fiancé by his shoulders and forced him to turn and face her. 'What exactly are your intentions towards me, Dr Williams? Am I to die a spinster?'

James got up and turned the television off. He sat back down onto the settee and held her hands, stroking the diamond in her engagement ring. 'You've been stalling and stalling for . . . how many years?' He raised an eyebrow and pursed his lips.

'All for good reasons,' she said, worried that he might blame her for wanting to keep her career going as long as possible. 'Which we discussed and agreed *together,* need I remind you? But *you* wanted to call off the plans we'd made for last summer.'

'Oh, come on, Kitty. You've seen the news. How can we marry under the threat of the Korean War and that brush with the authorities? I want our wedding day to be perfect.'

Kitty leaned forward and kissed him. 'Same.' She sat back and stared blankly at the silent television set. 'But there's still one elephant in the room, and we need to address it.'

'Such as?'

'George.'

James got up and walked into the kitchen. Kitty could hear him putting water on to boil for a cup of tea. She looked over to the group photo of his year at Trinity College taken in the summer when they had been graduating. Even from her vantage point on the settee, she could see a younger James, standing in the middle, flanked on either side by Timothy and George.

'I told you. I broached the subject,' James said, appearing in the doorway. 'And he swears blind that the government agents have just got hot under the collar about *all* physicists since the start of the Cold War. He insists they're making it up, and without evidence to the contrary, I'm inclined to believe him.'

'Well, those intelligence agents grilled us about him good and proper, for hours on end, and *I'm* inclined to think there must be something fishy going on with your chum for him to have piqued the interest of the secret service. And there's only one way to find out for sure,' Kitty said, climbing off the settee and following him into the kitchen. 'On our next day off, what do you say we go back up to the Lakes and confront him together? Maybe take in another few Lakeland churches while we're at it, and see if we can find our perfect wedding venue?' She put her arms around him and could see the trip was a done deal.

Some two weeks later, they packed their things into the Ford Anglia and made their way up north to Cumbria. George wasn't expecting them – a surprise tactic they'd agreed to use in a bid to flush out the truth. Fat beans of rain were bouncing off the car bonnet, lashing so hard against the windscreen that the windscreen wipers could barely keep up. James drove slowly, pushing the car along the climbing, bending roads.

'So, which church do you have your eye on this time?' he asked.

Kitty took a mirror out of her handbag and checked her reflection. Fatigue was etched into the delicate skin around her eyes. She hastily slid the mirror back into the bag, snapping it shut. 'Well, one of the junior nurses has got cousins in Ambleside, and she was saying that St Mary's is stunning inside. It's Church of England, and I'm Catholic, obviously. But you're C of E, so I'm sure we could get married there. I thought we could give that a go on the way.'

'Close to Windermere?' James asked, smiling. 'I rather like the sound of that. I'm sure we could find a hotel by the lake with a nice function room, where we could hold a small but elegant reception.' He squeezed her knee affectionately. 'Let's stop on the way.'

By the time they pulled up outside the imposing gothic church in the picturesque village of Ambleside, set against a backdrop of emerald green fells, the heavy rain had turned into a full-blown thunderstorm. Holding a picnic blanket over their heads, Kitty and James ran from the car into the church, giggling as the thunder crashed overhead.

Inside, sheltering from the squalling weather, Kitty gasped at the stone arched colonnade that ran either side of the aisle, propping the vaulted ceiling. Though the light was poor and the weather was as beastly outside as Lakeland weather could be, Kitty marvelled at how the stained glass in the tall gothic windows seemed to glow.

'It's got such a lovely feel, hasn't it?' she said. 'Nothing like the others. Look at those colours in the windows.'

James looked up at the ceiling and turned around slowly. 'I'm freezing cold and I'm soaked to the marrow, but this place has a warmth to it, don't you think?'

Kitty nodded and squeezed his hand. 'I can imagine our families sitting in these aisles. Can't you?'

Treating her to an electrifying grin, James picked Kitty up and swung her around, planting a kiss squarely on her lips. 'Let's do it, darling. Let's get married here.'

'At last,' Kitty said. 'This feels right.'

They found the vicar and made enquiries, dismayed to discover that there was no summer availability for a wedding until the following year.

'Can you wait?' James asked, looking crestfallen.

'We've waited this long,' Kitty said. 'What's another year?'

They set a date there and then for the first Saturday in June, 1952.

Buoyed by their decision, the last leg of the winding journey to George's house passed quickly, despite the lashing rain; so much so that Kitty had almost forgotten the reason for them visiting him.

Finally, they pulled into the steep little side road that led to his cottage on the hill.

'There's no way I'm going to be able to get the Ford up there in this weather,' James said. He stayed on the main road and pulled into a nearby passing place, where there was room for several vehicles. 'This will have to do. There's hardly any traffic on the road in this weather, as it is.'

With the rain biting into her exposed legs, and the freezing water spilling over the tops of her flimsy shoes and soaking her feet, Kitty linked James tightly. How she wished the picnic blanket offered better protection against the downpour.

'I can't see anything,' she said, peering into the distance. 'It's just grey.'

'Low hanging cloud,' James said. 'This is why we don't live in Cumbria. It's the place where clouds come to die.'

Slipping and sliding in the mud, they gingerly clambered up the steep little path to George's cottage.

'He'd better be in after all this,' James said. 'We'll catch our deaths out here otherwise.'

'There's a light on in his study,' Kitty said, pointing. Her spirits rose at the prospect of a warm fire and a hot cup of tea.

James climbed the steps to the rickety wooden porch and knocked on the door, and at first there was no answer. He turned to Kitty. 'Oh bother. Do you know, I reckon he might have gone to the pub and left the light on.'

Kitty stepped up beside him and knocked again. Again, there was no answer. She looked at James, searching his face for inspiration. 'I know,' she said, turning and climbing back down the treacherous stone steps, feeling the squelch as she made her way through the tussocks of ringing wet moss and overgrown grass to the window where a light shone. She looked through the rain-spattered glass and balked at what she saw: George was sitting at his desk, wearing headphones on his head, seemingly oblivious to the woman staring in at him through the window.

Kitty staggered back, trying to make sense of the scene she'd caught sight of. She shook her head and made her way back to the front door. She was just about to tell James, when the door finally opened.

'James! Kitty! Good Lord. Do come in, come in!' George seemed nonplussed at the sight of them initially, but his bafflement was soon replaced by a delighted smile.

Perhaps Kitty had imagined all she'd seen through the window.

'We were in the area, looking at churches for the wedding,' James said, shaking his friend's hand. 'Unsurprisingly, we got soaked to the bone, so I thought we might take liberties and avail ourselves of your hospitality before we set off back to Manchester. Is that all right, old chap? I mean, if you're busy . . .'

'Not at all. Not at all.' George ushered them inside, kissing Kitty on the cheek. 'My dear, you look perished. Come and dry off. I'll make some tea . . . or there's always some brandy or both. Ha ha.'

George immediately reached for his old stove-top kettle. He filled it at the butler's sink by the kitchen window, peering out. 'It does make one feel rather down in the mouth when the weather's filthy like this and one lives alone. I'm rather glad to see you both.'

Kitty could see that George was distracted. Now was her chance to make sense of what she'd caught sight of through the window. 'George, can I use your littlest room and try to wring some of this water out of my hair, please?'

'Of course, my dear. I'll bring you a fresh towel in just a moment.'

Before he could follow hot on her heels and stop her, Kitty scurried off into the living room, passing the laden bookshelves and the roaring fire. To her relief, she found not only the door to the privy standing open, but also the door to George's study. Checking that he wasn't behind her, Kitty stepped into the orderly little room and spotted the thing she was sure she'd glimpsed through the window.

On George's desk was an old-fashioned leather suitcase. It stood open, but instead of containing piles of clothing, Kitty could see it was kitted out with what appeared to be the knobs and dials of radio messaging equipment. The headphones George had been wearing were sitting on some paperwork to the side of the case. She could see that the paperwork showed blueprints for something terribly scientific-looking.

'I say. What are you doing in here?'

Kitty jumped and took a sharp intake of breath at the sound of George's voice. She turned around to find him standing in the doorway, a look of consternation on his suddenly deathly pale face.

Chapter 24

'Never mind, what I'm doing in here. I was looking for the privy, wasn't I? And I just happened to walk in here by mistake,' Kitty lied.

George turned slowly to look in the direction of the toilet and then turned his focus back to Kitty. The stern promontory of his brow cast shade over his narrowed eyes. 'But the other door is standing open. So I fail to see how you mistook what's obviously a study for the lavatory.' His cheeks were now flushed and his left eyelid had started to twitch. Like a radar searching for enemy on the horizon, his penetrating gaze tracked stealthily from Kitty to the cupboards and shelving of the study behind her. 'Now, I'd be very grateful if you could come out of there. I have a lot of sensitive scientific equipment in my study, and I don't appreciate being snooped upon.'

Kitty glanced over George's shoulder and caught sight of James, standing in the little vestibule, just behind his friend. George turned and bumped straight into James.

'Oh, sorry, old chap,' George said, chuckling nervously. His air of menace and subterfuge had gone.

James's expression was positively sombre. He didn't budge, forcing George back into the office. 'I say, George. You're not trying to shunt the blame for your suspicious-looking radio equipment onto my Kitty, are you?' he asked.

George looked from James to Kitty and back again. He opened his mouth, clearly searching for a plausible explanation for the suitcase full of what appeared to be espionage equipment. 'I, er . . . it's not suspicious at all.' He smiled and held his hand out to Kitty. 'And of course, I'm dreadfully sorry, Kitty. I never intended to imply you were—'

'What? Snooping?' Kitty said, feeling the adrenalin coursing through her veins and wondering if they were in any danger from this physicist, who had hitherto appeared benign, if slightly eccentric. *If he's concealing that suitcase full of radio-gubbins, maybe he's got a gun*, she reasoned privately. She cast her gaze around the rest of the study, looking for other signs of skulduggery. *How the heck did I get involved in this? It's like a bad noir film.*

'I tell you what,' George said. 'Let's put our feet up by the fire in the parlour and have a nice brandy. Perhaps a slab of parkin? I made it myself a couple of weeks ago.' He grinned. 'It really does get better with age. I don't believe you have to wait for bonfire night, especially not in the Lake District, where we're bedevilled by wintry weather all year round. And I can explain about the radio. It's entirely innocent.' He waved his hand dismissively as he pushed past James and wafted through to the parlour. 'You'll laugh when I tell you.'

Kitty stood at the threshold to the study. It was as if nothing more sinister had come to pass than her losing the way to the toilet.

'This is rubbish,' she whispered to James. 'You should have seen his face. It was obvious he'd been caught with his pants down.'

'Let's see what he's got to say for himself,' James whispered back, kissing her on the cheek and rubbing his hand supportively on her back. 'Go and freshen up. I'll see if he reveals anything to me while we're alone, man to man.'

Feeling instinctively that she'd happened upon an act of espionage, Kitty was so tense that she could only stand in front of the wall-mounted mirror, staring at her bedraggled reflection. She could hear the men – to the uninitiated, chatting in the parlour as if nothing had happened, though Kitty could hear the tightness in James's voice. He was rattled too, clearly.

'Come on, Longthorne,' she whispered to her mirror image. 'Pull yourself together. Act friendly. Pretend like nothing's happened. Get out of here, fast.'

Leaning on the little mushroom-coloured porcelain sink, she took deep breaths and willed a spell of dizziness to subside. 'How the hell did I get myself tangled up in this?' She looked up through the tiny window set high into the thick stone wall. 'Dad, give me strength to get through this. Watch over us. Watch over Ned.'

She flushed the toilet, making it sound as if all was normal. Back in the parlour, George had put a big band number on the gramophone. The place felt quite convivial, yet James was clearly examining his glass of brandy carefully, swilling the amber liquid around the crystal tumbler. He set the glass down, looking at it pointedly. 'Actually, old bean, I'd better not. Don't want to be squiffy on the drive home – not in this weather.'

George turned around to Kitty, smiling. He had the bottle of cognac in his right hand, and a cigarette wedged in the corner of his mouth, looking every inch the bon viveur. 'You'll have a snifter, won't you, Kitty?'

Why had James rejected the brandy, Kitty wondered? Was he concerned that George had perhaps spiked it?

'Ooh, I'll just settle for my brew, thanks.' She took her seat next to James on the old threadbare settee. Adjusting her skirt so it covered her knees, she felt her jaw aching from her fixed smile.

'All the more booze for me,' George said, merrily scooping up James's untouched brandy and pouring it into his own glass. He took his cigarette out of his mouth and knocked back a heavy swig of his drink, gasping when he'd swallowed. 'That will put hairs on my chest, no doubt.'

Perching on the arm of his easy chair, George dragged on his cigarette and eyed them both as if they were specimens under a microscope. 'You're still wondering about the radio equipment, aren't you?' He laughed.

'Well, now you come to mention it, we are, rather.' James laced his fingers together over his knees. He was sitting bolt upright. Kitty could see the tendon in his jaw flinching.

Kitty bit her tongue, realising that uncomfortable silence often drew the truth from liars more effectively than interrogation.

George shrugged. 'The telephone lines are always going down around here. The weather's so unbelievably temperamental.' He looked out of the window and pointed with the glowing tip of his cigarette. 'Case in point.' Taking a drag and exhaling slowly, he seemed to chew over his next words before he spoke aloud. 'So the radio's just a back-up way of communicating to the chaps at Windscale, when the other physicists on duty have questions. We work in shifts, you see? But the younger ones, especially, seem to think I work round the clock, just to service their ignorance. Ha ha.' He stubbed out his cigarette in a large cut-glass ashtray on the mantelpiece.

James nodded. He gave George a curt smile. Was he going to bring up the issue of the secret service investigation, Kitty wondered? Following their arrest at Belle Vue, James had told her he'd challenged George during a telephone call about George's alleged involvement with the Communist Party. But had that telephone call really taken place?

Her composure was flagging. The thirst for the truth could only be quenched with straight answers to difficult questions. 'And there was me thinking you're a communist spy,' she said, unable to hold her tongue any longer.

George froze, pressing his lips together; his brow furrowed and his eyes hooded. 'Is that what you really think, dear Kitty? You think I'm doing a Douglas Philips? A Julius Rosenberg, perhaps?'

'I don't think Kitty meant it like that,' James said, placing his hand on Kitty's knee and squeezing hard.

She was now certain that James hadn't discussed their arrest with George at all. 'Didn't I?' She pushed James's hand from her knee and turned from James back to George. 'Well, are you? Are you a Soviet spy? Is that radio equipment for sending atomic secrets behind the Iron Curtain?'

Plucking another cigarette from his packet of Dunhill, George chuckled and shook his head. He tapped the tip of the cigarette on the side of the pack and plugged it into the corner of his mouth. Then, he sparked his tortoiseshell lighter into flame and dragged hard on the smoke, exhaling a plume of blue smoke into the air, as if he was shooting the breeze in the pub. 'Deary, deary me. What a terrible impression I seem to have made on you, Kitty. I really must apologise. But I'll have you know I'm a Conservative man. It might not be terribly fashionable these days, but I come from a long line of committed Tories. God first, then King, then country. My uncle's a backbencher in the bloody House of Lords, for heaven's sake.' He looked at the red tip of his cigarette. 'He'd have his gamekeeper fill my behind with buckshot if he thought I was consorting with the Ruskies.'

'So, why did we both get arrested by the secret service last spring?' James asked. 'They grilled me for hours about you.'

'You were arrested?' George looked genuinely surprised by the news.

Kitty glared at James, realising her fiancé had lied about having challenged his friend on his alleged communist affiliations.

'Yes, I'm afraid we were,' James said. 'And it was you they were interested in.'

George held his hands up in a gesture of surrender. 'What can I say? The government is so obsessed with this Cold War nonsense that they suspect every physicist working with plutonium to be smuggling secrets out of the country. I mean, have they not considered that my reputation is beyond reproach? I've been working on developing atomic weapons for years. My efforts helped to win the war in Japan, for heaven's sake. How patriotic can a man be? And Windscale don't employ scientists that haven't been thoroughly vetted. I mean, why on earth would they endanger the nation by not doing due diligence on their workforce? Think about it!'

'I suppose so,' Kitty said.

'Westminster is stuffed to the gills with paranoid civil servants,' George went on. He poked himself in the temple emphatically. 'They've just got it into their dim heads that everyone working with plutonium is a security risk. Intelligence is rather a misnomer for those knuckleheads, I'd say.'

Kitty didn't know what to believe. Her head was spinning, though, and she'd had enough. She heaved herself off the old sofa and got to her feet, keen to get out of the cramped little cottage and breathe in the crisp Lakeland air. 'I'm afraid I feel rather lightheaded, James. Do you think we might get back on the road?'

'Oh, don't be a stick in the mud,' George said. 'You've got to believe me.' He picked up the receiver on a heavy old telephone that was on an occasional table next to the gramophone. 'I would say, let's telephone the boys at Windscale and they'll confirm everything I've said, but the lines are down, of course. Hence the radio equipment.' He set the receiver back in its cradle. 'Do stay.' He took another swig from his brandy tumbler. 'I have a pheasant hanging that I could slam in the range. It wouldn't take me long to rustle up a few potatoes from the vegetable patch.'

'No, it's very kind of you to offer, old chap, but I agree with Kitty.' James was also on his feet now. He laid a hand on Kitty's shoulder. 'We really ought to hit the road.'

George looked suddenly crestfallen. 'Oh well, if you must.' He walked out of the parlour and into the scullery, returning with a gentleman's black rolled umbrella. 'Do take this, though. I don't want you getting pneumonia on my account. And I hope with this little misunderstanding that you're not going to sack me as your usher.'

They took their leave from George and said an awkward farewell. Mercifully, it had finally stopped raining, though the ground was still sodden underfoot. When they had made their way gingerly down the slippery, muddy path, Kitty turned to James.

'Well? What do you think? Is he lying?'

Chapter 25

'Let's just get in the car, and then we'll speak,' James said, linking her by the arm and steering her across the rain-soaked road. 'The wind might whip our words back up the hill.'

Kitty shook herself loose from his grip. 'You're worried about hurting the feelings of a man with spy gadgetry in his study?'

James said nothing. He merely got into the driver's side of the car, leaned over and opened the door for her.

Irritated that her fiancé should be so wilfully gullible, Kitty clambered into the passenger seat and slammed the door a little too hard. She stared through the windscreen at the rugged scenery. The grass was the most florid green after the downpour, and wide rivulets of floodwater ran from the higher ground diagonally across the road, disappearing as they plunged over the roadside into some brook, to be carried away to the nearest lake. The place was stunning, but Kitty was desperate to go home.

'What are you waiting for?' she asked, still not looking him in the eye.

James started the engine and pulled away, that tendon in his jaw flinching yet again.

Their journey continued in uncomfortable silence until they left the winding country roads of Cumbria. Then, as the roads widened and straightened and flattened out into the more gently undulating Lancashire countryside, James finally spoke.

'Why are we letting George's odd behaviour come between us?'

'Oh, so you admit he's trying to make out black is white?' Kitty said.

'Part of me thinks he's trying to hide the obvious.' James shook his head and shrugged. 'Part of me thinks the notion that he's a spy is so outlandish, I'm inclined to believe his story about the telephone lines going down and the radio being an emergency back-up. Windscale is dealing with dangerous stuff, after all, and George is their senior man.'

'I think those agents in that basement last year made it very clear that something's genuinely going on with George.'

'What if they're wrong?'

'They're not idiots, James. Intelligence is their job. They wouldn't walk into your clinic and try to tell you how to fix someone's face. So why are you questioning their judgement? You should have challenged him on the subject last year after we got arrested. You said you would. You told me you had. You spun me a right web of lies.'

James changed down a gear to take a bend in the road. He rammed the gearstick into place noisily. 'You don't understand. I couldn't just bring it up, out of the blue. "Oh, by the way, George, the government seems to think you're a Soviet agent. Can you tell me all about it, old boy?!"'

Kitty felt irritation as a ball of hot acid in her chest. 'James, we've just seen the Rosenbergs sentenced to the electric chair. George has spy equipment under lock and key in his study. I caught him using it, red-handed, and there was a sheaf of scientific blueprints on the desk, too. I'm sorry, but I have no compunction in putting two and two together and making four.' She looked out of the window at the fat sheep that studded the fields. She mused that they were lucky to be so impervious to the wet weather, the hot topic of the Cold War and the stress and strain caused by human attachments. 'And you shouldn't have lied to me.'

'The longer I left it, the harder and harder it got to make the call to George. I knew you'd be angry with me, so I kept it to myself that I'd just let it go. I'm sorry. That was wrong of me.'

'But you can't let something like that go, can you? It's too damned important, James. It's affecting our lives. I think we need to . . . I don't know . . . inform the police or something. Telephone that Agent Riley or the other one. Townsend.'

James glanced at her, wide-eyed. 'No! Surely not. We have no real proof and a jolly good excuse for the radio equipment.'

'You're being wilfully naïve if you think that was a good excuse. If you won't go to the police, uninvite him to the wedding.'

'No! I certainly will not. Innocent until proven guilty, Kitty.'

Kitty glared at him, balling her fists. 'Are George's feelings worth risking our lives for? I mean, if he's innocent, the secret service will leave him be. But we can't do our duty as British subjects and not report what we saw.'

They both fell silent again for several miles. Kitty wondered how James could be so obstinate in his defence of his old friend.

'All this brouhaha George and Ned and the secret service are causing, yet here we are, giving each other the silent treatment. Because of them!' She turned to study James's face in profile. The setting sun bounced from the rear-view mirror onto his skin, making him look like he was a classical sculpture, painted in gold leaf. She sighed and reached out to stroke his neck. 'It's not on. But I don't want to ruin what we have because of all that.'

James reached over with his free hand and encased her hand in his. 'I agree. I love you, Kitty, and I don't want to risk our love, and certainly not our lives. Let me think about the George situation. Just hang fire, darling. I'm a patriot and I'd feel duty-bound to inform on someone if I thought they genuinely posed a risk to national security. But I do think Britain has caught the United States' Cold War fever.'

'What's that got to do with the price of fish?' Kitty asked.

'Well, Harry Truman has got himself all in a tizz since the Soviets detonated the atom bomb in '49. He thinks they're developing a hydrogen bomb, and that's where this race has come from. Truman can't be seen to fall behind in the race to acquire the even deadlier H-bomb. Meanwhile, the Soviets are supporting the People's Republic of China, who are behind the communists in North Korea. You couldn't make it up, could you? And all the while, Senator McCarthy is banging on about Reds in the White House.'

'But those are just newspaper headlines. What's any of that got to do with reporting George?' Kitty asked.

'It has everything to do with George and our arrest. I happen to think that the British intelligence service might well have caught the States' paranoia like the flu, forgetting that we're nothing like America. And I think there's an enormous margin for oversensitivity, potentially ruining lives . . . ending lives, if the Rosenbergs are anything to go by. So, if there's an outside chance that George is innocent, I won't be the one to throw him to the wolves. Does that make sense?' He glanced at her, looking for a reaction.

Kitty faced ahead, thinking of her own brother, who was also under suspicion. James had a point. Both men ought to be given the benefit of the doubt. She was a nurse, not a secret service agent or a politician. Who was she to dole out judgement, especially when the penalty for those found guilty was so high?

Chapter 26

'Now, Sister Longthorne,' Mr Thistlethwaite, the orthopaedic surgeon, said, bursting into Kitty's makeshift office towards the end of her shift. 'Dr Bourke has asked me to take a look at your young patient, Samuel Levine.'

Taken by surprise, Kitty looked up from her desk, where she had been writing up notes from the day. Thistlethwaite was standing before her in his white doctor's coat, all twitching bushy eyebrows, with a steel-grey thatch on his head and rogue wiry hairs peeking from his large nose. He leaned forwards, spreading his palms out on the desktop. He smelled of pipe tobacco.

'Oh? Dr Bourke never mentioned it during his rounds this morning.'

'Well, he and I spoke about it earlier over lunch. Bourke's concerned that the child isn't making progress with his physical therapy, despite a good deal of practice in leg irons and all that. He wanted a second opinion, and who better to give it than I?' He stood up straight, towering above Kitty.

Kitty got to her feet, feeling the fatigue from the day weighing down her already leaden limbs. 'Fine. Let me take you to him. He's about to go into his iron lung for the night. I thought he seemed to be doing rather well.'

'I'll be the judge of that, Sister.'

Concerned that Dr Bourke hadn't confided in her and that there might be something amiss with her lively minded little patient of whom she'd grown rather fond, Kitty led the orthopaedic surgeon down to Sammy's spot at the end of the ward. He and Gordon were poring over a *Dandy* magazine that James had brought in for them.

'Good evening, gentlemen,' Kitty said to the boys. She turned to Gordon and clapped her hands. 'Back into your chair, young man. The doctor here needs to examine Sammy.'

'Aw, can I watch?' Gordon said. 'I want to be a doctor when I grow up. Go on. Let us watch! Maybe I can help.' He clung to the wing of Sammy's armchair.

'Er, thank you, little Dr Spencer, but I don't think Mr Thistlethwaite here needs your assistance on this occasion.' She smiled and shooed the fast-recovering little boy back over to his own bed.

Kitty turned to Sammy, who was peering up at them with distress in his large eyes and furrows in his brow that befitted an adult, not a young child. 'Put your comic down for now, love. The doctor just needs to examine you.' She drew the curtain around his space, concealing them and the bulk of the iron lung behind the fabric.

With cracking knees, Mr Thistlethwaite crouched down so that his eyes were level with the boy's. He explained to Sammy that he wanted to look at his legs while he was standing up.

'I'm all right, aren't I?' Sammy asked. 'I've got callipers and braces now, like Gordon, and I can walk five whole paces.' He was smiling but that look of apprehension was still on the little boy's face.

The surgeon didn't answer. He merely helped Sammy out of his seat, probed the musculature of his thighs and calves and then stood back, eyeing the alignment of his hips and the growth of both legs. He asked Sammy to walk up and down, alongside his iron lung.

'Come on, Sammy. Show Mr Thistlethwaite what a cracking little athlete you are these days. We'll have you in the next Olympics, I reckon.'

Thistlethwaite shot her a disapproving glance, and for the first time in a long while, Kitty felt as though she had been silently chastised. When she saw Sammy struggling with his crutches to walk even a few steps, she realised that the surgeon was right. In trying to lift Sammy's spirits, she was giving him false hope of a full recovery.

'Thank you, young man,' Thistlethwaite said after the examination was complete.

Kitty drew back the curtain and asked Rijuta to help Sammy back onto his chair.

'Am I all right, Sister Kitty?' Sammy asked.

What on earth could she say to the boy? She searched for placatory words that wouldn't be lies. 'You'll be all the better once we get you tucked up for the night, and lovely Nurse Ghosh here reads to you. Eh? How about some Enid Blyton until your parents turn up for visiting time?'

For now, at least, Sammy seemed to have been successfully distracted. 'Ooh, yes please. Can I have the *Magic Faraway Tree*?'

Rijuta rummaged among the books on the ward's bookshelf and found the story in question. 'This one?' She waved it at Sammy, and Sammy beamed at her, holding his thumb aloft, his concern apparently forgotten.

Once Kitty and Mr Thistlethwaite had started the walk back along the ward and were out of earshot of the boy, Thistlethwaite cleared his throat and spoke quietly.

'I need to see his X-rays,' he said. 'Do you have them on file?'

'Of course.' Kitty led him back into her office, where she sifted through her alphabetically arranged files and found

Sammy's filed under L. She took out the X-rays of the boy's limbs, pelvis and spine. She passed them to the surgeon. 'These were done two weeks ago.'

Thistlethwaite held them up to the light and squinted. 'I need to look at these properly with the correct facilities, but I think we do have a problem with this boy. His paralysis is quite severe with muscles that are still almost entirely atrophied. He has acute scoliosis of the spine, and he doesn't seem to be responding to the usual treatments and therapies. Let me take these X-rays, please. I'll communicate with Dr Bourke directly, but I think you're going to have to call the parents in for a conversation about their son's future. Are they due to visit soon?'

Kitty nodded. 'At least one of them comes every day, without fail.'

'Right.' Thistlethwaite looked down at his scuffed brogues. 'It might take until tomorrow morning for me to confer with Bourke and then it's the weekend, so please ask them to attend Monday 9 July – for, say, eleven in the morning.'

'Oh, I'm afraid that's my day off. I'm taking my mother to the North-West Area Festival Fare Cookery Finals in town. It's her birthday treat, so I can't let her down.'

Thistlethwaite pushed his tortoiseshell spectacles up his nose. 'Well, it doesn't really matter who is on shift that day. Bourke and I are big boys. We don't need you to hold our hands when we're briefing parents on their children's progress or lack thereof.'

Shaking her head, Kitty felt frustration bite at the lack of regard doctors sometimes showed for the feelings of their patients and those patients' relatives. 'It's not that,' she said. 'It's just that you're delivering bad news, and I have a good rapport with the Levines. They'll be devastated.' She cast her mind back to the times when her own mother had been gravely ill, and her own father had been dying. 'When you get bad news like that, you can barely hear what's being said, let alone take on board the prognosis for the future and further treatment options. The Levines are going to need a familiar face to guide them through this.'

Thistlethwaite laughed. 'I rather think you're overestimating your own importance there, Sister. Sorry.'

Kitty folded her arms. Should she lecture this senior surgeon about her firm belief in the value of continuity of care? What was the point? 'Well, I'll make sure I pop in in any case.'

'As you wish.'

'Hello, Sister!' Esther Levine said, as she and her husband Dovid walked past the open door to Kitty's office at visiting time.

Kitty was preparing to do the handover with the Sister who was about to begin the evening on shift, but when she saw Sammy's parents, she got to her feet and ran after them.

'Ah, glad to have caught you,' she said. 'Can I have a word?'

Esther's eyebrows shot up. 'Is there a problem? Have the Spencers complained about us again?'

At her side, Dovid Levine rolled his eyes. 'If I had a tanner for every time that Gordon's father tried to start an argument with me, I'd be rich by now. Except he already thinks we *are* rich, just because we're Jews.'

'It's nothing like that,' Kitty said. 'And I don't want to bring politics onto the ward.'

'Being a Jew isn't political,' Esther said.

Kitty sighed and nodded. 'Yes, you're absolutely right. I'm sorry. But this is not about that. It's about your Sammy and his progress. You need to come in the day after tomorrow for a meeting with Dr Bourke and the orthopaedic surgeon, Mr Thistlethwaite. Eleven o'clock. Are you free?'

Esther and Dovid looked at one another as though they were communicating by telepathy.

'Well, we both work in a raincoat factory in Cheetham Hill,' Dovid said. 'I glue raincoats and Ethel's a machinist. Our boss is a bit of a tyrant, and if we don't work, we don't get paid. It's also a lot of travelling from our council house in Wythenshawe to Cheetham, and then back through town and out to Davyhulme, all in the same morning. Can we rearrange for the evening?'

'It's an important meeting,' Kitty said. 'The doctors have surgeries and clinics all day long. Eleven is when they can meet with you, and I'll personally make sure I'm there, in case you have any questions.'

Ethel, normally so buoyant, looked as though someone had punctured her, letting all the air out. 'It sounds rather serious. But Sammy's getting better, isn't he?'

Kitty's heart went out to these doting parents, who had been turning up every day for months on end, never appearing to lose hope for a minute that their boy would pull through and conquer the disabilities that polio had left him with. How would they cope with the news that their son might be wheelchair-bound for the rest of his life, having to spend every night in an iron lung? 'The doctors will be able to tell you more, now they've reviewed his progress. Just try not to let your imagination take you to terrible places. Sammy's out of the woods. Look!' She pointed to the end of the ward, where Sammy was still sitting in his chair, listening to Rijuta read *Magic Faraway Tree*. 'He's got a real thirst for stories, your boy. He's ever so bright. I'd say that's a rather different Sammy than the poor little lamb that I first met a year ago.'

She was itching to ask Dovid if he was still rubbing shoulders with Ned, either in the course of local Communist Party gatherings or on the streets, fighting with fascists. Now was not the time, however. The Levines had more to contend with than Ned Longthorne and the watchful eye of the government.

The morning of the Levines' meeting came around, and Kitty laid her clothes on her bed for her outing with Mam. Watching cookery competition finals in a draughty hall wasn't her idea of fun, but Mam had been looking forward to the event for weeks.

Kitty retrieved from her chest of drawers the greetings card she'd bought at the Post Office, and leaned on the top of her little dressing table to fill out the birthday wishes in her neatest handwriting. She signed the card from both her and James, putting three kisses on the bottom and thinking how strange it was to be celebrating yet another of her mother's birthdays without the prospect of her father possibly ruining the day. She made a mental note to take some flowers to her father's grave.

With an increasingly heavy heart, Kitty donned her uniform and made her way over to the hospital building. Almost as soon as she'd entered the reception area, she bumped into Grace, who was carrying a steel kidney dish, covered with a cloth.

'Kitty! Fancy bumping into you. I thought today was your day off,' Grace said. 'Isn't it Elsie's birthday? I was planning to nip round with a nice flowering plant or something, once my shift is over. Assuming Ned's out, that is.'

Kitty glanced at the time on her nurse's watch. 'It is Mam's birthday. I'm taking her into town in an hour to see that Festival Fare cookery competition final, would you believe it!'

Grace giggled. 'What a mouthful that is! I didn't think watching a load of old ladies cooking ration recipes was your cup of tea, our Kitty.'

'God give me strength,' Kitty said, chuckling. 'But I thought I'd nip in here first because I wanted to speak to the parents of one of my little patients. They've got a meeting with Mr Thistlethwaite about their son's condition. And you know what he can be like.'

'Oh, I certainly do. Thistlethwaite's good, but he's got all the bedside manner of a statue in Albert Square.'

'Well, I reckon this family might have questions or need a shoulder to cry on. It's the least I can do.'

Grace bit her lip. 'Any news on your brother?'

'You're still holding a candle for him?'

Grace merely shrugged and smiled sadly.

Kitty shook her head. 'We're still not talking. When I'm at Mam's, he's out. I couldn't tell you what he's up to, but then, turns out I never could.' She patted Grace on the shoulder. 'Don't give him a minute's thought. Ned Longthorne's very good at taking care of Ned Longthorne, and to hell with the rest of us. He's Bert's boy, all right. The apple didn't fall far from the tree.'

Grace chewed her lip ruefully, fingering the spot where her modest engagement ring had been. 'You're not wrong. Anyway, see you later at your mam's.'

Kitty continued on her journey to Thistlethwaite's office. The small waiting area outside was bustling with patiently waiting people, many of whom had body parts in greying casts that had been signed all over by friends and family in pen. But there was no trace of the Levines. She checked her watch again. It was five to eleven. Was it possible they had already gone in? She knocked on the surgeon's door.

'Enter.'

Poking her head into the office, Kitty happened upon an expectant-looking Thistlethwaite, seated behind his desk, clutching at some paperwork, his hair more dishevelled and wild-looking than ever. In a corner of the room stood a full human skeleton, which seemed to grin at her. On the walls were numerous framed illustrations, showing cross-sections of the human body, with the layers of muscle and sinew and the skeletal framework visible. There were full-sized models of an arm and a leg, mounted and displayed on top of a cabinet that was stuffed with medical tomes stacked seemingly arbitrarily – some standing vertically and others in piles on their sides – but there was no sign of the Levines.

'Sister? *You're* not Ethel and Dovid Levine.'

'No, sorry to disappoint. I didn't spot them in the waiting area, so I assumed they'd maybe come in to see you a bit early,' she said. 'I just wanted to say hello and show them a bit of moral support.'

Thistlethwaite wafted his papers in the direction of his examination couch. 'You may sit in on the meeting if you're that keen. For once, my clinic is running on time.' He glanced at the clock on the wall. 'They should be here any minute.'

Together they waited in awkward silence for some fifteen minutes, while Kitty looked around at the office, wondering whose skeleton it was and why the surgeon's secretary didn't tidy up for him. Thistlethwaite sucked on his pipe, reading case notes.

When Kitty could bear the waiting and the stink of the pipe no longer, she walked to the window. 'Do you mind if I open this? It's pleasantly warm outside today.' She didn't fancy spending her mother's birthday with her freshly washed and set hair reeking of pipe smoke.

'By all means.' Thistlethwaite looked at the clock again. 'Although I'm going to have to ask you to leave so I can call the next patient in.'

'It's not like them to be late,' Kitty said. 'Maybe they're outside, and your secretary hasn't sent them in.'

She opened the office door and looked around at the glum faces of those who were waiting. She turned to Thistlethwaite. 'No sign of them.'

The orthopaedic surgeon waved her away dismissively. 'If they turn up now, they'll have to wait until the end of the clinic or else rebook. Ask my secretary to send in the next patient on your way out, will you?'

After she had spoken to the secretary, Kitty took a seat at the back of the waiting area and watched the comings and goings of Thistlethwaite's patients. Every time she caught sight of a newcomer in her peripheral vision, she looked up, hoping it would be the Levines. There was no sign of them, however. After forty minutes, Kitty wondered if they'd perhaps gone to the polio ward, or even Dr Bourke's office, by accident. She left the orthopaedic clinic and made her way to her ward.

'Have you seen the Levines?' she asked one of her nurses.

They hadn't. She stopped by Dr Bourke's office and spoke to his secretary, but she hadn't seen Sammy's parents either.

Kitty had no option but to give up waiting and assume the Levines had forgotten the appointment or else had not been able to take the time off work. She thought it out of character for such committed parents and reliable time-keepers, but right now, she was running late for her mam's birthday outing. It was time to put her own family first.

Chapter 27

'Ooh, what a lovely card,' Mam said, running the tips of her arthritic fingers over the illustration of the stylish-looking woman on the front. She thrust it back at Kitty. 'Go on, love. Tell us what it says. I haven't got my reading specs.'

Kitty read out the message inside. Then she presented her mother with a gift of Helena Rubinstein rouge that she'd saved up for. 'Here you are, Mam. This'll put some colour in your cheeks.'

'Aw, rouge. Ooh, hey, I'm going to feel like Elizabeth Taylor wearing this. By heck, you're a smasher, what are you?' Mam planted a noisy kiss on Kitty's cheek.

Hugging her mother and savouring the heady smell of the Coty perfume and talcum powder that Ned had pilfered and given her as a gift several Christmases ago, Kitty pushed all thoughts of the Levines out of her overworked mind. 'Not half as smashing as you, Mam. Now come on, let's put the card on the mantelpiece, get on that bus and get into town.'

The Tunman Hall, where the north-west area cookery final was being hosted, was a vast, hangar-like place. Even in July, Kitty felt chilly. At one end were the spectators. Row after row of seating was filling up fast with mainly older women, all wearing their Sunday best.

'Ooh, the contestants have got a kitchenette cooker each,' Mam said, pointing to the other end of the hall, where the cooking would take place.

Kitty shunted her along. 'Get going, Mam, or we'll never get a seat.'

They sat behind two women who sounded like they came from Rawtenstall or Ramsbottom, judging by their strong Lancastrian accents.

'I wish to God they weren't wearing hats,' Kitty said. 'I can barely see.'

Between the millinery confections, Kitty glimpsed the competition area. Numerous kitchenettes had been set up. The contestants were already standing by their stoves, looking nervous. Kitty was surprised to spot a man among them. 'Look at that,' she said, grinning. 'Who'd have thought there'd be a feller competing with all these women?'

Mam shrugged. 'He might have been in the catering corps during the war. One of the women who worked at the Ford factory – her husband Harry did that in Wales. He got into a ruck with an officer, she reckoned, and cooked up the officer's pet rabbit for dinner.' She wheezed with laughter. 'Or maybe this feller works in a caff. Who knows?' She took her new spectacles out of her hard-framed handbag, pushed them onto her nose and studied the contestants in earnest. 'Blimey. There's a lot of old ladies from out in the sticks. Look at the cut of her from Rawtenstall.'

One of the women in front looked around and glared at Kitty's mother. 'That's my sister, if you don't mind,' she said. 'I happen to think she has a very strong chance of winning, so stick that in your pipe.' She turned back around to face the front.

Kitty looked at her mother and nudged her conspiratorially. 'You don't need that rouge now, Mam.'

Together, they giggled in silence, their shoulders heaving. Kitty savoured the moment, realising that experiences like this were few and far between, given how demanding her job was. She wondered if she might see more of her mother once she and James married. She then tried to imagine herself cooking for her own family at her own stove in her own kitchen in an elegant house in the suburbs. It felt like somebody else's dream.

'Hey, look at that,' Mam said, pointing to a man who carried a giant camera. 'They're filming it. Do you think it's *Pathé News*? Are we going to be on the television, our Kitty?'

'Looks like it,' Kitty said, half listening to the host of the competition, who announced that the contestants would all be making North Sea fish pie, with the pudding of their choosing.

'Those judges look like they've got a bob or two,' Mam said. 'Look at that one, with her mink ties.'

The competition got underway. At her side, Mam gave a running commentary on every step of the pie-making process, clearly delighted by the spectacle of other people's cooking mishaps and triumphs. Kitty's thoughts inevitably drifted back to the Levines.

Why hadn't they turned up to the important meeting about their son? Surely they wouldn't have missed it for the world, especially if there was the prospect of receiving bad news about Sammy's rocky road to recovery. The more she thought about it, the more Kitty realised that something was amiss.

'And the winner is . . . Mrs Cunliffe from Rawtenstall!'

Kitty was jolted out of her reverie by rapturous applause. How had the hours passed so quickly? The entire hall smelled of delicious cooking. She gathered her bearings and realised that the woman in front had turned to her mother.

'See! I told you my sister would win. Looks like you're the one with egg on your face, Mrs.'

'Oh, give over, will you,' Mam said. 'It's like you lot from the sticks have got nothing better to do than start an argy-bargy with strangers. Mrs Cunliffe can stick her fish pie.' She linked arms with Kitty, stuck her nose comically in the air and put on the upper-class voice she used for imitating James. 'Come along, Kitty. One simply has to celebrate one's birthday with a slice of *real* cake at Meng and Ecker tearooms.'

Together, they flounced out, giggling.

'Look, Mam,' Kitty said. 'When we've had tea and cake, I'm afraid there's an errand I need to run.'

Her mother narrowed her eyes. 'Oh, aye? Are you ditching your old mam on her big day? You're doing a Ned, aren't you?'

'No, of course not. It's just that you live more or less around the corner from the parents of this little boy on my ward.'

'And?'

'And I'm really worried about them. They should have come to the hospital today to see a surgeon, and they didn't. They knew it was important. Obviously, they don't have a phone. It seems daft to send a telegram and wait for a response when I can just nip round to see them.'

'Is it really worth interrupting my birthday celebrations for strangers?' Her mother's smile had faded. The corners of her mouth sagged, and the effervescence she'd displayed in the hall had gone flat like old pop.

'We'll go after Meng and Ecker. It won't take more than a few minutes to nip round on the way back to yours. I am sorry. It's just I've got a bad feeling, Mam. I hope I'm wrong.'

Chapter 28

'That slice of custard tart was a birthday present in itself,' Mam said, as they alighted from the bus to Wythenshawe. 'Real eggs and all-butter pastry. I think I'm going to dream about that until rationing's over. Never mind Mrs Cunliffe's North Sea flaming pie.'

'Not as nice as the sponge cake you used to make before the war,' Kitty said.

She linked her mother's arm, walking at a brisker pace than usual. The afternoon tea had been a real treat, but the nagging worry that something dreadful had possibly befallen the Levines had only become more acute with every bite she had taken of her food. The long, winding bus journey out to Wythenshawe had been agonising.

'Hey! You're going to break out into a run in a minute, our Kitty,' Mam said. 'Wait your hurry, Jesse Owens. I'm no spring chicken anymore.'

'Sorry, Mam. We're nearly there, now. I promise.'

As they approached the Levines' street, she could hear shouting – men's angry voices – and the ominous tinkle of breaking glass.

'Sounds like there's a bit of a to-do,' Mam said, slowing to a nervous standstill.

Kitty looked at her mother, dressed in her Sunday best. 'Listen, Mam. You go home. If there's any shenanigans going on, I don't want you getting tangled up in it. You're only a couple of streets away. Go.' She tried to pull away from her mother's grip.

Mam held her back. 'Don't you get involved, Kitty Longthorne. It sounds like there's a war going on just round that corner. It's your day off and it's my birthday, and this is above and beyond the call of duty.'

'I'm sorry, Mam.' Kitty bit her lip, feeling a rotter for interrupting her mother's celebrations, but knowing she had to do the right thing. 'These are decent people and they've got a paralysed little boy on my ward. Without them, he's all alone in the world. I've got to check they're safe. I couldn't live with my conscience if something had happened to them.'

Reluctantly, Mam let her go. 'I'll go and put a brew on. Any truck with yobbos, and you call the police.' She pointed to a telephone box some two hundred yards in the other direction. 'That's the only telephone box in the area. Just so you know.'

Kitty kissed her mother and shooed her off in the direction of her own street. Taking a deep breath, she rounded the corner to discover the source of the hullabaloo. She gasped at the sight of a mass brawl that had broken out on the very cul-de-sac where the Levines lived. There were at least thirty men lobbing bricks and other projectiles down the street at another group of men. Kitty watched in helpless horror at the sight of a young man carrying a beer bottle filled with clear liquid and stuffed with a piece of rag. She could smell the petrol from where she was standing. Open-mouthed, she watched as the youth took out his lighter and set fire to the rag. He hurled the bottle in among the rival gang. Kitty followed its trajectory through the air, watching the liquid inside ignite. When the petrol bomb smashed to the ground, it was a ball of flame.

Feeling lightheaded, Kitty tried to marshal her thoughts. She took note of the appearance of the fighting men closest to her. They looked no different from their opponents at the far end of the street. There was no sign of the Union Movement flag. Yet she could hear from the obscenities they were shouting at their adversaries that they were fascists.

'Cooee! Love! Do you want to come in?'

Kitty heard a shrill voice to her right. She looked around to see an elderly woman hanging out of her open parlour window. She wore a scarf in a turban over her hair, winged spectacles and a flowery apron. She was beckoning her to come closer. Kitty obliged, standing by her garden fence.

'I need to visit friends at the bottom of the street,' Kitty said.

'Oh, you don't want to be going down there, love,' the woman said, shaking her head. 'Fighting's been going on for hours. Since this morning. It's a siege.'

'Hasn't anyone called the police?'

The old woman looked at her, agog, rubbing together the lips of her toothless collapsed mouth. 'And get labelled a grass? Are you kidding? Folk round here know to keep themselves to themselves and just batten down the hatches. Those lads fighting – they know where everyone lives. But you can come in to shelter, if you like. I'm not proud.'

'It's kind of you to offer, but I'll pass, thanks.' Kitty was about to walk further into the fray for a better look, but she turned back. 'Say, have you seen the Levines today? They're the people I need to see.'

'The *Jews?*' the old woman asked. Those putty-like lips curled into a picture of distaste as she said the words. 'I'll not have anything to do with the likes of them.' She tugged on her thumb and four fingers, one by one, as she said five words, by way of explanation: 'The. Jews. Killed. Our. Lord.' She held her hand up with those fingers and thumb splayed. Then she slammed the window down and drew her curtain shut, ending the conversation.

'Charming,' Kitty said.

Steeling herself to be brave, she advanced a little further, crouching whenever a projectile fell close by. She tried to remember the house number of the Levines. Was it number twenty-three?

Ducking behind someone's garden gate, Kitty eyed the front doors of the houses, trying to work out in what order the numbering went.

'Is it odds one side and evens the other?' she muttered beneath her breath. Popping up from behind the gate to see where number twenty-three was, she realised with a sinking heart that the house was at the very head of the cul-de-sac, completely cut off by the fighting.

The front door of the house in whose garden she was crouching opened.

'Hey! You're trespassing,' an angry-looking man said. He was wearing slacks and a string-vest, putting Kitty in mind of her late father.

'I'm waiting to run over to number twenty-three,' Kitty said. 'I'll be gone in a minute, I promise.'

The man looked at her, scratched his head and then his belly. 'What's a nice girl like you doing trying to break through the ranks of that lot in the middle of World War Three? Are you potty? You'll end up with a black eye, or worse.'

'Why's nobody called the police?'

'It's not our business,' the man said. 'Besides, it happens a lot since *they* moved in.'

'They?'

The man gestured with his unshaven chin towards the head of the cul-de-sac. 'Jews. They're Bolsheviks. Commies. Reds. These lads, chucking the bricks – they're local lads. They've been trying to get 'em out since they came to live here.' He hitched up his trousers and peered beyond Kitty and the gate. 'Looks like they've finally managed it.' He smiled. The smile faltered. 'Now, sling your hook, lady.'

Horrified at the tensions that raged only streets away from her mam's peaceful house, Kitty left the man's garden. The mob had moved further along the street and she could see them fist-fighting with their opponents. Beyond the men, however, she caught sight of something that made her heart quail. Flames were licking at the windows of one of the houses, sending thick black smoke billowing into the perfect azure blue of a July afternoon sky.

'It's the Levines!' Kitty realised.

Retreating back down the street, Kitty ran as fast as she could to the red telephone box that her mother had pointed out. Heaving the heavy door open, she lifted the receiver and heard the dial tone. She tried to dial 999 with shaking fingers but let the dial swing back around too soon.

'Stop faffing, Kitty. Concentrate,' she chided herself.

Finally, she managed to dial the number successfully.

'Which emergency service do you require?' the man asked on the other end.

'All of them,' Kitty said, barely aware that tears were streaming down her face. 'Come quickly. There's a house fire, and a riot, and I'm worried an innocent family's being burnt alive.' She gave the address and her name and slammed the receiver back onto the cradle.

Panting and trembling all over, Kitty had to decide what to do next. She could go back to the safety of her mam's house and wait for the firemen to extinguish the fire, the police to deal with the thugs and the ambulance men to carry the wounded off to hospital. Then she pictured Ethel and Dovid, gasping for air in the flaming house, trapped behind doors they had perhaps barricaded for safety. Leaving the couple to die was not an option.

'Come on, Kitty. Time to be brave.'

Kitty stepped out of the telephone box and ran back to the Levines' cul-de-sac. She realised she needed to protect herself from the makeshift missiles that were being flung by both sides of the fray. Spotting a municipal rubbish bin standing by someone's side-gate, Kitty walked up the front garden path and snatched up the lid, holding it in front of her as a shield.

Taking a deep breath, she walked briskly towards the fighting, holding the lid at an angle so that her face and head were protected. Soon, she was among the men. All around her, they were wrestling, throwing knuckle-duster punches and trying their damnedest to wallop the living daylights out of each other with planks of wood and cricket bats. Kitty could smell their sweat and the testosterone on the air. She was sure she could taste the metallic tang of their blood.

Two entangled opponents blundered over to her, almost pinning her to a privet hedge. Kitty yelped and dodged out of the way, moving ever forwards. A half-brick whistled through the air and bashed against the bin lid with a heavy, dull clank. The impact almost knocked the lid from her grip, jarring her wrist as she held on for dear life.

How far was she now? She moved her bin lid aside to see if the fifty yards or so that stood between her and the Levines were clear. She was weighing up the odds of successfully sprinting through a gap in the fighting, when she caught sight of someone she hadn't expected to see.

Ned.

She was so tempted to call out to him, but Kitty realised that the man-mountain coming towards him with a balled fist, drawn back with deadly intent, would gain an advantage if Ned's focus waned for even a second. Did this mean that the fascists were fighting the communists that Ned had sworn he would have nothing more to do with? Were the communists trying to protect the Levines, or were the Levines just an excuse for a fight? Kitty couldn't be sure, but she could see a way through.

With the bin lid held in front of her, Kitty scurried through the middle of the fray and got to the other side. Looking up, she saw with horror that the Levines' house was now aflame in earnest. The glass had exploded in each window and fire licked through the apertures, kissing the dry terracotta roof tiles above. Sparks flew, landing on the neighbour's roof, and wily flames were licking along the wooden fascia beneath the eaves that connected the semi-detached houses. As if the devil himself was inside the Levines' home, belching out fumes from his poisonous gut, plumes of black smoke now climbed thirty, forty, fifty feet into the sky.

'Please let them live,' Kitty said beneath her breath.

Suddenly, above the loud crackle and roar of the fire and the jeering and shouting of the men, Kitty heard sirens and bells. She looked behind her and saw through the tangle of bodies that a number of vehicles were squealing to a halt at the mouth of the street. Two gleaming red fire engines, three police cars, at least three Black Marias and two ambulances.

'Kitty! Help! Over here!'

Kitty recognised the voice of Esther Levine. She crept towards the burning house and the voice, feeling the searing heat blasting in her face.

'Save us!'

This time, she heard Dovid's voice, though it sounded strangled and desperate.

Peering through the smoke, Kitty spotted the couple looking down at her from the only open window that wasn't billowing with flames. It was at the side of the house – the bathroom. She could see the Levines' faces were blackened by smoke. They were both coughing.

'The fire brigade's here,' Kitty shouted. 'The police too.'

'We've got to get out now!' Dovid cried. 'Right now! The fire's coming under the bathroom door.' He burst into a coughing fit. 'Find something that will break our fall.'

Hitching her skirt high and jumping over the low hedge, Kitty looked around for something they could jump onto safely. All she could find was some washing on a clothes line and their council rubbish bin. She dragged the heavy bin beneath the window. 'This is as good as it gets.'

'We'll break our legs,' Dovid said.

'Better broken legs than dead. Come on, now. Jump!'

There was a bang from inside the house. Esther screamed suddenly and a ball of fire shot past the two of them and out of the bathroom window, mushrooming upwards.

Were they dead? Kitty wondered. She could no longer see them. 'Esther! Dovid!'

Through the fiery mayhem, two flaming figures suddenly reappeared at the window and hurled themselves through the opening, onto the bin below. Snatching the washing from the line, Kitty quickly smothered the fire that had engulfed their clothing.

'It's going to be all right,' she said, wincing at the sight of their burns.

She looked up and saw the firemen running towards the house, carrying fat hoses. The ambulance men were only paces behind, ferrying stretchers.

'Over here!' she cried, motioning the ambulance men to come to her aid. She recognised them immediately as staff from Park Hospital. 'Scotty! Clive! Don! Trevor! Come quickly.'

'Sister Longthorne,' Scotty said. 'Whatever are you—?'

'No time for questions. These people are badly burnt. I suspect they have fractures to the legs as well. They need to be taken straight to casualty. I'll do what I can right now, and then I'll travel in the ambulance with them.'

'Right you are, Sister. Just tell us what you need and we'll do it.'

As the firemen started to douse the burning house with jets of freezing water that rained down on them all, Kitty administered emergency treatment to the burns as best as she could.

'Sammy!' Esther said, fixing Kitty with a look of utter desperation.

'He's safely tucked up on the ward,' Kitty said. 'Don't you worry about him. Let's get you both to the hospital to be seen to by the doctors.'

The police were breaking up the fight now, wielding their truncheons to bring the more unruly brawlers to heel. Police whistles blew all around in a bid to impose order on the chaos. There were barking Alsatian police dogs, straining on the ends of their leashes. Fascists and communists alike were being wrestled to the ground, their wrists roughly handcuffed together behind their backs, as the officers placed the brawlers under arrest.

Jogging alongside the stretchers towards the waiting ambulances, Kitty caught sight of Ned being grabbed from behind by a burly policeman even as he tried to lash out at an opponent with a hefty kick.

'Idiot,' she said softly. Some birthday present her brother's arrest would be for her mother. 'Mam!' Kitty then realised that the birthday girl would be sitting at home, all alone and wondering where everyone was, until Grace turned up after her shift had ended.

She looked down at the quaking, bewildered and badly burnt Levines and knew her mother would just have to understand. Kitty was a nurse, and her first duty was to her patients, even on her day off.

Chapter 29

'How are you feeling today?' Kitty asked, looking down at Esther Levine, who lay bandaged on her bed in the Burns ward. In the adjacent bed, Dovid Levine was sleeping.

'They've given me morphine for the pain,' Esther said through singed lips. 'My broken leg's been reset. I'll survive. We'll both survive.'

Kitty pulled the visitor's chair close to the bed. 'Is there anyone I can contact? Your parents? Dovid's family?'

Esther sighed. She spoke slowly. 'My parents are both dead. Dovid's father is . . . in Liverpool with his sister, Gittel. She's married now. Gittel Lieberman. I can't remember the address.'

Writing the name Gittel Lieberman down, Kitty nodded. 'I'll make sure her address is found and she's sent a telegram.' Kitty lifted the bandage on Esther's right arm and frowned at the florid skin beneath. 'Your burns look rough right now, but actually, they haven't penetrated as deeply as I'd initially thought, thank heavens. It's going to be very painful for a good while, but there may be surgeries that Dr Williams can perform on your facial burns.'

'Who's he?'

'He's our resident plastic surgeon. He's very experienced in these things.'

'I'm not bothered about my face. I just want to see my boy. Where's my Sammy?'

Kitty straightened Esther's sheet absently. 'Don't you worry about Sammy. He's just down the way, reading *Dandy* with his little pal.' She sat back and waited until Esther met her gaze. 'Do you want to tell me what happened yesterday?'

Esther looked away.

'It's no good you avoiding the issue,' Kitty said. She leaned in. 'The police have asked to interview you. Fifty-three men were arrested yesterday. Fifty-three! And you and your husband were the underlying reason behind all that fighting and damage to property.'

'We've lost everything,' Esther said. 'We've got nowhere to live. Everything went up in flames, didn't it? Our photographs, our keepsakes, the brass candlesticks my mother brought from Vilner . . .'

'You escaped with your lives. But the police are going to want to know why the fighting started in the first place. Why were you torched out of your own home, Esther?'

Esther's eyes filled with tears that started to run into her dressings. She winced. 'We're Jewish. That's why. Those fascist thugs were just looking for a scapegoat.'

'Could it also be that you and Dovid are both from Bolshevik stock?' Kitty asked.

Peering over at her sleeping husband, Esther didn't answer. 'I need to see my Sammy. Please. Can you bring him to me?'

Kitty shook her head. 'Not yet. We can't afford you getting any infection in those burns, and you don't want Sammy fretting, do you? You rest up.'

Leaving the Levines' bedsides, Kitty made her way to the ward where she knew Grace was on duty. Poking her head in through the doors, she spotted Grace helping an old lady onto a bedpan. She caught Grace's attention and gestured that she would wait for her in the corridor.

Presently, Grace emerged from the ward. 'Thank God you're safe.' She put her arms around Kitty.

Kitty squeezed her friend tightly and kissed her cheek. 'Thanks.' They broke apart. 'I'm so glad I bumped into you when the ambulances arrived outside casualty. Did you manage to explain to Mam how sorry I was to miss the end of her birthday?'

Grace nodded. 'Don't worry. We had fish and chips and watched television together. It was fine. I've promised to take her to the Band On The Wall to see me singing next week. Maybe we can all go.'

Looking down at her short nails, Kitty pursed her lips. 'Listen, there's something I didn't tell you yesterday.'

'Go on.' Grace narrowed her eyes.

'I spotted Ned among the rioters. I couldn't believe my eyes at first, but you can hardly mistake him for someone else, can you?'

Grace leaned against the wall and rubbed her face. 'Did you try to speak to him?'

'How could I? He was too busy punching some fascist's lights out, and I was too busy dodging petrol bombs and bricks. Anyway, I thought I should tell you he's been arrested. I saw him get carted off by some burly bobby. But I don't know what the charges are yet.'

'Do you think he'll be locked up overnight and get kicked out with a flea in his ear?'

Kitty exhaled heavily. 'The authorities have been watching my brother for a long, long while. Years, and not just for the communism fad.' She cast her mind back to the counterfeiting scam that their father and Ned had both been involved in, though Ned had evaded arrest then by boarding the first boat to Barbados. 'I have a nasty feeling they're going to throw the book at him. His bad decisions are catching up with him, I'm afraid.' She felt a pang of regret in her heart that the brother might finally be hoisted by his own petard. Along with the death of her father and the bombing of her childhood home during the Blitz, it felt like another piece of her world falling away.

Grace and Kitty embraced again – this time, wordlessly. Kitty rubbed the back of the sister-in-law she might have had, had Ned just behaved himself and been content with all he had. They parted, and Kitty could see the sadness in Grace's eyes.

'Don't let it get you down, chuck,' she said. 'You didn't come to England for our Ned. He followed you because he knew he was onto a good thing. You have a soft heart. And believe me, I've known our Ned long enough to say with absolute certainty that you've had a lucky escape.'

'He was only ever doing it for the right reasons,' Grace said softly.

'He started doing it for the right reasons,' Kitty said. 'And then, like everything else Ned has ever got involved in, he ended up doing it for the thrill of sailing close to the wind.' She glanced through the window in the door to Grace's ward and caught sight of the Sister glaring at Grace and looking pointedly at her watch. 'You'd better go. But one thing's come out of this . . .'

Grace looked at her expectantly. 'Go on.'

'I'm going back to the board of directors to talk about racial prejudice and the behaviour of some staff and patients towards anyone who isn't true blue. The Levines nearly burnt to death in their own homes, and not just because of their political beliefs. It's got to stop. I can't affect what goes on in the streets of Wythenshawe, but I can do something about what goes on in this hospital.'

*

'Why haven't Mummy and Daddy been to see me?' Sammy asked later that day as Kitty checked on his progress.

Kitty stroked the little boy's curls, wondering what to say. Really, it was up to the Levines themselves or else Dovid's sister to decide how to break the news to Sammy. Gittel had likely not yet received the telegram, however. 'They're a bit poorly at the moment, and can't make it in, I'm afraid. They telephoned to say they didn't want to pass their illness onto you, but they send their love.' How could she tell this small, poorly boy that his family home was now nothing more than a charred shell?

For the second time that day, Kitty cast her mind back to the loss of her own home during the Blitz, the devastation of having returned to her old street to find that the only item left standing had been an old oak sideboard. Was the rootless existence that her mother had been forced to lead, moving from squalid lodging to lodging, one of the reasons that Kitty had clung so steadfastly to her nursing career, relegating her relationship with James to second place? How might this terrible event affect a boy who already faced an uncertain future in a wheelchair?

'Are they going to get better soon?' Sammy asked. 'Because I really miss them. I miss home and my bike and my things, but most of all, I miss them.'

Kitty swallowed 'Don't worry, Sammy,' she said. 'They'll be over to see you as soon as they can, and in the meantime, I think your Auntie Gittel might be coming from Liverpool with your granddad. How does that sound?'

Finally, her words elicited a smile from Sammy. 'Smashing.'

*

At the end of her shift, avoiding the temptation to step out into the warm July evening air, Kitty made her way through the hot, stuffy corridors to James's office. The clinic was empty of patients, so late in the day, but she found him writing a letter. His tie had been loosened and hung at a rakish angle, the top button of his shirt was undone and his sleeves were rolled up to his elbows.

His serious expression gave way to a bright smile the moment he saw her. 'Kitty, my darling! The heroine of Park Hospital, rescuer of the persecuted few from burning buildings. I've been itching to see you all day. How are you feeling?'

Kitty edged round to James's side of the desk and planted a kiss on his forehead. James shunted his chair backwards and slapped his thighs, indicating she should sit on his knee.

'You look positively worn out,' he said. 'Come and let your fiancé hug your cares away.'

She sat on his knee and buried her face in his neck, drinking in the sandalwood smell of his aftershave, which was just about still discernible this late in the day. 'I think it might take more than a hug.'

James leaned to the side, turned to her and frowned. 'That bad?' He glanced up at the clock. 'I've got half an hour until the directors' board meeting. Tell Dr Williams everything.'

Kitty smiled and ran her hand through his thick, dark hair. 'Where to even start?' She puffed air out through her cheeks.

'You could start by telling me why you put yourself in harm's way like that,' James said.

Kitty looked at him askance. 'Are you kidding me? You would have done exactly the same thing in my position.'

James sighed heavily. 'Kitty, you're a nurse, not a fireman or a policeman. You shouldn't have risked life and limb to rescue the Levines. The emergency services are trained to fend off rioters and save people from burning buildings. You're not.'

Sitting bolt upright, tempted to climb down off his knee, Kitty frowned. 'The Levines would have both broken their necks, jumping out that bathroom window if I hadn't been there to break their fall with a bin. And it was me that rung the emergency services. If I hadn't—'

James was glowering at her. 'You can't possibly know that they wouldn't have been rescued anyway – without you needing to risk life or limb. Kitty, before you go rushing in where angels fear to tread, you need to remember that there are people who love you. I love you. Your mother loves you. Ned, for all the buffoon he is, loves you.'

Now, Kitty did dismount from her fiancé's knee. 'If you love me that much, why didn't you come and find me to make sure I was all right? Eh? Maybe I'd got burnt or beaten up.'

James shook his head. 'Darling, I saw you arrive with the ambulances. I saw you with my own eyes through the window.' He pointed to his window that had a clear view of the main entrance, obscured only by a potted spider plant. 'And news travels a darn sight faster down the hospital grapevine than any telegram or telephone call. I didn't come to find you because I knew you were fine and I had patients to tend to.'

Kitty balled her fists with frustration, realising there was some truth to what James was saying. She had been foolhardy to fight her way to Sammy's parents through that rioting throng. She could easily have been injured, sent flying, been burnt or maimed by falling, flaming debris. She stuck her chin out defiantly. 'Well, I did what I thought was right, and it turns out, I was right. Although I see your point, and I am sorry.'

'Are you?' James raised an eyebrow and smiled. He patted his knees and then held his arms out.

'Yes.' Relenting, Kitty sat back on his lap. She locked eyes with him. 'There. You've had your apology. And now, I need you to raise the issue of racial prejudice at the board again. The Levines have been torched out of their own home, and it doesn't take a genius to work out why. Lily Schwarz has been putting up with nasty jibes for years. The nurses from the colonies are still getting treated with disdain, and I don't like it.'

Wrinkling his nose, James looked around the office, clearly chewing over what she'd said. 'Well, we can hardly wheel the Levines upstairs to tell their story, but how about we get Lily, Grace and Rijuta to speak to the board, then?' He stroked Kitty's chin gently. 'Maybe Baird-Murray and Ryder-Smith need to hear it from the horse's mouth, so to speak. It will be harder-hitting from them.'

Kitty nodded. 'Good idea. When I leave here, I'll pop back to the nurses' home and see if they can come over. They might feel intimidated though. It's not easy to stand up in front of a room full of men like Baird-Murray and tell them something they don't want to hear.'

'Progress is never painless.' James shrugged. 'I'll back them up.' He kissed her knuckles. 'You know, you're not *so* dissimilar to your brother, are you?'

'What do you mean?' Feeling maligned, Kitty pulled her hand free, got to her feet and backed around the other side of the desk.

'Oh, come along now, Kitty. That wasn't meant to be an insult. I mean, like Ned, you're a champion of the underdog. A fighter for a good cause. You always have been. It's one of the things I admire about you.' He folded his hands behind his head and smiled. 'You have principles, and you stand up to be counted. Except, you have infinitely more common sense than your brother, thank heavens.'

'And I'm honest as the day is long!'

'Of course. You're a woman of utter integrity – that's just one of the reasons why you're the woman for me. And that's where you and Ned diverge somewhat. Ned's too easily swayed by money and opportunity for a cheap thrill.'

Kitty chewed the inside of her cheek, pondering James's observation. She ruefully acknowledged that it felt uncomfortably close to the truth, but she was in no mind to debate the pros and cons of her wilfully naïve brother. 'Listen, enough of that. Now, I need your help on something else too.'

Raising his eyebrow, James glanced at the clock again and started to roll down his shirt sleeves. 'Oh yes?'

'Your friend on the council. Do you think he can find some decent new accommodation for the Levines, once they get out of hospital? Maybe a nice house near Cheetham Hill, where there's an established Jewish community?'

James wrote a note in his desk diary. 'Leave it with me. I'll see what I can do. It's amazing the magic you can work when you know the father of an ex-serviceman whose face you put back together.' He winked.

'What have I done to deserve you?' Kitty asked, leaning over the desk and kissing him on the lips, acknowledging that their little spat was over.

Buoyed by James's kindness and inspired by his comments, that she'd always stood up for what she believed in, she left

James's office and marched straight over to Matron Pratt's room. It was time to stand up and be counted, not just for her patients, friends and family members, but for herself; for her and James. She knew James Williams was the love of her life, and she wouldn't make him wait another year to be married.

She knocked on the door, her pulse racing so fast and with such force that she could feel it pounding in her neck.

'Kitty!' Matron Pratt beckoned her into her office. She held her hand up. 'Just signing off on something. Give me a second, will you?' She inked her name on some document, pressed a blotter onto it, put the lid on her fountain pen and turned around, wearing a weary expression. 'How can I help?'

Kitty balled her fists determinedly. 'It's about getting married,' she said. 'I just want you to know that I intend to marry Dr Williams but I also fully intend to remain a nurse at Park Hospital. I don't know if you can sack me, but you need to know I'm not budging. I'm going to have my cake and eat it, like the doctors; like those nurses in Derbyshire. And if that means I have to travel to 10 Downing Street and stand outside until the prime minister listens to me, I will.'

Without waiting for a response, she turned and walked away, leaving the matron open-mouthed and wide-eyed. Then, Kitty searched the nurses' home, eventually finding Grace, Rijuta and Lily chatting in the small laundry. Grace was busy hanging her freshly washed smalls on a clothes horse, Lily was scrubbing a cardigan at the steel sink, using a back scrubbing brush, while Rijuta was carefully ironing a jewel-coloured sari. The piles of still-crumpled fabric lay in a heap on the clean floor in front of the ironing board.

'Ladies, it's time to speak up for yourselves. It's time to stand in front of that board and demand what you want.' She grinned, feeling a hot ball of determination fire up in her belly.

'What's got into you?' Lily asked. 'Did the old matron leave you what was left in her sherry bottle?'

'What are you on about?' Grace asked. 'We're doing our laundry.'

'No, you're not,' Kitty said, folding her arms, feeling the fatigue from the last few days drop away from her like a reptile's spent skin. 'You're coming with me to the board meeting of the directors to tell them about the truck you've been getting from the doctors and the other girls and the patients. Right now,' she pointed at them, 'you've got a date with destiny.'

Rijuta exchanged a bemused glance with Grace. 'Are you feeling quite well, Kitty?' she asked. 'Do you need a sit-down or a glass of water?'

'There's nothing wrong with me. I'm never better. Now put that iron down to cool, and come with me.'

Biting her lip, Rijuta continued to iron. 'Oh, I don't know about that, Kitty. I don't want to get the sack. There's people relying on me to send money back home.'

Kitty looked at Lily. 'Come on, Lil. Time to stand up for yourself.'

'I haven't got the energy, Kitty,' Lily said. 'The old matron never took my complaints seriously in all the years I've worked here. Why would the likes of Baird-Murray and his cronies listen? Besides, I got grease on my best cardy.'

Kitty turned to Grace for the streak of bravery and defiance that she knew her friend had. 'What about you? Don't you want to fight back?'

Crouching, Grace looked thoughtfully at her clean smalls on the bottom rung of the clothes horse. Then, she suddenly got to her feet. She turned to Lily and Rijuta. 'Don't make me do this alone, ladies.'

Together, the four nurses marched back over to the hospital and burst into the board meeting without knocking. Kitty knew she would get into a world of trouble, but at the moment when she saw the look of surprise on the men's faces and heard the cries of indignant outrage, she didn't care.

'I'm sorry to interrupt, gentlemen,' she said. 'Except, actually, I'm not sorry at all.' She locked eyes momentarily with James. The tendon in his jaw started to flinch.

'Sister Longthorne,' Professor Baird-Murray said, puffing on his cigar, 'this is very irregular. We are in the middle of a meeting and you are not an agenda item.'

James shifted in his seat and cleared his throat. 'Actually, chaps, I think we should hear the ladies out, since they've taken the trouble to come here in their own time.'

'Nonsense!' Sir Basil Ryder-Smith said. 'We can't have four girls barging in and interrupting directorial business. It's not the way this hospital works.'

James stood up, spread his hands wide on the board table and leaned towards the consultant radiologist. 'It's 1951, Basil. Maybe we should move with the times and listen to what these medical professional *women* have to say. They are our colleagues, after all. Not the domestic help.'

Kitty nodded her thanks, inwardly flushed with delight that he'd stood his ground with the other consultants, as he'd promised he would. 'Thank you, Dr Williams.' She turned to Baird-Murray, knowing she was reliant on getting his attention if she was to be listened to at all. 'Professor, this will only take a moment of your time, but this is a matter of the utmost importance that needs addressing urgently.'

Professor Baird-Murray blew his smoke towards her and then looked at the stubby, glowing end of his cigar. He raised his eyebrows. 'Fire away. But make it snappy.'

With a thundering heartbeat, Kitty told the board about what she'd witnessed happen to the Levines.

'How is this anything to do with the hospital?' one of the consultants asked.

Kitty tried to keep her voice loud and strong. 'They were already being picked on by the father of one of the other little lads on my ward. You should hear the unpleasant things said about them, just because they're Jews.'

'Nonsense. I don't believe it,' Ryder-Smith said. 'That lot are always moaning.'

'With all due respect, Professor, I'm Jewish,' Lily said. 'I get people having a dig at my religion all the time. My German accent, too.'

'And us nurses who have come from the colonies,' Grace said. 'We're supposed to be the heroines that have saved the National Health Service, but we're not even being paid what we were promised. And people think nothing of saying nasty things about our skin colour. Not just the patients but some of the other staff, too.'

'I'm sure you're looking for offence where there is none intended,' an ear, nose and throat consultant said.

'I'm doing no such thing,' Grace said, hand on hip. 'I'm Black, not green.'

Rijuta nodded. 'It's better on the polio ward, but before that, some of the adult patients wouldn't let me touch them or handle their food and drink, but they were happy to let me clean up after them. I'm a senior nurse with years of training behind me. I came to Britain to tend the sick. I didn't think I'd end up treated like this.'

They fell silent. Kitty could see that the doctors were absorbing what they had just been told. Dare she allow some hope to blossom that Park Hospital could become a more welcoming place, even as Manchester itself was riven by tensions?

Professor Baird-Murray broke the silence. 'I don't believe there is any law that says a British subject cannot pass comment on somebody's appearance, Sister Longthorne. This hospital seeks to uphold the law.'

'But last year, we did have a European Human Rights Convention, which, I believe, is being ratified in Britain this year, if it hasn't already been so. It includes nationalities within European countries borders – all entitled to the same rights.'

'Great Britain is a sovereign state,' Sir Basil Ryder-Smith said. 'We're not being held over a legal barrel by the Frogs or the Hun.'

James shook his head. 'Have some common human decency, man. How hard would it be to draw up a simple code of conduct for the hospital, asking staff and patients to behave in a gentlemanly manner towards each other, regardless of colour, creed or political beliefs?'

Kitty studied the professor's face, trying to ascertain whether or not he was absently puffing on his cigar or giving serious thought to what James had said.

'It would help Park Hospital cement its reputation as a trailblazer,' Kitty said, willing the stuffy old guard to relent. 'Isn't that what Bevan chose us for? Isn't that why we made history as the first National Health Service hospital?'

The professor scrutinised her with hooded eyes in silence for what seemed like an eternity. Finally, he looked at James. 'Very well. You want this? You can oversee some code of conduct nonsense that tackles the problem. We can't have patients' family members being burnt to a crisp on our account.' Then he turned to Kitty. 'Does Matron Pratt know about this little coup?'

Kitty shook her head. 'She had nothing to do with it. If there's a ringleader, then it's me and only me.'

'Then I shall ask her to dock your wages for insubordination, young lady,' he said. Was there a glimmer of a smile on his lips? 'You may go.' He clicked his fingers and pointed to the door. 'Out!'

Once back in the corridor, Lily, Grace and Rijuta rounded on Kitty, all wearing concerned expressions.

'Oh, Kitty, you're in trouble. I'm so sorry,' Lily said.

'We could have a whip-round to replace any money he takes off you,' Rijuta said.

Grace merely sighed and squeezed Kitty's hand. 'You're a good woman to have beside us in a fight, Kitty Longthorne.'

Kitty merely shrugged and then grinned. 'I'm not bothered about losing a couple of shillings out of my measly pay. The main thing is, we finally made some progress with those old dinosaurs. We won!'

Chapter 30

'Right, now we've got two new admissions before lunch,' Kitty told her senior nurses. Sitting behind her desk, she re-read the information that had been telephoned over from other hospitals. 'A girl's coming in from Pendlebury with minor paralysis – Hilda Deacon, aged seven. She needs a bed. And a boy's coming in from Booth Hall – Bobby Goodyear, aged nine. He needs an iron lung as he's apparently in quite bad shape.'

'Where are we going to find the space?' one of the nurses asked.

Kitty checked her discharge list and the notes from the night-shift Sister and Dr Bourke's rounds. 'Gordon Spencer and little Alice Keagan are both being discharged home in about an hour. Their parents are coming in to collect them.' She smiled, feeling like the sun was shining a little brighter through the window. Discharging patients who were well on the road to recovery was always a happy event. 'So I'll need the bed turning and the iron lung will need a full deep clean and safety check.'

She was just about to issue further instructions when she heard a man's voice, just outside her door.

'I'm looking for a Sister Kitty Longthorne,' the man said.

Kitty heard Rijuta respond. 'Oh. She's in a meeting at the moment.'

'I'm afraid this can't wait.'

'She's in her office. In there.'

One of the senior nurses in her office had started to speak, but Kitty held her hand up. 'Hang on, Gwen.' She looked over to the doorway and balked at the sight of a tall policeman, as he knocked on the architrave and locked eyes with her. He was so broad, he almost filled the entire space. 'Can I help you?' she asked.

'Sister Kitty Longthorne?' He toyed with the brim of his bobby's hat. The buttons on his uniform gleamed.

'Yes, I'm she.'

'Can I have a word?'

She glanced at the other nurses, some of whom were elbowing one another. 'Is this regarding one of my patients?' She chuckled. 'Only the average age is about six, so I don't think you're going to find any criminal element among them, unless there's a new law about persistent nose-pickers. Some of them are just about well enough to do that.' She smiled at the other nurses, but inwardly, she could feel her gut tightening. There was only one person this visit could be about.

'Actually, no. It's not about a patient. It's a . . . er . . . perhaps we could speak in private.'

Kitty ushered the other nurses back outside, beckoned the policeman into the office and closed the door. She gestured that he should sit in the visitor's chair and took her seat behind the desk, wishing the bulk of the desk could protect her from what was certain to come.

'Go on,' she said, sighing.

The constable cleared his throat. 'It's about your brother, Ned Longthorne. He's been arrested.'

'I know, I know.' Kitty massaged her forehead with her fingertips. 'I don't speak to him for ages, and then the first time I lay eyes on him, he's getting strong-armed onto the ground by a copper. Typical. He's been done for brawling, hasn't he?'

'It's rather more serious than that, I'm afraid. I came to tell you that he's being charged with grievous bodily harm and damage to public property, amongst other offences. He's been given a Legal Aid solicitor.'

'That's new, isn't it?'

The policeman nodded. 'Well, they introduced it a couple of years ago. It means your brother gets free legal representation because he's officially destitute.'

'But he works at the biscuit factory. He's a shop steward for the trade union, last I heard.'

The policeman looked down at his helmet, which he'd removed and placed on his lap. 'I'm told his employer sacked him.'

Kitty groaned, silently acknowledging that Grace had been wise to break off her engagement to Ned. '*There's* a surprise.' She didn't bother trying to keep the sarcasm out of her voice. 'What about bail? He's been stewing a day or two, now. When are we getting the idiot back?'

'He's already been to court for a bail hearing, but the judge has refused bail, I'm afraid.'

Kitty rolled her eyes, relieved that there was no mention of Ned's involvement with the Communist Party. 'Well, there's no money for bail, anyway. We're not a rich family. He'll have to rot in a cell until the case goes to trial.' Then she realised that something rather more serious was implied by what the policeman had said, and she could almost feel the blood drain from her face. She wrapped her arms around herself so that the policeman wouldn't see her shiver with adrenalin. 'Hang on a minute. I thought the only people who had bail denied were murderers and enemies of the state and that. Serious criminals. My brother's just an idiot, and a war hero to boot. Denying him bail's a joke, right?'

She let the words hang in the air, keen to see what, if anything, the policeman revealed next.

The policeman leaned back in the visitor's chair and crossed his left foot over his right. 'Seems the judge didn't see the funny side of it. The lad he gave a good kicking is in a bad way at the Infirmary. If you want to visit your brother, he's being held on remand in Strangeways until his trial.'

'Is that what you came to tell me?' Kitty asked. 'Only really, you should be telling my mother, and she lives in Wythenshawe.'

The policeman took out his notebook and a pencil. 'Well, actually, I need a statement. I understand that you were a witness to the riot.'

'Like I say, it was more of a brawl,' Kitty said, trying to see what he was writing in his pad. 'And I left with the ambulances.'

'Look, I attended the scene, Sister, and I saw the remnants of the Molotov cocktails and bricks that had been thrown by both sides.' His eyes narrowed and his gaze felt accusatory. 'I can tell you uncategorically that it didn't look like your average brawl to me. You're dealing with fascists and communists. We know Mr Longthorne is a member of the local Communist Party. And we know he's been a suspect in the past connected with a counterfeiting ring.'

Swallowing hard, Kitty felt as if the temperature in the room had dropped yet again. She cast her mind back to her father going to prison for having stolen a truckload of silk from the Dunlop factory during the war. Would she never be rid of the shame and embarrassment that came with being a Longthorne?

'My dad gave enough information to take the whole counterfeiting ring down,' she said, trying to hold the policeman's gaze. The last thing she wanted was to appear intimidated. Longthornes didn't back down. 'That's a closed chapter and my dad's pushing up daisies, so I don't know why you're bringing it up now.'

'I'm bringing it up because your brother's in hot water, as things stand. If the lad that he beat up dies, it's murder. The police has to find out exactly what went on that day.'

Kitty gripped the edge of the desk in a bid to steady herself. Might she be compelled by the prosecution to give evidence against Ned in court? Or could she give evidence to support him, since his solicitor could argue that he'd been defending the Levines? In truth, she didn't want to get involved in the matter at all as a witness, especially not if Ned's involvement with the Communist Party was under scrutiny by the powers-that-be. She hastily considered her options and came up with an excuse that she hoped would neither damn Ned nor involve herself any further.

'My memory of the day's a bit sketchy,' she said. 'I had a bin lid over my head for most of it – protection, like – so I couldn't really see what was going on. All I know is, I'd gone to check on the parents of one of my patients because they hadn't shown up to an important meeting with their son's consultant.'

'Do you normally visit patients, Sister?' The policeman was scribbling away in his pad. His mouth was downturned. His eyebrow was arched.

'They only live round the corner from my mam's, so popping round wasn't a problem. We were coming back from my mam's birthday day out, see?'

'What did you see?'

'Fighting in the street. I somehow battled my way through . . . I was just focused on rescuing an innocent couple from a burning building.'

'And your brother?'

'I didn't spot Ned until I was getting in the ambulance with the Levines. I was surprised to see him there. I don't know the extent of his involvement in any of it, but he does live locally with my mam, as I said, so maybe him being there was just a coincidence. Maybe he was just defending himself. And maybe, where he's concerned, the police are just getting the wrong end of the stick.'

Had she said the right thing? Kitty couldn't be sure. She neither wanted to lie, nor did she want to make matters worse for Ned. He was family, after all.

'Is that it?' she said. 'Only, I've got a busy ward to run and I've got nothing else to say.'

'That's all, Sister.' The policeman said, closing his notebook. 'For now, at least, though I can't guarantee you won't be called to testify in court.'

'But I don't want to get involved.' The very thought of standing in a witness box made Kitty's blood all but freeze in her veins.

He got to his feet and turned to her, grim-faced. 'It's not necessarily up to you. If the prosecution wants you to testify, you'll be compelled to do it. Don't leave town.'

Swallowing hard, Kitty hastened over to James's clinic as soon as she was able. She had to wait for what seemed like forever until he opened his door and his previous patient left.

'Kitty?' James said. 'You're as white as a sheet. Whatever's the matter?' He closed the door behind her.

Kitty turned to her fiancé with tears in her eyes. 'I've just had a copper on the ward, asking questions about our Ned's involvement in that riot outside the Levines' house. I think this is it, James. I think our Ned's going to prison. They're going to lock him up and throw away the key.'

James stroked her cheek, his black eyebrows bunching together as he studied her face. 'He'll need a character witness,' he said. 'I'll do it.'

'No!' Kitty stepped back. 'You can't. He's my brother and I love the bones of him, but we mustn't get dragged into this. How do we know this arrest isn't a pretext for Ned being tried for treason? I won't see you hang for him. Guilt by association, and all that.'

'Guilt by association, Kitty?' James said. 'Really? I like to think our legal system is robust enough to protect us against that.'

'Your memory's short, James Williams. Have you forgotten how we got snatched off the street and interrogated? Have you forgotten about that radio equipment in George's place?' She felt tears of fear and frustration prick at the backs of her eyes. 'Let's be honest. What can you even truthfully say in Ned's favour?'

Chapter 31

Later that week, when their time off coincided, Kitty and Grace caught the bus into the centre of Manchester and walked a quarter of a mile northwards to Strangeways Prison.

'If my mumma knew I was visiting a man in prison, I'd be for the high jump,' Grace said, looking around. 'I hope nobody from the church recognises me. I'll never be able to hold my head high again.' She pulled the brim of her hat a little lower on her head.

Kitty patted her shoulder affectionately. 'It's a good deed, what you're doing, and you'll be able to put your history with Ned into a box, and shove it in the dusty old storeroom of life experience.'

Grace chuckled. 'Yes. I suppose so. I wish it hadn't turned out this way.'

'Don't we both,' Kitty said, feeling her heart sink at the sight of the red-brick, Victorian wings that were like spokes on a wheel around the octagonal central building of Strangeways. The giant watchtower seemed to leer down at them. 'The last time I spoke to our Ned, I gave him a right dressing down. Now . . . what if he gets convicted?'

They climbed the hill of Southall Street, passing the courts, and found themselves in the shadow of the main entrance.

'It looks terrifying,' Grace said.

'There's a feller just been hung here. Took them seven minutes, from leaving his cell to falling through the trap door.' She shuddered and lowered her voice. 'I pray to God they won't change Ned's charges from GBH to treason.' Then, trying to lighten the mood, she nudged Grace. 'Guess how thick the walls are.'

Grace shook her head. 'Too thick for Ned to break through, that's for sure. Though it wouldn't surprise me if he sweet-talked his way out.'

Inside, they were shown to the visiting room and Ned was brought to them, clad in the prison's uniform. The side of Ned's face that hadn't been badly burned in the explosion at sea was unshaven – the shadow beneath his one good eye spoke to sleepless nights. On the scarred part of his face, the skin was waxen, as if he wasn't seeing enough sunlight.

'You look a mess,' Kitty said, wishing she could just embrace her brother; that they could go back to their childhood and try again to divert him from this fate.

'Ta,' Ned said. He only had eyes for Grace, though. The Adam's apple in his neck pinged up and down. 'Gracie. You came.'

Grace looked around at the barred windows and the visiting families of the other inmates. 'Maybe I shouldn't have done.' She tutted and sucked on her back teeth. 'I don't know why I'm even here.'

'Because you still love me?' Ned leaned forward. There was hope in his good eye.

'We had everything, and you threw it all away, Ned Longthorne.' Grace folded her arms and scowled at him. Tears started to roll onto her cheeks. 'How could you start with such good intentions – defending my honour – and end up in here? How, Ned? You chose a band of brainwashed Reds over me. Over our future.'

'I wanted to do what's right.' Ned spoke so quietly, he could almost not be heard. He looked down at his lap.

Kitty clicked her fingers until he gave her his full attention. 'No, Ned. You wanted to be popular.' She pointed at him in frustration. 'This is what you've *always* done. Dad did it too. You confuse being popular with being loved, and it's not the same thing. You stayed loyal to the wrong people, because that lot of commie idiots didn't pull you up when you said something stupid or kick you out when you'd gone too far. They told you what you wanted to hear. They used you as muscle, they pushed you into the spotlight and made you take all the heat when things went wrong. What did you get in return, exactly?'

'A sense of doing the right thing,' Ned said sullenly.

'Rubbish. You got paid in empty praise and a spell at His Majesty's leisure. You're a berk, Ned Longthorne. You never learn, and now you'll do time for strangers.'

Ned frowned and sat up straighter. 'Why did you come, Kitty?' He turned to Grace. 'And you. Did you come to gloat?'

Grace stood to leave, pulling her gloves back on with tears standing in her eyes. 'I came to say goodbye. So long, Ned.' She left the room.

Kitty remained at the table, studying her brother's anguished face. 'I came to wish you luck in the trial. You're still my brother and I still love you, you daft 'a-peth. Grace did right to leave, but me and you – we're blood. I'll always be here, even if it means visiting you in this godforsaken place. Idiot.'

Finally, Ned smiled. 'You're a good'un, our kid.'

'And you owe James a pint if you ever get out of here.'

*

When the trial came around two months later, Kitty sat in the viewing gallery, so nervous that she was barely able to breathe. On one side sat her mother, drained of all colour and seeming quite insubstantial, as though she were being projected into the courtroom like a clip from a film. On the other side sat James, stroking Kitty's hand.

'I'm dreading this,' Mam said. She turned to Kitty with a film of tears over her bloodshot eyes. 'What if that lad died and they do our Ned for murder? What if him rubbing shoulders with a bunch of commies gets him the death sentence?'

Kitty put her arm around her. 'Come on, Mam. You're overreacting. I'm fairly sure that lad's well out of the hospital by now. And Ned's too thick to be passing secrets behind the Iron Curtain.'

James leaned over so that Mam could hear him. 'Chin up, Elsie. Ned could charm the birds from the trees. He'll be fine and dandy.'

'Oh, I hope you're right, love.'

When Ned came into the courtroom, the expectant chatter of the jury and spectators grew so loud that the judge was forced to bash his gavel to bring hush to the place. Kitty caught sight of the courtroom artist, sketching Ned standing in the dock, wearing a suit and tie that James had given him. Ned looked at them and smiled weakly. He was sworn in and the case proceeded.

The evidence delivered by the prosecution seemed scant, Kitty thought. The lad who had been injured testified, although Ned's terribly young-looking barrister quickly discredited him as a Union Movement fascist. The only other witnesses called to testify against Ned were a woman from the Levines' street, who had apparently had her parlour window smashed by a brick that Ned had allegedly lobbed, and the arresting police officer, who had cuffed him. When Ned's previous boss climbed into the witness box to testify to his character, however, Kitty felt like she was being dragged down by a lead weight.

'That Ned Longthorne gave me nothing but trouble,' the manager of the biscuit factory said. 'The minute he started, he was terrible at sorting the biscuits. In fact, he ate most of 'em or stole them and took them home.' The man sneered at Ned. 'And then blow me, if he didn't get involved with the trade union, stoking up all manner of discontent and rabble-rousing. I didn't give a so-called war hero a job so he could fleece me for misshaped biscuits and then get everyone to go on strike.' He waved his fist at Ned. 'Bloody Red!'

'Order, order!' The judge banged his gavel again. 'Please contain your excitement, Mr Menzies. You're in a court of law, not the saloon of a public house.'

Menzies was led out, and Ned's barrister got to his feet. 'Your Honour, I'd like to call to the stand, Dr James Williams.'

Kitty held her breath as James made his way confidently to the witness box. He was asked to place his hand on the Bible to be sworn in.

'Now, Dr Williams – or should I say, Mr Williams, since you're a surgeon?' The barrister began. 'Is that correct?'

'That's correct, yes. I'm a consultant plastic surgeon at Park Hospital in Davyhulme.' James looked straight at the jury. 'And on the hospital's board of directors.'

'A pillar of the community.' The barrister turned to the jury and smiled. 'Ladies and gentlemen of the jury, this morning, the prosecution has asked you to hear testimony given as to the character of Mr Longthorne – all of it damning, and most of it circumstantial. For balance, I'd like to offer you the opportunity to hear a rather different story about Mr Longthorne.' He turned back to James. 'Now, I understand you've known Mr Longthorne for a long time. Can I ask in what capacity you're going to talk about his character today, please?'

'I'm his soon-to-be brother-in-law.'

A murmur of intrigue rippled around the courtroom. Kitty could see that people were obviously incredulous that this impeccably dressed, well-spoken doctor should have anything to do with the likes of Ned.

'Please tell the jury what you know about Mr Longthorne.'

A glimmer of a smile flickered on James's lips. 'Well, I first met Ned when he came back from the Far East. His sister, Kitty, was one of the junior nurses at the hospital – she was still just a friend at that time. She asked me to take a look at Ned because his injuries from an explosion at sea were dire. I reconstructed his face over the course of many surgeries. He seemed a charming chap – a little rough around the edges, but well intentioned and a real war hero. Obviously, at that stage, I only knew him as a patient, but Kitty and I began courting, and I got to know Ned better.'

Kitty's heart swelled with pride as she heard how confidently James spoke. Though all eyes were on him, including reporters from the *Manchester Evening News*, and though the court artist was sketching him with vigour, he sounded as if he were simply delivering a report to the board of directors at the hospital.

'How did you find Mr Longthorne, once you got to know him better?'

James shrugged. 'He's headstrong and a little naïve, but he's always had a good heart. He loves his family. He champions the underdog. I'd say Ned's jolly well intentioned but liable to be led astray by the wrong company.'

'Such as the Communist Party? We've heard from the prosecution that Mr Longthorne's a fully paid-up member of the Communist Party.'

'Yes. I believe Ned got involved in politics simply because he wanted to do something to defend his West Indian ex-fiancée against the fascist rabble that have been harassing Manchester's most recent immigrants. Naturally, I couldn't comment on what he was doing on that street on the day of the fighting. It's true that he does live only two streets away, and I don't doubt that any man would defend himself if a fascist attacked him apropos of nothing, on his way home.'

'Objection, Your Honour!' the prosecuting barrister shouted. 'That's hearsay.'

The judge ordered the stenographer to strike James's theory from the record, dismissed James, and then asked the prosecution and the defence to address the jury with their closing statements.

The prosecuting barrister took to the floor, damning Ned with great flourish as a trouble-maker, a communist threat to the status quo and a violent thug. Ned's barrister, however, delivered a heartfelt defence to jurors who seemed as though they might be lenient, when it came to the ill-conceived antics of a severely disfigured war hero.

By the time the verdict was to be read out, Kitty felt lightheaded, clinging desperately onto the hope that there was reasonable doubt in at least one juror's mind.

The judge peered over his pince-nez at Ned. 'Edward Longthorne. You have been charged with an array of serious crimes.' He read the list of allegations and turned to the jury. 'How do you find the accused?'

The head juror stood up and read from a piece of paper. 'We find the accused guilty, Your Honour.'

At her side, Mam groaned. 'Oh, sweet Jesus. My boy's going to prison.'

Kitty looked at James for comfort but could see only panic in his eyes. She turned to her mother, patting her hand. 'It'll be all right, Mam. You'll see.'

Mam shook her head. 'No, they're going to throw the book at him. He'll get life.'

'Just . . . just wait and see. It's not over yet.'

The judge ordered silence in the courtroom for sentencing. He stared down at a whey-faced Ned. 'Edward Longthorne, it is only thanks to your victim's recovery that you are not in this dock for murder. You have shown yourself to be argumentative and unwilling to obey rules. Nevertheless, I believe that your intentions were good, and you have an exemplary service record, having helped several Allied soldiers to escape a Japanese prisoner-of-war camp back in 1945. Taking your previous good behaviour and the testimony of Mr Williams into account, I sentence you to two years' imprisonment.' He banged his gavel and dismissed the court.

'Thanks, Your Honour.' Ned looked down at Kitty, her mother and James, grinning and giving a thumbs-up.

Kitty shook her head, but was smiling. 'He'll be out in eighteen months with good behaviour. I hope to high heaven he thinks hard about the company he keeps and the choices he makes while he's inside.'

Chapter 32

'Your burns are healing nicely,' James said, placing the dressings back on Esther Levine's face. 'Better than I could have hoped, actually.' He turned to Dovid, seated in the adjacent visitor's chair in James's examination room. Carefully, he lifted the dressing and peered at the skin beneath. 'In your case, it's as I thought. You're going to need a small skin graft,' he said, 'but I can carry out the surgery at Crumpsall Hospital and I'm confident of the result.'

Kitty, who had been perched on the edge of the examination couch in the corner, stood up. She smiled. 'So how's it feel to be finally getting out of the temporary lodgings where you've been staying?'

Esther gathered up her coat and bag. 'All we have is the clothes we're standing in and our lives. But I can't wait to have a home we can call our own.'

James dangled his car keys before them. 'Now, I deliberately booked your appointment late in the day. You're my last patients of the evening. Shall we go and see the new bungalow?'

'You're a good man,' Dovid said, draping his arm across Esther's shoulders. 'The thought of living near Cheetham is a dream. It's so nice and green in Crumpsall.'

'And the bungalow will make it easy for Sammy to whizz around in his wheelchair,' Kitty said. 'Speaking of whom . . .. Shall we go and get your boy?'

Esther beamed and clapped her hands together. 'Yes. In a day full of miracles, this is the best news of all. My boy's finally coming home.' She clasped Kitty in a bear hug. 'How can I ever thank you for taking such good care of my Sammy?'

Kitty chuckled and patted her on the back. 'It's my job,' she said. 'Though Sammy has been one of my favourite patients. I'm just sorry he won't be walking home.'

'We have to look on the bright side.' Dovid said. 'So many children have died from polio. But in our case, God's been good. We get to keep him.'

On the way out to James's Ford, they stopped at the children's polio ward and collected little Sammy, who was waiting for his parents with Rijuta by the doors.

'Look, Sammy!' Rijuta said as they entered the ward. 'Here they are. It's your mummy and daddy, come to take you home, at last.'

Kitty looked down at the tiny figure in the wheelchair, and her heart melted as the little boy gazed up at his parents with obvious love and undisguised glee in his large brown eyes. 'Hurray!'

Esther and Dovid fell to their knees and greeted the wheelchair-bound little boy with a flurry of kisses.

'Oh, bubbele, it's so wonderful to be taking you home – to our brand new prefab bungalow too,' Esther said.

'We've not even seen it ourselves yet,' Dovid said. 'But I'm told there's a garden for you to play in and a really lovely school nearby.' He took the handles of the wheelchair from Rijuta, thanked her and wheeled Sammy into the corridor.

Kitty and James followed behind, listening to the reunited family talk excitedly about their future. James surreptitiously took hold of Kitty's hand and squeezed it.

'So, little Sammy has come to terms with his old house having gone up in flames?' he asked quietly.

'Thankfully. That boy's got a lot to wrap his head around. Badly burnt parents who he didn't see for weeks on end. A new home in a new part of town. A life where he'll likely never walk again.' Kitty exhaled hard. 'Children are so resilient. Sometimes, it's overwhelming to watch them suffering on the ward, but the ones who get to go home just seem to bounce back, no matter how the odds are stacked against them.'

'I pray our children will lead wonderful, charmed lives,' James said. 'And I hope to God that by the time we have a family, there's a vaccine against polio. Maybe even other diseases that ravage childhoods.'

They reached the car, and Kitty helped to settle Sammy into the back seat with his parents, while James folded the boy's wheelchair and hefted it into the boot of the car.

In the dwindling autumn evening light, they made their way through town and over to the north side of the city. Kitty noticed how the main road up to Cheetham Hill village was studded with raincoat factories and synagogues. She cast her mind back to 1947, the time when Mam had moved to the dreaded Salford Brow, where they'd endured the harshest of winters in a cockroach-infested ice box of a flat. It hadn't suited her mam to live this side of town, but Kitty could see that Cheetham and the leafier suburb of Crumpsall would make a good home for the Levines.

'Here we are,' James said, pulling up outside a picture-perfect prefabricated bungalow. 'Newly built, with all mod cons. I've asked my pal at the council to deliver ramps for Sammy's wheelchair. I'm told they should arrive in the morning.' He reached into the breast pocket of his jacket and produced three sets of keys. He handed them to Dovid. 'All yours.'

Kitty grinned as she saw Dovid take the keys with a slightly trembling hand.

He wore a look of relief and shook his head. 'I can't believe this. I can't believe how lucky we've been because of you two. My son's life was saved, our lives were saved, and now we have a house we can make a home, in a lovely area, too.' He shook James's hand. 'You're a mensch, Dr Williams.' He locked eyes with Kitty. 'You too. Both of you are menschen. Do you know what that means?'

'I'm told it means we're decent sorts,' James said, blinking hard and starting to blush.

'You're more than that,' Esther said. 'Mensch is the ultimate compliment you can get from a Jew. And you both deserve it. Thank you so much for all you've done.'

'Well, we've got one more little surprise,' Kitty said. She climbed out of the car, walked around to the boot and opened it. Next to the folded wheelchair was a large box. She tried to lift it out, but it was too heavy. 'Give me a hand with this, will you, James?'

James came to her aid, and together, they carried the box up the path and set it down in front of the Levines' new front door.

'What's in the big box?' Esther asked, as she helped Sammy out of the car.

Dovid took the wheelchair out of the boot and glanced quizzically over his shoulder.

Kitty marched back down the path to show him how to open the chair. 'Well, for a while there, you three started to feel like permanent fixtures at the hospital!' she told Esther, levering the collapsed wheelchair open and locking the mechanism. 'So, word of how ill Sammy's been and how your house and your worldly goods went for a Burton travelled like wildfire round the hospital.' She smirked. 'If you excuse the pun. Anyway, we had a bit of a whip-round, and the collection went rather well. So, in that box, you'll find everything you need to set up – basics like bedding, pots and pans, crockery and that. The doctors were all asked if they had any spare furniture going, and James arranged for some bits and bobs to be put in ready for you.'

'Yes, you've at least got beds for the night, something to sit on and a cooker.' James had wandered back down the path. 'Here! I'll give you a hand carrying this strapping little fellow up the steps and over the threshold.'

Kitty noticed that tears stood in Esther's eyes. 'Ooh, hey, what's all this about? It's not a time for tears. You've got a new home to explore.'

Esther's chin dimpled. Her voice cracked as she spoke. 'I'm . . . I'm speechless.' She clasped Kitty's hands inside hers. 'I'll never forget this.' She shook her head vehemently. 'Never, as long as I live. Same goes for the other staff. I've never known kindness like it. Please thank them from the bottom of our hearts for their generosity.'

'I will,' Kitty said. 'They're not a bad bunch when they make an effort.'

'And please thank Ned, when you next see him. If you see him,' Dovid said. A shadow seemed to dim his smile. 'I know he's paid for our lives with his liberty. That's quite some self-sacrifice. He's a good man. An idealist. There aren't many left in the world.'

As Esther, Dovid and Sammy unlocked the door to the bungalow and stepped inside, Kitty thought about how it might feel to have her own house, instead of sleeping in the narrow, uncomfortable bed in the nurses' home, as she had for all these years. She imagined crossing the threshold of a spacious new family home, picturing all the life events that might come to pass under that roof. Married life. Children. Birthdays and Christmases. Family get-togethers. All the small memories that actually meant everything to a person when they eventually reached the end of their life.

She and James stood on the doorstep, arm in arm, peering into the small but perfectly formed prefab. It still had that fresh paint smell from its construction. The floors were bare of any covering, and the footsteps of the Levines and the squeaking of the wheels on Sammy's wheelchair echoed around the almost empty place. Outside, the garden was still little more than rubble and topsoil, marking the spot where a bombsite had been cleared. Kitty could see its potential, however. She turned to James, feeling satisfied.

'Time to go, my love.' She patted his arm and winked. 'Let's leave the Levines to their new life and head back to our side of town.'

They took their leave and drove back in near silence.

Eventually, Kitty was the first to speak. 'It's time for us to start our new life, isn't it?'

James brought the car to a halt at a red traffic light. He leaned towards her and kissed her tenderly on her cheek. 'Yes, 1952, darling – it's almost upon us. The first chapter in the story of James and Kitty Williams, husband and wife.'

1952

Chapter 33

'Let's get this gentleman seen by a doctor straight away,' Kitty told Molly Bickerstaff, as the ambulance drivers stretchered in an unconscious man whose limbs lay at untoward angles. His head was a bloodied mess. 'Set him up in bay three. Let's try to bring him round, but don't move his head.'

Molly looked at the patient and balked. 'He looks like he's been shot out of a cannon into a brick wall.'

'Not far from it,' Kitty said. 'Apparently he was knocked off his motorcycle on a country lane in Flixton.'

'A truck, going too fast, I heard,' the ambulance driver said. 'Truck skidded on some ice. Witness who called the ambulance said our daredevil, here, hadn't been wearing a crash helmet.'

Kitty shook her head and tutted. 'They never learn. One day they'll make crash helmets compulsory. You mark my words.' She turned back to Molly. 'See if Thistlethwaite will take a look at this patient. Tell him it might be a spinal injury.'

No sooner had she issued instructions than her attention was demanded by a heavily pregnant woman who had wandered into casualty in the throes of labour, only for her waters to break all over the floor.

'Help this lady up to the labour ward, nurse!' Kitty told one of the junior nurses. 'And somebody get a mop and bucket.'

Casualty had always been mayhem in early February, but since Kitty had moved shifts from her long stint on the children's polio ward, it seemed even more chaotic than ever. Standing in the packed waiting room full of people who had slipped on treacherous ice or else were brought low by all manner of winter illnesses, she was just musing that there was noticeably more traffic on the road when another ambulance driver ran in, shouting.

'Whatever is the matter, Clive?' Kitty asked, unable to make out what he was saying.

'The King is dead!' he said breathlessly. 'King George is dead. I've just heard it from someone who heard it on the wireless.'

Kitty looked at him askance. In her peripheral vision, she spotted those patients who had appeared to be half asleep in their chairs only moments earlier now craning their necks to see what the kerfuffle was about.

'Hang on,' she said. 'You heard it from who, exactly?'

'Trev. He went off shift, but hung around to have a brew with the other ambulance lads. They were sat round the fire in our little room, trying to keep warm between callouts, you know? And listening to the BBC, like. News comes on: "The King is dead."'

Clasping her hand to her chest, Kitty made her way over to the nurses' station in the busy casualty, where she knew a wireless had been kept since the war years. Lily was standing behind the counter, writing waiting times on a blackboard.

Almost tongue-tied by a mixture of excitement and dread, she waved to attract her friend's attention. 'Nurse Schwartz, put the BBC on the wireless, straight away, please.'

'Are you quite all right?' Lily asked. 'You sound rather wobbly.' Then Lily looked over Kitty's shoulder and saw that the waiting room full of the cold, exhausted and injured of Davyhulme had suddenly come alive. 'By heck. Whatever's going on must be pretty important to wake that lot up.'

She took the wireless out from a drawer, set it on the cluttered side full of paperwork and switched it on. It was already tuned into the BBC, but a woman presenter was talking about the Princesses Elizabeth and Margaret and some Royal visit or other.

Kitty looked at the clock. 'It's nearly twelve. They'll have the news on any minute now.'

Sure enough, they heard the pips that signalled the clocks were striking twelve, and the news was due to begin. Kitty heard the familiar voice of the newsreader, John Snagge, as he spoke with great solemnity.

'It is with the greatest sorrow that we make the following announcement . . .'

Kitty gasped as she heard with her own ears that King George VI was, indeed, dead. 'Fifty-six,' she said, turning the wireless off. 'That's no age at all, is it?' A lump in her throat and a tear in her eye took her by surprise. She wiped the tear away hastily. 'Deary me.'

'Heavy smoker, wasn't he?' Lily asked.

'Hundred cigs a day, I heard,' Kitty said, nodding. 'They say Princess Margaret smokes heavy, too.' She cast her mind back to the research that Park Hospital's own heart and lung specialist, Mr Galbraith, had taken part in. 'Galbraith said two years ago that tobacco was a killer. But I could have told him that myself. Watching my dad die from lung cancer was no picnic. Turns out not even royalty's immune to the dangers of smoking.' She sighed heavily.

Lily looked around surreptitiously. 'You'd think the professor would have given up his cigars by now, wouldn't you?'

'A man of his learning should know better. About lots of things.' Kitty thought about how the professor had put up such an almighty fight regarding the introduction of a code of conduct for staff and patients alike. At least progress was finally being made in that regard. 'But the King dying feels like the end of an era. Can you imagine saying, "Long live the *Queen*", and singing the national anthem: "God save our gracious *Queen*"? It sounds weird, doesn't it?'

Lily nodded. 'Weirder still when you were born a German.' She chuckled.

'A queen, indeed! She's very beautiful, is *Queen* Elizabeth. There'll be a coronation and everything, won't there? Blimey. And I suppose we'll get to watch it on the television, now.'

'Speak for yourself,' Lily said. 'No television in the nurses' home. I'll have to watch it at the picture house, like the other lesser mortals.'

Kitty patted her hand. 'You can come round to watch it on James's television *if* we can get the day off.' She gazed wistfully at a photograph of King George VI that hung on the wall of the ward. 'Fancy having another female monarch in Great Britain! A second Elizabethan era. Talk about a brave new world. Who knows what the future will bring, now?'

'Well, your wedding, for a start,' Lily said, smiling. 'Not long 'til June, eh?'

Mention of the wedding caused the wave of grief that had washed over Kitty since hearing the news to subside. 'The best things are worth waiting for. Better get your outfit sorted, Lil.'

Kitty slapped her hand down emphatically on the counter. 'Right. Back to it. The King might have passed away, but I've still got a casualty department full of people trying desperately not to shuffle off their mortal coil.'

*

With the wedding not far off, Kitty and James used any time off they could manage to look for houses. The following Saturday, on a fine, crisp morning, they headed out to Hale near the small market town of Altrincham to look at a 1930s house that James had his eye on.

'I can't wait for you to see it, darling,' he said, driving through a built-up suburban area called Timperley, which Kitty wasn't at all familiar with. 'There was a house up for sale on the adjacent road a year ago, but obviously, we weren't ready yet. Now, though . . .'

Kitty looked out of the car window, noticing how the elegant-looking, frost-covered houses seemed increasingly bigger, the further out of town that they travelled. 'It's green round here, isn't it? Everyone's got big gardens.'

'Perfect for young families,' James said. 'Hale Village is very sweet, though. There's a village butcher and a baker and a beautiful church. A train station with trains to Chester, Stockport and into Manchester.'

'Blimey. You know you're living in the sticks if you have to get a train to town.'

'Nonsense,' he squeezed her knee. 'You must learn to drive, darling, and then we can share the car. Perhaps we can get you your own little run-around.'

They headed into the outskirts of Hale, and Kitty whistled low as she looked at some of the enormous Edwardian houses that she could glimpse on either side of the tree-lined road. Each one was set in its own sprawling gardens. 'You're not taking me to see one of these piles, are you? These are like your parents' place. We can't afford that, even on your wages.'

James grinned. 'Nothing quite that grand. But it is a house we could grow into.'

He pulled onto what Kitty could only describe as a tree-lined boulevard and slowed the car in front of a handsome detached house, almost diagonally opposite a picturesque little red-brick church. The house sat in its own carefully tended gardens, where frosty rhododendrons, blue pines and the tangle of red- and purple-hued branches on deciduous trees and bushes looked like they had been dusted with icing sugar. Kitty felt like Alice, about to step into Wonderland.

'Is this it?' she asked. 'This house is what you're thinking of . . . for *us*?'

'It certainly is.'

She turned to see his face, still not sure whether he was joking or not. 'It must cost thousands.'

'I've got money saved,' James said. 'Plus there'll be the proceeds from selling my flat.'

Kitty puffed air out of her cheeks. 'Yes, but you're not talking about pin money, are you? I heard a two-up, two-down's over a thousand pounds. This is going to cost us an arm and a leg. We'll be too skint to raise a family.'

James took her face in his hands. Though their breath steamed on the air, his touch was warm on the cold morning. 'It's fine. I'm a consultant on the board. I don't work every hour God sends for nothing, Kitty. And besides, a long time ago, my folks offered to give some money towards a house – a wedding present.' He let her go, pulled on his gloves and got out of the car.

'A wedding present for you and Violet, by any chance?'

James didn't answer. 'Well, are you coming to see the place or not?'

The estate agent was already waiting for them inside the house. 'Dr. Williams, I presume?'

James shook hands with him. 'The very same.'

The agent turned to Kitty. 'And you must be the lady of the house? Pleased to meet you, Mrs Williams.'

Kitty laughed. 'Oh, I'm not Mrs Williams 'til the summer, love.'

Looking disconcerted, the estate agent handed her a sheet of paper that contained information regarding the house. 'Very modern, I'm sure.'

When the estate agent's back was turned, James nudged Kitty and winked. He took her by the hand. 'Time to explore.'

They were given the guided tour, and the house could not have been more different to her mam's council house in Wythenshawe or the Levines' prefabricated bungalow in Crumpsall.

'How the other half lives, eh?' she whispered, as the estate agent showed them the enormous living room with its grand Art-Deco fireplace that took centre stage.

'Regard the petrol-coloured tiles of the fireplace's surround,' the agent said with some flourish. 'The stepped mantel is hand-manufactured from solid oak, and covered with the finest ebony and walnut veneers. It wouldn't look out of place in a New York penthouse. A real feature, I'm sure you'll agree.'

Kitty looked up at the tall ceilings, decorated in fan motif mouldings. 'Isn't this all a bit old-fashioned now?'

'If you don't like it, we can change it, darling,' James said. He kissed her hand. 'This is the 1950s – anything's possible.'

The living room faced out onto a square, lawned garden. Kitty could suddenly imagine their future children playing there – perhaps playing hide and seek among the bushes or else swinging from a tyre attached to the sturdy bough of a what looked to be a winter-bare oak. The tree had clearly been there longer than the house. 'Flaming Nora, it's like a little park.' She squeezed James's arm. 'You'll have to take up gardening in your spare time.'

'Spare time!' James wheezed with laughter. 'There's a fantasy. No, I'm quite sure we'll be getting a gardener, darling. And you're bound to need a little domestic help, looking after this place, especially if you're juggling children and a part-time nursing post.'

Part-time? Kitty thought about the concept. She didn't personally know any nurses who were married, let alone who worked part-time. Following Kitty's impassioned visit to Matron Pratt's office, insisting that she be allowed to stay on at the hospital after marriage, the new matron had indeed advocated for her during a board meeting. It had been decided that Kitty would be the first nurse at Park Hospital to keep her post after marriage. With that particular battle won, there was now so much change ahead of her that as she walked up the rather grand staircase and looked around master bedroom, with its far-reaching views of the perfectly manicured surrounding area, she felt rather lightheaded.

'Are you quite all right, Kitty?' James asked, taking her by the elbow as she lurched to the side.

'It's excitement,' she said. She glanced through the open bedroom door and caught a glimpse of the pistachio-coloured bathroom beyond. 'I mean, look at this place. It's not just got an indoor loo, it's got a fitted bathroom suite, like in the Hollywood films!'

The estate agent showed them the bathroom. 'Yes, you'll find that this bathroom is fitted with sanitaryware of the highest quality and finish. You've got your cast-iron bath, enamelled in pistachio, with a matching porcelain WC, a large sink and . . .' He waved at something Kitty had never seen before. 'A bidet.'

'A bee-day? What's that for?' Kitty asked. 'Washing your feet or your smalls?'

'I'll tell you later, darling,' James said, clearly finding something amusing in what she'd said.

As Kitty walked around the three additional bedrooms, she could almost hear the sounds of the laughter of the children who were clearly currently living there. She imagined her own children in those twin single beds in the second bedroom. She imagined another, smaller child in the third bedroom. Then, there was a far smaller room that faced front.

'I'm getting a bit long in the tooth for *four* children, if that's what you're planning,' she whispered to James, as the estate agent climbed back downstairs to unlock the door to the frosty garden.

James peered into the box room. 'My study.' He nodded, clearly satisfied with what he'd seen. 'And if we only have one child, I'll think myself the luckiest man alive.' He put his arm around her and planted a kiss on her temple. 'We're career people, Kitty. I don't expect you to stay at home and have a child a year. You made that very clear, long ago, that you have no interest in that, and I love you all the more for it.'

By the time Kitty saw the back garden, she had quietly fallen in love with the house and had already mentally moved in and furnished the place. The ice crunched beneath her Morlands boots as she walked from the house to a holly tree at the far end of the garden. She looked back at the handsome home.

'Do you want it, then?' James asked, out of earshot of the estate agent. 'Is this to be Williams Towers?'

Kitty wrapped her arms around him and buried her head in his chest so that she could hear his heart beating strong, even beneath his many layers of clothing. 'It's perfect. Are you sure we can afford it?'

James kissed the top of her head and looked into the pale blue morning sky. 'I think we'd better have a trip down to Mater and Pater. Do you fancy watching the Royal funeral?'

Chapter 34

'Well, I didn't think my first trip to London would end up standing for three hours outside the Houses of Parliament,' Kitty said, stamping her feet to stop the jabbing pins and needles and get the blood circulating again. Gazing up at the Palace of Westminster, she felt a thrill of excitement, despite the sombre occasion and the discomfort of standing around on a February morning. With all its gothic-style turrets and gargoyles, she had never seen anything so grand before. She had never felt so British. 'If Mam could see me now,' she said softly.

She had wrapped herself up in thermal underwear, thick woollen stockings, a heavy dress that Mam had made for her out of some jumble-sale jacquard curtains, a cardigan that the old matron had knitted for her as a Christmas gift and her heaviest winter coat. Even with a muffler wound around her neck and a hat on her head, she was still cold.

Her breath steamed on the air. 'Is it nearly time, because I'm frozen to the marrow?'

James opened his coat and enfolded her inside it. 'They'll be bringing him out at any moment. Half past nine, I'm told. If it's any consolation, those dignitaries behind the gates have been standing there for over an hour.'

Kitty looked up and down the road, studying the other members of the public who had lined London's streets for the King's funeral. They were largely dressed in black or dark colours, and there was no waving of Union Jacks or excitable chatter. Some women dabbed at their eyes. Many men wore black armbands, with their wartime medals pinned to their overcoats. She knew she was taking part in a momentous occasion.

'Here we go,' James said.

Big Ben struck. Somewhere, a canon was fired, and a ripple of fascinated anticipation spread through the crowd. For a while, they could see nothing, but suddenly, they caught a glimpse of a coffin being borne by some military men – Kitty had no idea which force or regiment they were from, but they looked dreadfully impressive in their ceremonial uniforms. 'Who are they?' she asked James.

'Grenadier Guards, I believe.'

Through the tall gates, she could see the coffin being placed onto a carriage. The coffin was covered with a Union Jack flag and topped with several shining objects. Could one of them be the crown?

Big Ben chimed again, and the carriage was pulled out of Westminster Hall by sailors, dressed in full uniform. Slowly, they marched past where Kitty and James were standing. She couldn't quite believe that she was seeing the King's coffin with her own eyes. The coffin on its carriage was accompanied by finely dressed men, whom she assumed to be members of the Royal household.

Behind the coffin came cavalry, bearing the Royal standard. Before today, Kitty had never seen anything but dray horses pulling carts along Manchester streets. Now, she gasped at the sheer size and the gleaming flanks of the beautiful thoroughbred cavalry horses and the impressive sight of their riders.

Behind the cavalry came a gilded carriage so ornate that Kitty was minded of fairy tales. But who were the Cinderellas inside?

'Oh, here she comes,' James said, squeezing Kitty's hand. 'Our new monarch.'

Open-mouthed and with a racing pulse, Kitty peered inside the carriage and caught a glimpse of the young Queen Elizabeth II, her mother, the old Queen, Princess Margaret and a woman Kitty assumed to be the dead King's sister. They all looked terribly sombre.

Behind the carriage marched four men, one of whom Kitty immediately recognised.

'Hey, James. Isn't that Edward VIII?' She pointed to the man, whom she remembered had hit the headlines when he had abdicated because of his romance with the infamous American divorcée, Mrs Simpson. Hadn't Mam told her the socialite and Edward VIII had been rumoured to be Nazi sympathisers? 'God, how I wish Mam could see this. She'd be having an apoplexy.'

As the funeral cortege progressed, Kitty marvelled at the sight and sound of so many military bands, all playing their instruments and marching in step. The drumming of their feet on the ground and the banging of the big bass drum that accompanied each band seemed to reverberate up through Kitty's own legs. She could almost feel the hairs on the back of her neck stand on end as the pipers of the Scottish and Irish regiments passed.

'Flipping heck. Listen to them bagpipes! They're out of this world.'

Her eyes almost hurt from looking at all the bright colours and shining buttons of the servicemen's many and varied ceremonial uniforms.

'It's like something out of a painting,' she whispered. 'I'm glad we're not watching this in black and white on the television.'

By the time the procession was halfway through, Kitty felt overwhelmed and uncomfortably cold. She turned to James. 'Can we make tracks?'

James nodded. 'Better to beat the dash for the Underground, if we're to get back to my parents' place before tea.'

'Help yourself, everyone.' James's mother, Margery, set a large cake stand on the dining table. Its four tiers were laden with sandwiches towards the bottom, with fondant fancies on the top. 'Earl Grey?'

Kitty sensed that her future mother-in-law was staring right at her. She looked up to find her wearing the same predatory, judgemental expression she'd seen on hungry cats, weighing up the weaknesses of an unsuspecting bird or fieldmouse. 'Yes please.'

Margery leaned over the table and poured a stream of weak-looking tea from an elegant china teapot into Kitty's matching cup. Kitty looked at the colour of it. It didn't look like normal tea.

'Lemon?'

'Lemon??'

'You put it in the tea, dear,' Margery said, rolling her eyes.

'I know what to do with it.' In truth, Kitty didn't know what to do with it at all, but thinking quickly, she came up with an excuse that would make her sound less of the working-class oik that James's mother always succeeded in making her feel. 'I'm just surprised you've managed to get hold of a fresh one, what with rationing and all.'

James Senior sat back in his chair and laughed. 'Oh, my dear. We grow lemons in the orangery, along with . . . no surprises, here . . . oranges.' He guffawed.

'No need to be facetious,' James said, petting the exuberant family dog, Rufus, who sat at his side, panting and begging for scraps. 'You weren't growing citrus fruits last time we came, and not everyone has the luxury of an orangery at the back of their house.'

Convinced that the afternoon tea and stopover was going to be an excruciating game of her future in-laws making her feel like the hired help, Kitty took up her napkin, sitting up as straight as she could. She was poised to tuck the cloth into her collar, as every working-class person she'd ever dined with did, to save their clothes from stains. Fortunately, at the last moment, she remembered that in this grand house, middle-class etiquette applied. She laid the napkin across her lap.

'At least for afternoon tea, you don't have to think so hard about which knife and fork to use,' Margery said.

James set his gin glass down with gusto, making his tea cup and saucer rattle. 'All right. That's quite enough.'

'Whatever do you mean, James?' His perfectly made-up mother blinked at him innocently.

'Belittling Kitty.'

Margery clasped her manicured hand to her pearl necklace. 'I was doing nothing of the sort.'

'Oh really?' James narrowed his eyes at her. He turned to his father. 'You two have done nothing but dig, dig, dig at Kitty since we arrived.'

James Senior drained what was left of his aperitif and dabbed at his mouth with his napkin. 'Must you always bring the chip on your shoulder when you come to visit, James?

It's getting rather tiring and it doesn't befit a man of your standing. You're hardly a member of the lumpenproletariat, living in a slum, no matter who you're marrying.'

'Charmed, I'm sure,' Kitty said, wishing – not for the first time – that she could just slip outside and drive all the way back to Manchester.

James pointed at his father. 'See? That's what I'm talking about. Dig, dig, dig. That sort of snobbery doesn't befit a man of your intelligence.'

'Touché!' James Senior said, chortling. He clicked his fingers triumphantly. '*That's* more like it. A little witty repartee.' He took a sandwich from the cake stand and bit into it, grinning as he chewed.

'Father, this isn't a game,' James said. 'Nobody appreciates you playing devil's advocate and baiting us for sport. All you're doing is hurting our feelings, especially Kitty's.'

Kitty threw her napkin onto the table. 'I would say it was nice to see you both, but actually, it wasn't.' She turned to James. 'I'd like to leave now.' She tried to hold back angry tears but two leaked defiantly onto her cheeks. She wiped them away roughly with the sleeve of her cardigan.

'Absolutely.' James stood up and pulled out her chair. 'I'll get our coats.' He checked his wristwatch. 'Berkshire's not that far from Manchester. We should be home by midnight at the very latest.'

'Oh, darling, I wish you wouldn't be so hasty,' Margery said, standing in her son's way, offering him a fondant fancy on a side plate. 'It's really not necessary to leave.' She turned to Kitty. 'Please, do sit. We didn't mean to make you feel so unwelcome. It's just . . . the King's death and all.'

'Oh, king's death, my backside,' James said. He put a protective arm around Kitty. '"It's just . . . ?" I tell you what, "it's just . . ." It's just that, for all you consider yourself the social elite, Mother, you are a terrible hostess and clearly don't know how to behave in public.' He was stony-faced, his nostrils flaring with obvious indignation. 'I don't know why we're bothering to invite you to the wedding. We were going to tell you about a house we've seen that we'd like to buy. Once upon a time, you offered to help with a deposit, but clearly, that was when I was engaged to Violet, and that offer's now off the table because you can't help your overinflated sense of your own worth. And that's fine. We can manage on our own. When our children come along, you needn't visit us.'

'Don't be such a spoilsport,' James Senior said, gesturing that they should sit back down. 'Your mother's gone to the trouble of laying on tea.' He took a sliver of roast beef out of a sandwich and threw it to a grateful Rufus who barked his appreciation. 'I was rather looking forward to a nice dinner this evening, putting the world to rights over a very fine 1884 Merlot that I brought up from the cellar. I've already uncorked the damn thing.'

'I'm not interested in your wine, Father.'

'But I'm making boeuf en croûte!' Margery held a napkin to her eyes and was pretending to sob. 'It's always been your favourite, James.'

'Your bitter words would make every mouthful taste of dust, Mother. Please, don't bother on my account.'

'Oh, how could you think so ill of me, darling?' Margery turned to Kitty, bewilderment in her wide eyes. 'It's not that I was deliberately trying to make you uncomfortable, dear. I just tend to speak my mind, and I suppose that sometimes I can be a little brusque.'

James Senior heaved himself with cracking knees out of his chair, walked over to James and Kitty and slapped a meaty hand on a shoulder each. 'Now, your mother's not going to apologise, James, but this is the closest she's come to it in a long time.' He steered them back to the table. 'And I don't mind saying that I could have given more thought to my words.'

James looked at Kitty, clearly torn and wanting to take his cue from her. She sighed heavily, wondering whether it was worth storming out to make the point that she wouldn't allow them to speak to her like she was dirt. Might she irreparably damage James's relationship with his parents? Hadn't James put up with an awful lot over the years from the Longthorne men, with their criminal proclivities and reliance on him to right their wrongs, time after time? Wasn't Ned due out of prison, sooner rather than later, only because James had stood in the dock and given him a good character reference that he hadn't earned?

'Oh, go on then,' she said. She broke free of James Senior's grip and sat back down. *You can't pick your relatives,* she reminded herself.

The visit progressed more smoothly after that. Kitty regaled them with her outsider's view of the Palace of Westminster and the overcrowded, unfriendly grandeur of London generally. James updated them on the latest surgical advancements and the impact on his clinic of the Korean War and more traffic on the roads.

'So, tell us about this house,' James Senior said, over the boeuf en croûte, which had turned out to be nothing more exotic than Beef Wellington. He swilled his vintage Merlot around his crystal glass and took a large gulp.

'It's delightful,' James said. 'A modest detached house in Hale Village.'

'I wouldn't say it's modest,' Kitty said. 'It's grand. Three decent-sized bedrooms and a fourth, just about big enough for a study for James. The garden's about sixty foot.'

James beamed at her and squeezed her hand. 'Kitty will have a lovely kitchen with all mod cons, won't you?'

'Er, *we'll* have a lovely kitchen,' she laughed, nudging her fiancé. 'Don't think you're giving up cooking when we get married. I manage to burn water.'

His mother grimaced. 'A modest four-bedroomed house? It sounds terribly twee, James. I seem to remember there's a good number of Edwardian gentleman's residences and Art and Crafts houses in Hale and Bowdon. Why on earth are you settling for such a humble abode? I mean, a sixty-foot-long garden doesn't sound like a terribly exciting place for children to roam and explore.'

'It's more than enough for a starter home,' James said. 'And where would we get the money for something grander? You're already having to help us, as it is.'

James Senior cut a roast potato in two. 'You're a consultant with a Cambridge pedigree, for God's sake, boy. Stop crying poverty.'

'I work for the National Health Service. I'm a government employee. The pay's capped. It's not like the old days. And plastic surgery is so in demand that I barely have time for private cosmetic work.'

'The house is absolutely more than adequate for us anyway,' Kitty chipped in.

James Senior wasn't listening, however. 'Oh, come on, James! Being a plastic surgeon must be a licence to print money. All those debutantes with unsightly noses to bob and ears to pin back. All those ageing starlets who want nothing more than a nip and tuck for Christmas. Jack in the National Health Service nonsense and get a surgery on Manchester's equivalent of Harley Street. Take on solely private work and buy you and Kitty, here, a decent pile. Cheshire's nice enough, but it must be cheap compared to Royal Berkshire.'

Kitty wondered what James was thinking as he stared at his plateful of food. She could see that tendon in his jaw flinching. He was clearly irked by his father's words, and she could guess why. She put a comforting hand on his knee beneath the table.

Cutting a slice from his Beef Wellington, James blinked repeatedly. 'My patients need me precisely because they can't afford to pay. I prefer to stick to my hospital work and save any spare time I have for my home life.' He looked at Kitty with tenderness in those expressive brown eyes. 'You can't put a price on love.'

Kitty was grinning so hard that she barely heard James Senior calling his son a 'nincompoop idealist'.

By the time their weekend off had come to an end, the rift between James and Kitty and his parents had finally been healed, and they had pocketed a cheque for enough money to make the house in Hale a reality.

In the car home, Kitty watched the wintry twilit countryside speed by – exhausted but relieved.

'Are you ready to start a home together?' James asked.

Kitty spotted a small farmhouse that sat in the middle of a frost-covered field. It was roughly the same size as the house they hoped to buy. Despite the freezing fog that blanketed the land, with the lights on inside, it looked so inviting. She imagined the family that sat inside around the fire, listening to the wireless together on a Sunday evening, shutting the cold world out. 'I can't wait,' she said.

Finally, she truly meant it.

Chapter 35

'Hang on the bell, Nelly,' Mam said, as she crouched by Kitty's feet, trying and failing to put a pin in the hem of Kitty's wedding dress. She tutted. 'Oh, flaming Nora, I'm in my own light. I can't see what I'm doing for toffee.' She shouted through to Grace, who was icing the wedding cake in the kitchen. 'Gracie, love! Put the parlour light on, will you?' Mam sounded harried.

Kitty had been told to stand still, but she couldn't help but look down at the shining ivory silk of the full skirt, admiring her new matching shoes peeping out from beneath.

'Keep still, will you? And stand up straight,' Mam said. 'Every time you move, the hem goes skew-whiff. I can't have my only daughter walking down the aisle with a hem that looks half cocked.'

'Sorry, Mam,' Kitty said. 'I just can't stop staring at those shoes. Look at the pointed toes. They're gorgeous!' She stuck her right foot out. 'They make my ankles look so slim.'

Grace came in from Mam's kitchen. Her arms and middle were covered in a white dusting of icing sugar, as though she'd been stood in the snow. 'Ooh, that looks out of this world,' she said, smiling at the dress. 'I *love* that bodice, Elsie. It makes Kitty's waist look so tiny.'

'Hey, you cheeky beggar,' Kitty said. 'My waist *is* tiny. I don't think I've eaten a decent square meal since 1938.'

'None of us has,' Mam said, pushing a pin home through the fabric. 'Oh, well. Hitler might have bombed our old house to smithereens, but at least you'll look like a Paris model on your wedding day. Hurray for rationing.'

'Yes. And nobody needs to know the wedding dress is made out of the last of Dad's stolen parachute silk,' Kitty said. 'Hurray for the late, light-fingered Bert Longthorne.'

'And my bridesmaid dress is made out of Mr Galbraith's old bedroom curtains. Hurray for his wife's taste in Liberty fabric,' Grace said.

The three women laughed together. For weeks now, Kitty had been savouring every moment of the wedding preparations. Though they had only been able to get together in the evening, exhausted after a gruelling working day, there had been such a happy atmosphere in the house as Mam had fitted Kitty and Grace for their outfits in the parlour.

'Look at those appliqué flowers!' Grace said, leaning in to inspect the three lilies on Kitty's bodice that Mam had cleverly fashioned from the yellow felt of a rich woman's hat. 'You're so talented, Elsie.'

'They're gorgeous, aren't they?' Kitty said. 'And have you seen the lace trim on this little bolero jacket Mam's made to match?' She fingered the stand-up collar that was all the rage.

'Oh, good Lord, look!' Grace gasped and ran her fingers over the tiny ivory and yellow lilies on the lace jacket. 'Have you done this since the last fitting, Elsie? Where did you get this trim?' She looked down at Kitty's mother.

'An old Victorian tablecloth, would you believe it?' Mam muttered, barely able to make herself understood given she had pins wedged between her lips for safe keeping. Kitty watched as with skilled and swift fingers she retrieved the pins, one by one, and pushed them all into the hem. 'I found it at a jumble sale in Chorlton-cum-Hardy.' She paused and held a tape measure tight from the waistline down to the hem of the skirt. 'It's proper Nottingham lace, and all. I think the tablecloth came from a big, rich family. I took the lace panels out and dyed the lilies yellow by hand.'

Grace stood back to appraise the wedding dress. She clasped her hands together and nodded her head at Kitty. 'It's pretty clear where you got your brains from, Sister Longthorne. And it certainly wasn't your dad.'

'Shame I can't even sew a button on,' Kitty said, laughing.

Mam raised her eyebrow. 'In another life, I might have been a couturier, sewing sequins on ballgowns in London for some millionaire's debutant daughter.' She looked wistfully through the parlour window and sighed. 'Or maybe even in Hollywood, kitting out Rita Hayworth and Ava Gardner. Costumier to the stars, eh?' Then she looked up and met Kitty's gaze. She patted her foot affectionately. 'But who needs Hollywood bombshells when I've got my girl, walking down the aisle with her handsome doctor?' She grunted as she stifly got to her feet. 'By heck, now you've moved out of the nurses' home and over to your new house in Hale, it's like being visited by a minor royal every time you come for your tea.'

'Get out of town!' Kitty said. 'There's nothing upper crust about me and never will be. I'm living over the brush, for a start.'

'You're getting married next week!' Mam said. 'It's hardly living over the brush.'

Kitty allowed her mother to help her down from the chair on which she'd been standing. She slipped off her bolero and hung it reverentially on its hanger. Then she let Grace unzip the dress and stepped carefully out of it, trying her best not to tread on the newly pinned hem. 'I'm not married yet though, am I? You should see the faces of the neighbours when I introduced myself as Kitty Longthorne, not Mrs James Williams. I'm surprised they haven't complained to the council that there's a loose woman living next door.'

'That's hoity-toity types for you,' her mother said. 'They've got nowt better to do than gossip.' Mam clapped her hands at Grace. 'Right, young lady. You're next. Get yourself cleaned up and get into your bridesmaid's dress for the last round of alterations.' She took down Grace's Liberty-fabric dress from the lintel of the door where it had been hanging. 'This wedding might be small, but it will be perfectly formed, if I've got anything to do with it.'

While Grace got into her dress, Kitty put back on her normal clothes and wandered into the kitchen. She gasped when she saw the cake. 'Grace! This is a triumph! This could be from the finest patisserie in France.'

'Finest bakery in Barbados, you mean,' Grace shouted though to her. 'There's nothing fancy and French about the rum in that fruitcake.'

Feeling butterflies take flight in her stomach, Kitty took in the fine detail of the sugar flowers Grace had fashioned from fondant. She poked her head around the door. 'You're a genius, Grace. Those little yellow roses and lilies to match the bolero . . . I don't know how you do it. You and Mam – you're both artists.'

'Worth saving up everyone's sugar coupons for all these months,' Grace said. 'I might not be getting married to Ned, but I'm glad to be baking for one Longthorne who is getting wed.'

Kitty walked back into the parlour. 'That wedding cake's the best present we could ever have asked for,' she said. 'I just hope James manages to get it to the hotel in once piece, ready for the reception. Let's hope there's no stray sheep in the road to Ambleside.'

Taking a seat on the old sagging settee, Kitty realised that it hadn't been until she'd spent a week in her own freshly decorated home, where James had paid for all the floors to be fitted with brand-new wall-to-wall carpet and where the only bits of furniture had been what he had brought with him from the flat, that she realised Mam's house had a certain smell to it. Even in summer, it smelled of old frying, damp and dust. It was the smell of poor ventilation, a limited diet and small spaces. Kitty realised now that this was what poverty smelled like. This was why the hospital was still full of patients with respiratory problems and dietary deficiencies. She felt all at once glad to be marrying well, but guilty for leaving her humble origins behind.

'You all right, love?' Mam asked. 'You look a bit down. You're not having second thoughts, are you?'

Kitty shook her head. 'Not in the slightest. It's taken years for James to get me down the aisle. I'm just bone tired. I need a break. The wedding preparations are such fun, but moving into the house and all, and juggling work with everything . . .' She puffed air out of her cheeks. 'If I'm honest, I'm a bit nervous.'

Mam came and sat on the sofa next to her. She put her arm around Kitty. 'What about, chuck? Tell your mam, eh? Don't keep worries to yourself.'

Kitty nestled her head into her mother's bosom, drinking in the scent of lavender soap that cut though the other smells in the house. 'It's just . . . well, James's parents are at least behaving themselves, since he give them what-for on the day of the King's funeral. But I'm still worried about how they'll behave towards you.'

Mam kissed the top of her head and got up from the settee with a grunt. 'I'm not bothered by the likes of them. They're not fit to polish our shoes.' She got back on her knees and started to fiddle with the hem of Grace's bridesmaid's dress.

'I'll give them a Bajan-style tongue-lashing if they say a word out of place,' Grace said. She saluted. 'Bridesmaid's duties.'

'It's not just them, though. I'm going to miss our Ned, obviously. I had hoped he'd walk me down the aisle, now Dad's dead. But . . . Anyway, James suggested his usher, George, to give me away, but I'm not sure about him.'

'What's wrong with him?' Mam asked, pulling down the netting beneath Grace's dress.

Kitty shrugged. 'He's a lovely bloke, but I'm not sure I know him well enough to give him such an important role in my wedding. There's something about him that I'm just . . . He's a bit of an enigma, if I'm honest.' She toyed with the upholsterer's buttons on the arms of the settee.

'What about asking one of the other doctors in the hospital?' Grace asked. 'Galbraith? You like and respect him, don't you?'

'I'm not *that* close to him, though, and neither's James.'

'What about Richard Collins?' Grace smirked and winked.

Kitty burst into laughter. 'That would go down like a lead balloon. "Hello, Richard. I kicked you into touch after our second or third date, and my brother stole your best coat, but no hard feelings, eh? Would you like to give me away when I marry your arch rival?"'

'That's a belting coat,' Mam told Grace. 'I slept with it on the bed last winter when it got really cold. It kept me really toasty. You can feel the quality.'

As Kitty's laughter subsided, a thought occurred to her. 'I know exactly who can give me away in this brave new era,' she said.

'Who?' Mam asked.

Kitty stood and walked over to her mother. She crouched beside her and kissed the side of her head. 'You.'

'Get away, you rum pig,' Mam said, waving her away. 'I can't give you away. I'm the mother of the bride. It's not right. Giving the bride away is a man's job.'

Kitty helped the old lady to her feet and clasped both of her hands. 'Says who? Who's paying for this wedding?' She prodded herself in the chest. 'Me and James. And since when have the Longthornes ever done as they're told?'

Mam opened and closed her mouth. Her cheeks were flushed red. 'Ooh, I don't know, our Kitty.'

'Times are changing, Mam. Us women don't have to take a back seat and let the men have all the fun. That's the whole reason why I waited until 1952 to get married. I'm going to have my cake and eat it.'

Her mother giggled. 'Oh, you are a one, our Kitty. You've got a right rebellious streak in you. You might think you had nowt in common with your dad, but you're Bert Longthorne's girl, all right.'

'So you'll do it?' Kitty asked, searching her mother's tired-looking eyes for the sparkle of collusion.

Her mother grinned. 'Go on, then. It'll be my honour, love.' She dug her tongue into her cheek. 'And I can't wait to see that stuck-up Margery Williams's face when she sees *me* walking you down the aisle.'

Chapter 36

'How do I look?' Kitty asked. She stood in front of the full-length mirror in the Ambleside guesthouse bedroom, barely able to recognise herself. Her wedding outfit could have come from the pages of a fashion magazine. Lily had styled her hair into an elegant chignon, onto which she'd pinned the short veil. Kitty's make-up looked as though it had been applied in a Helena Rubinstein salon. Kitty turned to see herself from the back.

'A million dollars,' Lily said.

'Like a film star,' Grace said.

Kitty looked to Mam for her approval and saw tears standing in the old lady's eyes. 'Hey up, Mam. Don't be crying now. You'll make your mascara run.'

'You're the most beautiful bride in the world,' Mam said. 'Come on, love.' She dabbed at her eyes with a handkerchief. 'Let's get you wed.'

It was a short walk to the church. The clock had just struck eleven as Kitty walked past the rather grand parked cars of James's family and friends. She was so nervous, she was barely aware of how her new shoes pinched. Happily, it was a glorious day, and the June sunshine beat down on her.

'I'm boiling in this regalia, with that sun,' Kitty said. She looked down at her bouquet. 'I hope these flowers don't wilt,' she said, looking down at the cascading bouquet of yellow and cream flowers that had been dropped off at the guesthouse by the florist, only an hour earlier.

'They look fresh as a daisy,' Mam said. 'They smell a treat too. Florist was a local, wasn't she? Did you arrange her?'

Kitty shook her head, barely listening to her mother's words as she eyed the entrance to the church. It had been transformed with an archway of yellow and white flowers. 'George, the usher. He lives in the Lakes. Flowers are his wedding present.'

'They're glorious, aren't they?' Grace said, looking down at her small bridesmaid's posy. 'The lilies remind me of home.'

Stopping at the door, Kitty took a deep breath and held it, listening to the blood pulsating through her veins. 'This is it,' she said.

It dawned on her that she'd waited almost ten years for this event: from her very first day as a wartime trainee nurse at Park Hospital, when she'd fallen in love-at-first-sight with young doctor James, to standing there, peering through a crack in the door at the gathered congregation. Her husband-to-be stood at the front with his best man, Timothy. He was peering up at the large stained-glass window that blazed with colour on this bright summer's morning. From this vantage point in the vestibule, she could hear James's cousin, Lucinda, expertly playing a concerto on the church's piano. The scene was set. But where was George, the usher, to open the doors for them?

'Are you ready?' Mam asked.

Kitty exhaled hard through pursed lips. 'Ready as I'll ever be.'

'Are you sure about this?' Mam started to lift the veil up and over Kitty's face.

Kitty nodded. 'Completely sure. Mind my lippy.'

'I am minding your lippy.' The veil was in place. 'There. You look pretty as a picture. I only wish your dad and Ned could see you now.'

Kitty squeezed her hand. 'I love you, Mam. Thanks. For everything.' She let go and held her arm out for her mother to link.

Grace and Lily opened the doors to let them through. 'Good luck,' they both whispered.

The organ music began to play as Kitty took her first tentative steps down the aisle. In her peripheral vision, she could see her nursing colleagues on 'her' side of the church, and all of James's family, colleagues and friends on 'his' side. Towards the front, she almost didn't spot the old matron, who looked strange, wearing clothes and a hat that weren't a matron's uniform and cap. Her attention was stolen by James, though.

Standing at the front, the love of her life only had eyes for her. Kitty gasped as James flashed her a perfect white smile. Dressed in white tie, clad in an immaculately tailored black tailcoat and dress trousers and with his dark Brylcreemed hair gleaming under the church lights, he was more handsome than Rhett Butler in his heyday; more dashing than Rock Hudson or any of those Hollywood pin-ups. Kitty knew that she was still giddy as a kitten when it came to her love for James. She found herself picking up her pace to get to the front so she could stand by her fiancé's side.

'Kitty, you are simply stunning,' James said when she reached the altar. Tears stood in his eyes. 'I'm the luckiest man alive.'

'And I'm the luckiest woman,' Kitty said.

'Dearly beloved . . .' The vicar started to address the congregation about the solemnity of marriage.

Kitty was so overwhelmed by the significance of the occasion, however, that she barely took in what was being said. *I'm getting married,* she thought. *Me and James. We're tying the knot, at last. Oh, blooming heck, I think I'm going to cry.*

Before she knew it, the vicar was saying, 'If any man can show just cause why James and Catherine might not lawfully be joined together, let him speak now or forever hold his peace.'

A tense hush fell over the people gathered in the church, some of them no doubt remembering the scandalous incident of James jilting Violet at the altar of a rather different church in Bowdon. Kitty held her breath, yet silence prevailed and everyone seemed to sigh with relief as the ceremony continued. James began to say his vows. His voice cracked as he spoke. 'I, James Godfrey de Havilland Williams, take you, Catherine Longthorne, to be my wife.' Now, it was he who looked as though he might cry, yet his smile seemed to stretch from his lips right to the very roots of his hair. 'To have and to hold, from this day forward, for better, for worse, for richer, for poorer . . .'

Pure emotion welled within Kitty, pushing its way upwards, so that tears of joy and relief prickled at the backs of her eyes.

Now it was her turn to say her vows. She spoke haltingly, trying her very best to keep the wobble out of her voice. '. . . in sickness and in health, to love and to cherish, 'til death do us part, according to God's holy law.' She glanced at the cross on the altar and the religious scenes depicted in the stained glass. Then she looked back to James. 'In the presence of God, I make this vow.'

Kitty was dimly aware of Grace taking hold of the bridal bouquet. As Grace returned to her seat, Kitty caught sight of her mother, dabbing at her eyes. On the other side of the aisle, Margery and James Senior were watching her and James intently. The seat where George should have been was still empty.

Timothy took the rings out of his breast pocket.

With shaking hands, Kitty and James took the wedding rings from him and slipped them onto each other's wedding fingers.

'I now pronounce you man and wife,' the vicar said triumphantly. He addressed James. 'You may kiss the bride.'

Kitty found herself being scooped into a warm embrace by her new husband and kissed passionately on the lips. Abandoning all thoughts of smudged lipstick, she returned the kiss with vigour, almost disbelieving that a simple Hulme girl like her could be this fortunate and feel this happy. All around, the congregation was cheering and clapping.

Breaking apart, Kitty grinned at James. 'Am I dreaming, or did we finally get married?'

'You're not dreaming, Mrs Williams,' James said, holding her hands in his. 'We are most certainly married – *at last* – and I am the happiest man alive.'

Chapter 37

'What a lovely ceremony that was,' James Senior said, as James's side of the family posed together with the bride and groom for a photograph by Lake Windermere's edge. 'And what a beautiful bride you are, Kitty.' His eyes were somewhat bloodshot and slightly unfocused.

Kitty could smell champagne fumes on her new father-in-law's breath. She was tempted to tell him off for trying to peer down the front of her bodice as they all posed for the photographer, but in truth, she was just delighted that the wedding ceremony had been such a magical occasion. 'Thank you very much, James Senior.' She took a step away from his lascivious gaze. 'It was very kind of you to provide the champagne and wines for the reception. I'm sure everyone will have a ball, especially when my bridesmaid's band plays this evening. They're terrific.'

Margery was smiling at her, when she should have been looking towards the photographer. 'Do you know, I can't take my eyes off you, dear? You may not have been wearing a Christian Dior gown, but your dress *is* lovely. Who is it by?'

'Oh, a very skilled designer you might not have heard of.' Kitty looked over at her mother, who was standing within earshot, clutching a glass of champagne as if she were holding a Fabergé egg. 'Madame Elspeth from the House of Thorne du Longue.'

Mam snorted with laughter and turned away.

Margery looked perplexed but smiled nevertheless. 'Jolly good. Well, you do scrub up rather well, dear. I shall ask that the photographs are sent to *Tatler*.'

When the photographs were done, Kitty and James wove their way among their guests, greeting them one by one.

'Dr and Mrs Williams,' Matron said, holding her arms wide. To Kitty's surprise, she hugged and kissed them both. 'My heartfelt congratulations. I can't tell you how happy I am to see the handsomest couple in medicine finally wed.'

'I'm so glad you came,' Kitty said. 'It wouldn't be the same without you.'

Matron rubbed her arm. 'God bless your persistence, Kitty. You waited all this time so that you wouldn't have to sacrifice your career for love. Maybe one day, my wish will come true and *you'll* be the matron of Park Hospital.' Her eyes sparkled with glee.

'Don't rule it out, Matron,' Kitty said, grinning.

'Matron, I rather think retirement suits you,' James said. 'You're looking exceptionally well.'

Matron laughed. 'Oh, aren't you quite the charmer, Dr Williams? And there was me, thinking you such a serious young chap.'

'My wife brings out the best in me,' James said, putting his arm around Kitty.

Kitty rested her head on his shoulder and took in the tranquil scene of their nearest and dearest, toasting their union, with the shimmering blue lake in the foreground and the vivid green sheep-studded hills in the background. 'This is the best day of my life.'

*

As morning turned to afternoon and the wedding breakfast beckoned, Timothy shooed the guests inside the hotel and up to the function room where their reception was to be held. Everyone gasped at the sight of Grace's magnificent cake, and Kitty was relieved to take the weight off her feet and sit at the head table.

'My feet are killing me,' she said, as waitresses and wine waiters bustled around them, and the guests found their places at the five round tables that bordered a modest wooden dancefloor. 'I don't think I've sat down all day. I certainly haven't eaten anything since dinner, last night.' She hiccupped.

'Champagne on an empty stomach, eh?' James nudged her gently. 'Are you tipsy, Mrs Williams?'

Kitty shook her head. 'Not really. Well, maybe a bit.' She looked along the head table at the wedding party. 'But what I want to know is, where's George? He only lives down the road. What's his excuse for not coming?'

James shrugged. 'I haven't heard a word from him. It's a mystery.'

The food was served and Kitty was only too happy to finally tuck into a solid meal of celery soup to start, and chicken casserole, which had been prepared in a French style. It warmed Kitty's heart to see so many familiar faces from the hospital among the guests, all chatting away and wearing carefree smiles, which she saw too seldom inside the hospital's walls.

She bit into a mushroom, thoughtfully. 'Such a shame they wouldn't let our Ned out for this,' she said to James. 'He'd have loved chatting to this lot and lying and charming his way around the room.'

'That he would.' James raised his glass. 'To absent loved ones.'

They clinked glasses and Kitty swallowed down a lump of regret along with her white wine.

She was shaken from her reverie by Timothy leaning forwards and bypassing James's parents to bellow along the table. He slurred his words slightly. 'Did I hear you just mentioned absent loved ones?'

'Crikey, Timothy,' Kitty said. 'You might have had a few too many, but there's nowt wrong with your hearing. Keep it down a bit, will you? We're newly-wed, not deaf.'

'Absent loved ones?' James said. 'Yes. As a matter of fact, Kitty and I were just toasting her brother and father. Our mysterious missing usher, too. What of it?'

Timothy drunkenly held his finger aloft. 'I have a card here from Georgie.'

'You've heard from him?' James asked.

Timothy took an envelope out of his breast pocket and stretched out to pass it over everyone's food to James, almost knocking over Margery's wine glass in the process. 'No. The card arrived by post this morning in a larger envelope addressed to me. There was a note inside for me.'

'Saying?' James asked, looking down at the envelope on which was handwritten, *To the happy couple.* His brow furrowed. He slid the card into the breast pocket of his own tailcoat.

'Just that he was terribly sorry to be indisposed at short notice and couldn't make the wedding.' Timothy tried to scratch his nose and almost missed his face entirely. 'He said you're not to open your card until the day's over and you've got some time to yourselves.'

'I say, couldn't you have told us this a little earlier, old bean? We've been wondering where our enigmatic usher had got to.'

Timothy merely raised a glass and shrugged. 'Slipped my mind. Sorry.'

'What a day, eh?' Kitty said when they were finally alone in their honeymoon suite. She kicked off her shoes and started to unpin her hair.

'It couldn't have gone better. It really was the happiest day of my life, darling.' James shrugged off his tailcoat and the card from George fell out of his breast pocket.

Kitty picked up the envelope. 'Shall I open it?'

'Go ahead, Mrs Williams.' James slid his arms around Kitty from behind and looked over her shoulder as she opened the envelope and took out the card inside.

Kitty smiled at illustration of a bride and groom on the front. 'Congratulations! You're married!' She opened the card and a neatly folded letter fell out. First, she read the simple message that George had written in his sprawling, barely legible hand.

Dear James and Kitty,

What a handsome couple you make. Have a wonderful, memorable day, and thanks for allowing me to be part of your celebrations.

Love and best wishes,

George x

'Read the letter,' James said, kissing Kitty's earlobe.

Kitty unfolded the letter, giggling. She soon fell silent when she started to read the letter's contents.

'What does it say?' James asked.

Dear James and Kitty,

Forgive me. I will not be able to come to the

wedding after all. I've been rather naughty you see – with the very best of intentions, of course – and am forced to relocate at short notice. I shall miss you both immeasurably and I'll miss old Blighty too, but I'm told Moscow is rather lovely this time of year.

Please don't think ill of me. I'm sorry to have lied to you, but I never lied about you both being very dear friends.

Best wishes and enjoy a long and happy married life,

George x

PS: Don't believe all the horrid things they're bound to say about me in tomorrow's papers.

Kitty turned to James. The letter quivered in her shaking hand. 'I was right.'

The following morning, they lay in bed together, reading *The Times* and the *Daily Telegraph*. Both newspapers reported the same story on the front page.

DOUBLE AGENT DEFECTS TO USSR

James read aloud from the terrible story that emerged below *The Times'* headline. When he'd finished reading, he slapped the newspaper onto the counterpane. 'Well, I never. The damned fool was working for British intelligence on atomic weaponry and then passing the blueprints of everything he developed straight through to the other side of the Iron Curtain. They'd found out enough to arrest him, but Moscow tipped him off, just in time for him to escape.'

'They would have hanged him,' Kitty said. 'Good Lord!' She clasped her hand to her mouth, visualising George's dangerous expression when he'd realised she'd seen his radio equipment. 'Deary, deary me.' She looked down at the print in the *Daily Telegraph*. 'Says here he was part of a Cambridge spy ring, and they think other members might still be out there, evading capture.' She studied James's face. 'You don't think Timothy could be involved, do you?'

James blinked hard and shook his head slowly. He looked as if he were in shock. 'No. Tim's not interested in politics. He's not that idealistic, either.' He picked up the wedding card from George. 'Well . . . what a twist to *that* tale!' He raised an eyebrow and rubbed his chin. 'You think you know someone well, and then it turns out you never really knew them at all.' He set the card back down, looking at it dolefully. 'I must confess, I feel rather embarrassed to have been duped like this. And just the thought of all the lives he's potentially endangered by handing over such sensitive information . . . It really doesn't bear thinking about. I'm rather cross, now I come to think of it.' He frowned. 'What a perfect rotter George turned out to be.'

Kitty rested her head on James's chest. 'Hindsight's a wonderful thing, eh? You couldn't have known, James. Neither of us could. People like George . . . they're spies for a reason, aren't they? Secretive types, and good at lying. Don't let it spoil our day, love.'

She thought a little more about George's subterfuge, thinking privately that she should have contacted Agent Riley about George's messaging equipment as soon as she'd laid eyes on it. Yet she realised such self-recrimination was now pointless, and her thoughts turned back to her own life.

'When I first started working at Park Hospital, all those years ago,' she said, 'never once did I think I would find the man of my dreams *and* a job I'd want to do for life. I never thought for a minute that my brother would survive a

Japanese prisoner-of-war camp and then end up in prison, or that my dad would get out of prison and walk back into our lives, only to die a couple of years later. At times, I thought the war would never end or that rationing would finish.'

'It still hasn't.'

She chuckled. 'More's the pity. And I never thought I'd travel further than Blackpool, let alone sail the high seas to the West Indies. But I certainly never *ever* thought I'd be rubbing shoulders with double-agents and communists.' She sat up and locked eyes with James. 'It's all a bit much, if I'm honest. Do you think our lives might just calm down a bit, now?'

He carefully put a stray lock of her hair behind her ear. 'I certainly hope so because we need a little stability if having a family is going to be our next big adventure.'

'Are you ready for that adventure?' Kitty asked.

James grinned. 'I certainly am.' He looked at her with an eyebrow raised. 'Shall we start it . . . *now?*'

A smile spread across Kitty's lips. She glanced out at the view of Windermere, sparkling in the early morning sun. Suddenly, despite the many diseases that still required a cure, and the post-war poverty that had yet to be relieved, and the strange Cold War that had the world in its icy grip, it felt like everything was possible.

'We've waited long enough.' She draped her arms around James's neck and kissed him on the lips. 'It's the first day of the rest of our lives, James Williams. Let's start living.'

THE END

Acknowledgements

And so we come to the end of the Nurse Kitty trilogy. What a ride it has been – not just for my characters, Kitty and James, but also for me. Writing these historical sagas has been an utter joy. I feel privileged to have given a fictionalised account of the lives of the doctors and nurses working in the NHS's first hospital. I am delighted to have told a story of post-war Manchester, trying to find its feet after the devastation of the Blitz, going hungry during rationing that seemed to go on forever and forging ahead in the brave, new, cosmopolitan but politically fraught world of the 1950s. Thanks must go, first and foremost, to you, my readers, who have gone on this journey with me. I sincerely hope you enjoyed this last leg.

There are a few other folks without whom this book wouldn't have made its way into your hands. First, I'd like to thank my ever-loyal, tremendously funny and supportive agent, Caspian Dennis at Abner Stein. Thanks are also due to his brilliant, hardworking colleagues at the agency, especially Sandy, Felicity, Ray and Tom.

I'd like to thank the folks at Orion for the editorial input into this series – first, Sam Eades for commissioning it, and more recently, Rhea Kurien, who has edited this third book with such insightful aplomb. Thanks are also due to the sales, marketing and PR folk who get behind each book as it comes out.

Naturally, I would like to thank my family for their support and love which sustains me throughout the writing process. God bless their cotton socks for their patience and humour.

Finally, I'd like to thank the country's libraries, as I know a good deal of saga readers get their books on loan from their local library. Did you know that every time you borrow one of my books from a library, I get a few pence via the PLR (Public Lending Right)? Those pennies all add up, so if you can't afford to buy a paperback or an e-book of your favourite author's latest publication, give those nasty pirates, offering a freebie PDF download (and probably a nasty computer virus to boot), a swerve. There's no need to keep copyright infringement alive if you're short of cash. Simply support your local library. And those in charge of such things in the Government should take note: libraries are the beating heart of many a community and a real life-line for those who are getting on in years. Close them at your peril!

Goodbye, fair Kitty, and au revoir to my readers. Until we meet again with a new series...

Credits

Maggie Campbell and Orion Fiction would like to thank everyone at Orion who worked on the publication of *Nurse Kitty: After the War* in the UK.

Editorial
Rhea Kurien
Sahil Javed

Copyeditor
Clare Wallis

Proofreader
Jo Gledhill

Audio
Paul Stark
Jake Alderson

Contracts
Dan Herron
Ellie Bowker

Design
Tomás Almeida
Joanna Ridley

Editorial Management
Charlie Panayiotou
Jane Hughes
Bartley Shaw

Finance
Jasdip Nandra
Nick Gibson
Sue Baker

Production
Ruth Sharvell

Publicity
Sharina Smith

Sales
Jen Wilson
Esther Waters
Victoria Laws
Toluwalope Ayo-Ajala

Rachael Hum
Ellie Kyrke-Smith
Sinead White
Georgina Cutler

Operations
Jo Jacobs
Dan Stevens

Don't miss more of Nurse Kitty's adventures . . .

It's May 1945 and at 3pm, nurse Kitty Longthorne listens, together with the other surgical staff at South Manchester's Park Hospital, to Winston Churchill's broadcast on the radio. Germany has signed a declaration of complete surrender. The war is over in Europe and that day is to be celebrated as VE Day.

The mood in Park Hospital – still full of wounded American soldiers – is jubilant and hopeful, though Kitty is anything but. Her clandestine squeeze and the man she hopes to marry, James Williams has been giving her the cold shoulder for the last week, and she can't work out why. Furthermore, her twin brother, Ned, is still missing in action – his last known whereabouts point to him being in a Japanese prisoner of war camp.

It's 1949 and nurse Kitty Longthorne is still hard at work at Manchester's Park Hospital. The one-year-old NHS is inundated by the nation's sick and dying, made worse by a crippling labour shortage.

Now engaged, Kitty and James adore each other, but once they marry, she will be expected to leave the job that means so much to her. When she is offered the trip of a lifetime – a voyage by sea to Barbados to recruit nurses to join Park Hospital's ranks – adventurous Kitty is desperate to go. Her brother Ned has been there for years, and she simply cannot resist an opportunity to track him down and see what exactly he's been up to.

But what of her beloved James? What of the baby she suspects she may be carrying?

Returning home, Kitty has more to contend with than she ever anticipated. After paradise, will Manchester ever be the same again?